Benita Brown was born and brought up in Newcastle by her English mother and Indian father. She went to drama school in London where she met her husband who, also from Newcastle, was working for the BBC. Not long after, she returned to her home town where she did some teaching and broadcasting and brought up four children. She is now a full-time writer.

A Dream
of her Own

Benita Brown

HEADLINE

First published in 2000
by HEADLINE BOOK PUBLISHING

First published in paperback in 2001
by HEADLINE BOOK PUBLISHING

10 9 8 7 6 5

ISBN 0 7472 6618 2

Typeset by Avon Dataset Ltd, Bidford-on-Avon, Warks

Printed and bound in Great Britain by
Mackays of Chatham plc, Chatham, Kent

HEADLINE BOOK PUBLISHING
A division of Hodder Headline
338 Euston Road
London NW1 3BH

www.headline.co.uk
www.hodderheadline.com

To Norman, with love

Chapter One

Newcastle, November 1906

'And where do you think you're going?'

Mrs Mortimer's substantial figure filled the kitchen doorway, barring the way out. Constance stepped back in alarm. Behind her she heard Nella catch her breath. She could imagine her friend's expression of dismay.

They hadn't heard Mrs Mortimer coming. They had been laughing and too happy to care, for once, so they'd forgotten to listen for the officious swish of skirts and the jangling of the huge bunch of keys that marked the cook-housekeeper's progress along the corridors of the house.

'Well, I'm waiting for an answer.'

Constance met the woman's cool stare. 'I'm going to bed.'

Mrs Mortimer advanced into the room. The door slammed shut behind her, wafting in a draught of cold air from the basement passage. She raised her eyebrows and stared at Constance for a moment before turning her head to look around the kitchen.

In the ensuing silence Constance heard the coals shift and settle in the range and the faint hiss of the gaslamp. She glanced up and saw the whole scene reflected in the upper

1

half of the tall window above the sink. It was like a painting, she thought, such as she'd seen in the Laing Art Gallery.

No, not a painting, a photograph – one of those posed studies of 'Life Below Stairs'. The cook-housekeeper, in her starched white blouse and apron, staring sternly at the stone sink full of unwashed pans and the wooden bench next to it where the dishes waited to be dried.

Nella, in faded grey cotton, her thin little body seemingly held together by the ties of the overlarge apron, hunched forward over the table, a bar of soap grasped in one hand and a wooden scrubbing brush in the other.

And Constance herself, not much taller than Nella, standing upright, wisps of fair hair escaping from her mobcap to frame her face. John had told her that her features were delicate, that her complexion was like porcelain. If he were here now he would see that the fine bones gave an impression of strength rather than fragility and that her violet eyes could be dark with anger.

Mrs Mortimer turned once more to Constance. 'You cannot go to bed until you finish your chores.'

'But I thought that, as tomorrow—'

'Be quiet! It's not your place to think!' The woman gave a tight-lipped smile. Her thick fingers gripped a small brown envelope and she tapped it on the palm of her other hand. 'These are your wages.'

Constance clenched her fists, controlling the natural impulse to reach out for the packet. She sensed the woman was playing with her.

'As you are to leave us so early in the morning, Mrs Sowerby asked me to give you the money owing to you tonight. However, as I find you are not to be trusted, I think I had better keep it until you have finished in here.'

'It was my fault!' Nella cried out, and Constance spun

2

round to face her. She shook her head urgently but her friend ignored her warning glance and carried on, 'Mrs Mortimer, I said Constance should gan to bed. I divven't mind finishing off, meself, in the circumstances . . .' She had started boldly enough but her voice faltered under the woman's outraged glare.

'I was not aware that the running of this household had been given over to a mere skivvy.'

'But—'

Constance groaned softly. What would Nella do if she so enraged the most powerful member of the Sowerbys' staff that she lost her job? Looking the way she did it would be very difficult for her to find another position.

'It's all right, Nella.' Risking Mrs Mortimer's wrath Constance hurried towards the table and put her arm round the girl's crooked shoulders.

'Be quiet both of you! Nella, I have decided that you should go to bed immediately.'

'But why? The chores aren't finished, and you said—'

'Nella!' Constance breathed.

Mrs Mortimer ignored both interruptions and carried on. 'You will have to be up an hour earlier in the morning; the new girl will not be arriving in time to help you lay the fires.'

That's only just occurred to her, Constance thought. She doesn't really care whether or not Nella gets enough sleep. She just wants to punish me.

'Constance,' the cook-housekeeper continued, 'I will come back in exactly one hour with your money. You had better be finished by then.'

She turned and left abruptly. Her footsteps rang out along the stone passage towards her sitting room where her supper tray waited beside a cosy fire.

'Old cow!' Nella muttered. 'I hope the cheese in them

3

sandwiches she made herself gives her nightmares!'

Constance squeezed her shoulders. 'Hush.' She took the soap and scrubbing brush from Nella's hands and laid them on the chair next to the enamel pail. 'Go to bed, like she said.'

'But I wanted you to hev a proper night's sleep. It's your big day tomorrow.'

'I know and I'm grateful, but I shouldn't have let you persuade me. I should have realized that Mrs Mortimer would expect you to do the work of two until the new girl is broken in.'

'Broken in? That's a funny thing to say. They do that to horses, divven't they?'

'Yes, and that's all we are in this household, beasts of burden. I'm sure people like the Sowerbys don't think of us as human beings, otherwise why would we be treated this way?'

Nella looked up into her friend's face. She was small but if Nella's spine had been straight instead of twisted, she and Constance might have been about the same height.

Constance's eyes were blazing, and the two spots of colour burning in her cheeks highlighted her naturally fair complexion.

Suddenly, Nella grinned. 'Ee, Constance, this place'll be dull without you! What on earth shall I do when I want a good gripe?'

Constance's expression softened. 'You'll make friends with the new girl. In fact, you must, both for her sake and your own.'

'Must I?' Without warning, Nella's eyes filled with tears and, as they spilled over, she tried to brush them from her face with her bony little fingers.

'Oh, Nella,' Constance took a clean handkerchief from her apron pocket, 'Here, let me . . .'

She wiped her friend's face, guiltily acknowledging to

4

herself that Nella's distress at their parting was greater than her own. Poor Nella would have to remain here while she had a new and happier life to look forward to. 'Now, keep this hanky and go to bed,' she said. 'Leave me to get on with the work. I wouldn't put it past Mrs Mortimer to dock my wages if I'm not finished when she comes back.'

In fact it was just under an hour later that Constance placed the last of the dinner plates on the dresser and turned to face the empty kitchen. She was bone weary but she could hardly contain her elation. No more pans to scour, no floors to scrub, no carpets to beat, no more getting up in the cold and the dark to light the fires before the family was awake. Tomorrow was her wedding day.

Outside fog swirled from the shipyards on the River Tyne, up through the grimy terraces of Elswick and Scotswood, and on to settle like a shroud round the grand dwellings of the prosperous citizens who could afford to live in the sweeter air of Rye Hill.

In the upper windows of Dr Sowerby's tall town house, curtains were drawn against the chill of the November evening but down through the area railings, light spilled from the half-barred window into the yard at the foot of the worn stone steps.

Inside the basement room, Constance raised a hand to pull off her mobcap. Her long golden hair tumbled about her shoulders, the bright curls contrasting oddly with the faded uniform dress, the very drabness of which only emphasized her beauty. Unexpectedly she felt the threat of tears pricking her eyes and she pushed the cap into the pocket of her pinafore angrily. But it wasn't because she was leaving this hateful place that she felt like crying.

Often, when she was alone, disturbing memories came to

5

haunt her. Just now, as she had looked round the empty room, another kitchen had come to mind: larger than this one, brighter and full of the comforting smells of recent baking. Whenever she had gone down the back stairs to look for the kittens, the cook and the kitchen maids had always welcomed her. They had petted and spoiled her, taken her into the kitchen and given her milk and raisin cake.

Sometimes Robert would follow her, pretending that his only motive was to keep an eye on the younger child, and he would be fussed over and petted too. But she had been the favourite with the servants . . .

'So you're finished then?'

Mrs Mortimer observed her from the doorway. She was holding a candle and the light threw shadows upwards. Her eyes had disappeared into circles of blackness, making her podgy features resemble the grotesque mask of a pantomime clown. But she wasn't smiling.

Constance remained where she was, forcing the cook to step into the room. Mrs Mortimer glared at her. 'I'm glad you're leaving us, Constance, and it's just as well that you did not ask for a reference, for I would not have been able to recommend you to any respectable household.'

'Why not?' Against her better judgement, Constance was stung into responding. 'I've always worked hard. I'm sure you've never been able to fault me!'

'Not your work, no. It's your attitude I deplore.'

'I don't understand. I've never complained, never spoken out of turn.'

'Not to my face.' Suddenly the woman abandoned the air of refinement that she tried so hard to cultivate, and her voice rose harshly. 'Do you think I'm stupid, girl? Do you think I didn't realize from the moment you set foot in this house six years ago that, even when you were twelve years old, you

6

thought you were better than the rest of us?'

'That's not true! I couldn't help it if . . .'

'If what? Go on, finish what you were going to say.' Mrs Mortimer scowled.

'No, I'm sorry, I shouldn't have said anything. May I go upstairs, now? I'm tired and I still have to pack my belongings.'

The woman stared at her for a moment and then tossed the wage packet on to the table between them. 'Very well.'

As she reached the doorway she turned to face Constance for the last time. 'And mind you don't pack anything that doesn't belong to you. You haven't finished paying for the uniform dresses and the pinafores so they will remain Mrs Sowerby's property.'

As if I should want them, Constance thought, even though they have kept back payment from my pitiful wages for them. But she refrained from saying anything. In fact she didn't even move until she heard the cook open the door that led to the back staircase and mount the bare wooden stairs.

She must be going to bed now, Constance thought, and she let out a long sigh of relief. She loosened the ties of her pinafore and, for a moment, she was at a loss. Should she wash it and hang it on the pulley near the range? It would be dry enough to iron in the morning before she left.

No! Why should I?

Angry with herself for even thinking such thoughts, she pulled it over her head and folded it roughly. Then she tossed it on to the kitchen table that she had only shortly before scrubbed with strong soap and soda for the very last time. Let somebody else sort it out. Tomorrow she would no longer be answerable to any of them, she would be at nobody's beck and call. She would be Mrs John Edington.

But tonight there was one more thing she had to do. Taking a brass holder from the mantelpiece, she lit a candle and

7

threw the spent match in the dying fire. She picked up the packet containing her hard-earned wages and then she stepped up on to a chair and pulled down the chain that turned off the gaslamp. Then she hurried along the draughty passage to the back stairs.

On the ground floor, the entrance hall was long and narrow, and the dark colours of the walls and furnishings made it a sombre place, especially with the gaslamps turned down low. But Constance welcomed the shadows. She moved quietly; she had no wish to be discovered here. There was no reason for her to be 'above stairs' once her duties were over. Indeed, it was forbidden. Mrs Sowerby was convinced that all servants were unprincipled and deceitful, and ready to steal from her, given the slightest opportunity. Even the cutlery that they used in the kitchen was stamped with the words 'Stolen from Sowerby, Rye Hill'.

Suddenly a door opened on the first floor and the sound of Dr Sowerby's voice, raised in anger, spilled down the stairs. Constance froze and shrank back against the wall, hardly daring to breathe. Someone laughed mockingly, and the door closed abruptly. She heard footsteps in the upper passage and she was ready to dart back towards the door at the end of the hallway, but the footsteps echoed away from the direction of the stairhead and another door opened and slammed shut. Then there was silence.

She let out her breath in a ragged sigh and found that her heart was racing. I feel like a thief, she thought. She was aware of the bitter taste of anger – having to sneak about when her intention was quite honest. Even the matron of the workhouse was not so harsh as Mrs Sowerby! Constance's surge of resentment induced a feeling of recklessness and she no longer moved so furtively as she crossed towards the study.

However, she sensed she was safe enough; at this time of

8

night she had no fear that anyone would seek her out deliberately. Her notice had been given weeks ago and she doubted if any of the family would want to say goodbye or wish her well.

Dr and Mrs Sowerby would be upstairs in the first-floor drawing room, their daughter, twelve-year-old Annabel, would be in bed, and their son, Gerald, she guessed, had just stormed off to his room in order to get ready to go out with friends. The friends that his parents so disapproved of.

The fire in the study was burning low and the room was dark, but Constance did not waste time lighting the mantle. She went straight over to the wall opposite the door and raised her candle. There was something she wanted to see for the last time – an image she wanted to commit to memory.

'Why do you always look at that photograph?'

She spun round, her heart beating painfully against her ribs. Her hand shook and the candle sputtered and flared as melted wax fell back into the flame. Mrs Sowerby was in the act of rising from a wing-backed chair placed near the hearth. Constance steadied the candle and gazed through the smoky light at her interrogator. The dark fabric of the narrow choker collar that covered nearly all of her neck accentuated the paleness of Mrs Sowerby's face.

'Don't just stand there dumbly, girl. I asked you a question. Why do you look at the photograph? Answer me. What possible interest can it hold for a workhouse brat like you?'

The doctor's wife moved towards her, the silk taffeta of her skirts rustling across the floor with fluid menace; the sweet lily of the valley perfume that she favoured preceding her. Violet Sowerby was plump and matronly but her soft little hands could grip like a vice and her ladylike voice sound as shrill as any harpy's. She raised her hand and Constance flinched, but Mrs Sowerby simply took the candle from her and held it high to examine the photograph in question.

9

Her eyes narrowed as she studied the group of men in formal clothes. The caption written in copperplate on the mount at the foot of the picture read, 'The Infirmary Committee, Formed on the Occasion of the Royal Jubilee Exhibition in Newcastle 1887.'

'I've seen you linger and glance up when you are dusting.' She frowned. 'But I cannot imagine why. This photograph must have been taken before you were born. Dr Sowerby is in the front row, of course . . .'

So he was, along with some of the most influential men in the city, and that obviously gave his wife much satisfaction. When the Royal Victoria Infirmary was finally officially opened by King Edward and Queen Alexandra in July of this very year, 1906, Mrs Sowerby had bought a dozen each of the postcards in the series that Valentines had issued to commemorate the event.

She sent one to every single person in her address book, telling them all about the royal visit to Newcastle and being sure to add that she and Dr Sowerby had been guests at the civic banquet given for Their Majesties in the Assembly Rooms.

Vexation hardened Violet Sowerby's features even further. 'Well, are you going to tell me?'

'No.' Constance was composed now, and she stared back steadily. She had no intention of telling this woman, now or ever, that the tall handsome man standing in the back row of the photograph – at that time, one of the richest manufacturers on Tyneside – was Richard Bannerman, her father.

'How dare you speak to me like that!' Violet Sowerby exclaimed, and, for a moment, Constance thought she was going to strike her. But they were interrupted.

'Let the girl alone, Mother. She's leaving us in the morning to marry the little shopkeeper and you don't want to be the subject of malignant gossip amongst the tradespeople, now, do you?' Gerald's amused tones came from the doorway.

Violet Sowerby turned towards him but he moved aside into the hall. All else forgotten, his mother swept out of the room. Constance followed her. While they were talking, she would slip away.

'Gerald, I've been waiting to see you on your own. Are you going out?' Mrs Sowerby's voice had softened; she was almost pleading.

He was standing in front of a gilt-framed mirror and he concentrated on adjusting his wing collar and his white evening tie. 'Would I be dressed like this if I were going to endure another interminable evening at home with you and Father?'

'But, Gerald, you spend so little time with us these days . . .'

'Do you blame me? In this house I meet with nothing but disapproval.'

'Not disapproval – your father and I have been worried that you may be neglecting your studies – and perhaps that is because of the influence of some of your friends who have no need to earn a living . . .'

'I've already had to suffer one lecture from Father on that subject tonight. You both seem to forget that I am a grown man and that, thanks to Grandmother, I am financially independent. Save your breath, Mother. I'm going out.'

All the time he had been speaking he never once looked round. Now, he stared into the mirror with self-absorbed concentration as he smoothed his thickly waving red-gold hair. When he was satisfied, he looked to one side and spoke to Constance's retreating reflection. 'Pass me my overcoat, there's a good girl.'

She had almost reached the door at the end of the passage and she stopped and cursed herself silently for not having

11

been quicker. Gerald raised his eyebrows. 'Did you hear me?'

Constance hurried back and reached for the overcoat, from where he had tossed it over the carved wooden post at the bottom of the stairs. After handing Gerald the coat she tried to slip away again, only to earn a rebuke from his mother.

'I do not remember saying you could go.'

She turned once more and waited, keeping her eyes down. She thought it best not to betray her impatience or Mrs Sowerby would only harangue her the longer.

'Oh, let her go to bed now, Mother.' Gerald had put on his coat and was adjusting the ends of his silk scarf. 'No doubt she'll want to be as refreshed as possible for her wedding to Prince Charming.'

Constance felt her anger rising when he looked up and continued mockingly. 'I must say I was surprised when I saw him. Such a dapper little chap, sitting there telling you of his honourable intentions just as if he were a gentleman. I'm sure he could have the pick of the daughters of the more prosperous commercial families and yet he is content to marry a servant.'

'She's never been like a servant!' Mrs Sowerby's outburst was so vehement that both her son and Constance turned to look at her.

'What do you mean?' Gerald seemed genuinely surprised. 'As far as I know she has always performed her duties satisfactorily.'

'You are a fool, Gerald.' His mother's tone was scathing. 'Always taken in by outward show. Have you never noticed her manner?'

'I'm sure she's always appeared to be quite properly modest and reserved.'

'Supercilious and secretive more like! And her voice – it is not the voice of a servant!'

'No . . . you're right . . .' Gerald's murmur of agreement

betrayed surprise. He looked at Constance speculatively and then, suddenly, he walked over to her and lifted up a strand of her hair. 'And this hair . . .' He let the silky curls fall and placed his knuckles under her chin to raise her face. 'And these eyes . . . are they blue or violet?'

Constance held her breath. She was unnerved to find herself so close to him and her eyes widened with alarm as she found she couldn't avoid his amused gaze. She tried to turn her head away but he began to stroke the line of her jaw and the soft flesh underneath with the back of his fingers. She felt a pulse throbbing in her neck as she cringed at his touch, but pride made her raise her chin and hold his stare.

'And this soft skin,' he said. 'You are quite right, Mother. I wonder why I have not bothered to notice before how very unlike a servant Constance is.' Gerald's face mottled with sudden heat. His breath smelled of brandy.

'That's enough!' His mother's voice was sharp but Gerald took his time to drop his hand and step back. He was laughing but, when Constance saw the look in his eyes, she felt a frisson of fear.

'Constance, I have decided that you need not wait until tomorrow.' Mrs Sowerby's voice was cold. 'Go up and collect your belongings and leave now.'

'Now? But, until I am married in the morning, I have nowhere to go!'

'That is not my concern. You have no more duties here, there is no reason to stay.'

She stared at the doctor's wife, aghast. Mrs Sowerby had never been easy to work for but, as she was neither pleasant nor considerate to any of the servants, Constance had never taken it personally. Now she saw that the woman disliked her intensely and was enjoying venting her spite.

'Take nothing from this house that you did not bring with

13

you. If you do, I shall know where to find you. And be sure that you leave by the servants' entrance. Dr Sowerby will go down to lock up at eleven o'clock; you must be gone by then.'

Chapter Two

'Fancy throwing you out at this time of night – doesn't she know that's wicked?'

Nella stood shivering in her nightgown, clutching a shawl around her skinny shoulders with one hand and holding a candle with the other. The light gleamed on her pale, bony face and cast a cruelly exaggerated shadow of her crooked body on the sloping wall of the eaves behind her.

'If she does, she doesn't care.'

'Well, she should. All them improving texts she makes us read. What about "Do unto others as you would they should do unto you"? How would she like it if *you* threw *her* out on the street?'

'You don't think Mrs Sowerby believes in any of that, do you, Nella? That kind of thing is only to keep us in our place. "Be obedient unto your masters", that's all she's interested in!'

Constance pulled off the cheap cotton uniform dress and left it lying on the floor where it fell. Quickly, for the attic room was freezing cold, she put on one of her own blouses and a blue serge skirt. Then, she started to pull open the drawers at her side of the shared chest and toss the rest of her belongings on to her narrow iron bed.

Nella's small features were taut with worry. 'But, what

will you do? Where will you gan?'

'Hush, Nella, not so loud. If we wake the others, Mrs Mortimer will have something to say to us in the morning.'

They looked at each other. ' "Noisiness is considered Bad Manners" ' they intoned, each trying to imitate the cook-housekeeper's attempts at refinement.

Nella giggled. 'Old Mortimer'll be fast asleep by now, tucked up with her bottle of mother's ruin. And, besides, come the morning, she'll only hev me to scold. You won't be here.'

'Thank goodness!'

Constance stopped what she was doing and they smiled at each other. The prospect of freedom was marvellous and Constance knew that Nella was pleased for her, even though she was going to be left behind.

The moment was short-lived. 'But you heven't told me what you're gannin' to do – or where you're gannin'. Will you gan to John's?'

'No. His mother would be shocked if I turned up there without an explanation the night before the wedding.'

'Why can't you tell her what has happened?'

'Nella, you know I've never met her, but John has told me that, in spite of my circumstances, he's convinced her that I will make the perfect wife for him.'

'Of course you will. I knew the minute that I set eyes on yer ma that she was a real lady!'

'And me? Surely I'm just another workhouse brat?'

'Like me, you mean? The difference is that I was born there.'

'Oh, Nella, I'm sorry, I didn't mean—'

'Nivver mind. Anyone can see that you were born to better things. What happened wasn't your fault.'

'That's just what John said! He told me that when we first met he would never have guessed that I was in service and,

16

when I told him, oh, Nella, it made no difference to him!'

'He fell in love with you!'

'When I tried to tell him about what had happened he said it didn't matter. He said it was obvious that my family had fallen on hard times – like many another – and that he thought all the more of me for keeping my standards.'

'Spoken like a true gent!'

'But now, if I tell John's mother that my mistress has thrown me out, she might begin to question her son's judgement.'

'I suppose so . . .'

'I'm sure of it. And, besides, her health is not good. I wouldn't want to start my married life by upsetting my mother-in-law.'

'No, that wouldn't do, especially as you're all gannin' to live together. Ee, Constance—'

'Hush, don't fret. I'll go to John's friend's house in Fenham; his parents are away but his sister, Rosemary, should be there.'

John's friend Matthew Elliot had agreed to collect Constance from the Sowerbys' in the morning and take her to the church in his motorcar, but she had never been invited inside the grand house overlooking the Town Moor and she had no idea whether she would be welcome there now in such strange circumstances. Nor would she tell Nella that Rosemary Elliot was three years younger than she was and, at fifteen, was hardly old enough to be a proper chaperone. She did not want her friend to worry.

'Now, please help me to pack my things. And hold that candle steady; you don't want to set light to the place.'

'Divven't I just!'

Nella set the candlestick down on top of the chest of drawers next to the one Constance had brought up, which was almost spent. She took another from their precious hoard and lit it, dribbling wax into an old saucer and then securing the candle.

'Let's hev plenty of light for a change!' She grinned.

There was no gaslighting on the top floor of the Sowerbys' house, and Mrs Mortimer doled out candles to the maids' rooms parsimoniously, but tonight Nella didn't care about saving her ration.

Nella and Constance's friendship had begun when both were children in the old workhouse on Arthur's Hill. Nella had been born there and couldn't remember her mother, who had died when she was very young. When Agnes Bannerman and her daughter had arrived, obviously used to a better way of life, Nella had watched them with envious fascination. Constance and her mother had been aware of their silent little shadow and one day Agnes had invited Nella to sit with them at table.

After that she had attached herself to them like a stray kitten. But she was tough and wise beyond her years. She taught them the tricks they needed to survive in such a place and, in return, received the affection she craved. She would have died for them. Nella had told Constance time and time again how lucky she was that the Sowerby family had taken them on together.

She had tried to hide her dismay when Constance told her that John had proposed to her, and now she was doing her best to be cheerful as she helped her friend pack her clothes into a large flat cardboard box.

Constance smiled at her. 'If that's the last of my petticoats, you can help me fold my wedding outfit.' She held up the dove-grey grosgrain dress and examined it critically.

Nella clasped her hands together. 'Ee, Constance, it's lovely!'

'It was when my mother first wore it and, even then, it wasn't one of her best.'

She sighed. John's Uncle Walter owned a chain of

18

gentleman's outfitting shops, and John worked in the main branch in Grey Street, in the heart of Newcastle's smart commercial district. He was always smart and well groomed. Constance didn't want him to be ashamed of her tomorrow, especially as his uncle would be giving her away.

'Yes, well,' Nella said, 'yer ma was a lady and she had good taste. You've altered it to suit the fashion of today and that bit of lace you've added makes all the difference.'

'Do you think so?'

'You'll look more elegant in that old dress than Mrs Sowerby could ever look, for all the money she spends on herself!'

'I hope you're right.'

A moment later, Constance put the lid on the box and secured it with string. She had not had much to pack. The clothes she had worn when she came here six years ago at the age of twelve were long outgrown.

For the past year or two she had been altering and updating those of her mother's clothes that she had managed to beg. Just before Constance's twelfth birthday, Agnes Bannerman had died, worn down and made ill by nearly two years of the harsh workhouse regime. She had been small and slight just like her daughter. If she had been a larger woman, the matron would probably have kept her clothes for herself.

Nella suddenly cried, 'Ee, Constance, I'll miss you!'

'I've explained to you where John's house is, and you know you can come and see me on your days off. I want you to.'

Constance meant what she said, even though she had never told John about her friendship with Nella. She had met him on one of her solitary walks on her afternoon off and John thought she was all alone in the world. He didn't seem to care that she had no family and, indeed, he didn't seem to want to know about her past. He was so good-hearted –

19

surely he wouldn't mind if Nella visited now and then?

Constance took hold of Nella's hands. They were red and work-roughened, but her grip was firm. Constance knew that her friend's misshapen, undeveloped body held great reserves of strength.

Now Nella's eyes were shining. 'You're so lucky. You'll be mistress of yer own house!'

'Well, strictly speaking, John's mother will still be mistress, although he has explained that she will be willing to give up most household duties and responsibilities to me.' Constance smiled, her eyes sparkling in the candlelight. 'But I hope you don't think that's why I'm marrying him – for a house.'

'Of course not! You've told me. John is clever and kind and handsome!'

'He's not just handsome, he's – he's absolutely beautiful! Oh, I just can't explain . . . He's like a painting in the art gallery! When you meet him, you'll see what I mean!'

Nella's eyes were round and wondering. 'You really love him, then?'

'Of course I do! What a funny thing to say!'

'Divven't take me wrong – but you've nivver said much about the way you feel. You're very close, always have been. You know that, divven't you?'

'If you say so.' Constance hugged her and then took her shoulders and pushed her gently away. Nella sat on her bed and then grasped her friend's hands and drew her to sit down beside her.

'Tell me again. Tell me about the day that you met John.'

'You know that story as well as I do.'

'But I like to hear it. It's like . . . it's like a dream come true!'

'All right, but I must be quick. It's nearly time for me to go. It was a Sunday afternoon—'

20

'In June, wasn't it?'

'Yes, June. It was my afternoon off and I had walked up across the West Road and towards the Town Moor—'

'You've walked for miles about the city, haven't you? Old Sowerby doesn't care that we might have nowhere to gan on our days off!'

'Hush, I thought you wanted to hear about my meeting with John?'

'Sorry, gan on.'

'Well, I heard the music coming from the park—'

'A concert!'

'I went in and saw all the seats arranged around the bandstand, and I would have loved to have sat and listened but I was afraid that the park keeper would demand a fee and I had no money with me . . .

'Well, I was standing listening to the music. It was so lively that I couldn't help smiling and I didn't realize that I had started humming the tune that they were playing. Then suddenly I became aware that two young gentlemen had come to stand beside me and they were singing the words, ever so quietly—'

'I know the words, they're from *Flora Dora*!' Nella exclaimed. Then she began to sing. ' "Tell me, pretty maiden, are there any more at home like you?" ' Her voice, emerging as it did from such a deformed little body, was surprisingly strong and sweet.

'Hush, yes, *Flora Dora*. I turned to face them – I think I was blushing – and I saw John and his friend Matthew. They looked so handsome, John so fair, wearing a blazer and boater, and Matthew, tall and dark like—'

'Like an actor!'

'Yes, an actor, but a very prosperous one! Well, after a moment – I was embarrassed, you know – we all laughed. And

21

that was the start of it, the start of our friendship.'

'And the friendship led to true love!'

'Stop it, Nella. You make it sound like a tale from a penny novelette.' But Constance was smiling.

'And now, you're gannin' to be married.' Nella's excitement suddenly died. 'Hev you invited Robert to yer wedding?'

Constance let go of Nella's hands and rose swiftly. The smile had gone from her face and her eyes were wide with shocked surprise. 'Who?'

'Divven't you look at me like that! It's a natural thing to want to know. Hev you invited yer brother?'

'I have no brother!'

'Constance, how can you?' Nella stood up and stared at her accusingly. 'I heard yer ma telling you that you should write to him.'

'When?'

'When she . . . when she was dying. She said that when she went, Robert would be all the kin you had left.'

'You shouldn't have been listening.'

'I didn't mean to. I came into the room to see if I could do anything and you were crying. I stopped by the door . . . you didn't know I was there. Ee, Constance, I'm sorry.'

'All this time you've never said anything, never asked me about it.'

'I didn't like to. You always keep things to yourself. I thought you would only tell me if you wanted to.'

'You were right and I don't want to.'

'Divven't then!'

Constance sighed. 'Nella, don't scowl at me like that. I've got to go now, before Dr Sowerby locks up.' She took her coat and hat from the hook on the back of the door and began to put them on.

'Here, before you button yer coat up . . .' Nella held out

22

one of her hands. A twist of tissue paper lay on her palm. 'This is yer wedding present. Gan on ... take it ... that's right. Open it up then!'

Constance unwrapped the paper to find a necklace, a shiny little heart on a chain. Nella was holding her breath with anticipation.

'You shouldn't have spent so much!'

'Divven't worry, it's not real gold – and it's not a proper locket. I couldn't afford to buy one that opened. Still I divven't suppose you would have wanted a lock of *my* hair, or a picture of *my* ugly dial for a keepsake! But look at it – look closely.'

Constance held the heart up to the candlelight and saw that something was engraved on the front. Two letters were entwined there, *C* and *N*, the first letters of their names.

'Do you like it?'

'It's lovely.'

'I got it at that kiosk in the Grainger Market. I'd been saving up ever since you told me you were getting married. I couldn't afford one of them velvet boxes, that's why I want you to put it on now; it'll be safer that way. And wear it every day, mind, especially tomorrow, yer wedding day, promise?'

'I promise.'

'If you always wear it you'll always remember me.'

'I won't ever forget you, Nella.' Constance fastened the chain around her neck and began to button up her coat. 'And now I must be going.'

'No, I've been thinking.' Nella was animated. 'You can't gan out into the streets at this time of night. Even if John's friend will take you in, Fenham is at least half an hour's walk from here – there'll be drunks coming back from the town and all kinds of riffraff!'

'If they're drunk they won't take any notice of me.'

'For goodness' sake, lissen! You divven't have to gan. Stay

here until first thing. When I get up we'll gan down together and I'll make sure no one sees you leaving.'

'But what if Mrs Sowerby comes up here to check if I'm gone?'

'What! Mrs Sowerface come up to the servants' quarters! Hev you ever known that to happen?'

'Yes, I have. Remember when she thought poor Isabelle had stolen that brooch? She came up and supervised while her room was searched, and, when the brooch wasn't found, all the other rooms were turned upside down, too. She didn't go down again until precious little Miss Annabel came up and confessed that she had borrowed it to wear to a party.'

'Yes, well, she was angry then and she wanted to find her brooch.'

'Well, tonight she's angry with me and she wants me out of the house.'

Constance stared helplessly at her friend's stubborn expression until Nella turned away, her eyes wide and her lips pinched as she looked around the room. Suddenly, she darted over and began to strip the sheets and blankets from Constance's bed.

'What are you doing?'

'I'll fold the clothes up and put them at the bottom and, if Mrs Sowerby looks in, she'll see straight away that yer bed is empty and that I'm fast asleep.'

'But—'

'Give that to me.' Her task completed, Nella took the cardboard box from Constance's hands. 'I'll put this under me bed, see? I'll cover it with me shawl and it will do as yer pillow. You can have me top blanket. There's plenty room for you to stretch out, and old Sowerby will nivver dream of looking there. You'll be safe until morning.'

24

'No, Nella, no.' Constance took back her box and held on to it.

'Why not?'

'I wouldn't put it past Mrs Sowerby to look under the bed.'

'She won't!'

'She might. And, even if she doesn't, somebody might see us in the morning. If things go wrong you would lose your position here.'

'I divven't care!'

'But I do. Where else would you go?'

They stared at each other. Constance would have loved to go along with Nella's plan and stay for the night but she could not put her friend in danger of losing her place. The Sowerbys had got her cheap because of her disability and she might not find another employer willing to take her on, especially if she didn't have a reference. This job, hard as it was, at least provided adequate food and shelter.

Nella was staring at her and Constance lowered her eyes. She knew what the other girl wanted her to say but she couldn't say it. Finally, it was Nella who spoke. 'I know what you're thinking and it doesn't matter. Now cheer up and smile; after all, you're getting married in the morning!'

'One day, Nella, one day I really will be mistress of my own house and there'll be a place for you there, I promise you. Now, come here and look out of the window.'

'Why? What are you talking about?'

Constance put an arm round her friend's skinny shoulders and was almost overwhelmed by a wave of compassion. There was hardly an ounce of flesh covering Nella's twisted bones. 'Hush,' she whispered. 'Look down there. What do you see?'

'Not much; it's too foggy.'

'Exactly. The fog will make it safe. Nobody will notice me and, if I hear footsteps coming, I'll hide in a doorway till

25

they've gone by. I'll get to the Elliots' house in one piece, I promise you.'

Constance stepped out into the area yard and was engulfed in fog. She stood still for a moment to get her bearings, then she began to edge her way forward to the steps. Clutching the string ties of her box with one hand, she grasped the iron handrail with the other. Intent on putting one foot safely in front of the other, she did not look up until she had nearly reached the top. And then it was too late. Gerald was standing there, blocking the way into the street.

She was so startled that she lost her footing and began to fall. He lunged forward to grasp her arm and hold her steady. She looked up and the diffused glow of the streetlamp behind him illuminated her pale features. She had pinned up her hair but a few strands had escaped from under the brim of her hat and they curled damply, framing her heart-shaped face.

Even at this stage she expected him to step aside.

But then he spoke. 'Ah, the little bride.' There was something about his voice, throaty and unsteady, that made her jump back in dismay. Taken unawares, Gerald lost his grip on her arm and she went down one step.

'No – don't go. I've been waiting for you.'

Until that moment the fog had made what was happening seem unreal – dreamlike – but now Constance realized the full horror of her situation. She turned and stumbled down the steps, knowing she must get back into the house before Gerald's father locked the door.

Gerald only laughed. 'That's right, it's more private down there.'

'No!' Her scream turned into a terrified gasp of alarm as he swung out and knocked her the rest of the way down. She fell awkwardly, one leg twisting under her body and, before she could push herself up, he had plunged down after her.

She began to drag herself across the yard towards the door when she felt a forceful blow on her side. He had kicked her. She twisted round and faced him, fighting for breath, eyes widening with terror as he lowered himself on top of her.

He began to unbutton her coat and she tried to fight him off until he seized both her wrists in one powerful hand and forced them back on to the ground above her head. She felt him rive her blouse free from her skirt with his other hand and she moaned in distress as he began to finger her breasts.

Her reaction only excited him more. 'That's right – you like it, don't you?'

'No . . . no . . .'

'Yes, you do. You don't have to pretend. You've been waiting for this!'

He forced her legs apart with one of his own and Constance felt the weight of his body pressing her down on to the hard stone of the yard as he began to move rhythmically against her. Suddenly, his hand left her breasts and he lifted himself a little and pushed her skirt up above her waist. She felt him fumbling with his buttons and, having freed himself, he tore impatiently at her underclothes. She had barely got over the shock of feeling his hand on the soft flesh of her inner thighs, when he pushed his fingers inside her.

'No . . . no . . . no . . .' she sobbed at the hurt and the shame of it, until the hand that was holding her wrists seized her throat and pressed until she was silent. She could feel the chain of the necklace Nella had given her cutting into her neck. It was choking her. She tried to move but Gerald was too strong for her.

Her head began to pound. Over the hammering of her own heartbeat, Constance dimly heard the scrape of bolts shooting home in the door behind her. The hand that was grasping her throat moved up and took hold of her chin. She took a deep gulp of air as she heard him say, 'If you scream, I'll throttle you.'

He forced her head round so that she was staring up towards him. 'Keep your eyes open. Look at me.'

Above his head she could see the lantern shape of the streetlamp looking as if it was disembodied and floating in the mist. Gerald's face came nearer, blotting out the light. She could feel his breath, hot and damp on her exposed breasts, her neck and then her face as his lips covered hers and he kissed her savagely.

When he forced his way into her unwilling body there was a moment of pain so severe that Constance thought she would die. But there was no such release and the pain did not diminish, it grew even worse as Gerald began to move even more forcefully. She felt as if she were being torn apart.

The scream that she could not release echoed round and round inside her head until she felt that the whole world must hear her.

'Don't close your eyes, bitch. Look at me!' Gerald was enraged but there was no way she could obey him.

Mercifully, her senses began to fade and, long before he had reached his climax, Constance was unconscious.

Chapter Three

'Get up.'

The order came from just above her head. Constance stirred and pain stabbed her side. She groaned.

'Be quiet!'

She opened her eyes. Gerald was crouching over her. Before she could scream he clamped his hand over her mouth. It smelled of stale tobacco. She gagged and involuntarily bit into the firm flesh.

'Ach! You little bitch!'

Gerald snatched his hand back and slapped her face. The force knocked her head sideways on to the ground. The pain of the impact made her feel sick. Lights flashed behind her eyes. Before her head had cleared he brought his mouth closer and rasped in her ear, 'Now get up and go on your way. I don't want you causing any trouble.'

His tone was urgent, even menacing, but she couldn't obey. What was wrong with her legs? It was like a bad dream. She wanted to go – she *had* to go – and yet she couldn't move. Her vision gradually cleared. She stared through the gloom and began to make sense of what she saw just a few feet away from her – the bottom of the door. How long was it since she had heard the bolts shooting home? How long had she been lying here?

Gerald grabbed her shoulders. 'Didn't you hear me? I want you gone from here.'

He began hauling her up. She tried to bend her knees and push upwards but her feet slipped on the greasy surface of the yard and her limbs were not strong enough to support her.

'Can't you help yourself? For God's sake, don't fall down again!'

His anger shocked her into obedience and she found herself standing at the foot of the steps in the area yard. The street above was still enveloped in fog. The streetlamp did little to disperse the shadows.

'No!' She shied backwards when she felt the touch of Gerald's hands. He was kneeling and fumbling at her skirt.

'I'm only pulling your clothes down, you stupid slut. Making you respectable. Can't have you wandering the streets showing everyone what a little whore you are, can we?'

'No!' Her voice cracked. Memories started flooding back. She had been semiconscious, dazed with fright and half-suffocated, but she would never forget the shock when he had entered her, never forget the pain.

With the memory, the hurt renewed itself. She felt a stinging soreness between her legs. She looked at Gerald with loathing but he was bending down, picking something up from the ground near by.

'Here's your box.' He thrust it into her hands and then grabbed her arm and began to push her up the stone steps ahead of him. Her abused limbs shrieked in agony and she began to cry. She couldn't help herself.

'Stop that! You enjoyed every minute of it. In fact, I've done you a favour; I've given you something to remember. I guarantee the little shopkeeper won't be able to match me!'

They had reached street level and Gerald let go of her arm so suddenly that she fell back against the railings, clutching her box with both arms against her body like a shield. She was shivering with distress.

He glared down at her. 'Don't pretend you're injured. Don't go running to anyone telling them that I've hurt you – that I forced you. You asked for everything you got.'

'No . . .' she groaned, and shook her head despairingly.

Gerald grabbed her chin roughly with one hand and forced her to look at him. 'Oh yes, you did. My mother will vouch for the fact that you were acting provocatively – leading me on. She saw the way you looked at me. That's why she had to throw you out of the house. Do you think anyone would believe a little nobody like you rather than a respectable woman like my mother?'

It's true, Constance thought. No one would believe me if I told them what had really happened. And in any case who could I tell? Not John, dear Lord, not John . . .

Gerald caught the momentary flash of fear in her eyes and he went on more reasonably, 'You know it's in your own interests to keep quiet, don't you?'

'My interests?'

'Of course. Your bridegroom won't want shop-soiled goods, will he?' He laughed at his own feeble joke. 'No, you'd better keep quiet or you'll end up with nothing. No wedding and no job. My mother won't have you back and you've no hope of a reference. It would be back to the workhouse – or worse. It could mean the streets for you. I'm sure you know what that means.'

Constance raised her head and met his eyes. She had never felt such hatred in her life; it was all the stronger because she was powerless. Frustration benumbed her. Gerald mistook her stillness for passivity.

'There, I can see you're all right, so you'd best be on your way. I'll walk with you as far as the West Road. Where are you going?' He reached for her arm. 'Here . . .' Constance shrank away from him. 'Oh, very well.' Gerald shrugged and started walking up the hill.

She pressed herself back against the railings and waited. She held her breath, letting it out in a long, ragged sigh when the mist began to swallow him. Then, she took hold of the string handle of her box and, carrying it with one hand, began to walk slowly in the same direction. She had to go that way; the way downhill led only to the huddled houses of Scotswood and, eventually, the river.

The fog was not constant: it thinned and swirled, sometimes revealing the way ahead and sometimes appearing like an impenetrable grey veil. Each time it cleared a little Constance glimpsed Gerald's broad-shouldered figure ahead of her and she slowed down.

After a while he stopped and cocked his head on one side as if listening for her footsteps. When Constance stopped too, he laughed and started off again. And so he made a pantomime of their progress until he reached the wide road that swept down at right angles to the city.

Now she could hear other footsteps, voices, the jingle of a harness, then horses' hoofs on the cobbled road. Gerald raised his arm and she heard him shout, 'Halloa!' Coach lights pierced the murky air and a cab loomed out of the mist and drew up beside him.

He turned back to look at her and raised his arm again. For a moment she thought he was gesturing towards her, offering to take her in the cab, and she shook her head and backed away. But his arm moved downwards and something hit the pavement at her feet.

'Your purse,' he called. 'I almost forgot. It fell out of your pocket when . . . before . . .'

Gerald climbed into the cab. She heard him order, 'The

Haymarket – Alvini's.' The coachman cracked his whip and the cab lumbered downhill towards the city centre.

And then, when she was sure that he had gone, Constance began to tremble. At first the movement was barely perceptible but soon her limbs were shaking violently. Sobs racked her body and she tried to stifle them, but she could not stop the tears streaming down her face.

'Are you all right, hinny?'

Constance stared round wildly at the question. An old woman had appeared beside her. Her body was bent over, her head tilted sideways and upwards as she stared at her. Constance stared back, half wondering if the woman was real or just another part of her nightmare.

'Can't you speak? Wha's the marrer? Are you ill?'

The apparition thrust her wrinkled face closer; droplets of moisture beaded her grimy features, the sour-sweet smell of poverty rose from her clothes. Constance recoiled instinctively. 'I'm fine.'

'You don't look fine. You look fair done in.' The woman peered at her through straggled wisps of hair. She sucked her breath in. 'What's happened here? Do you want the pollis?'

'No, don't call the police. Nothing has happened. I'm just resting. I'll be going soon.'

'I seen him go.'

'What? Who did you see?'

'The gen'leman. I seen him get in the cab – but he spoke to you afore he went. What did he give you?'

'I don't know what you're talking about. No gentleman has given me anything.'

The mist was thinning now, writhing in smoky ribbons around the shrivelled form of her inquisitor.

'What's that then?' The old woman pointed to the ground

33

near her feet. 'He threw something. I heard it land . . .
heavy . . . looks like a purse.'

'My purse . . . I dropped it when . . . he was returning it.'

'Divven't you want it, then?' The old woman stooped and
snatched it up.

'Yes . . . my wages . . . It's all I have. Give it to me.'

'Wages! You must hev a good position. There's a half-
sovereign here!' She had opened the purse and tipped the
contents on to one filthy palm. Her fingers curled upwards
like a claw.

Constance frowned. 'There can't be.'

'I know a half-sovereign when I see one.' She thrust her
hand up towards Constance's face. There, amongst the small
change that was made up from her most recent wages and all
the rest she had managed to save from her monthly salary of
ten shillings, lay a bright coin that had not been there before.

'Whatever it was that you say didn't happen, he must hev
enjoyed hisself!' she cackled. 'And I divven't know why you're
looking so miserable – I know many a lass who'd be glad to
drop her drawers for half a croon!'

'You're disgusting! I didn't do anything. I don't want his
money!'

'Divven't shout, you'll have the pollis on us!' The woman
glanced over her shoulder, then moved closer and grasped
Constance's arm. 'Now lissen, you shouldn't be out on yer
own; you don't know how to look after yourself. Why divven't
you gan yem?'

'Home!'

The woman was disconcerted. She stepped back. 'Hev you
got some place to gan?'

'Yes.'

'It's not too far?' She edged away.

'No, not too far.'

'I'll be off, then.'

It was a moment before Constance realized that the woman had taken not only Gerald's half-sovereign but the purse as well, and all the rest of the money that it contained.

She began to laugh – thin high laughter that was more like crying. The Bible was right: *from him that hath not shall be taken away even that which he hath* . . . How wise Mrs Sowerby had been to prepare her servants for the vicissitudes of life – especially when it was her own beloved son who had caused them!

'Who's that?'

A door had opened a little way along the street and in the rectangle of light Constance saw the stocky figure of a man peering towards her. She forced herself to be silent and, before he could enquire further, she had darted across the road and vanished into the shadows.

Gerald slumped back in the cab as it rattled down Westgate Road to the city centre a bare mile away. The sexual release he had just experienced had been overwhelming, almost agonizing. At its peak there had been very little difference between pain and pleasure. For a while afterwards, all his senses had been intensified, but now that feeling of heightened awareness was beginning to dissipate.

He began to think of the meeting with his friends that lay ahead, and frowned. They would all be at the usual place, Alvini's, the fashionable restaurant next door to the Palace Theatre in the Haymarket, and he was very late.

He knew what they would say: 'Wouldn't they let you out again, Gerald?' 'Did Gerald's mama want to tuck him up in bed, then?' 'Did the pater insist he applied himself to his studies before he allowed him out to play?'

Once, when they had been playing cards and drinking for

35

some hours, and Gerald was beginning to worry about his reception when he returned to the house on Rye Hill, he had let slip how difficult his father and mother could be. The others were drunkenly sympathetic at the time but they had never let him forget it. Tonight they would assume that he had had the usual opposition from his parents and they would mock him for it. The banter wasn't always friendly. Sometimes Gerald imagined that the others, from much wealthier families than his own, were pleased to have an excuse to make fun of him.

But what if they knew the real reason why he was so late? He closed his eyes and tried to recapture the pleasure he had felt when he had had Constance so completely in his power. Could he tell them about this conquest of the little skivvy? No . . . Gerald sighed. That would hardly impress them. If his friends' stories were to be believed, deflowering servant girls was a rite of passage. No, they would hardly admire him for allowing something so banal to delay him.

Still, his spirits began to rally as the cab pulled up outside Alvini's. Perhaps he could embroider the truth a little – rather than a simple business transaction for which he'd paid her well, too well, he could hint that it had been some sort of assignation . . .

And then he had it. By the time he paid the cabby he was grinning. He needn't mention Constance's social position, but he could say that he had had a rendezvous with a beautiful girl on the very eve of her wedding. A girl who had made her attraction to him so plain that it was obvious that she was asking for it. What could Gerald have done but oblige her? Consequently, she would be going to her bridegroom tomorrow in a far from virginal state.

That would amuse them. It might even ensure that he wouldn't have to buy a single drink for himself all evening.

Constance hurried through the terraced streets, thankful that the fog was not so dense now that she was further away from the river. Her body was sticky with sweat and her legs were hurting but she could not allow herself to rest.

The houses at this side of the West Road were not so grand as those of Rye Hill but they were still respectable. She knew the area well; she had walked this way to the park many a time on her afternoons off. With nowhere to go and time to kill, she had enjoyed looking at the houses, the scrubbed front doorsteps whitened with soapstone, the shining brass, the immaculate net curtains, the neat flowerbeds in the tiny gardens. Lazy cats sunning themselves on windowsills, children playing tag or hopscotch until their mothers called them in for tea.

She had often wondered about the lives that were lived behind the neat redbrick façades. The children were nowhere near as privileged as she had once been. They had no wardrobes full of pretty clothes, no nurseries full of more toys than they could ever play with.

But when her happy childhood had ended so abruptly, Constance would have given anything to join in the simple street games, pick up the skipping ropes and the hoops and run in with them to one of those spruce little houses, sit at the table with its simple fare and stay there, safe, cherished and secure.

At this time of night all those children would be fast asleep, save one – she could hear the thin cry of a new baby and a shadow moved across the flimsy curtains in an upper window, but most of the houses were dark and still. Here and there, a passage light glowed dimly behind a frosted fanlight. A church clock began to strike the hour. It was midnight.

She had reached the park. There was no gate, and the gas lantern hanging from the centre of the wrought-iron entrance arch illuminated a path that cut straight through to the other entrance on Moorside Drive. There were other archways with lanterns at spaced intervals and she could see well into the distance. Her way appeared to be clear. And yet, she hesitated.

The kind of people who came here at night would hardly seek the light. Suddenly a muffled argument came from the shadowed pavilion, followed by a stifled scream and a curse. Constance stopped and listened.

'Gan on, hinny!'

'She's nivver said no before!'

Other voices called encouragement and then there was laughter. Constance held her breath. She was reluctant to go through the park but the only other way to reach the Elliots' house in its exclusive location on the edge of the Town Moor would be to walk round the perimeter. That would take very much longer and it was already past midnight. She had no choice.

Clutching her box to her body with one hand, she picked up her skirts with the other and, keeping to the very centre of the broad pathway, she ran as fast as she could.

As the last chimes of midnight faded Nella turned restlessly in her narrow bed. She had lain awake worrying about Constance out in the streets on her own and grieving for her own future without the only friend she had ever had.

She was cold. She had opened the window about an hour ago when she thought she had heard someone cry out. She leaned out as far as she could and peered down into the mist but could see nothing. The ensuing silence convinced her that she had imagined it and she moved her chilled head and shoulders back into the room.

But by the time she closed the window again, the damp air had seeped into every corner of the attic. Even the bedclothes felt clammy; Nella pulled her shawl around herself more tightly before burrowing down under the threadbare sheets and the rough blankets. Her skinny limbs squirmed around trying to find a more comfortable place on the lumpy horsehair mattress. She couldn't settle, her body was weary, but her mind was too active to allow her to sleep.

She must be there by now, Nella thought. She'll be tucked up in a warm bed in John's friend's house in Fenham. It wouldn't have taken Constance long to walk that distance.

During the years they had been working together in the Sowerby household, it had sometimes happened that Constance and Nella had the same afternoon off and Constance would allow her friend to go with her on her long walks about Newcastle. Nella had lived for those moments when she'd had Constance to herself, away from Mrs Mortimer's beck and call, and they'd been able to forget, for a while, the never-ending drudgery of their lives.

Nella loved the town, the busy streets and the throng of people. She couldn't understand why the parlourmaid, Isabelle, went on about the countryside and the farm near Allendale where she had been born.

Nella couldn't imagine walking for miles without seeing another house, and the idea of streams and trees and moorland being beautiful was baffling to her. What on earth would you do with your time off if you lived in the country? There were no cafés, no bandstands, no theatres. She had always been intrigued by the gaudy posters and the playbills posted on billboards and the gable ends of buildings.

Then, earlier this year, she had seen the London train disgorge a troupe of actors at the Central Station. She had stopped to watch them as the seemingly endless supply of bags and boxes and trunks was loaded on to a wagon. She observed the actors' brilliant clothes, their exaggerated

39

movements and the extravagant way they had of calling out to each other, and she was entranced. Ever since that day, Nella had been saving up to go to the Christmas show at the Palace.

But she also liked looking in the shop windows in the city centre, at the furnishings, the fabrics, and the fashions.

'Constance, you would look lovely in that blue tulle!' she had said once.

Constance smiled. 'So would you.'

'Me? Don't be daft!'

'But you would. We are about the same height, the same colouring—'

'No, Constance, no, we're not the same at all. You are bright – bright and beautiful – and I'm just faded, washed out and ugly as sin.'

'You're not ugly, Nella.'

'Amman't I?'

'No. You have a sweet little face.'

'And what about these little arms and these little legs? They're not sweet and shapely like yours are. They're more like sticks.'

'Nella, stop it!'

'And most of all, Constance, what about this twisted little back? If you dressed me in one of them fine dresses from Bainbridge's window, I'd look like Mr Punch in the sideshow.'

After that day, she remembered, Constance had hurried them past any display of fashion in the shop windows. Nella would see her friend's eyes linger regretfully on the new displays – the hats from Paris, the feather boas, the elegant parasols – and she longed to tell her that it didn't matter. Nella wasn't a bit envious of her friend's beauty, and she would have longed to stop and dream of how lovely Constance would look in that cream muslin day dress or the turquoise satin evening gown with the black lace draped and trailing romantically.

40

But Constance would hurry on, away from the shops and into the smart suburbs north of the city.

Here, Nella would observe a different kind of longing in her friend's eyes. As Constance gazed at the substantial terraced houses and the spacious villas in Jesmond she would grow silent – but there was no need for speech. Nella could see, only too clearly, what kind of hunger it was that was consuming her friend.

One day they had paused at an open gateway. They could see a neat lawn, almost velvet smooth, bounded by flowering shrubs. It was a late summer evening and the scents of the flowers lingered in the lengthening shadows. They stood very still, savouring the fragrance, then Nella saw that Constance was looking at the house beyond.

As they watched, a lady walked towards a table placed near the window and lit an oil-lamp. The soft glow revealed a graceful drawing room, not solid and oppressive like the Sowerbys', but light and airy, with small gilt-framed pictures on the walls. A gentleman appeared and the lady turned and placed a hand on his shoulder. They seemed to be smiling at one another as they drew closer. A moment later he broke away and drew the curtains.

Nella turned, grinning, to face her friend, and was frightened to see how very still Constance had become. Her eyes were wide and glittering in the dusk and she was clenching her fists tightly.

'Constance . . .' Nella whispered.

'Mm?'

'Constance, was . . . was your house like that?'

'What do you mean?'

'The house you had to leave. Was it like that?'

'No, Nella.' Her words, when they came, were like a sigh. 'Not like that. My father's house was much better than that.'

41

She turned abruptly and walked away. Nella scurried along behind her, not daring to question her further. They had never spoken of it again.

But Nella had thought about it often. From the moment she had first met Constance and her mother, she had known they were used to a much better life than the other poor souls who ended up in the workhouse. Agnes Bannerman never spoke of it. Never explained to anyone how she and her daughter had sunk so low but, although mother and daughter didn't ever complain, Nella grew to believe that they had not accepted what fate had brought them to.

One night, as they were preparing for bed in the bleak dormitory, Nella had heard Mrs Bannerman murmur, 'I'm so sorry, Constance. So sorry that it should come to this.'

Constance had flung herself in her mother's arms. 'We will go back there one day, Mama, we will!' Nella had heard her say.

Her mother hadn't replied. She'd simply held Constance tightly. But there had been tears shining in her eyes, and Nella, embarrassed, had turned away.

Well, Nella thought now, the poor lady was dead. But if there was such a place as heaven, she would surely be looking down this night and rejoicing that Constance was going to be married in the morning. She would be happy that her daughter was leaving this dreadful place that wasn't very much better than the workhouse.

Nella yawned and burrowed further into the pillows and the mattress. At last weariness began to overcome the cold and her sense of grief and loss. Her pinched features relaxed into a smile as she drifted off to sleep. Constance may not be going to live in the kind of grand house she had lived in as a child, but at least she was going to have her very own little house, be her own mistress.

And nobody would ever order her around or treat her like a servant again . . .

Chapter Four

'Wait here. Do not attempt to enter the house. I will ask if Mr Elliot will see you.'

The manservant looked down his nose at her. He was young and his sallow skin was at war with a rash of unsightly pimples. He was probably only an underfootman to be on duty as late as this, but his smart uniform and clean white gloves had given him a proper sense of the proprieties. He had decided immediately that this irregular late-night visitor should be allowed no further than the pillared porch.

He pushed the door until it was almost shut. Perhaps he's hoping that I'll go away, Constance thought. She heard his footsteps echo across a marble floor; then silence. She flushed as she remembered the look of suspicion on his face. She knew that she did not appear to be the class of person who should call at the front door of such a house. Her clothes were cheap and she was hot and dishevelled from her dash across the park.

While she waited she turned to gaze back down the wide gravelled drive. It had taken all her resolution to walk up and seize the bell pull. She had never been inside Matthew's house and she suspected that even John was not welcomed here socially.

One day, when they had been walking together, John had

brought her as far as the entrance. 'There, look, Moorside Towers, that's where Matthew lives.'

The tall wrought-iron gates were closed and they peered through the bars at the well-tended gardens and the neat box hedges which bordered the drive. The Elliots were hosting a weekend party at their country house in the Borders. Among the guests would be respectable land-owning families with eligible daughters; Matthew had been requested to attend.

'Why don't we walk up the drive and have a closer look?' she asked.

'Oh, I don't think so.' John coloured slightly.

'But you are Matthew's friend and the servants will recognize you; surely it will be all right?'

'No, it would seem ill-bred to gawp like common folk.'

He smiled his gentle smile, as if to take the sting out of his words, but she was cut to the quick. John did not know it but he had reminded her of how far she had sunk since the days when she would have known how to behave properly.

And then she was forced to acknowledge something else: if her father had not died when he had, if her mother had not been evicted from Lodore House, she would almost certainly not be standing here with John. Nor would she even have met him.

She had realized, almost from that first day in the park, that Matthew and John were separated by social class. For example, John, although he was well spoken and respectable, had to work for a living, whereas Matthew, since coming down from Oxford, seemed to do nothing at all. It had never occurred to her until the day John had remained so firmly outside the gates of Moorside Towers to wonder how the two young men had met or what formed the basis of their friendship.

She heard footsteps hurrying back across the hall and turned as Matthew flung open the door. 'Constance, what has happened? Don't say you have changed your mind? You haven't come to tell me that the wedding is off, have you?' His dark eyes were wide, his cheeks flushed, his voice unsteady as if he had been drinking.

Constance blanched. 'No! Why should I?'

He stared at her and then frowned as if making the effort to collect his wits. When he spoke, his voice was steady. 'But, come, what am I thinking of?'

He drew her in and closed the door behind them. They were alone in the brightly lit hall. Matthew was in evening clothes, but his tie had been loosened and the buttons of his white waistcoat were undone. A lock of his luxuriant dark hair hung over his brow and he raised a hand to push it back.

'Forgive me, I was about to retire,' he said, and then his eyes widened. 'My God, what has happened to you?'

'I have been thrown out. Dismissed without a reference!' She tried to sound amused, to make a joke of it. 'Mrs Sowerby said that as my duties there were over, I must leave *at once*!'

She made a theatrical gesture but Matthew did not respond with a smile. 'Did she attack you?'

'Attack me?'

'Strike you?'

'No, she was angry but she used no physical force to remove me.'

'Then what is this?' He placed long fingers gently under her chin and turned her face towards the light. 'You have a mark on your cheek. Is it a bruise?'

'No, it must be dirt; I fell down in the fog . . . See – my clothes . . .' In the bright light Constance had noticed for the first time the stains on her coat and her voice began to falter. 'As I told you, Mrs Sowerby said I must go and I thought . . .'

'My poor Constance. What a thing to happen on your

47

wedding eve. I'm glad that you thought of me and, of course, you must stay here. Come, give me your box. I'll take you to my sister's rooms; she will have everything you need.'

Constance followed him across the hall and, at the bottom of the richly carpeted stairs, he paused and touched a switch on the wall. Decorative wall lamps blazed into light; they curved up the length of the staircase, illumining the way ahead. The house was lit by electricity, just as her father's had been.

At the end of an upper corridor, Matthew paused at an archway. A heavy curtain was looped back to one side to reveal a vestibule with several doors leading from it. They were all closed.

Matthew gestured towards one of them. 'That is Rosemary's room. She will be in bed now, but—'

'Should we wake her?'

'She would never forgive me if she missed an adventure! But, here,' he opened another of the doors, 'this is her bathroom. You are welcome to use it whilst I go and inform her that she has a guest.'

He led the way in. Constance stared at the tiled walls with mirrors and glass shelves holding bottles of bath salts, essences and perfumes. A rich Turkish carpet lay on the marble floor and thick white towels hung on brass rails. The room was warm so she guessed that the rails were heated. There was another door set in the wall opposite the bath, but Matthew crossed to the stained-glass window on the far wall and adjusted the heavy maroon tasselled curtains. Constance went over to the bath; it was encased in panelled mahogany.

'You fill it like this.' Matthew came up behind her, leaned over and touched the taps. 'See, this one draws hot water and this one cold.'

'I know what taps are.'

'Oh, of course. I'm sure Dr Sowerby must have an up-to-date bathroom, but . . .'

'But not for the use of the servants.'

'Well, no.'

'Of course, you are right, Matthew. There is a bathroom in the house at Rye Hill and that is only for the use of the family.'

'Constance, please . . .'

She ignored his conciliatory expression and carried on, 'I was allowed to carry a tin bath up to my attic once a week and fill it with buckets of hot water – which I also had to carry up all those flights of stairs. My towels were those which were no longer fit for the Sowerbys to use, and the soap I had to buy myself, from my employers.'

'Don't be angry with me, Constance. I did not mean to belittle you.'

'Matthew, I'm tired, and tomorrow . . .'

'Of course. Your wedding day. I'll leave you now. Help yourself to anything you need. There should be spare robes and nightgowns in that cupboard. That other door leads directly to my sister's room. When you are ready she will be waiting for you. I'll see you when it is time to leave for church in the morning.' He closed the door behind him.

She sighed. Her head was aching and she felt bruised both outside and in. She was tired and she longed for sleep but, even more, she longed to be clean again.

As the bath filled, steam rose and surrounded her. It seemed to carry with it a flowery scent. She found a wide-necked jar of pink crystals on the floor by the side of the bath. The stopper was lying beside it. Rosemary must have forgotten to return it to its shelf. She sniffed it. Attar of Roses; that had been her mother's favourite.

Constance kneeled and scattered crystals liberally into the

49

deep bath, stirring them round. She watched the colour bleed into the water; ribbons of red swirling round her hand. Abruptly she rose and pulled off her clothes.

'Why, you have washed your hair. Come, Constance dear, you must sit by the fire and brush it dry.'

Rosemary Elliot had no sooner opened the door to Constance's timid knock, than she took her by the hand and led her across to the hearth. Matthew's sister was fifteen years old and, probably because of her sheltered upbringing, she was neither child nor woman. Constance, at eighteen, felt that she was much older, despite the mere three years that separated them.

Rosemary was almost as tall as her brother, and very slim. She had the same dark hair as Matthew – at the moment it hung almost to her waist in two long plaits – and the same dark colouring, but she had none of his dramatic good looks. A nose and chin that were too thin and pointed marred her oval face. And yet her eyes were like her brother's, large and brown and deeply expressive.

She wore a soft pink flannel robe over a long nightdress with pretty broderie anglaise flounces, but her body looked like that of a lanky boy. However, she spoke with all the authority of a young woman of her class and upbringing.

'Look, I have built up the fire. Sit on this ottoman and towel your hair for a moment. I will fetch you a brush and then I will go and pick up your clothes.'

Constance flushed. 'Forgive me, I should not have left them lying there . . . I'm tired – and a little confused . . .'

'Sit down, Constance. Matthew told me all about you and what has happened; no wonder you are confused!'

'What did he tell you?'

'My dear, don't look so alarmed. There is no shame

50

attached. Your employer threw you out of her house the night before your wedding, with no thought of what might happen to you. It is she who ought to be ashamed. Now, here is my hairbrush.'

No shame, Constance thought. What if I were to tell this confident girl what has really happened to me? Would she understand? Would she be horrified? Would she still want to help me or would she believe, as most of her class would, that I must be to blame?

'Would you like a hot drink?' Rosemary had come back into the room. 'Warm milk and honey perhaps? I always find that soothing.'

'Please don't bother. It's late, your – your household must be sleeping . . .'

'But it's no bother. Beattie has been hovering like a mother hen ever since Matthew woke me. She has her own little kitchen in what used to be the nursery and she will be only too pleased to make the drinks herself.'

'Beattie?'

'Miss Hannah Beattie, former nanny, kept on after I started school, out of sheer sentiment and now employed as my companion and to keep an eye on Matthew whilst our parents travel in foreign parts.'

Rosemary paused at the bedroom door, 'I'll give her your clothes, if you don't mind. Some of them appear to be torn. She'll sort through and see what can be done.'

She closed the door behind her. Rosemary was enjoying this 'adventure', Constance thought, and immediately she felt ashamed; the girl was good-hearted and generous. Constance could not imagine Annabel Sowerby putting herself out for someone she would consider to be one of the lower orders.

Constance stared into the flames. The nightdress she was wearing smelled of lavender and the flannel robe was soft and

51

comforting. She had had one like this when she was a child, and there had been times when she had sat looking for pictures in the nursery fire and brushing her hair dry just as she was doing now.

'Please, don't look so sad.' Rosemary had come back to kneel beside her. Constance was embarrassed to find the girl's face within inches of her own and she looked down.

Rosemary took hold of her arm. 'Whatever happened earlier, you are safe now and, just think, tomorrow you are going to be married. A whole new life, a better life, will begin for you. Look at me, Constance, you know that what I say is true, don't you?'

Constance looked up. Rosemary's eyes were shining. She is taken up with the romance of the idea, Constance thought, the idea of a friend of her brother's marrying a servant girl. She is kind and impetuous and apparently free from prejudice. Or perhaps, in spite of her sensible manner, she is just too young to have realized how unlikely this match is.

There was a tap at the door and Rosemary hurried to open it. After a murmured conversation, she returned with a tray. 'Here is your milk and honey. Beattie wanted to come in but I have told her how tired you are. You must sleep and be fresh for tomorrow.

'Look, while you were bathing, Beattie made up this bed – in the alcove here. When I was a child, if I was poorly, she would sleep here in order to look after me. But tonight I shall be looking after you.'

Constance allowed Rosemary to lead her over to the bed, help her off with her robe and settle the bedclothes around her. The cup of milk was placed on a small table.

'Now I shall put out the light. The glow from the fire should be sufficient for you to drink your milk by. Don't worry about anything. Matthew has everything organized for tomorrow. Good night, Constance.'

'Good night, Miss Elliot.'

'Rosemary. You must call me Rosemary, for I hope that we are going to be friends.'

'Good night, Rosemary. And – Rosemary . . .'

'Yes?'

'I – I don't know how to thank you. You've been so very kind – you and your brother . . .'

For a moment the younger girl looked disconcerted. It was as if she sensed but did not want to acknowledge the strength of Constance's feelings. She looked embarrassed.

Then, 'Oh, my dear,' she said, 'there's no need, no need. I'm sure Matthew doesn't want thanking and neither do I.'

'Nevertheless, I'm very grateful. I hope you'll tell him.'

'Yes, of course, but now you must drink up your milk before it gets cold.'

Constance watched as the girl placed a cinder-guard in front of the fire. She heard her put out the light, and then the soft rustle of bed linen as she settled in her own bed. After she had finished her milk, Constance lay for some time and watched the patterns that the flames made on the ceiling. The coals shifted and settled in the grate and, for a moment, the light flared, then died again. The room grew darker.

Constance felt enfolded by warmth and comfort. She had not slept in such a soft bed with such sweet-smelling linen since she was a small child, but she could not relax entirely. The scented water in the bath had eased the aching of her body; even the burning sensation between her legs had been replaced by a nagging tenderness.

She had taken the soap and washed that part of herself until she thought she had removed every sour trace of Gerald Sowerby – and yet she could not rid herself of the fancy that she would never be clean again.

Constance moved restlessly. Would John be able to tell what had happened? She had learned enough from gossip amongst the other girls in the workhouse to know what took place between men and women but she had only a hazy idea of virginity. However, she imagined that John would never have asked her to marry him if she had not been chaste.

Am I tainted now? she wondered. Has Gerald's action, even though it was against my will, made me impure?

When she had arrived here, earlier, Matthew had asked her if she had come to call off the wedding. For an appalling moment she had imagined that he had guessed what had happened, that her appearance had been changed by her ordeal, that her face somehow would reveal to the world what kind of woman she now was.

But, of course, that was impossible. Matthew could not know that she had been raped unless she told him. And she had told him simply that she had fallen down in the fog. He had believed her. She did not need, ever, to tell anyone any more than she had told Matthew. John would never know – *must* never know – what Gerald had done to her.

But if Matthew had not known what had happened, why had he asked her that question? And why did it seem so important to him?

Eventually, sheer fatigue overcame her need to find answers to these problems and she drifted off to sleep.

Some hours later, while Constance still slept deeply, apparently too tired even to dream, Nella was already stirring in the house on Rye Hill. Every morning of her life she faced the same agony as she swung her legs over the bed and her stiffened joints seemed to lock in protest. This morning there was no Constance to help her rise and ease her gently into her clothes, and by the time she was ready to go downstairs and begin her day's toil, there were traces of tears on her cheeks.

'What you need is a long soak in a hot bath,' Constance had told her once.

'Aye, and that's likely, isn't it?' she'd scoffed. 'By the time I gets the second bucket of water up the stairs the first lot's stone cold!'

'I'll help you next time.'

'Will you?'

But her friend had not been allowed to help her. A strict bath-time rota had to be followed and Mrs Mortimer had made sure that Constance was fully occupied when it was Nella's turn. But at least her friend had helped her in any other way she could, Nella remembered, and she was going to miss her more than she could say.

Constance had urged her to make friends with the new girl who would be arriving to take her place. 'Remember, the poor child will be straight from the workhouse, just as we were. We had each other but she will have no one. She'll be grateful to find a friend.'

'Even a friend who looks like me?'

'Nella, don't, please don't talk like that. She'll soon find out how good you are.'

Nella didn't hold out much hope. Constance and her mother had been so sunk in their own grief when they had first arrived at the workhouse that they had never really noticed how isolated Nella had been from the other children. She had attached herself to them as soon as she could and had been astonished at how they accepted her without prejudice. The confidence this gave her helped her in her dealings with the others. Now she was on her own again.

She felt her way cautiously down the stairs. It was pitch-black but Mrs Mortimer did not allow the servants to use candles on the stairs in the morning, and woe betide the lot of them if any dribbles of candle wax were found. Neither did she allow the gaslamps to be lit until she appeared, but luckily for Nella there was just enough life left in the coals in the kitchen range to light a taper and then a candle.

In spite of the lingering warmth, the kitchen smelled dank in the mornings, and Nella was glad the dim light didn't extend to the dark corners of the room where she could hear suspicious rustling sounds.

Cockroaches? Mice? Rats? Constance had always kept a broom handy first thing in the morning but Nella didn't think she would have the courage to wield it if she were faced with the reality of her nightmares.

She started work on the range. Today she would have to clean and light the black monster by herself and have it ready for Mrs Mortimer to start the breakfasts. The fires in the rest of the house would have to be lit before breakfast, too, and Nella was already dreading the idea of lugging the buckets of coal up the stairs. She wondered if the new girl had any idea what it was going to be like. Poor bairn. Nella found herself feeling sorry for her.

The bolts in the back door were almost too much for her, but Nella finally managed to tug them free and she opened the door that led out into the area yard. The coalhouse was directly opposite, stretching under the pavement. The street-lamps were still lit and Nella was thankful for the light that relieved the blackness. Otherwise the enclosed yard would have been almost like a dungeon.

Before she opened the coalhouse door she noticed something glinting on the ground and she stooped to pick it up. It was a fine chain made of yellow metal, like the chain of a necklace, but it was broken. Nella examined it closely. Was it the chain she had given to Constance? Had it snapped and had

Constance lost her wedding gift almost as soon as it had been given to her?

But where was the little heart? Nella looked all around the yard, even getting down on her hands and knees and feeling into every corner, but she found nothing. She went up the steps on all fours, looking carefully all the way, and even walked halfway up the street but there was no sign of the heart with their initials entwined.

Eventually she knew she must return to her duties and she made her way back. She hoped against hope that it wasn't Constance's necklace. She tried to convince herself that it was another chain that had fallen through the area railings by chance but in her heart she knew that that was unlikely.

Perhaps the heart is caught in her clothing, she thought. I hope so. But Nella could not deny the possibility that it might be lost, and the idea that her friend would be married without wearing her gift around her neck saddened her. Nella was about to slip the chain into her pocket when she stopped and looked at it more closely under the streetlamp. She tested it; it seemed quite strong. But then it had been cheap and perhaps there had been a fault . . .

Yes, that must be it . . . a weak link – otherwise why should it snap so soon without cause? She wondered how soon Constance had realized that she had lost it. She could guess how upset she must have been . . .

Chapter Five

'Have I hurt you?'

'No, you're very gentle.'

'But, Constance, you're crying.'

'No, I'm not, really—'

'Well, if those are not tears, I must have made your eyes water with the powder. Here, take this handkerchief.'

'Thank you.' Constance looked into the dressing-table mirror and dabbed her eyes, trying not to smudge the layer of pale peach-coloured powder that Rosemary had dusted so carefully over the mark on her cheek.

'If I had noticed that bruise last night I would have bathed it with some of Beattie's witch hazel,' Rosemary said. 'It must have happened when you fell over in the fog.'

'That's right.'

'Poor love! What a thing to happen on the eve of your wedding.'

'Yes.' Constance turned her head abruptly so as not to meet Rosemary's eyes in the mirror, and got a mouthful of powder.

'Ooops – sorry! Here, spit it out, use the handkerchief. Good . . . Look in the mirror. I don't think anyone will notice the bruise now.'

'Rosemary, if you're quite finished put that box of powder back in your mother's dressing room and mind you leave everything as you found it.' Hannah Beattie, small, round and flustered, was standing behind them with a hairbrush, a comb and a box of hairpins.

Rosemary smiled at her. 'Right oh, Beattie, dear, and you must take charge now. I have no idea how to dress hair, that must be quite obvious from the state of this bird's nest on my own head!'

'I'll tidy it for you when I've finished with our bride.'

Rosemary's companion turned to Constance and smiled as she put the box of pins down on the dressing table. 'I've a way with hair and fashion, you know, Constance.' She spoke in the soft accent of the Scottish Borders. 'I should have been a lady's maid, not a nanny.'

Rosemary turned as she reached the door. 'When the time comes for me to be presented at Court, you shall have complete charge of my wardrobe; it will save me having to worry about such frivolous things.'

'Stop blethering and hurry along, girl. It's getting late!'

'All right, don't nag!' The door swished shut.

Constance wondered at their easy banter. She knew that the Elliot family was immensely rich and that Hannah Beattie, even with the grand title of 'companion', was still only a servant. Yet, the two of them behaved as though they were equals. Nobody would have been allowed to talk to Annabel Sowerby in such a way. Everybody, from Mrs Mortimer down, had to address her as *Miss* Annabel.

The room was brightly lit and comfortably warm. Constance realized, with a twinge of conscience, that she must have been sleeping whilst the maidservant came in to make up the fire. Only yesterday, in the house on Rye Hill, she and Nella had carried buckets of coal up the stairs to every room. They had cleaned out the hearths and got the fires going before the family was awake. And that was after the mammoth task of cleaning and firing the kitchen range.

This morning, rather than a frugal breakfast of yesterday's bread and weak tea, she was enjoying freshly brewed coffee, toast and a dish of apricot conserve. And instead of sitting at the bare kitchen table in the terraced house on Rye Hill, she was propped up amongst feather pillows in a luxuriously furnished bedroom in a villa overlooking the Town Moor.

Rosemary had thanked the maid who had brought the damask-covered tray, and dismissed her before sitting down on Constance's bed. 'I didn't think you would want anything cooked,' she'd said. 'You must be feeling nervous.'

'Nervous? Why do you say that?'

'Why do you look at me so strangely, Constance? All brides are nervous and, although it is not proper for me to admit it, I do know why!'

The girl had then poured herself a cup of coffee and stayed for a while to nibble some toast but then she hurried off to issue orders to Hannah Beattie. Her companion had already started bustling in and out with items of clothing from Constance's box. Constance had been glad to be left alone for a while. Matthew's young sister was both excited and excitable and, in spite of her kindness, her restless energy was ener-vating.

After Constance's light breakfast, Rosemary had insisted on helping her to get dressed. It was then that she had noticed the bruise on Constance's cheek and she had hurried away to raid her mother's dressing table. The orange and gold box of powder, the delicate swan's-down powder puff and the linger-ing floral scent had brought back memories that had been deeply buried, and Constance had been shaken by their re-emergence and their intensity.

How many years had it been since she had crept into her mother's room to play with the exquisite little jars and scent

61

bottles on the dressing table? Her mother had caught her experimenting with the tiny papers from a book of *papier poudré*.

Instead of scolding, Agnes Bannerman had brought out the bottles of complexion milk, nail polish and liquid rouge, and an array of coloured pencils and tubes. She explained to Constance how everything must be applied so delicately that no one would ever guess that a lady's complexion was anything but natural.

'*Come, I'll show you how to do it!*'

When Constance looked into the mirror, she had almost expected to see the reflection of her mother's face smiling indulgently as she dipped the powder puff into the gold-rimmed box.

But, of course, it was not Agnes Bannerman smiling at her, it was Rosemary Elliot. Constance had not been able to stop the tears brimming in her eyes.

And now, Hannah Beattie had just finished arranging her hair. 'Stand up and let me look at you. Mm, I can see what you've done with the dress. You've got rid of the bustle and the train to give it a more modern line.'

'How can you tell that?'

'Don't look so crestfallen, Constance. Nobody but the most avid follower of fashion, like me, would guess that you had altered anything at all. But it must have helped that the dress was very well made in the first place. Did your employer give it to you?'

'No, it was my mother's.' Constance had answered spontaneously and she was disconcerted to see the appraising look Beattie shot her.

'Your mother's? I see. Poor Constance, it must have been hard for you being in service. Forgive me for saying this – Rosemary is much too unworldly to have noticed – but I

62

couldn't help perceiving that your speech and your manners are not those of a servant. At first I thought you might have been a lady's maid or even a governess, but then I saw your hands.'

Constance glanced down at her work-roughened hands and then she thrust them behind her in an embarrassed gesture. 'They spoil the effect, don't they?'

'Yes. You must wear gloves. Do you have any?'

'Only knitted mittens. They'll hardly match my wedding outfit.'

'Then that shall be my wedding present to you. I have a pair of pale grey silk gloves that I have never worn, and also the dearest little grey velvet toque with a veil.'

'But I couldn't . . . You mustn't—'

'You cannot wear that bonnet, sweet as it is. I have too many hats; they are my weakness. But my round country face was not meant to have a toque perched on top; it will look much better on you.'

'Quite right, Beattie, dear.' Rosemary had come back into the room. 'And I am going to give Constance this velvet cape; I never wear it and it will look much better with her dress than a navy serge coat!'

Constance gazed at herself in the cheval glass. Her new hat tilted forward dangerously on top of the curls which Beattie had piled high; the veil almost matched the smoke-coloured lace she had sewn round the high-standing collar of her dress. Her hourglass figure was accentuated by the fullness of the bodice, the tiny waist and the skirt, which smoothed over her hips and then flared out a little at the knee. If only Nella could see her.

Nella! Constance remembered how she had promised to wear the necklace she had given her and she glanced over to the bedside table. Had she put it there when she went to bed?

She couldn't remember. She had been so distressed last night that it was no wonder she'd forgotten what she had done with it. But the necklace wasn't on the table and she frowned as she tried to recall exactly what she had done the night before.

She had taken her clothes off in the bathroom and left them there . . . Rosemary and Hannah Beattie had gathered them up and sorted them out for her. This morning, Miss Beattie had packed all Constance's things neatly into her box. The necklace must be there. But wait a moment . . . the chain . . . hadn't she felt . . . no . . . Hastily she suppressed an unwelcome memory.

'Is something worrying you, Constance?' Rosemary was looking at her anxiously.

'No . . . no, nothing at all.'

'Then, please stand still, if you don't mind,' Rosemary ordered, 'whilst I arrange the cape around your shoulders.'

Constance turned back obediently. She had decided not to make a fuss about the necklace now. But she was sorry to break her promise to Nella . . .

'It's a pity that this cape is black.' Rosemary stepped back and stood with her head tilted to one side. She looked at Constance through narrowed eyes. 'But at least it is short, and if you take this matching muff,' Rosemary had been holding a muff made of black velvet and now she gave it to Constance, 'I will pin a little nosegay of silk flowers on it. They are the same violet-blue as your eyes. You will have a bridal muff instead of a bridal bouquet!'

'But this was meant to be a quiet wedding,' Constance started to protest. 'John said there would be no fuss.'

'It is hardly making a fuss to have you looking beautiful on your wedding day. And you do look beautiful, Constance, very beautiful indeed!' Rosemary clasped her hands together, her eyes were shining.

Beattie smiled approval before turning to chivvy the girl.

'Come along, child, let me dress your hair. We mustn't keep Matthew waiting.'

Constance stared at them. 'Are you coming with me?'

Rosemary answered. 'Of course we are. I was horrified when I learned that my brother had intended simply to take you to the church and then leave you there with no friends to see you married.'

'But that's all right. John said that his family would be sure to make me feel welcome.'

'That may be so. However, Beattie and I have persuaded Matthew that you must have some family of your own!'

'Nella, stop daydreaming. Take Alice with you and carry more coal to the rooms upstairs. Did you hear me, girl?'

Nella and the new girl, Alice, had just finished washing and drying the family's breakfast dishes. Nella dried her hands on a kitchen cloth and turned to face her tormentor.

'Yes, Mrs Mortimer.'

'And for goodness' sake wipe that crabby look off your face. It's enough to turn the milk sour.'

Mrs Mortimer didn't see Nella's even crabbier response because she turned immediately to a thin-faced, smartly dressed little man who was sitting at the table with a large cup of tea and a slab of fruit cake. An open notebook and pencil lay on the table next to his plate.

While the cook settled herself opposite to him, he looked up and his narrow features cracked into a sly smile as he gave a wink in the direction of the two girls. Nella knew it wasn't for her benefit, it was for Alice's. The new girl was pretty and, although she was only twelve, she already had the rounded figure of a ripe young woman.

Mrs Mortimer had not noticed this by-play and by the time she was seated, the man was concentrating on sinking his sharp, white teeth into the rich, dark cake.

'Now, Mr Askew,' the cook said, 'let me give you our order for next week.'

The cook-housekeeper began the important task of ordering the weekly groceries for the Sowerby household. Nella knew the reason why she wanted everybody out of earshot. With Isabelle and Martha still tidying and dusting upstairs, and herself and Alice safely occupied with the fires for the next half-hour or more, Mrs Mortimer would be able to order whatever stores she pleased.

Mrs Sowerby, like most of the mistresses round here, gave her cook-housekeeper complete charge of the books, only checking them cursorily once a month. Mrs Mortimer controlled the stores, the still room and the linen cupboard, and as she dealt with all the tradesmen there was ample scope for a little cheating. Mr Askew was a high-class grocer but Nella was sharp enough to have worked out long ago that he must be in cahoots with all the cooks round here.

I'll have to remind Constance about what goes on, she thought. Constance had told her that she didn't know how many servants John and his mother kept. Well, whatever the situation was, Nella didn't want her friend to be cheated.

Ee, Constance, she thought, and her mind flew back to what she had found that morning and her fruitless search in the street.

'Nella! I thought I told you to see to the fires? Get along with you!' Mrs Mortimer was having difficulty remaining ladylike. If Mr Askew had not been there, she would have been bellowing by now.

Nella became aware of Alice snivelling at her side. 'Stop that!' she hissed. 'If she thinks you're frightened, it will only make her pick on you whenever she can. Now, hawway!'

She pushed the poor girl before her out of the room and then she deliberately let the door slam shut. 'Sorry, Mrs Mortimer!' she yelled over her shoulder. Then she mouthed the words, 'Noisiness is considered Bad Manners!' in the direction of the closed door to the astonishment of the ever more frightened Alice.

Nella looked at her compassionately. 'Come on then.'

'What are we supposed to do?' The girl's voice was hardly raised above a whisper.

'We're gannin' to climb all them stairs and see to every fire in every room. We'll clean and tidy the hearths and we'll fill the coal scuttles.'

'But—'

'Yes, that means gannin' up and down with buckets of coal until every blessed fire and scuttle is seen to. And not just this once – we'll do that regularly all day long and that's only part of our duties here.'

Nella soon discovered that Alice was good-natured and biddable, and seemingly unaffected by her crook-back appearance. Nella knew very well what she looked like and she had braced herself for that certain look on the new girl's face when they first met just after the staff's frugal breakfast. She had imagined that the girl's eyes would widen with disbelief and that then she would either smirk openly or look away sharply to hide her disgust and embarrassment.

Alice had not reacted in either of these ways. She had looked at Nella with huge, brown eyes that were filled with fear, and begged her, without a word being spoken, to be kind to her.

Nella had been more moved than she wanted to admit. Her immediate thought was of how she would tell Constance. 'You told me to make a friend of her and I hev,' she would say. And she meant to. But not before she had taught her her duties and

67

to do so she might have to be harsh. It was for the girl's own good.

'For goodness' sake, watch what you're doing!'

Alice, already tired after only two trips up and down the back stairs, had lurched against the wall and tipped the scuttle she was carrying so that half its contents went bouncing back down the stairs leaving a sooty trail of coal dust.

'Ee, I'm sorry!'

Nella thought the girl was going to pee herself with fright.

'Divven't apologize to me – it's you that's gannin' to hev to clean it all up. As soon as we've finished seeing to the fires yer next job is to scrub all the back stairs from basement to attic and get rid of every trace of this mess or Mrs Mortimer will eat you alive!'

Alice swayed and leaned back against the wall. Her breasts were heaving as she gasped for air and the features of her soft pretty face seemed to be dissolving as she began to cry.

'Stop that!'

The girl blanched and almost choked with fear. Oh God, she must think I'm just like the wicked witch in the fairy tales, Nella thought, and her voice softened. 'Hawway, we've nearly finished the fires and I'll help you with the stairs.'

'Oh, will you? Oh, thank you, miss.'

'I'm not "miss", I'm Nella, and if you're a good girl, I'll keep you right here.'

The girl's look of gratitude almost made Nella feel ashamed of herself. Almost, but not quite. It would be no good being too soft with her; she would have to learn the hard way just like Nella herself and Constance had done.

Constance . . . she thought for the hundredth time that morning. I wonder if you're missing me as much as I'm missing you. No, why should you be? This is yer wedding morning.

Nella tried to imagine what the church would be like . . . blazing with candles and full of the colours and scents of bonny flowers . . . And Constance would look so beautiful that her new family would all fall in love with her straight away . . .

The image shattered when her fingers curled round the cheap little chain she had slipped into her apron pocket earlier that morning. As she felt the tiny links she remembered something that had happened the night before. She had thought she had heard someone cry out and she had risen from her bed to open the window and peer down into the fog-filled street.

She had seen nothing and she had gone back to bed. But, somehow, that cry had come back to haunt her and she knew that she would not easily forget it.

The journey was only about twenty minutes in Matthew's motorcar to Heaton, where John lived. Constance knew that it would have taken about three-quarters of an hour or more to walk there. She had never travelled in such a way before, although she had seen motorcars in the streets of Newcastle during her walks on her afternoons off.

She was sitting in the back, the covered part of the vehicle, in between Rosemary and Hannah Beattie. A large rug covered their knees and feet but Constance still felt the chill of the November morning. It must have been worse for Matthew, who was in the open driver's seat at the front. He was an astonishing sight in his long waterproof coat, peaked cap and goggles, but Constance barely had time to wonder at the strangeness of it all. Her mind was wholly occupied with what was to come.

She had longed for this day . . . dreamed of marrying John and of their future life together. She ought to have been feeling as blithe as any bride on the way to her wedding but, instead, she could only grieve about what had happened the night before.

'Nervous, Constance?'

Rosemary was peering at her through narrowed eyes, a frown puckering her forehead. Constance realized inconsequentially that the girl was short-sighted.

'A little.'

'Don't worry. As I said, that's only natural, but do try to smile.'

'Very well, if it will please you.'

Constance forgot her worries long enough to hope that she hadn't sounded snappish. Rosemary's concern for her was touching so she tried her best to respond but her smile did not reach her eyes and she knew it. She took her gloved hands out of the muff and raised them to adjust her veil, pulling it down a little further. Then she turned to look out at the passing streets.

The rain had stopped but it was still quite dark. Light spilled out of open doorways on to wet pavements. It was a Saturday morning and the small shops that they passed were already busy. A queue had formed outside the baker's, huddling in towards the window and away from the edge of the dripping awning above them.

An aroma of freshly ground coffee filtered out from the Italian grocer's on the corner, mingling with the smells of frying bacon coming from the small workman's café next door.

A greengrocer was arranging boxes of fruit on a raised stall outside his window when one of the boxes tilted too far and some oranges dropped out. They rolled across the pavement, bounced down on to the road, and spun on into the path of the car. Matthew made no attempt to avoid them. He laughed as he drove straight over them and turned to grin at Rosemary, who joined in. But Hannah Beattie tut-tutted at the waste.

'I'd be grateful if you'd keep your eyes on the road, Matthew. We don't want any mishaps on the way to the wedding.'

'Sorry, Beattie, dear.'

Constance couldn't see his eyes because of the goggles. She thought his voice sounded strained.

As they sped away she turned and looked back at the squashed fruit. The beautiful bright skins had split open and the pulp had burst out and was smeared across the road. They were despoiled . . . ravaged . . . No one would want them now . . . She closed her eyes and turned back to face the way they were going.

The church where she was to be married was on the corner of the street where John and his mother lived. The building was tall and grim against the winter skyline, and a wide flight of steps led up to a massive wooden door.

John was waiting at the top, one half of the door was open and he was sheltering from the cold wind just inside the archway. Another figure stood a little to one side, taller and thickset. Constance guessed that this would be Walter Barton, John's uncle and the head of the chain of gentlemen's outfitting shops.

Long before the car drew to a halt at the kerb John had hurried down the steps to greet them. Rosemary and Beattie helped Constance out of the car as if she were made of spun glass. Matthew had already got out of the driver's seat; he pushed his goggles up on to his forehead and spoke to John. Constance thought that he looked embarrassed.

'Slight change of plan. This is my sister, of whom you've heard so much, and her companion, Miss Beattie.'

'I'm pleased to meet you, Mr Edington.' Rosemary was smiling; Hannah Beattie was polite but seemed to look at John askance.

71

John murmured a polite greeting and then turned to watch in surprise as Matthew divested himself of his protective coat. Matthew leaned forward and began to talk quietly.

Constance was distracted when Rosemary took her arm. 'Your bridegroom is so handsome!' The younger girl's face was pink with excitement. 'You will make such an entrancing couple, won't they, Beattie?'

'I dare say.'

Matthew straightened up again and Constance heard him say, '. . . furthermore, they thought it very strange that I was not going to attend a friend's wedding.'

After a slight pause, John replied, 'Oh, that's all right, my mother isn't coming to the church, as a matter of fact. This damp weather could be fatal for her.' Then his face cleared and he grinned. 'But do wipe your face before you come into the church. Those goggles have left black circles round your eyes!'

Constance was perplexed. She had not realized until that morning that Matthew was not going to be a guest at the wedding. Also, it was obvious that John had never met any of Matthew's family before today. Probably, that could all be explained by the fact that they were separated by social class.

John turned towards Constance and his wry amusement turned to pleasure. 'My darling girl, you look exquisite!'

'So do you!'

John laughed. 'Thank you, but I think you are supposed to say "handsome" or some such thing. Now come along, my uncle is waiting for you.'

Matthew had already begun to escort his sister and Hannah Beattie up the steps towards the entrance of the church. His tall elegance was oddly accentuated by the figures of his skinny schoolgirl sister and her plump little companion.

Constance withdrew her gloved hand from her muff and placed it on John's arm. 'Wait!'

'What is it?'

'John—' She looked up into his face. He was not much taller than she, and he only had to incline his head slightly. His dark blue eyes were full of concern.

'Constance, you look so grave. Is something worrying you?'

'John, what did Matthew tell you just now?'

'He told me how that ogress Mrs Sowerby threw you out and how you'd had the good sense to go to him for refuge. He also told me that Rosemary insisted that they should all accompany you to the church. Now come, we must hurry.'

But Constance resisted for a moment longer. 'John . . . I want to tell you . . .'

A slight frown of impatience marred his almost perfect features but his voice was as kind as ever. 'Tell me what?'

'I – I love you.'

His frown disappeared and he leaned forward and kissed her brow. 'Then you had better come and marry me.'

He took her hand and they hurried up the steps. At the top, after the most perfunctory of introductions, he left her with his uncle and he hurried inside the church and down the aisle. She gazed after him with a growing sense of anxiety.

I ought to have told him . . .

'Well, Constance, you must take my arm.'

'Oh, I'm sorry.'

She turned to look up into the face of Walter Barton. His dark hair was greying and his moustache and short, neatly trimmed beard gave him a distinguished air. He looked the prosperous retailer that John had described him to be and, at this moment, he seemed puzzled.

'Constance?'

'Yes, Mr Barton?'

'My nephew tells me that you have been in service?'

'Yes.'

'A lady's maid?'

'Well . . . I . . .'

'No matter.' He frowned, but not unkindly, and patted the gloved hand that she had placed over his arm. 'The organ has begun to play and it seems I have been given the role of your father so we had better proceed.'

As Constance and Walter Barton began to walk towards the altar, their footsteps seemed to echo unnaturally loudly on the brown and yellow tiled floor. The church was lit by hissing gas jets but they barely lightened the gloom of the high-vaulted interior. Areas of yellowish light alternated with pools of darkness.

The place felt cold and smelled damp and musty. Constance was chilled to the bone and yet her skin felt clammy. Her underclothes were clinging uncomfortably and she became aware of a trickle of perspiration running down between her breasts.

There were only very few people gathered in the pews at the front of the nave. Someone turned and stared at her: it was Hannah Beattie. She caught Constance's glance and gave a small smile and a nod of encouragement. Next to her, Rosemary grinned and gave a little wave but her brother seemed to be trying to merge into the shadow of a stone pillar.

Constance focused on the backs of two men waiting before the altar. One she had never seen before but she knew him to be Albert Green, a young man who lived next door to John and his mother. The other was John. His bright blond hair shone, somehow, through the gloom.

Suddenly, he turned and smiled at her and her love for him rose up and overwhelmed her. In that moment she managed to contain her anxiety and push it down into the hidden well of

74

strength that had sustained her in all the miserable years since her father had died.

Her doubts faded. She would never reveal what Gerald had done to her. She knew that she ought to have trusted John, ought to have given him the chance to prove his love for her. But she also knew that she would rather die than run the smallest risk of losing him.

Chapter Six

'Well, at least you won't be losing your son, Frances. They'll be living here with you, and no doubt the girl will be only too pleased to look after you.'

'The girl?'

'Don't be difficult, you know who I mean. John's wife – Constance.'

Frances Edington, propped up amongst the cushions on a chaise longue set well back from the hearth, watched as Muriel Barton stared into the mirror above the mantelpiece and attempted to secure errant wisps of hair with tortoiseshell combs.

She must have overheated her tongs, as usual, for the curls fluffed over her forehead were frizzed and lifeless. I suppose she imagines that that dated style she adopts gives added height and character to her plain round face, Frances thought.

Muriel was small and she had grown stout over the years. The effort of holding her head back and raising her arms was making her breathe heavily. For a moment, as Frances watched her brother's wife, an expression of sheer dislike animated her pale features; but then she dropped her head and began to cough gently into a large white handkerchief. The coughing fit was not too serious but, when it passed, Frances examined the handkerchief anxiously for spots of blood. There were none.

At the hearth, Muriel was swaying slightly. Even though the fire was kept banked down because of Frances' lung condition, it was warm enough to make her overweight sister-in-law more uncomfortable the longer she stood there. At last Muriel seemed to have arranged her hair to her satisfaction and she stepped back and turned round. Still breathing heavily, she tucked her blouse into the waistband of her skirt and pulled down the jacket of her emerald green woollen suit. It was trimmed with black braid, and the frogging on the front gave comical emphasis to her great rounded bosom.

No amount of money could compensate for taste, Frances thought, but that did not stop Muriel adopting an air of superiority. Frances averted her eyes and looked down at the handkerchief she clasped in her hands.

'You need not have stayed here with me, Muriel. You should have gone to the church,' she said.

'And watch my daughter's heart break in two? No, let her father comfort her; he is as sorry as she is about your son's choice of bride.'

'Are you sure about Esther's feelings? She could hardly have married John: they are first cousins.'

'Oh, cousins do marry, you know, especially when family interests are concerned.'

'You mean money?'

'Yes, and why not? Walter has worked hard since your father died; he has made Barton's even more prosperous. Since Grandfather Barton willed that John should inherit only when he married, why should my husband not have hoped to keep the money in the family?'

'And yet I sense that *you* have never been so keen that John and Esther should marry?'

'No.'

Frances looked at her coolly and Muriel pursed her lips and raised her chin like a stubborn child. Then, in the continuing silence, she flounced over to the window. Even although it was mid-morning, little light filtered through the cream lace curtains. Muriel twitched them aside and gazed out. Her expression of amused contempt was reflected in the glass.

She has chosen to forget that she once lived in a house like this, Frances thought. Once, her brother, Walter, and his wife also looked out into a tiny yard where brick walls enclosed a coalhouse and an outside privy, but now they lived in a gracious villa in a prosperous suburb.

At her home in Jesmond, Muriel looked out with proud satisfaction on to a landscaped garden surrounded by luxuriant shrubs and mature trees. That was obviously where her thoughts had taken her for she murmured, half to herself, 'I'm thinking of putting in a pond,' before she let the curtain fall and turned to face the room again.

Frances felt her coughing fit returning. She raised the handkerchief to her lips and began to cough gently at first, but then the spasm grew in intensity until her whole body was shaking. She saw Muriel make a *moue* of distaste before hurrying over and snatching up a carafe from a small table. She poured a tumblerful of water and held it out to Frances.

The coughing subsided a little and Frances took the water. 'Thank you.'

'You know, Frances, it need never have come to this. Grandfather Barton was prepared to send you to Switzerland for a cure when this trouble of yours was first suspected.'

'That was years ago. I was young, and thought myself immortal.'

'You mean you wouldn't leave Duncan.'

'The price my father expected me to pay was too high. I

79

loved Duncan. How could I take his son and abandon him?'

'Huh! He didn't hesitate to abandon you – and the way he did it!'

'Muriel, this is pointless.' Frances began to cough again and the handkerchief she was holding to her mouth spotted with blood.

Muriel looked frightened but when the spasm receded she said, 'I can't understand why you've never engaged a properly trained nurse.'

'You know very well that we cannot afford it. As you would be the first to point out, my husband left me almost penniless and my father had washed his hands of me.'

'Walter has always been prepared to pay for whatever care you needed.'

'I know that, Muriel, it's just . . . it's just that John didn't think we should be too beholden to his uncle. He—'

'Rubbish! Your son was frightened that anyone Walter appointed might carry tales back—'

'Muriel!'

'Well, then, it is just as well that John is marrying a girl who's used to hard work. She'll be able to look after you as well as taking over the running of the house.'

'And that would not have suited Esther, would it?'

'Of course not. We've brought her up to expect more . . .'

'More than you had as a girl. Is that what you were about to say?'

Muriel Barton's small brown eyes filled with annoyance but then she shrugged and turned to survey the table placed slightly to the back of the dining room. It was set with ham, cold roast beef and salmon, all in beds of salad. There were two cut-glass bowls containing trifles and, in the centre, there was a three-tier wedding cake decorated with royal icing.

'Very clever, Frances.'

'Clever?'

'Generous but not exactly *à la mode*. You would hardly want to intimidate your new daughter-in-law, would you, by making her wedding breakfast too genteel?'

'I don't know what you mean.'

'No? Well, you never have moved in quite the same social circles as we have, have you?'

'Perhaps I haven't cared to.'

'Of course not, my dear. Quite apart from the fact that you have had to look to Walter for any little extras, even this wedding breakfast, it must have been a great strain for you, carrying the burden of such a scandal all these years. No wonder you have preferred a quiet life at home.'

'Mrs Edington?' The door had opened and a young house-maid came into the room.

'Yes, Polly?'

Frances turned her head and smiled at the girl, glad to be spared more of Muriel's venom. She knew that she should try not to rise to any of her sister-in-law's taunts but she was becoming increasingly weary of the woman's airs and graces. However, sometimes her brother's wife managed to sail too close to the truth. The wedding breakfast, for example.

She could have made the refreshments more 'refined', as Muriel would have put it, especially as Walter had been good enough to help out with the expenses. Why hadn't she? Perhaps she, too, had hardly thought it appropriate for some little servant girl.

'Mrs Edington,' Polly's face was flushed and her hair was escaping from her cap. Her white pinafore was creased and stained; she had not stopped since rising before dawn that morning, 'shall I light the gaslamps? It's already as dark as night out there.'

'Yes, thank you, Polly, here and in the hall. And then you'd

81

better tidy your hair and put on a clean apron. It won't be long before the guests arrive.'

Constance walked out of the church on John's arm and looked up at the heavy black clouds and darkening sky. She hoped it wasn't an omen. John squeezed her hand and whispered, 'There, it's all over, and it wasn't such an ordeal, was it?'

It's almost as if he's reassuring himself, she thought wonderingly. As he leaned towards her, she imagined that he was going to kiss her. She half-closed her eyes but he pulled away when he heard the others begin to emerge from the doorway behind them. They waited whilst their guests walked to each side of them and began to make their way down the steps. John's eyes followed Matthew and his party until they reached the pavement.

Rosemary and Hannah Beattie had their heads together. Rosemary had a white paper packet in her hands. She opened it. Constance could hear her laughing. Matthew stood a little apart as if trying to detach himself from his sister's gaiety. The other guests, hesitant at first, began to gather round the little group.

Constance turned her head as a gust of wind blew stinging drops of moisture into their faces. They looked like tears. John brushed his cheek with his fingers before turning to say, 'We'd better go, it's starting to rain again.'

'No, it's not rain, it's sleet. Oh, John, on our wedding day!'

They clung on to each other as they hurried down the now treacherous stone steps. When they reached the bottom, Rosemary, her face flushed with excitement, raised a hand and showered them with rice.

'Hurrah!' Albert Green, John's best man, roared approval.

Hannah Beattie applauded but the other guests seemed to be unsure what to do. It's no wonder they're so quiet, Constance thought. The church was as cold as the grave and now the wind is freezing.

But Rosemary was irrepressible. She caught at Constance's hands and blurted out, 'I've asked my brother to take you and John home in his motorcar.'

'No, that doesn't matter,' John said. 'You've already been too kind.'

'No, Matthew has agreed to my plan. The rest of us can walk, but this is your special day!'

'I don't mind, John.' Matthew stepped forward. 'I'll take you home, unload Constance's box, and then take Rosemary and Miss Beattie back to Fenham.'

'Oh . . .' Rosemary's smile vanished. 'I thought we would be going to the wedding breakfast. I mean . . .' She flushed as, behind her, Hannah Beattie cleared her throat. 'Of course, how rude of me, we have not been invited.'

'Then let me invite you now.'

They all turned as Uncle Walter spoke. He was standing with a tall dark-haired girl dressed in crimson, whom Constance took to be John's cousin, Esther. Esther was staring moodily ahead. She had strong features and bold dark eyes, and the biting wind had given her a high but not unattractive colour. She would be beautiful if she allowed herself to smile, Constance thought. I wonder why she looks so out of humour?

'No, really, sir,' Matthew said. 'Mrs Edington is not expecting us.'

'Nonsense, my sister will be only too pleased to welcome three more guests. Now, I suggest we hurry before this sleet turns into a snowstorm.'

By the time Matthew had put on his coat and his goggles, and Constance and John were settled in the back of the car, the others were halfway down the street ahead of them. Constance watched them. Rosemary and Hannah Beattie led the way and Albert Green and his parents walked just a little way behind. Constance knew that the Greens lived next door to John and his mother, and that father and son both worked at the Central Station.

She remembered Matthew saying to John that day the three of them had sat in the teashop planning the wedding, 'I suppose that strapping young railway porter shall be your best man.'

'Albert is not a porter, he's a bookings clerk – and destined to climb even higher in the service of the London and North Eastern Railway Company. Or so his mother assures us,' John had laughed.

'Well, porter or clerk, he will be by your side on your wedding day and I shall be jealous.'

Constance watched the rueful look that passed between them and she frowned before she asked, 'But, John?'

'What is it?'

'Why can't Matthew be your best man? After all, he is your best friend.'

'I suppose you'll have to know. My mother doesn't altogether approve of Matthew.'

'Whyever not?'

Matthew and John glanced at each other and then Matthew smiled at her. 'Let us say that Mrs Edington thinks her son should stay within his own social class. A ridiculous notion in the twentieth century, I know, but perhaps she imagines that people like me will lead him astray.'

All the while Matthew was talking even his eyes had been smiling so that Constance did not know whether to take him seriously. He and John so often teased each other. After that they had changed the subject and Constance had forgotten about the exchange – until now, when they were on their way to John's house in Matthew's car. It was only a short journey from the church on the corner. They would soon be there.

John gripped her hand. 'What are you thinking?'

She was glad that her veil partly obscured her expression. She did not know why, but she felt that John would not want to be reminded of her question that day.

'Constance, is something the matter?'

'No. I was just wondering . . .'

'Wondering what?'

'Wondering why your cousin Esther looks so cross.' Constance pointed to where the tall young woman strode ahead through the swirling sleety flakes, not waiting for her father, who was politely walking behind the others.

'Look!' Constance's eyes widened as Esther overtook the Green family and then actually pushed Rosemary Elliot aside as she went past.

'Don't worry about my cousin. Esther will always find something to sulk about. Goodness knows what has set her off today.'

Just as John spoke, the car drove past them all, and Constance glanced back admiringly at Esther Barton's glossy dark curls piled high under a fur-trimmed hat. Constance caught her eye and was shocked at the venom she saw there.

'Cold, sweetheart?'

Constance turned to find John looking concerned. 'Yes.'

'You're shivering. But don't worry, the journey's over. You'll soon thaw out when we get inside.'

Constance watched her new husband as he opened the waist-high, wrought-iron gate of the small grey-brick terraced house. He took her hand and led her up the short path to the front door. The others had waited and now they followed them. At one side of the path, dividing it from that next door, was a tall privet hedge, and at the other side, a tiny square of garden crowded with frosted shrubs. She had never been invited to this house. Since John had proposed to her, and she had accepted, there had hardly been time.

After that first casual meeting in the park, when the band had been playing, John had asked her to meet him in the Willow Tea Rooms the following week. Constance had hardly been able to contain her excitement but, when the day came, she had not really been surprised that Matthew was there too. Indeed, over the next few months she had been unsure whether or not John was truly courting her. He seemed to enjoy her company, otherwise why seek it, but they were hardly ever alone together.

And then one day he had turned up without his friend. John offered no explanation but he had been flatteringly attentive, making Constance deliriously happy. That was the first time he had reached for her hand and held it as he walked her home. Before parting he had brushed her lips with his own. She could still remember the disturbing sensations his first kiss had aroused.

There had been so few kisses after that; they had not had the opportunity. Matthew had even been there, walking a little apart, when John had asked her to marry him. She had been overcome with happiness as she agreed and she had longed for John to take her in his arms and embrace her. But, with Matthew so near, John had simply raised her hand to his lips instead. But he had looked at her with eyes so full of emotion, she was sure she had seen the glint of tears.

'You're supposed to carry the lass over the threshold, you know! I'll give you a hand, John, if you can't manage it!' Albert Green was standing behind them.

'Albert!' His mother hissed. Her large, protuberant eyes stared up anxiously at the son who dwarfed her.

'I only meant because John's such a little fellow, Mam. Not much bigger than his bonny bride. I mean—'

'Albert!' This time his father rebuked him. Mr Green was

as tall as Albert, but he was thin and so pale that he appeared almost bloodless. Constance wondered how the pair had produced such a robustly handsome son.

Acute embarrassment made Mr Green address the ground near her feet. 'I'm sorry, Mrs Edington. Our lad's more brawn than brain but that's no excuse for bad manners. What will you think of us?'

For a moment Constance was at a loss. Mrs Edington? Of course, he means me! *I* am Mrs Edington! 'Oh, I don't mind.' She smiled radiantly up at Albert, who grinned back.

The next moment happiness engulfed her as John, with surprising strength, swept her up into his arms. 'No thank you, Albert, I am quite capable of carrying my bride myself!'

'I'm sorry that I cannot get up to greet you, Constance.'

'That's all right, Mrs Edington. John has explained that you are not strong.'

'Not strong?' Frances Edington smiled faintly. 'I hope he has been a little more precise than that.'

'Yes, he has.'

After introducing them, John left them alone together while he instructed the maid to arrange more chairs at the table. Constance looked at her mother-in-law. She was so unlike John. He was small with angel-blond hair, fair skin and delicate features. His mother had long limbs and a large frame, although it was wasted now with illness.

Before ill health had made her complexion so pallid, she must have been as boldly dark and attractive as her brother's daughter, Esther, Constance thought. But it was undeniable that, even although she was gravely ill, her beauty still lingered. In fact the consumption had added something – an air of drama, of tragedy that may have made her even more attractive.

Mrs Edington was wearing a plain, dark blue dress and her black hair was parted in the middle and fell in two raven wings before being drawn back into a heavy knot on the nape of her neck. The severe way she has of dressing her hair suits her, Constance thought. In contrast to her hair, her face was unnaturally pale but as she smiled up at Constance, two pink spots appeared and glowed faintly in her cheeks.

Frances assessed her daughter-in-law. She had had so little time to get used to the idea and this was not what she had expected. She remembered the day John had told her that he was getting married. How surprised and how apprehensive she had been.

'I thought you would be pleased,' he had said. 'I will come into my inheritance, at least some part of it, and if a child is born, Uncle Walter will not be able to withhold the full amount.'

'Of course I'm pleased that you are marrying, but I hope it is not just for the sake of the money your grandfather willed to you. Are you sure that . . . I mean the girl—'

'Don't worry, she has nobody, no family to object to her alliance with the son of a scoundrel.'

'John!'

'I'm sorry, I know that you loved him.'

'John, I only meant . . . the girl is a servant.'

'Constance is poor but she's quite respectable. Don't you trust me? My good taste?'

'Of course. But will she . . . ? I mean, will you be happy?'

'What do you want to hear, Mother? Believe me, Constance is perfect. She is young, she is beautiful and she adores me. How could I not be happy?'

He had seemed so eager, so like any young man who had found the girl that he wanted to marry, that she had tried to suppress her misgivings. But there had been so much left unsaid. And now Constance was actually married to her son and she realized that she had been staring for rather too long.

'I'm sorry, I don't mean to make you feel unwelcome. If I seem distant it's because I tire so easily.'

'Can I get you anything? Something to eat? Or perhaps a cup of tea?'

'Do you know,' she smiled up at Constance, 'as it's your wedding day, I think I would like a glass of wine.'

'I guessed you might and here it is, madam!' John reappeared beside them. He was carrying a plate of cold roast beef sandwiches cut into small triangles and a glass of red wine. 'Polly has prepared this for you so that you can join in the festivities without tiring yourself too much.' He turned to smile at his new bride. 'Would you move that small table a little nearer to my mother? Good. Now we should join our guests.'

As the others were taking their seats, Muriel found time to approach her sister-in-law. 'Quite a surprise, eh, Frances?'

'Surprise?'

'Well, what kind of servant girl is it who speaks and dresses like a lady and is friends with the daughter of Sir Hubert Elliot?'

Frances glanced at her unexpected guests, her expression unreadable. 'Matthew Elliot is John's friend.'

'Really? You've never said anything about it.'

'Why should I?'

Suddenly, Muriel's small eyes and mouth formed three speculative circles as something occurred to her. 'She's not some castoff of young Elliot's, is she?'

'What are you talking about?'

'Constance. Some governess or lady's maid that the lad has got into trouble? John's not marrying her to do his rich friend a favour, is he?'

'How dare you?' The spots of colour in Frances' cheeks intensified and burned an angry red. When she began to cough, Muriel sidled away.

From her seat at the table Constance had seen the vexed exchange and, not knowing what was the matter, she half rose to go and see if there was anything she could do for Mrs Edington. But the little maid was already hurrying over to her. John took Constance's hand and pulled her down again.

'Don't worry, I could see before that my mother was getting overtired but I didn't want to banish her from the wedding feast. Polly will see to her; she's used to it. Our guests are waiting to begin the meal.'

Constance looked around. There were seats for ten people at the dining table. She had been placed between John and Uncle Walter, John on her right and his uncle on her left. Opposite to her Albert had settled himself between Rosemary and Hannah Beattie and she could see his cheery face towering over the wedding cake.

Round the corner, on John's right, Esther stared moodily at her plate and did not even look up as her mother settled herself officiously on the seat beside her. At the other end of the table, and next to Walter Barton, Matthew sat and stared almost as moodily as Esther, although he did respond politely every time John's uncle spoke to him.

On Matthew's left sat Mr Green, stiff and awkward to find himself in such august company. Constance noticed that Hannah Beattie tried to engage him in conversation but the poor man replied with words of one syllable and looked longingly in the direction of his wife, who had donned a large white pinafore and was helping Polly serve the guests.

Constance looked beyond the table and noticed, for the first time, how low the fire burned in the grate. There was not enough heat to warm this high-ceilinged room. Polly had taken

Constance's cloak away when she had first arrived and she was still cold. How few pictures there are on the walls, she thought, and how few ornaments on the mantelpiece or the sideboard. It is somehow bleak – and yet still preferable to that vulgarly overfurnished dining room at Rye Hill.

The rooms at Lodore House had never been overfurnished. Her mother had created areas of space and light that enchanted all who came there. And yet not everyone had been pleased. She remembered something Robert had said: *'Grandmother Meakin says that your mother just couldn't wait to empty this house of anything that reminded you of my mother. She said it's quite indecent the way that she gets Father to agree to anything!'*

Why had she thought about her half-brother now? She had put him out of her mind for years until that moment last night.

'Hev you invited Robert to yer wedding?'

The question had taken her by surprise. She had not realized that Nella knew about Robert. She had certainly never talked to her about him in all those years in the workhouse. She hadn't even seen him since the day before she and her mother had had to leave Lodore House.

Captain and Mrs Meakin had come to take their grandson home with them to Berwick. They had made it quite plain that they wished to have no more to do with their late son-in-law's second family. They would be happy if Robert never saw his stepmother or his half-sister again.

'You haven't touched your wine.' John was smiling at her. He took the glass and put it in her hand.

'I'm not used to wine. I'm not sure . . .'

'Drink just a little. There, do you like it?'

'Mm, yes, I do.'

Constance looked down into her glass. The light from the gas chandelier above the table sparkled on the rim for a moment but the dark red liquid inside it remained dull and impenetrable. She took another sip. It tasted rich and sweet; it was strangely warming; at last the ice in her veins began to thaw. The tight knot in the very centre of her being began to ease a little.

She looked around the table. It was all so strange. This was her wedding day; these people, most of whom she'd never met before, were her guests; this house was now her home; she and John would live here together . . .

As she drained her glass she was overwhelmed with love and gratitude.

Chapter Seven

'Her followers call her Gypsy, you know.'

The wedding guests were beginning to leave. John and Matthew were talking beside the door and Rosemary had hurried round to sit next to Constance.

'Who? What are you talking about?' Constance asked.

Mrs Green was helping Polly clear the dishes away. Rosemary leaned close, and dropped her voice to a whisper. 'Esther Barton, your husband's cousin. I know her from school.'

'Which school?'

'The Girls' High School in Jesmond.'

'Esther Barton is at school with you?' Constance glanced over towards the shapely young woman who had gone with her mother to talk to Frances Edington.

'Not now – she left at the end of the summer term. She stayed on until she was sixteen. I have no idea why as she never had any hope of going to college.'

For the first time since she had met her the night before, Constance saw Rosemary adopt a superior air. 'But of course you don't have to be intelligent to attract admirers.'

'Admirers?'

'Well, there is no denying that she is handsome. Although those dark good looks are supposed to be unfashionable, quite a few of the more empty-headed junior girls were her devoted slaves.'

Rosemary's long nose was shiny and her hair was beginning to escape from Beattie's tidy arrangement. Constance realized that, in spite of her poise and air of sophistication, in many ways, Rosemary was still a child.

Her own formal education, provided by the workhouse, had been over long before she was Rosemary's age. She had been put out to service the minute that she was twelve and she'd had to grow up quickly. She had been a bright pupil, she knew that, and her lonely walks around the city on her days off from the Sowerby household had taken her to museums, exhibitions and art galleries in a constant search for knowledge.

She had never ceased to regret the life that she had lost when her father was ruined. Almost certainly she would have attended the same high school as John's cousin Esther; most of the daughters of the local professional and business families went there, or to the convent school. But she was surprised that Rosemary Elliot was a pupil there.

'Rosemary did not want to go away to boarding school.' Hannah Beattie had come to stand behind her charge's chair and she'd seen the surprise on Constance's face and guessed the cause. 'Within reason, her parents like to indulge her wishes.'

'Constance, be careful.' Rosemary was frowning.

'Careful?'

'She doesn't like you.'

'Who?'

'Esther. I've seen the way she's been looking at you and I'm sorry, it's probably my fault.'

'Rosemary, Constance doesn't want to hear this kind of schoolgirl blether.'

'No, really, Beattie, dear, Esther has been glowering at Constance all day and I'm sure it's because she sees that we are friends.'

'Why should Esther dislike me because of that?'

'It was something that happened at school. Caroline Blakey, my best friend – at least I thought she was – betrayed me!' And now Rosemary sounded just like an indignant child – like twelve-year-old Annabel Sowerby when she had been denied her own way.

Constance suppressed a smile. 'Betrayed you?'

'Yes, she joined the ranks of the Gypsy's followers. She would watch her with great cow eyes and simper after her and generally behave in a sickening way. It was all the more exasperating because, until I befriended Caroline, she had been too shy to talk to anyone.

'One day, when I could stand her look of slavish adoration for Esther no longer, I told her how foolish she was to imagine that there was anything inside that romantic-looking exterior other than greed and self-regard. It was the end of our friendship. Unfortunately, Caroline repeated my remarks to her new beloved. That, and the fact that women like her will always despise my kind, is why Esther Barton hates me.'

'Your kind?'

'Women with brains in their heads. Women who want to be equal to men rather than be owned by them.'

'Rosemary, you have gone much too far.' Hannah Beattie was vexed. 'You should not be talking like this to Constance about one of her husband's family and, furthermore, you should not be bothering her with your unconventional views on her wedding day.'

'You hold those views too, Beattie!'

They glared at each other as if no gulf of age, upbringing or enormous wealth lay between them, and Constance wondered again at their easy familiarity. She remembered her childhood at Lodore House: her own nursemaid, Frazer, had been cheerful and kindly but, even when she had cause to scold her, she had respected the division of class between them and had always addressed her as *Miss* Constance.

'It's all right, Miss Beattie,' she said. 'I don't believe that Esther dislikes me because of anything that Rosemary has done.'

'Oh, Constance,' Rosemary was contrite, 'Beattie is right. I should not have said anything to upset you on this day of all days!'

'I'm not upset.'

'Truly?'

'Truly.'

Rosemary smiled and then put her arms round Constance and hugged her. But, before she drew back, she whispered, 'However, I still think that you should be careful.'

'I will be.'

For Rosemary was right, of course. Constance had known since their eyes had met on the way home from church that Esther Barton disliked her. She also knew that it had nothing to do with Rosemary Elliot.

'Well, Constance, I haven't had a chance to talk to you yet.'

Esther's mother was standing regarding her from the other side of the table. While she and Rosemary had been talking, Polly and Mrs Green had finished clearing away and all that remained was the top tier of the wedding cake. Muriel Barton looked at it and her lips thinned into an imitation of a smile. 'I suppose you'll be keeping that for the christening?'

'I . . . I suppose so.'

'Have I embarrassed you?'

'Rosemary and I will leave you to talk to Mrs Barton,' said Hannah Beattie.

She looked at her charge, and Rosemary got up obediently, took Constance's hand and said, 'We'll talk again before we go.'

The two of them moved off and Constance rose to face the older woman. 'No, I'm not embarrassed. I know it is a custom to keep one tier of the bridal cake for the christening of the first child.'

'And there will be a child?'

'Who can say? I hope so.'

'Now, I have embarrassed you. You're blushing. Perhaps that's natural modesty, but I suppose you know very well how much John needs an heir?'

'No, we've never spoken of such things.'

'Haven't you? Surely he has told you that he comes into his full inheritance the moment he becomes a father. I imagined you were very happy to marry him in the circumstances.'

'Circumstances?'

'Your own.'

'My circumstances? You mean because I'm poor?'

'No, not that.'

'Then, I haven't the faintest idea what you're talking about!'

'Don't adopt that tone of voice with me. You may have married my nephew but, as far as I'm concerned, no amount of airs and graces will make people forget that you're only a little jumped-up servant girl who has probably tricked John into marrying her!'

Constance felt the blood draining from her face. Her eyes dilated. What did Muriel Barton mean? Could she have guessed? No, surely there was no way she could know that Gerald Sowerby had raped her. She swayed forward and put both hands on the table to steady herself. She heard Muriel Barton's indrawn breath.

'So there is something. I knew it.'

97

'No! There's nothing! What reason would I have for tricking him? I love John and he loves me.'

For a moment the other woman's tight-lipped smile faltered; she frowned. 'Love? You believe that he loves you?' But then she shrugged. 'Quite a performance. He's chosen well for himself.'

Constance watched her walk away. She had not been entirely surprised by the woman's animosity but was bewildered as to its cause. At first she had thought that, as Esther's mother, Muriel Barton might not view her favourably. It was obvious to Constance that Esther wanted John for herself.

But that was not why this woman disliked her – was suspicious of her. It was more than that. She had hinted that perhaps Constance had reasons for tricking John into marrying her. And she had cast doubts on something Constance preferred not to think about: John's reasons for marrying her.

'Mrs Edington, I've got to go now.' Mrs Green was buttoning up her coat. 'Albert and his father are both working late shifts tonight and I've yet to put up their bait boxes.'

'Oh yes, thank you for all your help today.'

'I was pleased to do it. Your husband has been good to Albert, giving him samples from the shop, shirts and so on. I've always been happy to keep an eye on his mother for him on Polly's day off but, of course, she's got you to look after her now.'

'Yes.'

'By the way, Mrs Edington said it would be all right for me to take some of the leftovers for my menfolk.'

'Of course.'

'I'll be going then but, remember, if you need help . . .'

'Help?'

'When John's mother . . . when she gets a bad turn. I'm just next door. You're welcome to call any time.'

98

'Thank you, I'll remember that.'

Mrs Green hurried away to take her leave of Frances Edington.

'I see that you have made a friend.'

Constance spun round. Esther Barton was pulling on her gloves. She was ready to leave and her crimson coat and vivid colouring made her conspicuous in the drab setting of the dining room. Friend? Was she referring to Rosemary Elliot?

'Mrs Green.' Esther's dark eyes expressed amused boredom as she glanced towards the brisk little woman who was now shepherding her husband and her son towards the door.

'I heard her inviting you to call next door. I can't imagine why you would want to, but then I suppose you are used to that kind of person.'

'I'm not sure what you mean.'

'Oh, yes you are.' Esther's voice rose and her air of sophistication wavered. 'Don't pretend to be so clever and ladylike.' Suddenly, she became aware that she was being observed by Rosemary and Hannah Beattie, and her chin tilted defiantly.

She assumed her air of worldly wisdom again but she made no attempt to lower her voice. 'And don't imagine that it will be any advantage to have Rosemary Elliot as a friend. Rosemary has no *savoir-faire*, no sense of who is the right kind of person; she treats everyone as though they were her equal. But she will forget you as soon as she takes up with another of her lost causes.'

'Esther, our carriage is here.' Muriel Barton appeared beside her daughter.

'Oh, thank goodness. I can't wait to get home.'

Mother and daughter swept out of the room without another word to Constance.

Walter Barton did not leave with his wife and daughter but

not long afterwards he came to say goodbye. 'I must go now, but I'll try not to keep John too long.'

'Keep him? I didn't know that he was going anywhere.'

'Didn't he tell you? John must come back with me to head office. It is Saturday, all the branch managers must make their reports and there is certain business that must be attended to even on his wedding day.'

'I see.'

'Don't sound so forlorn. I'll send him home to you as soon as I can. Certainly in time for you to have a romantic little supper *à deux*!' Walter Barton took her hand and Constance felt that he, at least, held no animosity towards her.

Rosemary's face was flushed and earnest as she took her leave. 'Constance, you must let Beattie and me call on you, and you should come to us.'

'Yes, yes, of course. And, Rosemary, thank you. I'm so grateful to both of you, not just for your generous gifts—' both Rosemary and Hannah Beattie began to smile and shake their heads and Constance hurried on— 'I'm truly grateful to have had friends here today.'

Matthew was waiting for them by the door. He did not come over to say goodbye; he simply inclined his head and smiled faintly before following Rosemary and Hannah Beattie out.

Everyone else had gone and John and his uncle helped Frances Edington rise from the chaise longue. She looked drained of strength but she smiled at Constance. 'Walter will take me up to my room so that you and John can have a moment together.' Her breathing was shallow and Constance sensed the effort as she continued, 'I'm very tired. Polly will help me to bed. Come and see me in the morning.'

Walter Barton lifted his sister up into his arms and carried her out of the room as if she were a child.

Constance and John were alone but she felt strangely reluctant to face him. The gaslight above her dimmed, flared and then steadied again as a lamp was lit upstairs. John was behind her and she turned, expecting him to embrace her, but he took hold of her shoulders and held her at arm's length, smiling ruefully.

'I have neglected you, Constance.'

'No, you had to talk to your guests.' Why had she said that? He had spent most of the time talking to Matthew.

But her answer had pleased him. 'And you also. What do you make of my family?'

'I like your uncle.'

'Do you?' He sounded surprised. 'Why?'

'He seems to be kind.'

'In that case he must have decided to like you. If he had not, he would seem to be very unkind. But what of Aunt Muriel and my cousin, Esther?'

'They . . . I don't think they—'

'They're monsters, both of them. Admit it!'

'No, not monsters, it's just that I don't think they like me.'

'Of course they don't! But don't look so wounded. Surely you realize that it's of no importance? I like you and that's all that matters. Now, come with me. I've just time to show you my wedding present before Uncle Walter carries me off to the hub of the Barton empire!' John took her hand and led her out of the room.

The passage was narrow and the stairs only wide enough for one person. John hurried up ahead and pulled her along behind him until they reached the landing at the top of the main stairway. He stopped and said, 'Close your eyes!'

'Why?'

'Your wedding present, it's in the room ahead. I want to surprise you.'

Constance closed her eyes and allowed him to lead her.

'No, don't open them yet!'

They had stopped outside a door at the back of the house. John let go of her hand and, after a few seconds she heard a key turning in the lock, then she felt a slight draught as the door opened.

'Stand there a moment while I light the lamp.'

Constance waited. Her heart was racing. She had caught John's excitement but it was more than that. What kind of present was it that had to be kept in a locked room? She laughed nervously.

'Now, give me your hand and come in, but keep your eyes closed until I tell you to open them.'

He led her forward; the air was cool on her face. He let go of her hand and she heard him moving away from her and then the rattle of metal rings being dragged along a brass pole as he closed the curtains.

'Now, now you may open your eyes.'

Constance stared around the room. There was a fireplace with coals neatly laid but unlit, two velvet-covered easy chairs set near the hearth and, nearby, a low occasional table. A small silver box was on the table and, for a moment, her gaze lingered on the burnished metal reflecting in the polished rosewood, but then her eyes were drawn towards the object set on a larger and more workmanlike table near the curtained window. John nodded his encouragement.

'A sewing machine?' She suppressed a feeling of disappointment. Was this her wedding present? She was good at dressmaking; she had excelled in the lessons in plain sewing in the workhouse and gone on to teach herself much more. But this was only because she had been determined never to accept the badly fitting standard uniform or the cast-off charity clothes that the other girls had to wear.

What had she imagined would happen when she married John?

She remembered one day when they had been walking through the new arcade in town, taking refuge from a late summer shower. The arcade was brightly lit and the shop windows attractive. Matthew was with them, as always.

He stopped before a display of dressmaking fabrics and exclaimed, 'Do look at that blue velvet. What do you think, John?'

'It's charming.'

'Not charming – magnificent! I can't wait to see her ladyship draped in that!'

John laughed. 'What about the emerald taffeta?'

'No, too bold. But there's enough choice here for a whole new wardrobe, don't you agree?'

'Yes, so long as they'll allow me a trade discount.'

'Ah, the trade discount! Won't you ever allow me to forget that you're just a little shopkeeper?'

Constance had looked quickly at John's face to see if he had been hurt by Matthew's jibe but he was laughing. She stood and waited, half pleased and half puzzled, as they discussed the fabrics and the styles of the new clothes they intended for her without once asking her opinion. At last she had decided it was all a game, they were not really planning a new wardrobe for her, it was simply a light-hearted fancy.

'Constance?' Now John was staring at her and he looked piqued.

'I'm sorry. Did you say something?'

'Yes. Not just a sewing machine, Constance, look.'

He pulled open a drawer in the table to reveal scissors, pins, tape measures and chalk. Constance did not have time to take it all in before he took her hand and hurried her across the room again.

103

'Come and look in the cupboard.'

He opened the door and then stood aside like a conjurer as he gestured towards the shelves set on the wall. They were full of bolts of cloth. Constance recognized the colours and textures; he must have gone back and bought up the whole window display, even the emerald-green taffeta.

'John, there's so much!'

'Ah well, the fabrics are Matthew's gift, but the sewing machine is from me and so is this.'

He leaned into a recess behind the cupboard door and brought out a dressmaking body form. 'There you are, my wedding present. A complete sewing room!'

'John, I . . .'

'Aren't you pleased?'

'Of course, but—'

'I thought you would be delighted.'

'I am. It's just that I don't know if my sewing skills are good enough. I might not be able to—'

'Oh, my dear, surely you don't think that you're going to have to sit here and sew all by yourself?' He smiled again, his hurt vanished. 'That I'm going to lock you in here every night like the miller's daughter in the fairy tale, and expect to find a room full of newly made garments every morning?'

'Well, what—I mean, are you going to get a dressmaker?'

'No, not exactly.'

'Then what?'

'We are going to make your new gowns together!'

'Together?'

'Yes, you and I. I have some marvellous ideas – designs. You know that some of the best couturiers are men, don't you?'

'Couturiers?'

'High-class dressmakers. Doucet, Paquin, Poiret, Worth!

But I haven't time to tell you properly now. My uncle has ordered a cab and it will be here soon.'

'John, do you have to go?'

'I must, even although I would rather stay and tell you all my plans.'

Constance watched as John closed the cupboard and then reached up to turn off the gaslamp. He took her hand and guided her towards the door. She had never been so close to him, so completely alone and in such an intimate situation. She found that she was longing for him to stop and turn towards her and perhaps take her in his arms. But, as her heart began to race, the memory of Gerald and what he had done to her suddenly intruded. She gasped and pulled her hand free.

'What is it?' John was instantly concerned.

'N-nothing . . . the dark . . .'

'Look,' John pulled the door wide open and they stepped out on to the landing, 'there is nothing to fear.'

But she found that she was still trembling and John's smile was infinitely kind. 'My poor darling. I had no idea that you were such a child. So sweet, so innocent.'

'Oh, John, I'm sorry.' Her cry was involuntary.

'Don't worry, dearest, I think I will love you all the more for that. Now, I really must go.' He closed the door and began to hurry down the stairs.

'John – don't – not yet!'

Constance followed him and stopped halfway down. At the bottom, in the narrow passageway, John was buttoning up his coat. Polly waited to hand him his hat. He took it and turned to smile up at Constance.

'My dear, you can see that Uncle Walter is impatient to be gone.'

The front door was open and Walter Barton stood on the step. He wore a bowler hat and an overcoat with an astrakhan collar. He bent his head and a match flared as he lit a cigar, then, as he drew on it, he straightened up and looked out through the swirling snowflakes before turning and calling, 'John, the cab has arrived.'

John hurried out to join him without looking back, and Constance sighed. She wished that he could have appeared more reluctant to leave her. She roused herself to call, 'You haven't told me what time you will—'

But Polly had closed the door behind him.

Constance wondered what she should do. How should she occupy herself until her husband came home? She could not return to the sewing room for John had locked it after them and taken the key. Mrs Edington had gone to her room and did not wish to be disturbed until tomorrow, and now Constance realized that she did not even know where she was going to sleep tonight.

Constance felt dangerously near to tears. This was not how she had expected to be treated on her wedding day.

Chapter Eight

'Would you like me to show you around?'

Polly stood at the bottom of the stairs, peering up at her. The girl looked tired, exhausted even, but she was smiling. Her smile revealed large uneven teeth which, set in her long sallow face, made her look plain, even comical. But her light brown eyes were full of a lively intelligence. Constance guessed her to be no more than fourteen or fifteen.

'I would like that. My husband seems to have forgotten that I am a stranger in this house.'

'Don't be hard on him. Master John would know that I'd look after you.'

Constance realized how critical she must have sounded. 'Yes, I'm sure he did.'

She knew her voice was strained so she was not surprised when Polly hurried on in John's defence, 'Mr Barton shouldn't have taken him off like that. It's not fair on your wedding day, is it? Master John must be as upset as you are!'

'I suppose so.' But Constance thought disconsolately that John had seemed more upset because he had not been able to tell her all about his dressmaking plans rather than by the fact that he had to leave his bride on their wedding night.

'I'll show you upstairs first – where your clothes are and everything. Do you mind going on ahead? We don't want to invite bad luck on your wedding day.'

'That's just a superstition about passing on the stairs, Polly.'

'Mebbees, but I'm not going to risk it!'

The girl grinned and Constance couldn't help smiling. 'Very well.'

At the top, with the sewing room straight ahead, Polly excused herself and squeezed past on the first landing. Here the stairs turned back on themselves and only a short flight of three more steps took them to the narrow corridor that headed towards the front of the house again.

'The door straight ahead of us leads to Mrs Edington's room; you'll see that in the morning. Master John's room is next to his mother's so's he can hear her if she needs him during the night. But I suppose he'll be sleeping in here now.' The girl stopped at the third door, the one nearest to them, and smiled at Constance, her head cocked to one side and her eyes slyly curious.

She is wondering if I know what will happen in here tonight, Constance thought. Polly almost certainly does know, but she's not sure about me. She doesn't know whether I am a lady because I speak like one, or a servant because she has heard everything that has been said today.

'Well, then, are you going to stand here all night?' Her embarrassment made her sound brusque and she regretted the look of hurt surprise that replaced Polly's smile.

The girl opened the door and stood aside so that Constance could enter first. A small fire glowed in the hearth. Points of warm light sparkled on the fender and on the brass bedstead. The curtains were still open but the sky outside was dark. It could be only early evening and yet it seemed as if the sun had never risen on this, her wedding day. In a recess on the fireside wall Constance saw there was a wardrobe.

'I've hung your clothes up in there and your underwear is

in the drawers at the bottom,' Polly said. 'Your nightdress is under your pillow.'

There was a mirror set into the door of the wardrobe. The glass reflected the pale mound of the eiderdown and, as her eyes grew accustomed to the flickering firelight, Constance turned to look at the bed. All the bedclothes were white – white pillowcases with frills of broderie anglaise and a white sheet turned down over a white eiderdown cover. White for purity.

'That's all new, all that bed linen. Master John chose it hisself – bought it at Bainbridge's. It was delivered only three days ago and I've had the devil of a job getting it washed and dried and ironed in time!'

Constance knew this would be to remove the size, which gave a glassy slipperiness to new linen. She ran a hand over the cool coverlet, feeling the raised, silken stitches of the self-coloured embroidery. Polly was watching her action, grinning.

'If I hadn't softened the sheets up a little you'd have slid straight off the feather mattress on to the floor every time one of you turned over! I'll light the lamp, shall I?'

She didn't wait for a reply. First, she hurried over to close the curtains and then she came back to the fireplace and, stooping, took a spill from a jar on the floor beside the hearth. She held it into the flames until it flared into light, then she lit the overhead mantle.

As she raised her arms to perform this task, Constance caught the smell of stale sweat and saw the stains on her faded cotton dress. Yesterday I was wearing a dress not much better than that, she thought. Yesterday . . . So much had happened since she had tossed her unwashed apron on to the kitchen table.

Polly raised the spill to her lips and blew out the flame, then nipped the smoking wick with her fingers before

109

replacing it in the jar. 'Look, there's the night table.' She pointed towards a marble-topped washstand in the other recess. On the stand there was a large basin and jug, a saucer with a tablet of soap in it and a pile of clean towels.

'And here's the jerry.' She opened the door set below the marble top to reveal the chamber pot. 'There's a netty in the back yard, of course, but you won't want to be nipping out there on a freezin' cold night!'

'Polly, thank you, but—'

'I'll show you the front parlour now, if you like. It's a cosy little room. Master John told me that the two of you would have your supper there by the fire.'

'I'll come downstairs when I'm ready, but first of all I would like to wash. Would you bring me some hot water?'

'Right oh!'

Polly took the water jug and hurried away. She did not shut the door and Constance closed it after her and leaned against it for a moment. She dropped her head into her hands. Polly's chatter had wearied her. The girl had been friendly but polite at first, and then she had seemed to grow more unrestrained, less respectful. Is it something she senses about me? Constance wondered. Can she have guessed that the new Mrs Edington was little better than a skivvy until yesterday? Surely not. Constance raised her head and found herself staring at her work-roughened hands. She thrust them behind her.

It was obvious that Polly adored John, she had been so quick to defend him. But why should I be surprised? Constance thought. He is so handsome, so gentlemanly ... *Every Maiden's Dream!* She smiled as she remembered a romantic novelette that she and Nella had giggled over by the light of one of their precious candles.

Isabelle had found a secret hoard of penny romances, stuffed at the back of the wardrobe when she had been cleaning

110

Mrs Mortimer's bedroom. She'd taken to surreptitiously borrowing one or two at a time and sharing them with Constance and Nella before replacing them and taking some more.

'Fancy that great lump of sour lard reading romantic stories like this!' Isabelle had exclaimed.

Nella's eyes were huge. 'Mrs Sowerby would hev a fit if she knew we was reading them. First of all, she doesn't think servants, not even housekeepers, should hev any spare time and, secondly, if they hev, they ought to be reading the Bible!'

'Perhaps Mrs Mortimer finds more comfort in these stories than she would in the Bible,' Constance had said, but the other two had not known what she meant.

There was a knock at the door. Polly had returned. 'Here's your hot water,' she called.

'Put the jug down, Polly. Just leave it there, I'll get it in a moment.' She found she could not face the girl just yet.

'Right oh.'

Constance gripped the door knob and leaned forward to listen to Polly's footsteps receding. When she was sure Polly had gone, she opened the door and took up the jug of hot water. She poured the water into the flower-patterned basin; steam swirled about the surface before rising into the dark corners of the room. A moment later Constance had taken off her dress and taken a clean flannel and the bar of soap. She held it to her nostrils; it smelled of carnations.

The act of washing herself was soothing. She looked down into the water in the basin, now curdled with streaks of soap. Polly would bring her hot water whenever she wanted. She would never again have to creep down first thing in the morning to wash in icy water at the kitchen sink.

She picked up a towel. It was thick and soft, unlike the thin worn-out rags Mrs Sowerby had considered good enough for

111

her servants. Until yesterday Constance had shared a freezing garret with poor, crippled Nella; tonight she would be sleeping in this warm, comfortable room with her husband.

John was so kind, so gentle, and they loved each other. When they were in each other's arms she would be able to forget Gerald's savagery, she was sure of it. Poor John. Why had she imagined that he had not been sorry to leave her? It wasn't his fault that his uncle had insisted that he return with him to the office. If he had not expressed regret it must have been because Walter Barton was waiting and could hear what they were saying. Yes, that would be the reason . . .

Constance buttoned up her dress and smoothed her hair. She opened the door and went back to pick up the basin. Then, smiling, she put it down again. Polly would come and get it. She felt more cheerful now. Surely it wouldn't be long before John came home, and what had Uncle Walter said before he left? That she and John would have a supper '*à deux*'? Until then she would sit by the fire in the front parlour. Polly could bring her a cup of tea.

When the bell rang, Polly paused with her arms up to her elbows in the greasy dishwater and glanced round and up at the glass-fronted wooden box on the wall near the door. Huh! It hasn't taken her long to settle in to her new way of life, she thought.

Walter Barton had had the system of bells installed in the modest house in Heaton so that his invalid sister could ring for help from whichever room she might be in. But it was not Mrs Edington who was demanding Polly's presence now – or rather it was, but it was the new Mrs Edington, and the indicator showed that she had found her way to the front parlour.

Polly dried her hands on her pinny and hurried along

the narrow passage to answer the summons. She gave a peremptory knock at the door and went straight in. Master John's wife was standing by the window, gazing out into the street.

I don't know what she's looking at, Polly thought. There's not much to get excited about round here and, besides, it's dark.

Then it occurred to her that she might be looking for her bridegroom to come home and, in spite of everything, she felt sorry for her. Polly moved towards the window and she couldn't help seeing how lonely the poor young woman looked as she gazed out into the swirling snow. It was wet, more like rain, Polly noticed. She hoped the damp wouldn't bring on one of John's mother's bad coughing fits.

His new wife seemed to have only just realized that she was no longer alone and she turned to face her. For a moment she looked as she had when she had first arrived here earlier that day – unsure of herself, shy even – but the look vanished almost immediately.

'My goodness, Polly, your apron is very dirty.'

Polly's warm feelings melted away. 'This is the second one today. Mrs Edington told me to change before the wedding guests arrived.'

'And she was right to do so.'

'But if I change again that's all three to wash.'

'Nevertheless, you shouldn't come into this part of the house looking as if . . . as if . . .'

'As if I'm the only one here to do all the work?'

Her new mistress's eyes widened. She looked taken aback by the surly tone but Polly didn't care. She'd been up since five o'clock this morning because of all the extra work and she was tired and disappointed. In a house as small as this, she hadn't been able to help overhearing some of the conversations leading up to the wedding. She knew that Master John's chosen bride had been in service – she'd heard him telling his mother what a help Constance would be to her – and Polly had been expecting . . . Expecting what, exactly?

As she looked at her now, small and dainty and as pretty as a china ornament, she realized that her half-formed hopes for a friend, someone to share a little of the work around the house, had been no more than a foolish dream. Oh, the lass might have work-roughened hands – Polly had seen her trying to hide them in the folds of her dress all day – but she spoke and carried herself like a lady. More of a lady than the mistress, if the truth were admitted.

John Edington's new wife may have been working as a servant but that could only be because her family had fallen on hard times. The state of the clothes that Polly had put away for her bore this out. Although the undergarments were all darned and threadbare, one or two of the dresses were made of good quality stuff and they looked as if they had once been fashionable. Yes, Polly decided, this young woman's marriage had rescued her from life as a servant and it looked very much as if she was determined never to soil her hands again.

Now, she was smiling sweetly at her. 'Polly, I'm not criticizing you.'

'No?'

'No. I know what it's like having to keep your aprons cleaned and ironed.'

'Do you?' Polly wondered what was coming next. Was she going to offer a bit of help after all?

'So this is what you should do. You must keep one clean apron hanging on the back of the kitchen door at all times so that, if you're summoned to any other part of the house you can change quickly and look more presentable. Isn't that a good idea?'

'I suppose so.'

If the new Mrs Edington had noticed Polly's sulky expression, she chose to ignore it. She walked towards the hearth. 'Now, I wonder if you would fetch me some more coal for this fire? I presume that the fire in the dining room was banked low because of Mrs Edington's consumption, but she isn't likely to come in here tonight, is she?'

'No, nor never.'

'I beg your pardon?'

'Mrs Edington doesn't often come downstairs these days.'

'Oh, I see. Well, then—'

'Yes, I know, I meant to build it up for you, but I just forgot. I've had so much to do today.'

'Yes, this has been an exceptional day. It won't always be like this.'

'Is that all, then?'

'No, when you have seen to the fire, I would like you to bring me a cup of tea.'

'Right oh.'

'And, Polly, we shall have to agree about what you're going to call me.'

'What do you mean?'

'Well, I've noticed that you have avoided calling me Mrs Edington – or anything at all, for that matter – so I've decided that, to avoid confusion, you should call me Mrs John. I think that's the way it's done, don't you?'

'If you say so, Mrs John. I'll fill the coal scuttle, then.'

'Good. Oh, before you go, would you close the curtains for me? Your arms are so much longer than mine.'

Once back in the kitchen, Polly slammed the kettle down on the hob so hard that water shot out of the spout and raised a cloud of hissing steam in the fire. She was angry. Not with the new Mrs Edington, who was only behaving as anyone would expect, but with herself for having imagined that things might be going to be different around here.

In truth, she knew that she didn't have much to complain about. The Edingtons were kind employers but they couldn't afford to take on any more help than Polly, and the work was hard, especially now that Mrs Edington seemed to be failing fast. Polly was on her feet from morning till night and the only break she got was her one afternoon off each week when Mrs Green next door came to sit with Mrs Edington out of the sheer kindness of her heart.

Polly missed her mother and father and her large family of brothers and sisters. They were only a short walk away in Byker but she hardly ever saw them and she was lonely. They all thought she was lucky to live in a warm house, have plenty of food on the table and a bed to herself, even if it was only a truckle bed stowed under the kitchen table and pulled out each night.

She might have the work of two or even three to do but, as her mother had pointed out, most of the time she was left to get on with it in her own sweet way. She had an uneasy feeling that that was going to change.

'Gerald! Would you look at your sister?'

'Why on earth should I want to do that?' Gerald Sowerby paused at the top of the stairs and closed his eyes in a weary gesture of resignation. He had hoped to leave the house without encountering his mother but she must have been listening for him.

'Don't be difficult. You know what I mean.'

He opened his eyes and turned to face her; she was hurrying towards him. Her left hand was pressed against the base of her throat and she was picking at the lace of her choker collar with her small white fingers.

She looked tired; the vibrant red of her velvet gown only accentuated her pallid complexion. Her right hand held a lavender-soaked handkerchief and she brought it up to dab at her face before she continued, 'Annabel's fever has risen. I think she's delirious.'

'Father will be home soon.'

'He was called to a confinement. He could be hours yet.'

'But what am I supposed to do?'

'You are studying medicine, surely you can tell me.'

'I can only tell you what you already know. Annabel was bilious when she came home from Ursula's party and now she has a fever. It won't hurt to wait until Father comes home.'

'Gerald, please!'

'Oh, very well.'

He followed her to his sister's bedroom. He was sure that there was nothing seriously wrong with the girl. She had probably overeaten, as usual, at her friend's birthday party, and she had made herself sick. As for having a fever, she would be overheated because his mother had insisted on piling on extra bedclothes and building up the fire in her bedroom. The warmth met them at the doorway and Gerald shrugged off his evening cape and tossed it on to a chair on the landing.

As he entered the room Annabel shrieked, 'Get out! I don't want you here!'

Gerald raised his eyebrows and turned to go.

'No! She doesn't mean you!' His mother grasped his sleeve. 'She's taken against the skivvy. Each time Nella comes in to see to the fire, Annabel nearly has a fit. I'm sure it's a sign of delirium.'

'Of plain bad temper more like,' Gerald muttered.

But when he turned to look in the direction of the hearth, he shuddered involuntarily. The maid called Nella was kneeling as she built up the coals with swift, precise movements. In

117

the light from the fire Gerald fancied that the point of her chin and the tip of her nose grew towards each other like those of a witch. Each time she leaned in towards the hearth, the odd, twisted hump of her shoulders was thrown into sharp relief against the firelight.

His mother watched her impatiently for a moment and then she called out, 'You can go now, Nella.' The odd little creature got up. 'But fetch up some more coals.' Nella picked up the empty scuttle.

'No, no, no! I don't want her in here,' Annabel wailed.

She was propped up in bed within a mound of fat pillows and her long fair hair hung in limp rat's-tails round her face. Her usually fair complexion was flushed and blotchy. She had pushed the bedclothes back and Gerald could see that her nightgown was creased and clinging to her plump adolescent body. Scattered across the front of the garment there was a pattern of brown stains. Probably dried vomit, he thought, and he could barely control his distaste.

'Wait.' He raised a hand to stop the little crookback before she hurried from the room.

'Yes, sir?' She stopped and the look she shot him almost made him flinch.

My God, she really is ugly, Gerald thought, and I'm sure she dislikes us whereas she ought to be eternally grateful that my mother has given her employment. Many of my friends' parents would not have her anywhere near them.

'You wanted something, sir?'

'Yes, Nella, I do. Before you bring the coals, you are to bring a basin of cool water and some towels and flannels.'

Gerald glanced down at the bony claws clutching the handle of the brass coal scuttle and grimaced with distaste.

'And wash your hands first.'

'Yes, sir.'

118

Even before Nella had left the room, Annabel said, 'I don't want that disgusting little creature to come anywhere near me. Why can't Constance bring the coals?'

Mrs Sowerby's expression of concern hardened for a moment. 'Constance doesn't work here any more. Now let me cover you up and make you decent. Your brother is almost a doctor and he has come to look at you.'

She hurried over to the bed and tried to pull the bedclothes up around her daughter but Annabel only pushed them away again.

'Why doesn't Constance work here? Have you dismissed her?'

'Yes.'

'Why?'

'She had to go. She was insolent; insolent and dishonest.'

Gerald's eyes widened with surprise. It had been obvious last night that his mother did not like Constance but he had not realized the depth of her antipathy. Even now, with the girl safely out of the house, she was prepared to lie about the reason that Constance had left their service.

Why? Of course his mother had always been possessive. She had not liked it when he had spoken to Constance, teased her about her wedding to her Prince Charming. She had liked it even less when it became obvious that the girl was flirting with him.

His loins quickened with remembered excitement as he recalled the way the pulse in her throat had throbbed when he'd stroked her skin, the way her violet eyes had widened with agitation, a sure sign of her arousal. And then, instead of retreating from him, as any decent girl would have done, the minx had raised her chin and stared brazenly into his eyes, a clear invitation if ever there was one. No, his mother was not stupid. She had guessed what was going on.

But that was not all of it. She had obviously detested Constance long before the incident in the hallway last night. Was it simply because the girl did not behave as a servant should? Her manner and her speech set her apart from the usual run of workhouse skivvy.

Considering how quietly and efficiently she carried out her duties, why had Constance never been promoted above stairs? Could it be that she had never shown sufficient gratitude for being rescued from the workhouse? Had never known her place?

Gerald realized then that in all the years that Constance had worked for them, his mother had probably made her life a misery, culminating in that astonishing act of malice last night when she had thrown her out on to the streets. She had not cared what could have happened to the girl.

What *had* happened to her?

Gerald flushed. He found that his breathing was shallow and that his face was bathed in perspiration. He took a handkerchief from his pocket and dabbed at his brow. The room was warmer than ever; a sickly sweet miasma of vomit rose from Annabel's bed and seemed to engulf him.

'*Stop* it, Mother. I'm too hot!' Annabel pushed the bed-clothes away as her mother made another attempt to cover her up.

'But, darling, I must make you decent.'

'Leave her, Mother. You will only make her condition worse.'

His mother looked up at him distractedly, and, at that moment, his sister drew up her legs and began to writhe furiously. Her mother sprang away as Annabel kicked out and sent the sheets and blankets flying. They slithered to the floor, Annabel's foot caught in her nightgown and, as she gave one final kick, the fine fabric tore from the neck almost to the waist.

'Annabel!'

His mother darted forward and pulled the torn edges across his sister's body but not before Gerald had seen the ugly red stain which started midway down her neck then ran down to spread out over and almost encompass her right breast. He had known the blemish was there, of course. When Annabel was a small child, the mark had been like a faint pink blush above the collars of her baby clothes. As she got older she was able to wear higher collars and Gerald had almost forgotten about it.

However, he had had no idea that the birthmark was so extensive, nor that its colour had intensified so angrily over the years. Poor old Annabel, he thought. That will spoil her chances.

He glanced at his mother and suddenly realized why she was so fond of those high, boned collars. She'd been wearing chokers or something like them for as long as he could remember. He wondered what his father thought about it, how it made him feel. But then perhaps he hadn't seen it very often. Women like Violet Sowerby almost certainly preferred the dark.

'Nella, come here.' His mother had succeeded in covering Annabel with the top sheet, and she turned as the little crookback appeared carrying a basin of water. There were some towels folded over her arm. 'Put the water and the towels on the table and go and fetch a clean nightgown for Miss Annabel. Gerald, would you wait on the landing for a moment?'

'Mother, I really must go.'

'*Must* go? Why?'

'My friends are waiting for me.'

'But I want you to look at Annabel.'

'I've looked at her.'

121

'Gerald, please be serious!'

'I am being serious. I don't think there's very much wrong with her. She has obviously eaten something that has disagreed with her and that, as well as making her bilious, could have given her a slight fever.'

'A *slight* fever!'

'Yes, *slight*. At least it was until you covered her with blankets and got Nella to build up the fire.'

'But she had to be kept warm.'

'No, she ought to have been cooled down.'

'But, Gerald—'

'You wanted my advice and I'm giving it to you. Nella must bathe Annabel in the cool water I asked her to bring, then you can make her comfortable in a clean nightgown.'

Nella had already dipped a flannel into the basin and was wringing it out. Gerald stopped talking and watched, fascinated, as the skeletal fingers grasped and squeezed the cloth. Her bony wrists twisted in opposite directions until every drop of excess water had been extracted. Nella was much stronger than she looked.

'Gerald?' His mother was staring at him and he was suddenly infinitely weary of the whole episode.

'Give her only water to drink. Don't pile the bed up with extra blankets and don't put one more lump of coal on that fire!'

'But—'

'If you won't take my advice, ask Father when he comes home.'

He turned brusquely and made for the doorway but then paused and frowned. Annabel had been quiet while he had been talking. Too quiet. She hadn't even objected when Nella had approached her with the flannel and towels.

Perhaps she really was ill, Gerald thought. Perhaps he

122

ought to stay until his father came home. He didn't want any trouble from that quarter, any accusations of neglect. How aggravating.

He looked over his shoulder towards the bed. His sister was sitting up amongst the pillows again, but she had both hands wrapped around her body and she was clutching herself as if she were in pain. Her eyes were glassy. Gerald turned and took a step back into the room. At the same moment his sister groaned and was sick all over the bed. The little crookback stepped aside neatly, but his mother had not been so fortunate. Her red dress was covered in yellowy-green, evil-smelling gobs of vomit.

'Annabel?' Gerald hurried to her side and she looked up at him. Her eyes were moist but her cheeks were already a better colour. The blotches had gone, to be replaced by an even, rosy pink. She wiped her mouth with the back of her hand.

'It's all right, Gerald. You can go out with your friends. I feel much better now.' Brother and sister smiled at each other as their mother hurried from the room.

'Nella,' Violet Sowerby screeched, 'come to my room and take my dress away to be cleaned. But first you must see to Miss Annabel.'

'Will you be all right, now, Annabel?' Gerald's mood had lightened now that the prospect of having to do something about his sister's condition had been removed.

'Yes, really. You may go to Alvini's.'

'How do you know that I go there?'

'Oh, everybody's older brothers go there, all the time. I think you go there every night, just about. But, Gerald?'

'What now, nuisance?'

'One day you must tell me what goes on there.'

'Perhaps, Annabel, perhaps. But now, forgive me if I don't

123

give you a brotherly kiss before I go. The fact is, odious child, that you stink.'

Annabel hurled one of the stained and foul-smelling pillows at him and they both laughed. Gerald turned to go and nearly collided with the little crookback. The wet flannel she was grasping dropped on to his polished evening shoes.

'You fool,' he snarled, and then stopped when he saw the look on her face.

She was looking at me like that when I woke up this morning, he remembered. She detests me. The misshapen little monster is not just angry with the world in general, it's me she hates. But why? I've hardly ever spoken to her. What can have happened to make her loathe me so?

Chapter Nine

'Frank, you must go and help your brother.'

Gianfranco Alvini looked up and frowned. He was studying a diagram of the human circulatory system. His papers and medical textbooks were spread out across the green chenille cloth. The pool of bright light cast by his reading lamp did not extend to the person standing at the opposite side of the table. He sat back, blinking. As his eyes adjusted to the dimmer light of the overhead gasolier, he saw his mother looking at him anxiously. He sighed and she seemed to shrink into herself at this sign of his displeasure. But she persisted.

'Please, Frankie.'

Maria Alvini had been nearly forty when Frank's older brother, Valentino, had been born twenty-four years ago but now, were it not for her severely styled white hair, it would be hard to guess that she was much older. She had never been a conventional beauty but she had good bone structure and expressive eyes.

Her husband, Alfredo, many years younger than she, had needed money to turn his ice-cream parlour into a high-class restaurant, and Maria's prosperous father, who had no sons of his own, had seen him as a good investment. Maria had loved Alfredo; she had been a good wife and it was her tragedy that he had died before her.

Now, she stared unwaveringly at the younger of her two sons; the unrelieved black of her widowhood giving her fine-boned, sallow features a dramatic appearance.

Frank closed his eyes for a moment and rubbed the muscles at the back of his neck with the fingers of one hand. Then he flexed his shoulders and stood up, lifting his jacket from the back of his chair.

'I am sorry to interrupt your studies,' his mother said. 'I know how hard you work and how much it means to you to succeed. But who else can I send?'

'No one. Of course I'll go. What is it this time?'

'He is with those young men again. The same who were here last night – and nearly every night. The ones who think it is clever to make fun of him. They have invited him to their table. Mr McCormack does not want to offend them – they are good customers – but he thinks Valentino should be persuaded to come away. He sent Jimmy up to tell me.'

'Valentino is drinking?'

His mother shrugged and raised her hands in a helpless gesture of acknowledgement. At times like this she looked wholly Italian; yet her own mother had been English; a wealthy confectioner's daughter whose inheritance had been the start of the family fortune.

'Tell Valentino that if he comes up now, I will make hot chocolate for him, hot chocolate and a slice of cake – *torta di cioccolata*.' His mother smiled as she followed her younger son to the door.

'You treat Valentino as if he were a child.' Frank could not hide his impatience and his mother looked wounded.

'He is a child.'

'He's twenty-four years old.'

'You know what I mean.'

Frank looked at her. She was small and he was only of

126

medium height. There could be no denying that they were mother and son: they had the same spare build, the same mobile features. But now his mother's eyes were huge with emotion, and Frank saw the glitter of tears.

'Don't cry, Mamma. I know what you mean.'

He was just about to open the door when she grasped his arm. 'I love you equally, Gianfranco, you must believe that. But Valentino needs me more than you do.'

'I know that.'

'And, after all, you are the lucky one.'

'Lucky? Explain.'

'Oh, I know Valentino is the heir. Your father did not live long enough to see . . . to realize that his firstborn, his handsome boy-child, did not mature quite as he should into manhood. But you – you inherited your father's intelligence. I think that is much more valuable.'

'Perhaps.' Frank smiled wanly. 'And now I must go and bring my big brother home to Mamma.'

Jimmy Nelson was leaning against the bannister. Madame Alvini never allowed the staff from the restaurant to enter the family's private quarters on the top floor of the large old building in the Haymarket. After the young waiter had knocked and murmured his message through a half-opened door, he had waited patiently at the head of the stairs.

'Well, then, Jimmy.' Frank's expression was weary. 'Are you going to help me carry the master upstairs?'

When speaking to her staff or to tradespeople, his mother had always referred to her husband as 'the master' and since he had died she had transferred that title to his elder son. The staff went along with the pretence although they knew that it was Madame Alvini herself who ran the business, helped by her younger son, Frank.

'I don't think it's come to that.' Jimmy grinned. He was

127

only fifteen but was already much taller than Frank. He was thin and undernourished-looking; the bony wrists protruding beyond the celluloid cuffs of his shirt appeared to be extra large and out of proportion to his spindly arms. His pale unformed features were touchingly childlike, in spite of the downy growth of pale blond hair that he was desperately encouraging on his upper lip.

'How much has he had to drink?'

'Not much. Mr McCormack's been keeping an eye on the situation – seeing that your brother's glass gets filled up with water and taking the wine away from him. But the young gentlemen have ordered spirits, and the restaurant's getting busy now that the Palace is out. Mr McCormack thought I'd better come for you.'

'Quite right.'

By now they had descended one flight of stairs and were on the floor where the private dining rooms were situated. Frank noticed that so far only one was occupied, its door closed. If a door was closed, no member of the restaurant's staff would blunder in without knocking first. Customers who booked private rooms expected discretion.

They went down one flight further to find Patrick McCormack, the head waiter, hovering just outside the wide-arched entrance to the main dining room. He was a tall, black-haired, handsome man whose ramrod gait and clipped moustache made him look more of a gentleman than many of the restaurant's customers.

'Ah, Mr Alvini, I apologize for disturbing you, but . . .' The man's blue eyes were clouded with anxiety.

'That's all right, Patrick. I know you wouldn't do so if it weren't necessary. My mother is happy to trust your judgement.'

McCormack inclined his head slightly. We're lucky to have

him, Frank thought. God knows what we'll do when he finally saves up enough money to open a restaurant of his own.

'Now,' Frank sighed, 'where is he?'

The head waiter dismissed Jimmy, who hurried towards the staff entrance to the kitchen at the end of the landing. When the boy had gone, he moved into the shadow of the looped back velvet drapes of the dining room. 'Look,' he breathed, 'over there.'

Frank could see Valentino sitting at a table on the far side of the restaurant. He recognized the three men who were with him.

'I'll follow you across there, Patrick,' he said to the head waiter, 'as if I were a customer and you were taking me to a table. Let's not make this too obvious. My mother would never forgive us if we caused my brother any embarrassment. You understand?'

'Of course.'

Patrick McCormack led the way as confidently and as convincingly as the actor he had once been. Frank was happy to fall in behind his broad black-clad shoulders. Patrick was the only member of staff to wear a jacket. The other waiters wore black waistcoats over their white shirts, the sleeves of which were kept back neatly with metal armbands. As Frank strode across the room they moved efficiently from table to table, taking and delivering orders.

Elaborate gasoliers illuminated the large room from above and, in the centre of each table, there was an ornate brass oil-lamp combined with a container of fresh flowers. Ivy leaves and ferns trailed artistically across the white damask table-cloths. More than half the tables were taken and the noise level of laughter and animated conversation was already rising.

Frank looked around at the gentlemen in evening clothes and the ladies – there were fewer of these – in low-necked, tight-waisted gowns. The women's hair was piled on the top of their heads with the front puffed and padded out in the current fashion. Some wore flowers in their hair, at their wrists or pinned to their bodices; some had jewels glittering at their throats and their ears; all were beautiful.

And it was their beauty that revealed the true nature of the restaurant's clientele. The men were exactly the sort of prosperous citizens that Frank's father, Alfredo Alvini, had set out to attract, but they did not bring their wives here, and especially not to the private dining rooms on the upper floor.

One or two of the customers, both male and female, acknowledged Frank with a smile or a wave. The women had respectability of a kind: none of them walked the streets and some devoted their attentions to only one admirer. Frank did not despise them, but he understood why his mother preferred never to make an appearance in the restaurant, although she worked ceaselessly behind the scenes.

Suddenly the head waiter stopped and drew Frank aside. 'See, Mr Carmichael and his friends have been trying to persuade your brother to drink more than is good for him.'

Frank noticed that Patrick had not referred to Valentino as 'the master' although he would have done if he had been speaking to Madame Alvini. Valentino had not seen them approaching. When at last he looked up and saw them, he smiled with delight. 'Franco! Are you joining us?'

Behind him, Patrick McCormack coughed discreetly and Frank half turned to face him. 'Do you want me to stay?' the head waiter asked.

'No, it's all right, Patrick. I've kept you from your duties long enough.' Frank turned back to face his brother. Valentino's handsome features were still wreathed in smiles. His companions at the table were also looking at Frank but their gaze was not so welcoming.

130

He knew them all. Warren Carmichael and Leonard Russell, both the sons of prosperous local families, were regular customers. So was Gerald Sowerby; but he also knew Gerald as a fellow student at the Medical School.

'I don't think your brother wants to join us.' Leonard Russell, who was sitting next to Valentino, leaned back in his chair and gazed at Frank through half-closed, insolent eyes. His sallow features arranged themselves into a sardonic challenge. 'And besides, there isn't room, is there?'

'No room?' Valentino frowned for a moment and then the smile returned. 'Oh, I see – we need another chair. I'll get one.'

He stood up suddenly, knocking the table as he did so. Warren Carmichael grabbed his glass just as it was about to tip its contents into his lap. He laughed. 'Steady on there, Alvini. You're like a young carthorse!'

Gerald, who had also had to grab his glass, scowled. 'Don't bother to get another chair. Russell's right. Your brother doesn't want to join us. He's come to spoil your fun.'

'Spoil my fun?'

'He's come to take you home. He doesn't like you making friends with us. Isn't that right?' Gerald stared up at Frank insolently.

Valentino looked at his brother and scowled. It was the scowl of a small child who had been crossed, Frank thought, but the trouble was that Valentino had the body of a man, a very big man, and, although he very rarely lost his temper, it was better not to risk provoking him.

'I don't want to go home yet. I'm enjoying myself.'

'For goodness' sake sit down again, then.' Warren Carmichael, his podgy face flushed with drink and shallow good humour, grinned up at Valentino. 'Tell your little brother to go away and stop pestering you.'

131

'That's right,' Gerald Sowerby added. 'I mean, who's the master here, you or Frank?'

Valentino frowned. 'Master?'

Frank could see Patrick McCormack glancing at them across the crowded tables. Patrick raised his eyebrows questioningly. Some of the diners seated at nearby tables were looking up at Valentino's massive form. They had heard him raise his voice and they could sense trouble.

Frank smiled a small tight smile and shook his head at the head waiter almost imperceptibly, then he turned his attention once more to his older brother and his companions. He knew that it amused them to make fun of Valentino, but he didn't want his brother to know that.

'Valentino is the master here. We all know that. In fact, that is why I have come for him. We need his advice on a matter of business.'

'You need Valentino's advice?' Warren Carmichael looked incredulous.

Leonard Russell's thin lips curved into a sneer and Gerald sniggered. Thankfully, Valentino didn't hear him and his expression became solemn as he focused on Frank.

'Business?' he asked. 'You need me on a matter of business?'

'Yes, we need to consult you. You'll have to come with me. I'll show you the papers.'

'Ah, the papers.' His older brother's expression cleared and he smiled as if he now understood everything. 'I'll come at once.'

More heads had turned. Valentino had drawn himself up to his full height and Frank had to admit that he looked impressive. The elder brother had his father's powerful physique combined with his mother's beauty. Frank knew that women found him heartbreakingly handsome. The tragedy was that his difficult passage into the world had done something to the brains confined within that noble-looking skull.

Valentino looked down at the other men graciously. 'I have to go. You will forgive me?'

The three of them looked openly scornful and, before any one of them could say anything, Frank said, 'Thank you for inviting my brother to your table. However there was no need for you to be quite so generous with the wine—'

'That's right,' Valentino interrupted, 'very generous – I shouldn't have allowed it. Patrick,' he called, and the head waiter came hurrying over.

'Yes, sir?'

'These gentlemen are my guests tonight. They may order anything they please; there will be no charge.'

'Very well, sir.'

Frank could see that it took all Patrick McCormack's acting skills to hide his displeasure and he cursed himself for not foreseeing what Valentino might do. But how could he have done? Usually his brother was quiet, good-natured and biddable, it was only when the drink lubricated his poor wits and loosened his tongue that he could take you by surprise.

As he led Valentino back through the crowded dining room Frank could see heads turning to watch their progress. One or two faces registered derision, but most of the regular customers were prepared to be compassionate. Here and there a woman's face showed open admiration for his brother's good looks.

I wonder if they know, Frank thought, and if they do know, whether they care? He knew that his mother often worried that some scheming woman would trap her elder son into marriage. Valentino was outwardly prosperous and handsome, and the fact that he was slow-witted might be an added attraction to a woman who was not altogether scrupulous.

Once married to him she might treat him cruelly.

On the next landing Frank saw Jimmy Nelson coming out of a private dining room, looking worried. He was so preoccupied that when he looked up and saw Frank and Valentino he jumped and dropped the empty tray.

'I didn't hear you coming. What a fright!' He stopped to pick up the tray.

'Is something the matter, Jimmy?'

'Matter? Why should there be?'

'I thought you looked worried.'

'Did I?' Jimmy couldn't meet his eyes.

'You're not having trouble with the customers, are you?'

'What kind of trouble?' The lad's response worried Frank even more.

'They're not giving you a difficult time – you know, being unpleasant, being mean?'

'No, nothing like that.' Jimmy's composure was returning and Frank began to think that he had imagined that the lad had been upset. 'Not mean, definitely not mean. Generous to a fault, in fact. The meal isn't over yet and they've already tipped me well over the top.'

'Why would they do that?'

'Said that I had to bring them a bottle of the best champagne. Said they knew what went on in restaurants – labels being soaked off and cat's piss being foisted on ignorant customers. Said I was to make sure that they got the genuine article. Hence the tip.'

By the end of his little speech Frank got the impression that Jimmy had convinced himself that all was well.

'I see. Are you to bring the champagne now?'

'Yes. Got to make sure I bring it back myself.'

'Well, take your time, then.'

'Why? What do you mean?'

'Don't hurry or they'll think you've brought them any old cat's piss. Make them think you've searched the cellar, outwitted the wine waiter. Get it?'

'Got it!' Jimmy's young face cracked into a grin and he hurried downstairs.

Valentino had been waiting patiently, completely uninterested in anything that had been said. He followed Frank up to the family's private apartment without protest. He's tired, Frank thought, and the wine has made him sleepy. With any luck he'll go straight to bed.

But their mother was waiting with the chocolate cake and, at the sight of it, Valentino's eyes lit up like those of a greedy child. He allowed Maria Alvini to lead him over to the table, drape a napkin around his neck and present him with a large slice of cake.

When Frank murmured to his mother that he wanted to go back downstairs for a moment, she barely acknowledged him. But before Frank could close the door behind him, he heard Valentino say, 'But where are the papers?'

'Frank?' His mother called out helplessly.

'The papers, Mother,' he said. 'Remember you wanted Valentino to look at the papers? Wait, I'll get them.'

He hurried back into the room and opened the roll-top desk in the corner. He extracted an old ledger. The pages were yellowing and the ink was fading but it was big and looked impressive.

'Here you are,' he said as he placed the ledger on the table next to the plate of chocolate cake. 'Perhaps you would check the figures? It would be a big help for Mamma.'

'Would it?' Valentino was looking up into their mother's face.

'Yes, my son. I don't know what I would do without you.'

135

He began to turn the pages of the ledger at the same time as biting into the cake. Rich dark crumbs scattered over the neat rows of accounts. Frank watched their mother surreptitiously dab at her eyes with her handkerchief as his brother ran a finger along and down the columns of figures. He nodded and smiled as he reached the bottom of each page.

It didn't matter that the ledger was years old and that the figures were now meaningless. Valentino couldn't read.

Frank stopped Jimmy just as he was about to knock on the door of the private dining room. He put a finger to his lips to indicate silence and then took the tray from him. He indicated with a turn of his head that the young waiter should go back down to the kitchen.

As he pushed the door open he heard a gasp and then stifled laughter. The heads of the two men, one fair and one dark, moved quickly away from each other. Frank glanced at the table. There was a small stain on the cloth where a wine glass lay on its side, the rim resting on the edge of a serving dish of salmon mousse moulded in the shape of a fish; very little had been taken. The plates in front of the two men contained barely touched food. And yet there were already two empty wine bottles on the serving table. And now they had ordered champagne.

'I didn't hear you knock, Alvini.' Matthew Elliot stared at him coolly.

'I'm sorry, sir. Your champagne.'

'Well, did you knock or didn't you? And I thought I told young Nelson to bring the wine back himself.'

While Elliot was talking, his friend, John Edington, the little shop assistant, watched with simpering admiration. Frank felt the muscles of his stomach tighten with distaste.

'I did knock, Mr Elliot, and I thought I'd better bring the

champagne myself in case you accused my young waiter of serving you cat's piss.'

John Edington gasped softly and Matthew Elliot's eyes widened for a moment before he decided to take it in good part. His handsome features expressed amusement. 'I was only joshing the lad. Truth to tell, I just wanted to make sure that he came back himself.'

'And why was that, sir?' Frank's usually mobile features remained impassive and his voice was level.

Elliot was disconcerted. 'Well . . . you know . . . he's quick, intelligent; we'd like to encourage him . . . take an interest . . .'

'I see.' And Frank was afraid that he did see. He would tell Patrick that young Jimmy Nelson was not to wait on the private rooms for a while. That is, not the private rooms where two gentlemen were dining alone.

He put the tray with the ice bucket down on the serving table and withdrew the bottle of champagne. 'Veuve Clicquot, sir?'

Elliot raised one hand and pushed the white linen napkin down to reveal the label. This was natural enough but it was the way his indolent gesture managed to suggest that he suspected Frank of cheating that riled. Frank concealed his irritation. Sir Hubert Elliot's son was a good customer who spent freely.

Matthew Elliot always dined in a private room with one friend in particular and, for some time now, that particular friend had been John Edington. The private dining rooms were opulent, too opulent for Frank's taste, but the customers liked that style. Gold brocade draped the walls, the dark red carpet bore an oriental pattern and the ruby velvet curtains were permanently closed, ensuring that the atmosphere was intimate. There was a day bed in the corner of each room.

137

Frank would have thought that someone with Matthew Elliot's education would find the décor ostentatious, even vulgar, but then he would know very well that a more discriminating establishment would not have entertained his friends. He had never before this evening been quite so supercilious, but perhaps something had upset him.

The two men watched as Frank uncorked the champagne and filled two glasses. He stood back a little. 'Shall I send someone to clear the table?'

'If you like,' Elliot said. 'I don't think we can eat much more; we are too – excited.'

Frank looked from one to the other. He noticed now that John Edington's colour was high and his eyes were shining. In fact they looked unnaturally bright. But he didn't look happy. Frank was curious. 'Excited?'

'Yes.' Matthew Elliot raised his glass and gestured towards his friend. 'In fact we must congratulate Mr Edington. You see, he got married to his sweetheart, Constance, today.'

'I see.' Frank began to withdraw.

'Wait a moment, Alvini. Send some fruit and cheese in, will you? My friend has hardly touched his food and I suppose he should eat and make up his strength—'

'Matthew, no—' It was the first time John Edington had spoken. His voice was unsteady.

'Do you think I'm being coarse? Don't just shake your head.' He stared at his friend for a moment and his look was almost hostile. And then he smiled up at Frank. 'Alvini, I'm not being coarse, am I? Isn't that the kind of joke little shopkeepers make on their wedding day?'

'I'll send someone to clear the table, sir.'

'Oh, no. I can see by your expression that even you think I'm being coarse—'

'Matthew, stop . . .' John Edington reached across the table

138

and took his friend's hand but Matthew shook him off angrily and emptied his glass of champagne in one swallow.

Just as Frank reached the door he called out, 'Send another bottle of this, whatever it is, up with the cheese, will you? I must make sure that John is fortified against the perils of the night.'

As Frank closed the door behind him he thought he heard the sound of muffled sobs.

Chapter Ten

In any other circumstance I should be enjoying sitting alone here by the fire, Constance thought. She had found an embroidered footstool and had put her feet up and settled back into the cushions. She'd tried to cheer herself up by imagining what Nella would think if she could see her now, but she frowned when she realized that Nella would immediately ask her where her new husband was. And what he was thinking about, leaving her alone like this on their wedding night!

Constance supposed that, in spite of his promise, John's uncle, Walter Barton, was keeping him late discussing business. It may even be something to do with the inheritance that Muriel Barton had mentioned. What had she said? That John would come into his full inheritance when he became a father? Constance had not known what Mrs Barton was talking about, but she remembered how angry she had been at the woman's hints that she might have married John just for his money.

So perhaps John's uncle had kept him to discuss family matters once the shop takings had been dealt with. But surely he would have warned her that this was going to happen instead of telling her not to be upset and that John would be home in time for them to have an intimate supper together. She glanced at the mahogany mantel clock; its brass face showed ten past nine. It would be a late supper.

But, even though John's continued absence was both worrying and hurtful, the soft hiss of the single gaslight and the crackle of the fire were comforting. Constance remembered other fires, other hearths . . .

The nursery fire at her father's house and the floor strewn with toys and picture books, the gleaming little hearth in her mother's sitting room where Constance would lie on the soft-piled rug and listen entranced to her mother's tales of her childhood in Le Touquet. The imposing fireplace in the library where her father would sit with the newspapers, the dogs stretched out at his feet, gazing up at him with half-open trusting eyes.

Then, last night she had dried her hair in front of the fire in Rosemary Elliot's room in the grand house in Fenham. The house that John had seemingly never set foot in.

Last night . . . Constance shuddered when she remembered what had happened after Mrs Sowerby had so cruelly thrown her out of the town house on Rye Hill.

Suddenly she sat up straight and dug her fingers into the soft plush on the arms of the chair. Is that why John had not come home? Had he discovered what had happened to her the night before? That Gerald Sowerby had raped her, had taken from her the only thing she had to offer John: her innocence.

No, it was impossible, wasn't it? Surely even Gerald Sowerby would not seek John out to tell him what he had done.

Constance hunched forward and stared miserably into the flames. If only John would come home!

A sudden gust of wind sent the smoke back down the chimney and a small cloud billowed out into the room.

Constance turned her face away until it dissipated and then kneeled down to sweep the soot and ash up from the hearth.

As she settled back into her chair she half smiled to think how instinctive her action had been. Mrs Sowerby would have rung the bell and called for one of the maids to do that. Should she have rung for Polly? Uneasily she examined something that had been nagging at her conscience. The Edingtons' maid had looked pinched and exhausted; Constance realized that she had probably been doing the work of three maids and yet she had not hesitated to add to her burden by giving her fresh duties.

And yet I am not a servant here, Constance thought. John has not married me to turn me into a household drudge. I am the mistress of this house, or at least I will be when . . . when . . .

Constance did not allow herself to continue that train of thought. John had told her that his mother was an invalid but it was not until today, when Constance had met Mrs Edington for the first time, that she had realized how gravely ill she was.

So what did I imagine life would be like as John's wife? she wondered. What did Nella say only last night? '*You're so lucky. You'll be mistress of yer own house!*'

'*I hope you don't think that's why I'm marrying him – for a house,*' she had replied.

And she had tried to tell Nella how much she loved John, how, ever since she'd first met him, she had dreamed of being his wife. At first the dream had seemed to be an impossible fantasy and then, when he had proposed to her, she had hardly been able to believe that it was really happening – that she was going to spend the rest of her days with John who was so handsome and so kind.

But had Nella instinctively touched on another truth? Nella had known that Constance was used to a much better life than that of a servant. She had surely guessed that Constance dreamed of returning to that life. Of dressing in velvets and silks just like her mother had done, of wearing jewellery and being driven in a carriage or a motorcar.

Well, she had driven to her wedding in a motorcar but it had not been John's. If it were only the desire for worldly goods that Constance craved, she should have married her husband's friend, Matthew Elliot. And then she reminded herself how unlikely a match that would have been. No one like Matthew Elliot, from the upper reaches of society, would consider marrying an orphaned servant girl.

No, she was lucky that she and John had found each other. He had fallen in love with her and married her, and taken her away from a life of backbreaking drudgery. But surely she had learned something during those miserable years? She must never allow herself to behave like Violet Sowerby. Constance rose from her chair and walked to the other side of the hearth. She seized the tasselled bell pull and rang for Polly.

'Yes, Mrs John?'

The girl had forgotten to knock but Constance did not reprimand her. Polly stood just inside the door, wearily unaware of the sooty smudge trailing down her cheek, and her hair escaping from her mobcap, untidier than ever. Her sleeves were pushed up above her bony wrists almost to her elbows and her hands were red raw.

'My – Master John is not home yet,' Constance began.

Polly blinked. 'I can see that. I mean, yes, Mrs John?'

'You must be tired.'

'Yes.' She looked surprised.

'What has been arranged for supper?'

'Some nice sandwiches, two kinds, ham and salmon, cut dainty, like. There was plenty left over from the wedding breakfast so there's more than enough for the two of you. And there's a slice or two of wedding cake. It's all waiting on a tray with a teapot and two of the best china cups.'

'Good. I want you to cover the tray with a clean cloth and bring it in here. You can leave it on that table by the window – it's cool over there – and then you needn't wait up for Master John coming home.'

'But the tea – it'll go cold.'

'You needn't make the tea yet, Polly. I've noticed there's a small hob on this grate. Have you – we – got a kettle that'll fit?'

'Oh yes. Mrs Edington used to make tea for herself regularly when she was still able to spend her days in here.'

'Right then. Bring everything in, as I say, and then you must go to bed. You've had a long day.'

Polly's face flushed; she stared at her for a moment as if she was going to say something, but then she turned and hurried out. As the door closed behind her a gust of wind rattled the window and the russet-coloured curtains moved slightly. Constance went over to the window and moved one curtain so that she could look out into the street. There were still a few snowflakes swirling in the wind but the snow wasn't lying. The roofs of the houses opposite glowed damply in the light from the streetlamps.

Where was John?

Frances Edington knew that her son had not come home yet. Ever since her brother had carried her upstairs and Polly had helped her to undress and get into bed, she had lain awake and tried to make out what was happening in the house around her.

She was tired, exhausted even, but her mind had not allowed her to sleep.

She was becoming a prisoner in this room. She spent more and more of her life here and, when she was too tired to read, she would lie listening to the sounds from beyond her door, and try to imagine exactly what was going on.

She knew when Polly woke up and began to clean the grate in the kitchen. She heard John's kind-hearted greeting to the girl every morning when he went downstairs for breakfast. He was always cheerful, no matter how late he had returned home the night before.

Then Frances would sit up and smile in anticipation when she heard his footsteps returning upstairs to say goodbye to her before he left for work. How eagerly she would wait to hear him returning home again. He always came straight up to see her, bringing her newspapers, magazines, perhaps a new book from the circulating library.

And then there were the sounds from outside the house. Usually she was awake in time to hear the tradespeople – the milkman and the baker – bringing their deliveries in horse-drawn carts. Then, a little later, after the men had gone to work and the children to school, the butcher and the grocer would arrive. The people who lived in this street were not prosperous, but neither were they poor, and the sounds outside were a testament to how comfortably they could afford to live.

Except for her and John. Making ends meet was as much of a struggle as it had been when Frances had eloped with Duncan and her father had refused to help. And when Duncan had left her, her father had relented – but only a little. Over the years she and John, even with the salary he earned from Barton's, could hardly have stayed living in this house if it had not been for her brother's kindness, and she would certainly not have been able to afford a maid.

But now John had married and things would be different. Not just because his wife would be able to help to look after her, but because John would now come into part of his inheritance. And once a child was born there would be more. Frances sighed. She knew why her father had insisted on a child before John gained his full inheritance, and she almost hated him for it.

But what of John? Surely he hadn't married the girl simply for financial reasons? No, Constance was lovely – more than that, she was truly beautiful, and she was well-mannered and well-spoken. Surely any young man could fall in love with her, no matter what her background.

And Constance? It was obvious that she adored John. Would that love be strong enough to withstand any horror she might feel if she discovered what kind of man John's father had been? Frances wished that John had not been so quick to assure her that Constance had no family to object to her alliance with the son of a scoundrel.

The carriage clock on her bedside table began to chime. Frances turned her head wearily. Quarter-past nine. The clock had been a present from that scoundrel – the husband she had adored. She sighed and acknowledged bitterly that now it was not her husband's behaviour that was worrying her, it was her son's.

This was his wedding night and where was he?

Frances began to cough. She pushed herself forward from her mound of supporting pillows and clutched at one of the clean rags left handy on the night table. She wiped her lips but, before she had time to examine the sputum by the light of the oil-lamp which was always left burning, the coughing fit worsened. The pain in her chest became so severe that she found herself gripping handfuls of the eiderdown and pulling it in towards her chest in an effort to press the pain away.

As the cough and the pain subsided she found that tears were streaming down her cheeks.

Polly stood in the narrow hallway and listened to the dreadful sounds coming from upstairs. How long had Mrs Edington been coughing like that? Until a moment ago, Polly had been in the kitchen and she wouldn't have heard anything with the door closed. That's why Mr Barton had had the bells installed: so that his sister could summon Polly quickly if she needed help.

The bell pull was right next to the bed. Mrs Edington hadn't summoned her. Polly hesitated: should she go up anyway? She gripped the tray she was carrying more firmly and looked towards the door leading into the front parlour. Or should she send Master John's new wife up? It would give her something to do instead of sitting moping by the fire . . .

While Polly stood there, undecided, the racking coughs subsided and then stopped. After a moment Polly heard a half-moan, half-sigh of distress and she could imagine Mrs Edington settling back into her pillows. She wouldn't go up then. But perhaps she'd better mention it.

Polly balanced her tray and knocked on the front-room door. Barely waiting for an answer she hurried in to find Mrs John, as she wanted to be called, sitting staring miserably into the fire. Poor little thing, to be kept waiting like this on her wedding night, Polly thought, but she stopped herself feeling too sorry for her. After all, she reminded herself, there she is, sitting by a nice warm fire giving orders like Lady Muck, while I'm skivvying, fetching and carrying just like I always do. But it was nice of her to say I could go to bed now. Perhaps she'll be all right when she's settled in a bit.

Polly put the tray on the table by the window as she'd been instructed and then hurried back to the kitchen to fetch the small kettle. Master John's wife looked up and smiled weakly when she returned. Polly took a fire iron and pulled the hob forward before placing the kettle on it.

'There,' she said. 'The water'll heat up nicely, and when Master John comes home you can push it back and boil it up.'

'Thank you, Polly. Now off you go. I won't need you any more tonight.'

'Right oh. But . . .?'

'What is it?'

'Mrs Edington, she's been coughing.'

'Yes, I heard her. I thought that you must have gone up to her.'

'No. I was going to but then she stopped. If she's sleeping I don't want to disturb her.'

'I understand. Don't worry, I'll listen out for her.'

Polly hesitated. 'Her medicine's on the table. But will you be able to . . .? I mean have you ever . . .?'

'I'm used to invalids, if that's what you mean. My mother died in the wor— I mean when I was younger.'

'Oh, I'm sorry.' Polly started to walk towards her but Mrs John shook her head and waved her away. The poor lady obviously didn't want to be reminded. 'Right, then. Good night, Mrs John.'

'Good night.'

Once back in the kitchen, Polly pulled the truckle bed out from under the table, and tugged the chain that turned off the gaslamp. She knew it was daft but she never took her clothes off until the room was dark. At home there were so many brothers and sisters that modesty required all kinds of shifts

149

and turns, but here there was no one to spy on her or make cheeky comments and yet she still could not bring herself to strip off with the light on.

Not that she stripped off exactly. She didn't own a nightgown so she slept in her underwear and, if it was cold like it was tonight, she kept her woollen stockings on too. Then, the same as every night, she hung her dress over the back of a chair and slipped beneath the blankets on the truckle bed which she'd pulled right across in front of the fire.

Usually she fell asleep as soon as her head hit the black and white striped ticking of the pillow, but tonight she found that her head was spinning with strange thoughts.

She couldn't help thinking about Master John and his pretty little bride and what they would be doing tonight when he came home. Polly squirmed as she felt a stab of feeling at the pit of her stomach. It didn't hurt but it was uncomfortable and yet strangely pleasant. Polly knew what men and women did – she couldn't help knowing, growing up the way she had, with her mam and her dad and all her brothers and sisters sleeping so close together shared out between two tiny upstairs rooms.

When her oldest brother, Geordie, got married and brought his lass, Ida, home, they'd had to share with the younger children until they got a couple of rooms of their own. But by the time that happened, Ida was six months gone.

Master John would be no different from her dad or Geordie, she supposed. And that was probably why he hadn't come home yet. No doubt he was out on the town with that swell friend of his, getting drunk as a boiled owl.

Polly was glad that she wouldn't have to deal with him if he did come home blotto. She could stay here until the morning, warm and snug in her own narrow bed, with the kitchen smelling pleasantly of good food and the glow from the hearth to comfort and reassure her.

Yes, she worked hard but life here was good compared to the life of her sisters and her mother. Perhaps she would never get married. It might be better to remain an old maid rather than have to be some man's drudge and be worn out having baby after baby year after year.

But if she didn't get married she wouldn't be a bride, she wouldn't have a wedding day. She could imagine herself walking down the aisle of the church carrying a beautiful bouquet of flowers. Just before she drifted off to sleep, Polly sighed as she found that the young man waiting for her at the altar was Albert Green . . .

Nella waited until the sound of regular breathing from the other bed told her that Alice was asleep. Then, pushing the bedclothes back, she swung her feet over the lumpy mattress on to the bare wooden floor. It was cold, the draught under the door was like a howling gale, and Nella reached for her shawl and pulled it over her shoulders.

The Sowerby house might be grand, Nella thought, but these flamin' attics are like the most miserable hovels on earth. In summer it's boiling hot up here under the eaves and in winter it's like ice.

In the cold light coming through the dormer window Nella glanced at her new roommate. Alice was sleeping like a baby. Well, she was a baby, wasn't she? And that was probably why she had cried herself to sleep. Nella had heard the muffled sobs but she had lain still, pretending to be asleep. She could have comforted her, Constance would have wanted her to, but she had something else to worry about.

Now, satisfied that the new skivvy was sleeping the blessed sleep of exhaustion, Nella moved her aching limbs painfully across the floor towards the chest of drawers. She groped for

151

the matches, pulled the candle in the saucer forward and lit it. The flame wavered and then steadied; Nella turned to see if the slight scraping noise the match had made had woken Alice but it hadn't.

Nella's clothes were hanging over the rail at the bottom of her bed. She reached into the pocket of her dress and took out the small golden coloured heart. She held out her hand and examined the heart in the light of the candle. There they were, the two letters engraved on the front, *C* and *N* entwined. The first letters of their names. This was the wedding gift she had given to Constance.

Very early, when she'd gone out to the coalhouse and had found a broken chain and she had hoped against hope that it was not the chain she had given to Constance. And, if it was, then she had imagined that one of the links must have been weak. But she had not found the little heart. Not until later that day.

Nella grew even colder with horror when she remembered the scream she had heard the night before. So she hadn't been imagining it: it had been Constance who had cried out for help and there had been no one to go to her aid. No one to help her when he had attacked her.

Oh, how she hated him!

She remembered the moment after breakfast when she had been cleaning the grate in his bedroom. He had been lying in bed, snoring like a drunken pig, and she had set the fire, lit it, and tried to get out before he woke up. In her haste to leave the room she had stumbled over the clothes he had left strewn about on the floor. She would have left them there and hurried out but something was glinting in the turn-up of one of the legs of his trousers. She crouched and pulled it free – and felt like seizing a fire iron and beating him over the head.

She was crouching there, feeling sick with shock and rage when he spluttered and stirred. She turned her head to find him staring at her. Startled, she thrust the golden heart in her pocket and fled.

Whenever she had had a moment throughout the day she had taken the golden heart from her pocket and stared at it. Then she had put it back into her pocket where she could almost feel it burning through the thin stuff of her dress and branding her skin.

She wished she could brand him!

She would have to see Constance and find out what had happened. Perhaps her friend had been able to fight him off. He was big and hefty, but if he'd been drinking – and he probably had been – a nimble lass would have been able to outmanoeuvre him, knee him where it hurt and dodge away.

Would Constance know about that? Where to hurt a man? Any woman would, wouldn't she?

Poor Constance. What a thing to happen on the night before her wedding!

She would have to go and see her at the first opportunity.

Constance will tell me whether Gerald Sowerby has hurt her, Nella thought, and if he has – if he has – I'll find a way to kill him!

'Constance . . . Constance, sweetheart . . .'

She stirred and opened her eyes. John was standing over her. She moved her head and found that her neck was aching. She frowned, but as soon as he saw that she was awake, he smiled and kneeled down beside her. He took her hand.

'You're cold, I'm sorry . . .'

'Sorry?' Constance turned her head to look at the hearth. A few embers glowed amongst the ashes but the fire was past saving. How long have I been sleeping? she thought. She glanced up at the clock. Midnight!

'John!' She turned to face him and he reached for her other hand and held them both tightly against his chest.

'I know, I know – and, Constance, I'm so sorry,' he said.

'But, John, why? This is our wedding day . . .'

'There – there was so much to do, so much to talk about—'

'Talk about? With Uncle Walter? Have you been talking business all this time?'

'I . . . I don't know what to say. The time just flew . . .'

'I don't understand. Your uncle promised that he would send you home in time for us to have supper together. Polly has left everything ready for us . . . there on the tray.'

'You haven't eaten?'

'No, I waited for you!'

Constance realized that her voice was shrill and she also realized that she couldn't care less about missing her supper. It was the fact that John could do this tonight of all nights that upset her. Surely he should have wanted to hurry home to her?

He rose to his feet, bringing her up with him. 'Do you want something now? Shall I ring for Polly and tell her to make you a hot drink?'

'Polly is asleep. I told her she could go to bed hours ago.'

John released Constance's hands and stepped back. 'Then I shall make you a cup of tea.' He had seen the kettle in the hearth and was about to kneel and put it on the trivet when Constance reached out a hand to stop him.

'John, it doesn't matter. I don't want anything. I just . . .'

She could feel the tears pricking at the back of her eyes and, the next moment, John had taken her in his arms.

'Oh, my poor darling,' he said. 'I have been thoughtless. Will you forgive me? Please say you'll forgive me!'

'Yes . . . but why? Oh, John . . .'

He caught her open mouth with his, and between kisses he murmured against her lips, 'Hush . . . my sweet . . . We mustn't start our life together with a quarrel . . . must we?'

'No, but . . .'

His lips were moist, his kisses gentle, tender, sweet . . . Constance found herself responding, melting against him. But there was something on his breath. Was it wine? Had he been drinking? Had he and his uncle been celebrating his marriage? If that were so, it was only natural . . . but to come home so late!

She stiffened and made a moan of distress. He pulled away and held her face in his hands. They were warm and soft and his touch was sure. He held her so that she had to look into his eyes.

'Hush, sweetheart.' He pulled her forward and kissed her brow. 'Come, my darling . . . come up to bed.'

Polly must have banked the bedroom fire up well for it was still glowing and the room was not too cold. John, murmuring something about respecting her modesty, went to his old room to undress. Constance was grateful that he had not chosen to light the lamps; there was something reassuringly comforting about undressing by firelight.

She felt a little lost and uncertain. She realized that in spite of the romance of their courtship she hardly knew her husband. They had so seldom been alone together. But she had been sure that John loved her as much as she loved him. Otherwise why should he marry her?

Why had he stayed out so late tonight?

Had he really been unable to refuse his uncle's hospitality? He hadn't really answered her but then he had seemed so ashamed, so regretful, so eager to make up with her . . .

Constance lay the last of her undergarments on a chair. She

shivered. Where was her nightdress? Oh yes, under the pillow. She should hurry; John would be returning soon.

John . . . I love him so much, she thought, and he is here with me now and he is right, we should not begin our life together with a quarrel.

She took her nightdress from under the pillow and suddenly wished that she had been able to afford a new one. She wondered what Polly had thought about the numerous darns. Well, at least the mends were neat. By the time John returned she was in bed.

There had been so little intimacy between them that Constance hardly knew what to expect. Once in his arms, she surrendered herself to his kisses and they were infinitely sweet. To her delight, she felt her body beginning to respond to his feathering caresses. A tremulous pleasure began to build up inside her and suddenly she became possessed of an urgent desire to be as close as possible to him, for the two of them to become one. Then, just as he was about to enter her, she had a moment of terror.

Would John be able to tell that this was not the first time for her?

She must have drawn back and tensed up because John whispered, 'Don't be frightened, sweetheart. The last thing I want to do is hurt you. Try to relax.'

But she couldn't relax and she could feel her muscles resisting him as he pushed his way in. *This is my husband*, she had to remind herself, he loves me and I love him. I must not let the evil that Gerald did spoil my wedding night.

John held her and soothed her as he moved inside her. Her terror faded as she succumbed to the joy of being in his arms but the pleasurable feelings had gone – died away. She was left with a puzzling sense of disappointment.

After it was over there were traces of tears on her cheeks.

John found them there and kissed them away. Constance could have sworn that he had been crying too.

Chapter Eleven

December

'There's a woman at the door what wants to see you.' Polly sounded cross – no, not exactly cross, put out and a bit unsure of herself. Constance looked up from her mending; the girl was scowling. Constance held her patience.

'*Who* wants to see me,' Constance corrected her, 'and what is her name and what does she want?'

'I dunno.'

Constance was vexed. In the weeks since she had been here, Polly had behaved herself well enough. The two of them had achieved an uneasy truce, but now she hadn't even remembered to knock; she had barged in and was giving every sign of being in a proper fret. Perhaps it was because of all the extra work over Christmas. Constance glanced at her; at least the girl had remembered to put on a clean white apron before going to the door. Constance decided to exercise patience.

'Did you ask her what her business was?'

'Yes. She just said she wanted to see you.'

'And her name? You did ask her name, didn't you?'

'Of course I did. It's Miss Nicholson.' With a raise of her

eyebrows Polly conveyed that this was very unlikely.

Constance frowned. 'I don't know a Miss Nicholson.'

'Right.' The girl looked relieved. 'Then I can send the little witch on her way.'

Polly was out of the door before Constance had time to rise to her feet. Dropping the socks and the darning wools, she called out, 'Polly! Come back!'

'Yes?' The girl popped her head round the door. 'She's still standing there, mind, and there's a fair old draught from the door.'

'Show her in.'

'But—'

'Show Miss Nicholson in – and for goodness' sake, try to be polite!'

Polly raised her eyebrows and pursed her lips together sulkily but she did as she was told. Constance heard her say, 'This way, Miss Nicholson,' and a moment later her guest entered the room.

'Nella!' Constance exclaimed.

'Constance – ee, Constance!'

They hugged each other, then stood back and stared for a moment before they both exclaimed at once, 'How nice you look!'

'And you smell lovely,' Nella said, 'like a rose garden!'

'Attar of Roses,' Constance told her. 'John bought it for me when I told him that I liked it.'

'Mind, you really suit that colour,' Nella said. 'It's like cornflowers – matches yer eyes. And velvet – that's not cheap. Been shopping, hev you?'

'No, we made it.'

'We? You and yer ma-in-law?'

'No. I'll tell you later. But look at you – such a smart skirt and jacket!'

'It's not a jacket, it's a bolero. Isabelle gave it to me – and the skirt and blouse. She helped me alter them to fit. And that was a fair puzzle, I can tell you.'

'That was kind of her.'

'Well, she said she was sick of navy blue – she wanted the new red. And, of course, her mam still buys her clothes for her even although Isabelle's a working woman.'

'And did she give you that hat?'

'Does it look daft? A straw boater in winter? It's the only hat I hev...'

'No, Nella, with your hair up like that, the hat looks just fine.'

Constance became aware that Polly was staring at them, wide-eyed. 'Polly,' she said, 'go and make a pot of tea and – wait a minute – are you hungry, Nella?' She didn't wait for an answer but hurried on, 'And make up some sandwiches; we've plenty of cold roast beef left, haven't we?'

Polly nodded.

'Sandwiches then and some mince pies and Christmas cake.'

The girl lingered.

'What is it?' Constance asked.

'Do you want enough for two?'

'Yes, Polly, of course. What are you thinking of? My friend and I shall take tea together by the fire here.'

When the door closed behind the young maid, Constance drew the other armchair up nearer to the hearth and motioned Nella to take it. She gathered the fallen socks and darning wools and stuffed everything into the workbasket on the small table next to her chair before adding some coals to the fire and sitting down.

Nella had been staring at the holly and the ivy arranged along the top of the gilt-framed mirror above the fireplace, and at the red satin bows tied to the brass candlesticks. 'Bonny,' she murmured and then glanced round to see Constance wiping her hands on a handkerchief. 'You should hev asked me to do that. You might hev dirtied yer bonny frock.'

'No, you are my guest. Oh, Nella, it's been so long!'

'Yes, well, I would've come sooner – I wanted to – but yer letter said everything was fine.'

Constance looked startled. 'Of course everything was – is – fine. Why shouldn't it be?'

Nella looked levelly at her friend and then tugged at the drawstrings of the small pouched bag that was tied to her belt. She took out a letter. Constance glanced at the curling edges and guessed that it had been much read.

'I was worried about you until I got this,' Nella said.

'Why worried?'

'Never mind, I'll tell you later, but I was planning to ask Mrs Mortimer to change my afternoon off so that I could come here sooner – and this arrived.' Nella was scanning the letter as she spoke. 'It was kind of you to write, Constance; I didn't expect it. It was nice of you to think of me.'

Constance had written the letter one afternoon only a few days after her wedding, sitting in this very room, this very chair, because she was bored and lonely. John's mother was sleeping after a light lunch in her room – in fact she hadn't left her room since the day of the wedding. Polly was in the kitchen and John was at work.

Constance had nothing to do to fill her time until teatime, when, she had told Polly, she would take a tray up for her mother-in-law and, uneasy with her thoughts, she had sought comfort by writing to her old friend. She had written what Nella would be expecting to hear – that she was blissfully happy.

'I realized that I'd been fretting about nothing when I read

162

this,' Nella said. 'I mean, the wedding sounds just like a dream – and yer new friends, Rosemary Elliot and Miss Beattie, coming to the wedding breakfast . . .'

Constance looked at Nella keenly. Had she detected just a hint of jealousy when Nella had mentioned her new friends?

'And how beautiful and sweet yer ma-in-law is, and how much you like her, poor lady. So-oo . . .' Nella sighed. 'I thought I might hev been worrying needlessly.'

'Worrying? Nella, you've said it again. I wish you would explain yourself.'

'I didn't write back – you know me writing isn't as good as yours. Well, you always used to help me, didn't you?' Nella put the letter back into her purse and she looked as if she was going to take something else out when there was a knock on the door. She withdrew her hand; it was empty. 'That'll be the girl. Shall I open the door for her?'

'Why?'

Nella laughed. 'You're turning into a proper fine lady, aren't you? Because the lass'll be carrying a tray and if I open the door there'll be less chance of her spilling anything. By the way, Constance,' she said over her shoulder, 'thank you for saying to the lass that I was yer friend.'

Constance looked at Nella while Polly arranged the tray on the table by the window. She could see that she was itching to help the girl and she shot her a warning glance. Nella sat down and watched impatiently while Polly lifted the table, tray and all, and brought it nearer to them.

'Thank you, Polly,' Constance said. 'Now if you could just bring the small kettle and place it on the hob, we'll be able to fill up the teapot without bothering you.'

'Yes, Mrs John.'

Nella's eyes widened but she didn't say anything until Polly had returned with the kettle and left the room again.

'Yes, *Mrs John!* Ee, Constance, I can't get over the change in you. You look as though you belong here!'

'But, I do.'

'Of course.' Nella's smile faded.

'And what about you? *Miss Nicholson* indeed! Do you know I almost didn't know who it was. To me you've always just been Nella.'

'Do you want me to pour the tea?'

'No, take this plate,' Constance rose swiftly, 'and some of these sandwiches,' she offered the serving plate, 'and let me look after you.'

While they enjoyed their meal together, Constance told Nella about her wedding day surprise – her sewing room – and how John seemed to take endless delight in planning a wardrobe for her. When she told her that it was John who had helped her make the dress that she was wearing and that John had ambitions to be a couturier, a sort of high-class society dressmaker, she was worried that Nella would find that peculiar.

But her friend seemed to be enchanted by the whole idea and thought it was very romantic that John should want to dress Constance in beautiful clothes. 'Ee, Constance,' she said, 'real sweethearts, aren't you?'

And all the while Constance watched and was touched by Nella's obvious delight at the unexpected feast. In the few weeks she had been John's wife, Constance had not forgotten the near starvation diet at the Sowerbys' house. She decided to ask Nella to come and take tea with her on every one of her afternoons off. Then she wondered why she hadn't called before this. It was as if Nella had read her mind.

'I hevn't had any time off since you left to get married, you know. Once I'd got yer letter and realized that everything was

164

all right,' Constance frowned and was about to interrupt but Nella hurried on, 'yes, once I realized that you were fine, I sent you that note saying I'd be along to see you when I could. Did you get it?'

'Yes.'

'Well, I traded in all my time off so's the old cow would give me Boxing Day.'

'But that was yesterday.'

'I know. And Miss Annabel had a party for her friends so old Mortimer decided that I couldn't have the time off, after all. Not that I was allowed into the parlour – I might have frightened the children out of their wits – no, I just had to slave away in the kitchen. Lucky I couldn't afford to book a ticket and I'd decided to queue for the gallery.'

'Nella, I'm not sure what you're talking about.'

'The Christmas show at the Palace. You know I've been saving up for a ticket all year. I've been looking forward to it for so long, I could hardly wait. I wanted to gan on the opening night! But at the last minute old Sowerby said I couldn't hev the time off and I'd hev to gan the next night. I was mad, I can tell you, but in a way it's worked out well because I've been able to come and see you. I expect you had folk round on Boxing Day too?'

Constance smiled and shook her head, 'No, Nella. You know how poorly John's mother is? Well, we were very quiet. John's uncle, Mr Barton, sent round a hamper – Nella, you've never seen such treats – but poor Mrs Edington was hardly well enough to enjoy them.'

'Oh, what a shame.'

'On Christmas Day John and I took a tray up so that we could share our meal with her. Yesterday she slept for most of the time and John and I were alone together downstairs.'

'And the girl? Polly?'

165

'My neighbour Mrs Green came to help and to sit with John's mother for a while, so I sent Polly home yesterday afternoon, although I had the impression she would rather have stayed here. But there was so much food going to waste I thought she had better take some of it to share with her family.'

'Ee, Constance, you are kind. That lass doesn't know she's born, working for a mistress like you!'

Constance felt uncomfortable. She remembered her first day here and how, almost unthinkingly, she had quite effortlessly shed all those years of servitude and adopted the role of an employer. Of course, she *had* been born to better things . . .

'So you're happy, then, Constance?'

'Yes, of course.'

Her answer had come too quickly, it had been too emphatic, but Nella didn't seem to have noticed. She was fiddling with the drawstrings of her purse again. In the silence, Constance found herself babbling. 'This house is so comfortable and John is so kind, oh, Nella you wouldn't believe how gentle he is— What's that?'

Constance's throat constricted. Nella had taken something out of her bag and she was holding it out towards her. Constance stared at the monkey-like paw, the small fingers bent and curling upward around the object that lay in Nella's palm and glittered in the firelight.

'You didn't say anything in yer letter about losing me wedding present,' Nella said.

'I . . . what . . . how. . .?'

'Don't shake yer head, Constance. It is the necklace I gave you, and divven't worry. I realize that you wouldn't want to hurt me and I know you didn't lose it deliberately. I know what happened.'

'Do you?' Constance shrank back in her chair. 'How? How

166

do you know?' All kinds of emotions churned up inside her. My God, has Gerald been boasting about what he did to me? she thought, panicked.

'Well, I guessed.'

Nella told Constance about finding the broken chain the next morning. About worrying about the cry she had heard the night before and then about finding the heart in the turn-up of Gerald's trousers.

'He attacked you, didn't he? He must hev been lying in wait for you outside the house. Constance,' Nella put the chain and the heart on the table and leaned forward, staring at her earnestly, 'he didn't hurt you, did he?'

'Hurt?'

'Well, of course he must hev hurt you but he didn't hev his way? You fought him off, didn't you, Constance?'

'I . . . yes, I fought him . . .' And it's true, I did, she thought. And I must make Nella believe that I got away from him. I couldn't bear it if she knew, if anyone knew, what happened to me. It's too shameful, too degrading. 'Yes, I fought him and – and I managed to run away.'

'I thought you would but I wasn't sure. I was gannin' to come and see you as soon as I could but then yer letter arrived and you sounded so happy. I mean I'm yer best friend, amman't I? If anything dreadful had happened, you would hev told me, wouldn't you?'

'I . . . well . . . yes . . .'

'So he didn't spoil things? Well, of course he didn't. I mean if he had, John would hev been able to tell that you weren't – you know – pure, wouldn't he? And, unless the man's a saint, you wouldn't be so happy right now!'

It was dark when Nella took her leave later that afternoon, and there was a biting wind.

167

'Wait,' Constance said, and she shut the door again. She ran upstairs and came down a moment later with the black velvet cape that Rosemary Elliot had given her to wear at her wedding. 'Here, put this round your shoulders. If you're going to queue for a ticket you might die of cold before you get in to see the show! Go on – you can keep it.'

'No, Constance, I can't take that. It's much too good for the likes of me!'

'Don't ever speak like that!' Constance exclaimed. 'Nothing could ever be too good for you, Nella. I insist that you take it. Think of it as a Christmas present.'

Constance hoped that Nella would never guess how much her action had been prompted by guilt. Guilt because she hadn't allowed herself to worry about the necklace since she had first missed it on the morning of her wedding. It was easy enough to excuse herself; she had been thrown out on to the street and raped the night before, and she had been in turmoil wondering whether she ought to tell John what had happened.

Why had she never admitted to herself that the chain of the necklace had been broken when Gerald had – what had Nella said? – 'attacked' her? In her heart she had known it – she could even recall the pain as the chain had been pulled so tightly against her neck – but it was something she hadn't wanted to remember so she had pushed the thoughts away.

Poor Nella, she thought. Her gift was given in love and friendship. I can never tell her what really happened that night.

'Constance, did you hear me?' Nella's voice penetrated her dark thoughts.

'Sorry?'

'I asked you what John will hev to say about you giving away yer things.'

'John will not mind at all; I've told you how kind he is. And, anyway, next time you come I'll show you my sewing room. Soon I'm going to have more clothes than I will ever be able to wear in one lifetime!'

Constance made Nella promise to come back as soon as possible, and she watched her friend as she hurried down the path. Once she had closed the gate behind her, Nella seemed to vanish into the winter gloom very quickly and Constance was reminded of Polly's description of her as an ugly little witch.

Poor Nella, she wasn't really ugly. In spite of her sharp features her face could actually look appealing when enthusiasm or happiness made her open her eyes wide – blue eyes. And Nella's hair, although not quite so golden, was soft and baby-fine. If only her bones hadn't been twisted so cruelly, she might even have been considered attractive.

Constance closed the door and went along to the kitchen. She was surprised to find Albert Green in there with Polly. Albert was sitting at the table with a cup of tea and a piece of Christmas cake. A sprig of mistletoe was tucked behind one of his ears and he must have just said something amusing because Polly was laughing self-consciously as she sliced a loaf of bread.

Constance stared at the girl wonderingly. She looked happy and pleased with herself, and almost pretty. But surely Albert Green, with his good job at the Central Station and his sturdy good looks, could do better for himself than a mere skivvy?

Almost as soon as the thoughts had formed in her mind Constance realized their significance and she was ashamed of herself. Her own John had fallen in love with her and married her, hadn't he? And when they'd met she'd been working in the Sowerbys' house: a skivvy, just like Polly.

Albert saw Constance first, and got to his feet awkwardly. Polly looked up and her smile turned into a scowl. 'You told Albert's ma that he could come and get some of the leftovers for his bait.'

'I know I did.'

'Well, he's going on the late shift tonight and I thought it wouldn't harm if I made his sandwiches up.'

'Polly, that's fine. I just came along to say that I would take up Mrs Edington's tray when it's ready.'

'She hasn't rung down yet.' Polly looked up towards the row of bells defensively.

'That's all right. I thought I would take her tea up, anyway, and wake her up. I don't like the amount of time she spends sleeping.'

'When she's sleeping at least she's not coughing.'

Constance ignored the rough edge to the girl's voice because she knew how fond of Mrs Edington Polly was. 'I know that, Polly. It's just that I'm worried that she's sleeping her life away . . .'

Her words trailed off and the three of them found that they could not meet each other's eyes.

Albert spoke first. 'Well, then, if Poll here sets up the tray, I'll carry it up for you before I go.'

'There's no need for that—' Polly began, and he raised a hand and smiled at her.

'For goodness' sake, lass, you aren't half prickly at times. Can't you see when folks are trying to make life easier for you?'

Frances Edington looked more frail and more beautiful than ever. But so thin. It seemed to Constance that she was fading

170

away. It was becoming harder and harder to tempt her to eat anything. She watched while her mother-in-law nibbled at the bread and butter and sipped the beef tea that Mrs Green had sent in.

She wiped her lips when she had finished and sighed as she sank back into the pillows. 'You are happy, aren't you, Constance?'

Constance stared at her mother-in-law. Why had she asked that today? 'Of course I am.'

'John . . . John is good to you?'

'Yes.'

'You know that he came into part of his inheritance when he married you, don't you? And that this has made life easier for us?'

'I do.' What was John's mother implying? That John had only married her in order to get some of his money? She would never believe that. There must be many a girl who would have been delighted to marry John; even girls who would have brought some money of their own to the marriage. He didn't have to choose a penniless servant girl.

'My life has become easier too, remember,' Constance said. 'And John has been generous and thoughtful.'

'Thoughtful? Do you think it is thoughtful to be always working so late?'

Constance was perplexed. It was obvious to everyone how much John and his mother cared for each other and yet Frances seemed to be criticizing him. She was watching Constance anxiously, waiting for her reply.

'John has explained how he feels that he must work hard in order to convince Mr Barton that he should be made a partner.'

'He told you that?'

'Yes. That is why he stays late after the shop has closed, going over the books, studying the accounts.'

'I see.' Frances closed her eyes and was silent for so long that Constance thought she had gone to sleep. But then she asked, 'And tonight? Is he working late tonight?'

'Yes, I think so. He said that he might have to stay late so I was not to wait up for him.'

'Poor Constance.'

'No, it's all right, really it is. Some evenings, no matter how tired he is, we go straight to the sewing room after supper. We spend hours there together. Sometimes I have to remind him that we must go to bed. John is not just helping me to make clothes, he's working for our future. He says that I will want for nothing—'

'Nothing except . . . except . . .'

Constance did not discover what Frances Edington had been going to say next for, after a soft sigh, she seemed to drift off to sleep. It was unfair of her to criticize John, Constance thought. He was sweet and kind to her and so gentle. If married life was not quite what she had expected she was prepared to accept that it was her own foolishly romantic dreams that had been at fault. Dreams in which she saw herself and John spending endless love-filled days in each other's company. But real life wasn't like that.

Nella had imagined it the height of happiness that her friend would no longer be at anyone's beck and call, that she would be mistress of her own house. Well, yes, she was enjoying that role in spite of Polly's awkward ways. John's mother was too ill to want to run the household any longer and John seemed grateful to leave most of the housekeeping decisions to his new wife. But if only he would spend more time at home with her, and not just in the sewing room . . .

She thought about her childhood at Lodore House. Her father had worked long hours too, and her mother had spent

172

many an evening alone. But they had been in love and happy together. Constance was certain of that.

John was working hard, just like her father had done. She must try to conquer these feelings of dissatisfaction. No . . . she had nothing to complain about . . .

Chapter Twelve

Frank stood at the window and looked out over the Haymarket. It was not even five o'clock but the sky was dark. There were plenty of people about. No doubt many of them were working people finding time to spend the Christmas boxes given them by their employers the previous day. They hurried across the thoroughfare; dark huddled figures silhouetted by the warm inviting glow of the shop fronts.

It was a good day for trading, not just for the shopkeepers but for the Alvinis too. The coffee shop below the restaurant had been busy since it opened at seven o'clock this morning, first with the early workmen and the tradespeople and then, as the day drew on, with women shopping: women with their friends, with children, or even with their husbands, who might be taking an extra day off work.

But by now the clientele would be changing again. A few office workers, let out early and taking the opportunity to have a hot drink and read the newspaper before setting off for home, and, as usual, the theatregoers. Those with tickets arriving early and waiting for their friends, those without tickets fortifying themselves with hot coffee and, perhaps, a brandy before joining the queue.

And tonight, when the show at the Palace was over, those members of the audience who could afford the boxes, the dress circle and the stalls might round the day off by coming to the restaurant upstairs. Not so many would do this while this particular show was playing, though. A pantomime was a family entertainment and Alvinis was not a restaurant where men brought their families. Frank frowned. He wished it wasn't so but he didn't see how he could change things. A certain reputation had been established while he was still a child and people had long memories.

He moved back from the window; the glass was cool and, no matter how the lights of the city sparkled, the scene outside was cold. He longed for warmth. He had never been to Italy, neither had his mother, but she often joked that they were not meant to live in this cold northern climate. Their very bones craved the sun of the land of their ancestors.

Frank pulled the curtains closed and faced the room. He had cleared his medical books from the table in time for the family's evening meal. The chenille cloth had been covered by one of white linen and his brother, like a child, was helping his mother set out the cutlery. Valentino was smiling and eager to please, and tonight, in his new suit, he looked more handsome than ever.

Maria looked handsome too. She was wearing black, as she had ever since she was widowed. The dress was not new, but the bodice was well tailored and every seam was boned, which made her waist look impossibly tiny. The pointed front of the bodice and the leg-of-mutton sleeves were a trifle out of date, but the touch of creamy lace that softened the high neckline was a recent addition, and the cameo brooch at her throat was matched by her small pendant earrings. The jewellery made from carved shell and mounted in silver had been a gift from her husband when they married. Alfredo Alvini had had them sent from Italy.

While Frank watched, his mother hurried through into their

176

small kitchen. When she reappeared, she had put on a white apron and she was carrying a large soup tureen. Frank moved towards her. 'Let me take that.'

As he placed the tureen on the table he wondered, not for the first time, why his mother insisted on always cooking herself. It would have been so easy to have meals sent up from the restaurant, and they would be of the highest quality, but she would not hear of it. He watched her fondly as she tied a napkin around his brother's neck and ladled out the soup for all three of them.

She must have sensed that he was watching her for she looked up and smiled. 'What are you looking at, Gianfranco?'

'You, Mamma. You're beautiful.'

She laughed. 'And you are clever and Valentino is hand-some. Yes, we are a remarkable family! Now perhaps you will sit down and we can begin. After the soup we are having cold meats and salad. I want to be quick tonight.'

'Of course. We mustn't make you late for the theatre.'

Frank sat at the table and, as his mother broke her bread, she said to him, 'Frankie, why don't you come too? There will be room in the box.'

'But surely one of us should be here – for the restaurant?'

'Mr McCormack will be here,' his mother answered. 'You have often said yourself that he is quite capable of running the place without you – you and Valentino, I mean.' She glanced at her elder son but he went on eating, making no indication that he was following the conversation.

'That's true,' Frank said, 'but I have another reason.'

'Don't tell me. Your books! You want to read your books and do your learning here on your own while Valentino and I are out.'

'Do you mind?'

'Of course not. I am just sorry that you have so much else

177

to do . . .' she broke off and glanced at her elder son, 'that you cannot devote yourself to your studies, and, even when you have qualified and you are a doctor, you will have to help your brother with the business.'

She had lowered her voice and was looking at Frank earnestly. He reached across and took her hand. 'Don't worry, Mamma, I can manage.'

'Aren't you coming with us, Frank?' Valentino had finished his soup and was staring at him. Frank wondered how much he had heard – and how much he understood. 'I would like to but I can't. I have to study. I am very grateful that you are taking Mamma to the pantomime. It will be such a treat for her.'

'Yes, a treat.'

Valentino's eyes were shining. And so were Maria's. As their mother collected the empty soup plates together and took them to the kitchen, Frank saw that she was close to tears.

Nella threaded her way quickly through the crowds in the Grainger Market. High above in the vaulted ceiling, sparrows swooped and chattered among the looped garlands, setting them swaying when they landed for a moment. The tops of the brightly lit stalls were festooned with evergreens, and the columns dividing the stalls were twisted round with tinsel.

She paused for a moment when she saw a group of children gathered round a toy stall. On the shelves at the back of the stall there were rows of doll's houses and, on the counter, there was a display case full of miniature furniture. Nella, hardly taller than the tallest child, watched as a small girl, encouraged by her mother, pointed towards a dining table and a set of chairs. Another child, probably her brother, was already clutching a box of skittles.

The mother and her children were in decent but shabby clothes, hardly better dressed than the other children who were observing with such envious eyes. Nella wondered if the money they were spending was a Christmas gift. The stall keeper lifted out the furniture and the small audience gave a collective sigh.

Nella turned and hurried on her way. The lights, the colours and the smells of the market enveloped her. She breathed in deeply, savouring it all. The sharp, sweet evergreens, the fruit, especially the oranges, the roasting chestnuts, the cheeses and the coffee, the sawdust underfoot, the hurricane lamps hanging in some of the stalls, the rows of geese and turkeys, all mingled in an intoxicating mix, carrying her along amidst the hubbub of excited voices.

In the central arcade a giant Christmas tree was hung with coloured baubles, strings of gold and silver bells and concertinaed paper lanterns. Nella had to crane her neck to see the Star of Bethlehem perched at the very top. Suddenly a small boy pushed against her and she almost fell.

'Stop shovin', will you!' a woman called, and she grabbed the boy's arm before turning to smile at Nella. 'Sorry, miss,' she said. 'He's that excited.'

'Don't worry, it was an accident. I don't mind.'

The woman and her child vanished into the crowd and Nella stared after them wonderingly. '*Sorry, miss*,' the woman said, and she sounded so respectful, as if she thought I was something better than a skivvy, Nella thought. It must be the clothes, especially the velvet cape that Constance has given me.

But there had been something else about the woman's expression. Nella frowned. Or rather it was something that hadn't been there . . . The woman had looked up at her and smiled – and remained smiling. There had been no dawning

179

look of horror and no embarrassed aversion of the eyes before she turned away. Hadn't she noticed the way Nella looked?

It *is* the cape, Nella realized. But not because it's of such good quality. I was still righting myself from nearly falling over and the way the cape was draping must have hidden my twisted shoulders.

For a moment Nella was so happy that she felt like crying. Just for once she had been treated like a normal person.

The old man at the jewellery kiosk took the broken chain from her and looked at her suspiciously. 'I don't remember selling you this.'

'Well, you did.' Nella reached into her bag and brought out the heart. 'Along with this.'

He peered over his half-moon spectacles at her and suddenly grinned. 'Yes, I remember. Had it engraved, didn't you? Didn't recognize you, all dressed up like a lady.'

Nella smiled and, emboldened by his words, said, 'So now that you know who you're dealing with, are you sorry you sold me something so shoddy?'

'What! The cheek of it!' But he responded to her grin. 'This chain is no worse than any other for the same price. It's had rough treatment, that's why it's broken.'

'Can you mend it?'

'Easily.'

She watched while the jeweller took off his spectacles and clamped an eyepiece in one eye. He took up the chain and what looked like a tiny pair of pliers and removed the broken link. 'Too far gone,' he muttered, before opening up another link and repairing the chain. Then he threaded the heart back on to it. 'There you are.'

'Thank you.' Nella reached into her bag.

'No, I'll not charge you for the mending, and furthermore, as you're such a toff, I'll give you this to keep it in.' The old

180

man reached below the counter and brought out a small red velvet box.

Nella's eyes widened and he laughed as he arranged the necklace in the box. 'Got to keep on the right side of grand ladies like you, haven't I?' He winked as she put the box into her bag. 'Now, mind you call again!'

'I will, and right now I'll take that hatpin, the one with the pearl bead on top.' Nella handed over her sixpence, knowing that the pearl, as big as a pigeon's egg, couldn't possibly be real, but it was the most beautiful creamy ivory colour and she would give it to Constance as a belated Christmas present.

As she made her way towards the exit on Nunn Street Nella thought that she had never been so happy in her life. She had seen Constance and set her mind at rest. Constance was obviously happy and comfortable and she had been so pleased to see her. Just because she'd gone up in the world, she hadn't forgotten her. In fact she'd made a point of calling Nella her friend in front of that vinegar-faced servant girl.

They'd had tea together beside the fire – and what a tea! And Constance had told her she must come again, and given her this lovely cape. When Nella had left Constance's house she had felt as if she were walking on air. It had taken her more than twenty minutes to walk to the tram stop on Shields Road but she had had plenty time. It had been only five o'clock and the show didn't start until seven.

Once the tram had rattled into town, Nella decided that she had time to hurry to the market and get Constance's chain mended. She'd seen the way Constance had looked at the necklace – she could guess how upset she must have been. Well, now it was mended *and* was in a beautiful little box. Constance would be so pleased.

Ten minutes later Nella reached the Haymarket and stopped in dismay. The queue outside the theatre was halfway down

Percy Street. How could that have happened so quickly? There was nothing for it but to go to the end. As the people ahead of her moved up slowly, Nella became more and more anxious. She watched the lucky folk with booked seats in the stalls and the dress circle arrive and go into the theatre.

Whole families arrived together, groups of friends, young couples, and a party of lads and lasses who had been whiling away the waiting time in Alvini's coffee shop below the restaurant and were already in high spirits. Nella watched enviously as they hurried into the foyer. They were laughing and joking in such a friendly way. How nice it would have been to have come with a friend tonight. With Constance.

And then another couple came out of Alvini's – or rather the door next to the café entrance, the door that led to the restaurant above. Nella stared with fascination at the huge man and the tiny woman who must have been mother and son. For, although the bright-eyed little woman was holding on to his arm and gazing up at him tenderly, she was years older than he. Apart from that, Nella recognized the kind of love that shone in her eyes. It was a mother's love. This tiny, well-dressed woman was looking at the tall young man the same way that Agnes Bannerman used to look at Constance.

Nella watched as they walked the short distance to the main entrance of the theatre and she saw the commissionaire hurry forward and hold the door for them. She also saw the way the women looked at the man. Not just the other more prosperous theatregoers, but also the women in the queue along with Nella. The group of girls standing behind her fell silent, and then one of them sighed. After that they all started giggling and making remarks that Nella could only describe as coarse.

Fewer and fewer people were arriving now. She knew it was drawing nearer and nearer to seven o'clock and when she saw the commissionaire closing the doors to the main entrance, she nearly despaired.

Just as she reached the ticket office she heard the music start inside the theatre and a great cheer from the audience. The lady behind the small glass window smiled as she gave the tickets to the young couple ahead of Nella and told them to hurry up the stairs. Then, as Nella slid her money on to the counter, she said, 'Sorry, pet,' and propped up a card against the glass. It said: 'HOUSE FULL'.

The girls behind her complained loudly and then one of them said, 'Hawway, let's try the Pavilion!'

'But that's not a proper pantomime,' another one said.

'That's right, so there might be a few tickets left, and it'll be better than nothing. If we run, we'll not miss much!'

But Nella couldn't run, of course. And, besides, no other show would do. She wanted a proper Christmas entertainment with a transformation scene and the audience joining in some of the songs. 'Oh, no!' she exclaimed. She felt the tears come to her eyes. 'Please let me in.'

The woman wore a high-collared maroon dress with dark red bugle beads embroidered on the front. Her hair was swept up severely, but she had a kind smile. 'There's no seats left, pet.'

'I divven't care. I'll stand at the back.'

'That's not allowed. And besides, do you know what it's like up there in the gods? It's so steep that it's bad enough just sitting down in the back few rows. You'd not see a thing if you were standing.'

'But I wanted to come yesterday when the show started and I couldn't – and I've saved all year – and by the time I get another afternoon off it'll all be over!'

Nella felt the tears trickling down her face and she rubbed them away with cold fingers. The woman looked concerned.

'Don't cry, pet. Look, can you afford the upper circle?'

'The upper circle? But I thought all them seats was booked?'

'They are. But sometimes we get a return – or someone doesn't turn up to collect their ticket. I've got one here, if you want it.'

Nella stared at the bit of pink paper that the woman had placed on the counter. If she took it, she might not be able to afford to get a cab home and Mrs Mortimer would give her hell if she was late back.

'Do you want this ticket or not? You'll have to hurry, the overture's nearly over.' As she spoke there was a burst of applause from inside the theatre.

'I'll take it.'

Nella decided that the only way to get to her seat without falling headlong was to sit down and edge along and down each step on her bottom. The woman in the ticket office had said that the gods was steep – well, if it was worse than this she never wanted to sit up there!

Once she had bought her ticket it had taken her agonizing minutes to get up the brown and cream painted stairway to the entrance to the upper circle. Her bones were aching – screaming at her – by the time a pasty-faced youth in a threadbare evening suit stopped her at a set of brown-painted double doors with big brass handles.

'You can't go in now,' he said.

'Why not? I've got a ticket! Look! You can't stop me seeing the show!'

'Hush! I didn't mean that you couldn't see the show. I just meant that you'll have to wait until the first scene's over.'

'Why?'

'Because you'll disturb the other folk in the row as you go to your seat.'

184

Nella saw the sense of this. 'Well, can I stand at the back?'

The lad looked her up and down as if assessing her trustworthiness. 'I suppose so,' he said at last. 'Here, give me your ticket.'

Nella fumed with impatience while he examined the ticket and tore it in half. She could hear music and singing and then a burst of laughter; she could hardly bear to miss much more. The lad gave her her half of the ticket back and leaned towards her smiling. 'You're in luck,' he murmured. 'Why didn't you say you were a friend of Ethel's?'

'What?'

He grinned at her puzzled expression. 'That's the ticket she tries to keep for her cronies. Front row, right at one end. If you promise not to make a noise you can sidle down and slip into your seat right away.'

But when the young assistant took her through the doors, guided her along behind the back row and then left her at the top of the steep rows of seats, Nella almost grabbed on to him and asked him to please help her down. But he had gone. So here she was, not sidling, but bumping down on her bottom and trying to make out what was going on on the stage at the same time.

She kept her eyes on the scene below her. She decided that it was like a picture in one of Miss Annabel's storybooks. At the back of the stage there was a big curtain with a picture of a pretty little village on it. And at each side of the stage there were a couple of tall thin curtains a few feet apart with trees painted on them.

By the time she got to the bottom row and eased herself up on to the end seat, she had worked out that the lively bunch of people singing and dancing were jolly villagers, and the lady with impossibly blonde ringlets, a blue-checked dress and a red cloak was Little Red Riding Hood.

She was disappointed, but only for a moment, that Lucy Lovekins, the actress playing the part of Red Riding Hood, wasn't a real little girl; that her figure was too rounded, not to say buxom, and that her childish tones were a bit too sugary sweet. Soon Nella was lost in a fairytale world, willing to suspend her disbelief and accept anything that the wonderful, magical beings on the stage told her. She leaned forward, rested her arms on the plush padding in front of her and gave them all her attention.

One tier below, at the opposite side of the auditorium, Maria Alvini watched her son and smiled ruefully. Valentino had pulled his chair forward to the very front of the box. He was enchanted with the story; he nodded in agreement when the little girl's mother told her to go straight to her grand-mother's house and not to speak to strangers. He shouted out a warning when he saw the wolf hiding behind a tree and, when the woodsman asked the audience whether he should sharpen his axe and take it with him into the woods today, Valentino's voice could be heard shouting 'Yes!' above all the others.

During the interval, when refreshments were sent in to the box, Maria could hardly persuade him to move back and take his eyes from the orchestra playing in the pit below. Then, when the curtains were raised once more, the grandmother suddenly got up from her bed and came forward and begged all the children in the audience to sing to her and cheer her up.

She asked them to sing a song she was sure they all knew, 'Daddy Wouldn't Buy Me a Bow-wow' and when they began, Valentino turned to his mother, his eyes shining.

'I know that song!' he said, and he began to sing.

On stage, Harry Bodie pushed up the frill of his mobcap and looked up into the royal box in amusement. He had noticed the big good-looking man and his childlike enjoyment of the show and, for all his fine clothes and his well-built manliness,

Harry had realized that there was something childlike there. Something not quite right. And now the big galoot was singing his head off even although it was just meant to be the children in the audience. Behind him the faded little woman who must be his mother was dabbing at her eyes with a handkerchief.

Suddenly the audience, children and grown-ups alike, yelled out, 'Look behind you!' and Harry dropped back into the character of the grandmother and turned to face the big bad wolf. He ran upstage and grabbed his prop rolling pin and then followed a knockabout routine that had the audience in stitches and left Harry and Sam Slater, who played the wolf, out of breath. And, of course, it was worse for Sam in that skin.

At the end of the routine they finished up front centre stage, shaking hands and agreeing on a truce which would last long enough to have a singsong. Sam went to get a sack of bonbons and Harry ordered the lowering of the song sheet.

'Here we are, lads and lasses,' he said, ' "The Song of the Sparrow".'

The members of the audience who knew the song clapped in anticipation and the orchestra began to play.

> Poor little sparrow, lost and alone,
> Poor little sparrow, so far from home . . .

Harry went through the words first and then Sam joined in. After that he called for everybody to sing and he pointed out the words with a giant pointer.

'Let's make a game of it!' the wolf called on cue and Harry began to set one half of the audience against the other. They sang in turn while Sam decided who was best and started throwing bonbons out into the audience.

'Why don't we have all the posh folk in the dress circle

next?' Sam said. 'You know, the ones who live in Je-esmond!'

'Oo-ooh!' the rest of the audience called dutifully.

The people in the circle sang out good-naturedly.

'I bet the upper circle could do better than that!' Harry said, and started them off.

The upper circle was more raucous than the stalls or the dress circle and they began lustily enough but then a strange thing happened. Harry was aware that some of them had stopped singing, and then some more and he could hear people shushing and saying, 'Listen, who is it . . .?'

And then he heard her. One voice, sweet and true, rising above the others. He stared up and cupped his ear until he located where the voice was coming from at the front of the upper circle at the end of one row.

> Poor little sparrow, lost and alone,
> Poor little sparrow, so far from home . . .

Harry leaned towards Sam and said quietly, 'Go and get them to raise the house lights, will you? Upper circle only if they can.'

> He fell from his nest ere his feathers were grown,
> And now he must wander and evermore roam . . .

The voice went on, clear as a bell, even though everybody else had now stopped and when the lights came up there she was. She was so far away that he could only make out a pale sweet face and a slight frame robed in dark hues. But it didn't matter what she looked like, of course. Just look what greasepaint did for Lucy! No, it didn't matter what the girl looked like, not when she had a voice like that.

When the song ended, the audience applauded

spontaneously and, after a while, the lights were dimmed and Harry got the show going again. But not before he had noticed the reaction of the big man in the box. He had risen to his feet and he remained standing in spite of the fact that his mother was tugging at his sleeve and no doubt urging him to sit down. It was obvious that he couldn't even hear her as he stared up at the girl in the upper circle.

Chapter Thirteen

April 1907

Constance removed her black three-quarter-length coat and handed it to Polly. She lifted off her black lace veil, laid it on top of her coat, then caught at stray wisps of hair and smoothed them up with cold fingers.

Cold . . . she had been cold all day.

'Take my things to my room, Polly, and then come down and help Mrs Green.'

'Yes, Mrs Edington.' Polly, more subdued than usual, hurried upstairs, leaving Constance in the narrow hallway. The others had preceded her into the dining room but she needed to be alone for a moment.

She lowered her head and rested her chin on clasped hands while she tried to deal with the more disturbing images of the day.

The glass-sided hearse, the carriage horses bedecked with black ostrich feathers, men in top hats, and the cross of white flowers on the black-draped coffin . . . The church as dank and cold as a grave, and then the fleeting sun in the watery sky above the dripping trees in the graveyard . . .

John had not wanted her to go but, for once, she had stood

firm. And now she was chilled to the bone.

Polly had returned and she glanced respectfully at Constance, who was no longer Mrs John, before opening the door to the dining room and standing back to allow her to enter first.

The air in the room was cool. There was no longer any need to keep the fires banked low. Constance beckoned Polly over to the hearth and asked her to build up the fire; then she turned to look at her three guests. The last time that John's family had been here together, the three-tiered white-frosted wedding cake had taken pride of place on a table decorated with white flowers and ribbons, but now the table was draped with black crêpe and everyone was in mourning.

John's uncle, Walter Barton, looked distinguished in mourning clothes, whereas his Aunt Muriel looked faded and drab. Esther, in black, looked older than her seventeen years and very stylish; although her features were just a little too bold to be truly ladylike.

Constance became aware that Esther was staring at her and looked away. She felt ashamed. I should not be thinking like this – making frivolous judgements about John's relatives on such a day.

'Come and sit down, Mrs Edington.' Mrs Green was at her side. 'Your guests can't begin without you.'

Constance allowed herself to be led to the table where she took her place next to John. He had been talking to his uncle, who sat at the head of the table, and she caught the words, '. . . my father should be told.'

'Don't worry,' Walter Barton replied, 'my solicitor, Mr Silverman, will take care of that. I imagine that you would prefer Duncan not to get in touch?'

'It's been so long. I think that would be best, don't you?'

'You know my feelings. But, after all, he is your father.'

192

John's father, Constance thought. Until recently I believed Mrs Edington to be a widow . . . until she began to talk about him.

'Constance.' John turned and took her hand as she sat down next to him. He looked at her searchingly. 'Are you all right, my love? You look pale.'

'I'm fine, John, really. Just a little tired.'

'Do you want to go upstairs and lie down? You've done so much these last few days.'

Constance heard Muriel Barton sniff ostentatiously. She glanced across the table to find both mother and daughter watching her through narrowed eyes. She forced herself to smile at John. 'No, really, and I haven't done much at all, not as much as I would have liked.'

It was true. For the last week or two of Frances Edington's life John had hardly allowed Constance into his mother's bedroom. She remembered the day, just a week or two ago, when she had been sitting with her mother-in-law trying to persuade her to eat something. Frances had pushed the tray aside and taken Constance's hand. She'd gripped it painfully and Constance had looked at her in surprise, such strength in a woman who seemed to be wasting away before her eyes . . .

Frances' face was as pale as parchment but there were two feverish spots of colour burning in her cheeks. Her other hand lay on her breast, fingers splayed, pressing down as if to stop any coughing fit before it started. Her voice was low and Constance wasn't sure whether she knew what she was saying.

'I loved him from the moment I saw him . . . Duncan. There could be no one else for me, no matter what my father said . . .'

A spasm of pain passed across her face and her breathing became laboured. Minutes passed before she spoke again. 'He

193

loved me, I'm sure of that . . .' She closed her eyes and lay quiet for so long that Constance thought she had gone to sleep. She tried to remove her hand but Frances responded by gripping her even more tightly. Constance looked up to find the sick woman staring at her urgently.

'Do you think he would come if he were told?'

'Told what?'

'Told that I was dying – no, don't deny it. John could write and tell his father that I am dying. Surely he would come!'

Constance shook her head. 'But how can he come to see you? I thought . . . I thought he—'

'You thought he was dead.' Frances laughed bitterly, and Constance held her breath, terrified that the laughter would bring on a coughing fit. But then John's mother said, 'He might as well be dead. He's never mentioned here; in fact my family would prefer it if he were dead.'

That was the only time that Constance saw her mother-in-law cry. For a moment her dark eyes glittered and then tears welled up and began to stream down her cheeks. 'He couldn't help it. He loved me, I believe that, but he loved his . . . the other one more . . .'

'Mother, please don't cry. I can't bear to see you so unhappy.'

John was standing in the doorway. Constance did not know how long he had been there. He came over to the bed, took one of the clean rags from the bedside table and began to dry his mother's tears. 'Go downstairs, my love,' he said to Constance. 'I'll sit with her until she is calmer.'

The next day John hired a nurse and Constance was banished from the sick room. She told John that she wanted to help, that she loved his mother, that she wanted to be with her, but John would not be moved.

'Constance, we have to face the fact that her life is drawing to a close.'

'All the more reason why—'

'No, my love. You're not being reasonable. My mother's life is ending but a new life is beginning. You are carrying my child. I must protect you.'

She had not been able to argue with that . . .

'Mrs Edington, drink this.' Mrs Green had brought a cup of tea from the kitchen and was holding it towards her.

'Thank you – and thank you for helping like this.'

'You don't have to thank me. I'm your neighbour, aren't I? I was always pleased to help your ma-in-law and, now that she's gone, I'll be here to help you. I promised her.'

'Did you? When?'

'One afternoon when I was sitting with her. She asked me to come and help you when your – when your time comes.'

Constance's eyes widened. 'She knew?'

'Master John told her. He wanted her to die happy, I suppose. But don't worry. I won't tell anyone – not until you want me to.' Mrs Green returned to her self-imposed duties of serving the guests.

Die happy, Constance thought. That's a strange phrase. Mrs Green knew better than most that Frances Edington's death had not been easy. She had not faded away and passed on peacefully in her sleep. The final coughing fit had torn her lungs apart. Constance, crouching by the fire in the room below and trying to block her ears to the hideous sounds, had suffered agonies of distress and helplessness.

But she supposed she knew what their neighbour meant. Frances Edington had loved her son and it was only natural that she should want him to marry and have a family of his own. Poor lady, she would never see her grandchild but

195

hopefully it had given her some joy to know that one was on the way.

'This is all very tasteful, Constance.' Muriel Barton interrupted her train of thought. John's aunt sipped the red wine that John had served to his guests and surveyed the cold entrées. With the help of *Mrs Beeton* and Mrs Green, Constance had provided game pie, beef galantine, chicken medallions and a selection of savouries including eggs in mayonnaise, anchovy croutes and angels on horseback.

'Thank you.'

'Where did you learn how to prepare food like this? At the house where you were a servant?'

'Of course not, Mother,' Esther said. 'She was just a skivvy in Dr Sowerby's household, weren't you, Constance?'

How does Esther know that I worked at the Sowerbys'? Constance saw the way the girl and her mother were looking at her, their mouths twisted into smug little smiles, and knew instinctively that they had made it their business to find out about her. They must have been waiting for the opportunity to gloat. She felt her gorge rising but she controlled her anger and glanced towards John, hoping for support, but he was deep in conversation with his uncle. He had not heard his cousin's insulting remarks.

That was just as well, Constance realized. After all, this was the day of his mother's funeral. She breathed deeply and smiled across the table at mother and daughter. 'Actually, these are recipes that I remember from my childhood. I used to love going down into the kitchen and watching cook, especially if my parents were giving a grand dinner party.'

'What are you talking about?' Muriel Barton's puzzled expression was comical and, for a moment, Esther was completely taken aback. Then she laughed.

'She's playacting, Mother. Pretending that she comes from

some sort of grand family when we know for a fact that the Sowerbys got her from the workhouse.'

'I know but, Esther,' Muriel Barton was frowning as she turned to her daughter and said quietly, 'that doesn't mean that she was born there. All kinds of people end up in the workhouse and, remember, she doesn't speak like a skivvy.'

Esther frowned and glanced at Constance before shrugging and replying, 'It's playacting, no more than that. I'm sure of it.'

After that they left her alone and Constance was grimly amused to see that, no matter if they despised her, they wolfed down the food greedily. Esther will be as stout as her mother one day, Constance realized, and was not ashamed to admit that that gave her some satisfaction.

But then she remembered that even though John's family had taken the trouble to find out something about her, John had never questioned her about her past. But that's because he loves me, she thought. He fell in love with the person I am, not my family or my background. She had accepted that at first but increasingly lately she thought it strange that John had not wanted to know more about her former life. Surely if you loved someone you should want to find out all about them.

She sighed and looked down at her plate. When Mrs Green had filled it she had looked at the amount of food in despair. But now she was surprised to find that she was hungry. She was pleased that her appetite was returning. For a while she had been sickly and delicate, as she knew that many women were in the early stages of pregnancy. She had had no one to advise her and nothing to go on except her memories of women in the workhouse.

Now, since her visits to the doctor, visits upon which John had insisted, she realized that she must have become pregnant straight away, probably on her wedding night. John had been overjoyed. He had taken it as an excuse to treat her like Dresden china and, although he was happy to hold her in his arms and soothe her if she felt unwell, they had not behaved like husband and wife since the moment the pregnancy was confirmed.

The meal came to an end and Constance was pleased that the Barton family did not want to linger. Before they left, John's aunt took her aside and said, 'I see that you will soon have need of the christening cake, Constance.'

Constance brought her hands to cover her belly instinctively. Her dress was made of black taffeta and, although it was fitted, the full bodice pouched over the belt, concealing her thickening waistline.

Muriel gave a thin smile. 'Oh, the pins and tucks are artful but did you think it didn't show?' She continued, 'Well, I probably wouldn't have noticed if you hadn't filled out at the top as well. John must be delighted.'

'Yes, he is.'

'How far gone are you?'

'Really, I—'

'No matter. So long as you produce a healthy bairn – or at least a live one – that's all he needs to come into his full inheritance.'

Constance glanced at John as he came back into the dining room after seeing his relatives to the door. She said, 'The table, it must be cleared. Polly has been working since early this morning.'

'Don't worry. We'll take advantage of the excellent Mrs Green and you shall come into the sitting room.' John walked over to the mantelpiece and was just about to pull the bell rope when Constance stopped him.

'No, don't do that, John. Mrs Green is our neighbour, not a servant. I'll go to the kitchen and get her.'

John looked at her askance. 'I was about to ring for Polly, whose place it is to answer the bell. I intended to instruct her to tell Mrs Green politely that I should like to speak to her.'

Constance saw that he was smiling, and of course he was right, she had no idea why she was being so sensitive. Perhaps it was part and parcel of being pregnant. She allowed John to lead her into the sitting room at the front of the house. The gaslights were burning and the curtains had remained closed since the day Frances Edington had died; the atmosphere in the room was stuffy.

John settled her in an armchair, brought her a footstool. 'Would you like a rug?'

'No, thank you.'

John glanced at the clock on the mantelpiece.

'What is it, John?'

'Constance, my love, I have to go out.'

'Out? *Today*? But where are you going?'

John dropped to one knee beside her and took her free hand. 'I have some business to attend to.'

'Business? Surely not! Surely your uncle wouldn't expect you to go to work on the day of your mother's funeral?'

'Sweetheart, I don't mind. And you mustn't. I'll tell Mrs Green to warm the bed for you and when she's finished helping Polly to clear up, I'll ask her to help you settle for the night.'

'John, I'm not an invalid!'

'I know that. But you're precious to me and you must allow me to look after you.'

He leaned forward and kissed her on the lips. The action was gentle, tender, and Constance realized that neither his kiss nor her response to it had been passionate. She remembered the early days of her marriage and how her senses had

199

been roused by his nearness, by the gentleness of his caresses. And yet, those feelings had come to nothing. John's love-making had hinted at a rapture, a fulfilment that each time she had felt must surely be about to consume her. But it never had. And, once he had learned that she was expecting a baby, the lovemaking had ceased altogether.

In fact some nights, when he had come home particularly late, he had gone to his old room to sleep. He said that she needed her sleep and he didn't want to disturb her. And now he was about to go out and leave her alone on the day of his mother's funeral – just as he had on their wedding day.

As John paused in the doorway to smile at her, Constance was surprised to feel a spurt of anger. She gripped the arms of the chair and, instead of returning his smile, she bit into her lips and turned her head to stare into the fire.

'Constance?' he murmured softly, but she didn't reply.

She went on staring into the flames until the door had closed behind him.

After he had gone Constance sipped the wine without enthusiasm. When Prudence Green brought her a cup of tea and a tray of sweet pastries she thanked her and told her that she must go home to her husband and Albert. She was, Constance maintained, perfectly capable of getting herself off to bed. But her neighbour hovered by the door, seemingly reluctant to leave.

'You will drink that tea up now, won't you? Don't let it go cold.'

Constance sipped the tea obligingly and found it a little too sweet but she smiled her thanks.

'Mrs Edington,' her neighbour said, 'would it be all right if Polly came next door to us for an hour or so? The girl needs a break – a bit of company. I'm worried that she might just brood sitting in the kitchen all by herself.'

'Polly? But of course, if she would like to.'

'Thank you. I'll make sure she doesn't stay too late.'

Constance didn't know whether she ought to feel rebuked. Surely she couldn't have been expected to feel responsible for Polly sitting alone in the kitchen? Suddenly she had an image of the house as a doll's house with the maid doll in the kitchen and the mistress doll in the parlour. One sitting on a wooden chair by the range with her feet on the fender and the other sitting in a plush chair with her feet supported by an embroidered footstool.

That was how it should be, shouldn't it? But her neighbours, the Greens, where did they fit into the doll's house? They were neither masters nor servants. Even though Mrs Green paid a woman to help her scrub through every week and do the washing, they would never aspire to be called middle class. They were respectable working people who could afford to live in a decent house, that was all.

Constance remembered Esther's scorn on her wedding day. What was it that she had said about Mrs Green? '*I see that you have made a friend . . . I suppose you are used to that kind of person.*'

That kind of person . . .

She sighed and sipped her tea again. Well, whatever Esther had meant by that, Constance realized that the Greens seemed to fit somewhere in between the parlour and the kitchen, not quite friends but definitely not servants. And she saw that their independent working status gave them a kind of freedom from the ridiculous rules of society.

But meanwhile Polly was next door enjoying companionship and comfort and she, Constance, was alone. Where were her friends? Who exactly were her friends? Rosemary Elliot had promised that she and Beattie would visit, and they had at first. They had called two or three times and taken tea with her, and Rosemary had even repeated her invitation to Constance to call upon her at Moorside Towers. But Constance had not done so. On reflection she knew that she would not want to be a guest in a house where her husband could not enjoy the same footing.

As John's mother's condition had worsened, Constance and Rosemary had agreed that the visits should end for a while. They had stared at each other, knowing what was meant by the words 'for a while', but neither of them cared to say it out loud. And now Constance knew there would have to be a suitable period of mourning.

And Nella. What of Nella? When they had said goodbye on the day after Boxing Day, Constance had urged her to come whenever she could, but Nella had never returned. She had not called from that day to this. At first Constance did not think too much of it. Perhaps Nella had made friends with the new maid as Constance had told her to. Perhaps she was looking out for the girl – keeping her company. But surely she would not forget about her old friend? Not Nella.

Eventually, Constance had written to her but, so far, there had been no reply. She could not imagine what had happened. She had not realized how much she would miss her cheery company.

In spite of Mrs Green's entreaty Constance found that she had allowed her tea to get cold. She took another sip and then placed the cup on the tray. She might as well go to bed.

Matthew stretched languorously on the battered, old horsehair sofa and turned to smile at John. 'It's after midnight. Shouldn't you go home to your little wife?'

'She'll be asleep.'

'How can you be sure?'

'I told our obliging neighbour that I was worried about the

effect the day might have had on Constance and I gave her a sleeping potion to slip into a cup of tea.'

'Is that safe?'

'Quite safe. I got it from the doctor. He agreed that Constance might need help to relax after everything that has happened.'

'Well then, put some more coal on the fire and I'll open another bottle of claret. Hungry?'

'Yes, quite.'

'See what's left in the hamper, there's a good chap.'

John filled their plates with cold chicken, cheese and small bread rolls while Matthew poured the wine. He turned to John and smiled. 'Why don't we sit on the floor in front of the fire. Here, help me spread the rug. Now it will be like a picnic only instead of in the countryside we are in our own little house.'

'But it won't be ours for much longer, will it, Matthew?'

Matthew frowned. 'No. My father is determined to extend his garage into this unused stable block, then these old grooms' quarters will be given over to the mechanics.'

'And then?'

'Then? You and I will just have to find somewhere else.'

Chapter Fourteen

After she had finished her song, Nella remained centre stage
and bowed her head. There was a long moment of silence
before the applause began. She drew herself up and stared out
beyond the proscenium arch into the darkened auditorium.
She couldn't see the audience but she could smell them, the
odours released by shabby clothes, unwashed bodies and sweat,
hair pomades and cheap perfume.

She could also sense their enjoyment. It was almost
tangible, the approval, the love, even. And above all she could
hear them. First the hands clapping, then the feet stamping
and then, as they rose to their feet, the cries began.

'Bravo!'

'Encore!'

'More! More!'

She allowed herself to glance into the wings where Harry
Bodie was grinning and giving the thumbs up.

' "The Song of the Sparrow",' someone in the audience
called out, and other voices took up the cry. Nella glanced
over into the orchestra pit where the conductor was smiling up
expectantly. She nodded and the conductor raised his arms
theatrically. The audience saw the gesture and settled down
again. The music began and Nella started to sing.

Harry edged forward and stared at the slight figure still

standing centre stage. That was where she always stood. Nella never moved about the stage like the other performers did. She couldn't – or at least she wouldn't. The long dark grey cloak that she had designed herself was padded cleverly across the shoulders in order to hide her twisted back and she had schooled herself to walk, almost glide, on to the stage as gracefully as possible.

No one could know what effort and pain it cost her to walk and hold herself like that for the duration of her act, least of all the big man in the box who had become her most devoted follower.

Harry peered beyond Nella and up towards the box overhanging the stage. He was there again, as he was most nights. He had followed Nella around all the theatres in the North East ever since her theatrical career had begun just after Christmas, and Harry fully expected that he would follow her even further when her growing fame began to get her bookings further afield.

It was not unusual, of course, for the girls to acquire followers. And Nella was destined for stardom, that was already obvious. Harry remembered the first time he'd heard her sing at the pantomime in Newcastle. Even then, he'd found it hard to believe that she'd had no training. Her voice, pure and strong, had echoed down from the upper circle like the voice of an angel. She seemed to know instinctively how to project and fill the theatre. She had a natural talent. A talent that he'd been only too keen to sign up and train.

And the little crookback was beautiful; there was no doubt of that. Once the good food and rest periods that Harry had insisted on had filled out the hollows in her face and had added a bloom to her young skin, she began to take on the ethereal attraction of a romantic medieval princess in a painting by Rossetti. She always secured the hood of her cloak far enough back on the top of her head so that her babysoft, pale gold ringlets framed her face, and the soft, fluid folds of the expensive velvet cloak hung gracefully to the floor, concealing her body entirely.

Harry sighed. That poor malformed body – who could have guessed that it contained a voice so perfect and a spirit so strong. He remembered watching Nella gripping the brass handrail as she came painfully down the stairs from the gods the night of the pantomime . . .

After the finale, Harry had pulled off his costume and hurried into his ordinary clothes and, without even stopping to clean off the greasepaint, he had hurried out of the stage door and round to the exit she should emerge from.

The last of the boisterous theatregoers had hurried into the cold and dark of the winter night and Harry began to wonder if he had missed her when, at last, she appeared, clinging on to the rail for support as she came down the stairs. He tried not to show his dismay at his first sight of her twisted body and, summoning up his acting skills, he was able to smile as he stepped into her path.

'What do you want?' Her stare was half suspicious, half belligerent.

'Don't be afraid. I'd like to speak to you.'

'What about?'

'Your singing. But not here, it's cold.'

'Too right. It's bloomin' perishing and I've got to get back. Step aside, if you divven't mind.'

'*Don't* mind,' Harry corrected automatically. 'You should say *don't* mind.'

Nella's eyes widened. 'I *beg* your pardon. Who do you think you are to correct me like that!'

Harry grinned at the sheer spirit she showed. Her eyes had flashed and the angry animation had hinted at how expressive

207

her face could be. If only it weren't for those poor twisted bones . . .

'Well, answer me, then. Didn't yer mother give you a name?' she demanded. She had drawn herself up so that her body almost appeared to be straight and Harry laughed out loud.

'That's it,' she said. 'If you've just come here to mock me then will you kindly step aside so's I can get a cab and get back before I'm locked out!'

'No, don't go!'

'I've got to. Me job depends on it.'

Nella began to push past him. Harry didn't want to catch hold of her and frighten her. The strange little thing looked quite capable of twisting out of his grasp and vanishing into the night like Rumpelstiltskin. 'Wait!' he almost shouted. 'I told you I wanted to talk to you about your singing. Your voice – it's beautiful.'

'Is it?' She was out on the pavement. Frost sparkled at her feet and her eyes shone as she looked back at him. 'Well, thank you. But I've still got to get a cab back to Rye Hill.'

'Is that where you live?'

'Aye, if you can call it living.'

Nella shrugged and turned away from him. Harry hurried after her as she made her way towards the cab rank. He could see the steam issuing from the horses' nostrils, hear the subdued chatter of the cabbies.

'How about if you never had to go back there?' She ignored him and hurried on. 'What do you do there? Work in one of the big houses?' She had almost reached the first cab in line and Harry raised his voice even further. 'Is that what you are? A skivvy?'

She turned and faced him. 'Yes, that's what I am. Now I don't know why you're tormenting me like this, but will you please let me go or I'll lose me job and me home an' all!'

'Do you like being a skivvy?'

'Huh!'

'I'm serious.'

The cabby was just about to help her up into the cab when she turned and spat out, 'And I'm serious, too. Haddaway and stop botherin' me!'

'You heard the lass,' the cabby said, and he stared at Harry's face, still covered in greasepaint. 'Haddaway back to the theatre, Mr Bodie, and get one of the chorus girls to oblige you.'

At that point Harry had almost given up. The shame of it – to be judged to be so hard up for female company that he should be pursuing a shabby little crookback through the streets of Newcastle. His outrage must have shown for he heard Nella say, 'Ee, I divven't think it was *that* he was after. He was just gannin' on about me voice.'

'That's right,' Harry said, 'and it's *my* voice and look where it's led me. I only wanted to do you a good turn, offer you a better life in the theatre – stardom, riches, even – but you seem determined to remain in servitude for the rest of your miserable existence!' He knew he was overacting but he was beginning to enjoy himself. 'Take her home, my man. Take her back to Rye Hill. And just to show there's no hard feelings, please allow me to pay the young person's fare.'

He was just about to drop the money into the cabby's outstretched palm when Nella placed a hand on his arm. 'Wait a minute.' Turning to the cabby, she asked, 'Do you know this man?'

'Aye, it's Harry Bodie, the comic actor.'

'Actor-manager,' Harry murmured.

'Famous, he is,' the man continued, 'but that's no reason for chasin' innocent young lasses.'

209

'Oh, for goodness' sake—' Harry began.

'You were the grandmother!' Nella exclaimed.

'That's right. Doubling up as the Baron and—'

'And you're in charge of this troupe?'

'For my sins, I am.'

'And you really think that me voice is good enough for the stage?'

'More than good enough.'

'And what about the way I look?'

'That's a problem.' Harry had known that it would be no good lying to her. 'But it's not insurmountable.'

'Insur . . .?'

'We can solve it. Believe me.'

'So you're really offering to take me on?'

'I am.'

'Right now?'

'What do you mean?'

'I mean that if you really want to give me a job, it'll hev to start right now because you've delayed me so long that Dr Sowerby will hev locked up and I'll hev to sleep in the coalhouse – and if I dare show me face in the morning Mrs Mortimer will take the greatest pleasure in dismissing me.'

'*My* face,' Harry corrected gently. 'You should say *my* face,' and dropping the coins into the astonished cabby's hand as a gesture of goodwill, he took hold of Nella's arm and led her back across the slippery cobbles to the theatre.

Lucy hadn't been pleased, but she found it hard to refuse Harry and she had agreed to take Nella back to her digs with her that night and keep a motherly eye on the girl until she could fend for herself in the strange new world she had entered so unexpectedly . . .

And now Harry knew that his instinct had been right. Just a few months on and already word had got around that Nella

Nicholson was an act worth seeing. Her admirers had begun to refer to her as Little Sparrow after the song which she had made her own.

And Nella had nothing to reproach him with. Harry was taking his cut but he was straight with her and already she was earning as much in a week as she had once earned in a year – more like five years – as a domestic servant. If he had anything to do with it, she was going to be very rich indeed. And Harry, as her manager, would do very nicely, thank you.

He smiled with pleasure and anticipation as the audience at the Hippodrome finally, and reluctantly, let the curtain fall for the last time.

Jimmy Nelson had to run to keep up with Valentino. He saw the way the women looked at the master as he strode through the concourse of the Central Station. Not a chance, Jimmy thought. Some of them were bonny enough, but even if they had been a better sort of woman rather than the whores that hung around the entrance at night, Valentino wouldn't have given them a second glance.

The master had eyes for no one except the little singer Nella Nicholson, and that was why Jimmy had been wrenched away from his duties at the restaurant and given this strange but exciting new task of accompanying Valentino to the theatre. Over the past weeks, they had been to shows at theatres all over the place: Ashington, North Shields, South Shields, Gateshead, Jarrow and Sunderland, and tonight they had been to the Hippodrome at Blyth.

Goodness knows what would happen when Nella Nicholson began to travel further afield. Jimmy couldn't see the master giving up his passion for the singer. Perhaps the Alvinis would have to let him stay away for the night – get rooms in a nice hotel. I'll need some smarter clothes if that happens, Jimmy mused, as well as a bit more spending money.

Valentino was no longer in sight. Jimmy wrenched his mind back to his duties and ran through the pillared entrance out into the April night. He was worried. One night, not long ago, one of the trollops had approached the master and offered her wares. Jimmy remembered how Valentino had stared down at the poor painted thing uncomprehendingly until, growing impatient, she had started to get nasty.

When her smiles turned to snarls, the big man stiffened and, when she began to screech he grew angry. Usually he was as meek and as biddable as a lamb; otherwise his ma, old Madame Alvini, would never have let him out with only Jimmy in charge. But when his anger was roused it was swift and violent, and all the more dangerous because his poor brain was so addled.

'Piss off!' Jimmy yelled at the girl. 'Piss off before he clouts you one!'

The girl began to back away but, from the corner of his eye, Jimmy saw a man detach himself from the shadows. The man was big, but not as big as Valentino. Jimmy watched as he cocked his head to one side and seemed to sum up the situation; then the man shrugged, grabbed the girl and pulled her away.

'Look, Mr Alvini, look at this!' Jimmy hurried towards him, holding out the postcard that he had bought in the foyer of the theatre.

'What – what is it?'

Valentino was still staring after the retreating girl. Hesitantly Jimmy reached out and tugged at his sleeve. Valentino blinked and glanced down.

'Look – I bought it for you – a present.'

Jimmy pulled the master over to stand under one of the gaslamps hanging high in the roof space of the portico. He

212

relaxed when, at last, Valentino looked at the card and smiled.

'Little Sparrow!'

'That's right, Mr Alvini. Nella Nicholson. That's for you – you can keep it.'

Valentino had forgotten everything else and been totally absorbed in looking at the postcard. Jimmy had been pleased with himself. When he'd seen the cards for sale in the theatre, he had bought one hurriedly, intending to give it to the master as a nice surprise when they got home. Now it had served as a useful distraction.

Perhaps they remembered the incident because, ever since that night, the girls had confined themselves to looking. Jimmy was amused to see that some of the young men looked at Valentino too. He knew what kind of young men they were who hung around the station at night, one or two of their sort dined in the private rooms at the restaurant and sometimes made life awkward for him. Not that this lot could have afforded to eat at Alvini's.

But tonight the whores of both sexes kept their distance.

They could easily have walked back to the restaurant from the station but Jimmy decided that they'd better take a cab. Valentino's brother always saw to it that he had plenty of spare cash and he never questioned Jimmy's use of it. Not that he would ever cheat Mr Frank, he respected him too much. In Jimmy's opinion Gianfranco Alvini was much more of a gentleman than most of the customers of the restaurant.

Frank must have been watching for the cab from the upstairs window for he was waiting at the door. He hurried out across the pavement.

'Everything all right?'

'Fine. Your brother really enjoyed the show.'

'I'm sure he did. But what I meant was, did he . . .?'

'Don't worry. No trouble. Never is.' Jimmy had never

213

mentioned the incident with the street girls. Why worry folk when nothing had happened?

'I'm very grateful to you, Jimmy,' Frank said. And then, 'But it's late. Why don't you take a cab home? Here, I'll pay.'

'Not likely! I mean, no thank you. I'll walk home, if you don't mind. I'd never hear the end of it if I turned up in a hansom in Raby Street. And, anyway, if I leg it I should catch the last tram.'

'All right. Good night, Jimmy, and thank you.'

'Good night, Mr Alvini.'

Frank Alvini closed the door and locked it before taking his brother up to the family's living quarters. Valentino didn't give him any trouble. Frank hung up his older brother's clothes and waited until he was settled in bed and breathing evenly before he closed the door quietly and walked softly across the landing to knock on their mother's door.

'It's all right, Mamma, you can go to sleep now.'

There was no answer and Frank smiled. His mother always pretended that she was asleep but Frank knew that she didn't settle on the nights that her elder son was out of the house. He imagined her lying in bed in a state of anxiety bordering on terror until she heard Valentino come home again.

Frank was soon in bed himself and he sighed as he reached out to turn off the oil-lamp on the bedside table. There was a pile of medical books on the table and he had promised himself earlier that he would do at least an hour's reading before he went to sleep but his mind was too troubled. He didn't know what they were going to do about this obsession his brother had with the little actress. They had hoped it would wane but instead it seemed to be growing more intense with each passing month.

Frank guessed that, unlike a child, Valentino's power of

214

comprehension would never develop further than it had already. Unlike his body, which was growing more and more powerful. And that was where the danger lay. Usually good-natured, Valentino could lose his temper if he were crossed, and with such physical strength and so little maturity who knows what he might do.

They had had to give in to his requests – more like demands – to let him go to see Nella Nicholson wherever she might be performing, and so far Jimmy Nelson had been an intelligent and adequate escort. But, if this obsession with the singer continued much longer, Frank knew that they would have to decide what to do about it. Meanwhile he should probably consider paying Jimmy more and, luckily, they could afford it. Alvini's was doing well. So well that Frank felt guilty that he had no desire whatsoever to continue in the business once he was qualified. And that was another problem.

Constance was also lying awake. The dying embers in the bedroom hearth gave out a warm glow but she felt far from comforted even when she pulled the clean sweet-smelling bedclothes more closely around her.

She was alone. She couldn't remember how long ago it had been when John had told her that rather than disturb her at nights he would return to sleep in his old room. He said that she needed all the sleep and rest she could get for the sake of the baby.

But did he not understand that she could neither sleep nor rest when she was left alone like this? She didn't even know what time he came home these days, nor where he had been. Some nights she tried to remain awake to listen for him but either exhaustion overcame her before he came home or he was too quiet for her to hear him.

But he always appeared in the morning, bringing her

breakfast tray himself, and he was otherwise so sweet and kind to her that she could not bring herself to reproach him. He gave her a generous allowance, said she could order anything she liked for the household or for herself, but he never once asked her how she spent her days or whether she would have liked his company.

She had tried to talk to him about his work at Barton's but he was obviously bored by that. He became much more animated when discussing the future that he still hoped to make for himself as a couturier. At first that had drawn them together. He had been willing to spend hours in the sewing room, designing and making clothes for her. But when her body began to change with the pregnancy he had suggested that she should let him do most of the work.

Most times he went in the sewing room by himself. Now and then he would ask Polly to make up some sandwiches and go in there and lock the door after him. He had explained that he needed peace and quiet in order to concentrate on his designs. Sometimes Matthew Elliot called and Constance was hurt when he was allowed to enter the sewing room – after all, it was supposed to be her room – but John explained that Matthew had agreed to invest some money in the venture and that they had to discuss the details. Details that he seemed to think would be beyond a mere female's brain.

Constance turned over in bed as she felt the baby move within her. She must sleep for the child's sake. John would get upset if she looked tired and she knew he was right to do so. He was as eager for the birth of this child as she was and he constantly urged her to take care of herself. But how much nicer it would have been if he stayed at home more often and took care of her himself.

John had instructed Polly and Mrs Green to make sure that

she had everything she wanted but what she wanted was her husband's company. Just to be with him, just to talk to him. She had nothing in common with Polly or her neighbours and she was bored. That was why she had started walking again.

She remembered how on her days off from the house on Rye Hill she had walked for miles around the city and into the suburbs. She thought she must know the shops, the streets and the houses by heart.

Sometimes she and Nella had even ventured down to the Quayside where you could still spy some high-masted sailing ships. They would watch, fascinated, as the steamers arrived at the wharfs and began to discharge their cargoes. There were baskets of fruit and potatoes, cheese, butter and eggs, bacon and lard. And then there was the livestock: squealing pigs and unprotesting sheep being driven on shore; great droves of cattle, the poor beasts hustled and prodded and beaten and dragged away to a fate that Constance and Nella hadn't wanted to think about.

Once, daringly, they had picked their way across the cobbles and the tramlines and ventured into The Baltic, a waterside café. There was a wooden floor, brass-rimmed, tile-topped tables, and the place smelled of salt herring and strong coffee. They ordered a pot of coffee and sat and observed the family groups of tall, fair-haired Scandinavian emigrants waiting patiently for the call to board the ship that was to take them to America.

'Lucky folk, they are,' Nella said wistfully. 'Off to a new life in the New World. I wish we could get on one of them boats.' She turned her head to look out of the window and across the Quayside towards the Tyne-Tees Shipping Company dockside office. 'How about that boat over there?'

Constance had laughed. 'And what would you do in Hamburg? You can't speak German!'

'Germany? Is that where Hamburg is? Ee, Constance, you're so clever!'

Now Constance smiled as she remembered. Days like that had cheered their miserable existence and given them so much to talk about when they had to return to the forbidding house on Rye Hill.

But in those days she had never walked across the Town Moor. She had never been able to bring herself to approach the house where she had spent her early childhood. The grief and the pain caused by what had happened, what she had lost, had still been too acute.

But now, now that she had a home of her own again, even though it was nowhere near as grand as her father's house had been, she had begun to feel the urge to visit Lodore House once more. The bitter, sleety winter had given way grudgingly to hesitant, showery sunshine and the parks and gardens were fresh and bright and full of the hope of new life.

Suddenly Constance was overcome with longing to see the spring flowers in the gardens at her old home, the gardens where she and Robert had played. She pictured them now, the lawns, the formal pathways bordered by well-trimmed shrubs, the rose garden, and the walled garden where, on her mother's instructions, everything was allowed to grow just a little wild.

The daffodils and narcissi would be clustered beneath the old trees, there should be primulas, hyacinths and tulips – and was it too early for the wallflowers? Her mother had loved wallflowers; their sweet, distinctive fragrance seemingly released by the spring sunshine and their vibrant colours – mahogany, gold, magenta, and pink – were a promise of the summer to come.

Too tired to fight the pain and the pleasure of her memories Constance gave herself up to reminiscing. Before she drifted off to sleep she decided that, if the weather remained fine, tomorrow she would pay a visit to the place where in all her young life she had been happiest.

Chapter Fifteen

The sky was overcast and the air was cold. The few people Constance encountered in the streets seemed to be in a hurry to get indoors again and, apart from a solitary man walking a dog, Exhibition Park was deserted. Once she left the park and struck out along one of the paths that crossed the moor she was completely alone except for the cows.

The cows belonged to the Freemen of the city who had the right to graze them on the Town Moor. She glanced at them warily. She wasn't exactly frightened, but the beasts were large and solid-looking; she found that she was more than usually anxious about her own safety. She supposed it was because she was pregnant.

She remembered one long ago summer day when she had walked on the moor with her mother and Robert. The cows had been grazing lazily. Then they suddenly began to move more purposefully. She and her half-brother stood and stared wide-eyed with curiosity as the strange creatures with big liquid eyes and velvety noses ambled towards them.

For such ungainly looking beasts, they covered the ground quickly and they were close enough for Constance to wonder at the long, lolling tongues and see the flies crawling on their steaming flanks before she felt her mother seize her shoulder and pull her backwards. The three of them ran all the way home across the tussocky grass, laughing and shrieking half with fright and half with sheer high spirits.

It was only when they reached the safety of their own garden gate that Agnes realized that she had dropped her parasol, probably when she had seized hold of the children. Robert offered to go back for it but Agnes said it was of no consequence and that, anyway, the cows might have eaten it by now.

'Oh, no, Mama,' Robert said. 'I don't think they would eat it, although they might have trampled it, I suppose.'

Constance remembered how serious, how concerned, his expression had been and how her mother had looked at her stepson lovingly before bending down to kiss him.

'You *are* a good boy,' she'd said. 'I shall tell your father.'

Her mother had loved Robert, Constance was sure of it, and she had tried to make up for the fact that he had lost his own mother. And Robert had loved both Agnes and his little half-sister, she was equally sure of that. So, no matter how kind his grandparents might have been to him in the years since their father had died, her half-brother had been the loser too. She wondered if he ever thought about their shared childhood.

Constance was approaching the wall. Six foot high and made with big grey stones, it was the barrier between the ordered cultivation of the gardens of Lodore House and the rough moorland. There was a large wooden gate set into the wall but she doubted that it would have been left open. Whoever lived there now probably kept it bolted just as her parents had done.

Who did live there now? With a shock she realized that in all the years since she and her mother had been forced to leave, she had never wondered about Lodore House's new residents. In her mind she had been able to see no family other than her own inhabiting the spacious rooms or relaxing in the gardens which had been her mother's joy and her father's pride.

With both hands, but without much hope, Constance took hold of the heavy metal ring and turned it. The latch lifted and the gate swung open a little way. She took a step forward and then hesitated. Was there someone in the garden?

She stood very still and listened but she could hear nothing except the leaves of the trees rustling in the cold breeze. She pushed the gate further open and noticed how it scraped back over a clump of weeds growing in the middle of the garden path. Her eyes followed the path as it led away from her, winding between lawns that needed cutting and shrub borders that needed trimming. Was the house empty then? Had it remained empty and waiting for her to return all these years?

No, she didn't think so. The gardens, at least the parts of them that she could see, were not exactly neglected, they were just not as carefully tended as they had been in her father's day. Suddenly she remembered how they had looked the last time she had seen them, drenched with rain, the leaves dripping, the lawns thick with water.

It had seemed to Constance that it had rained ever since the day of her father's funeral . . .

Constance hugged her knees as she crouched on the window seat in the library. She had hidden behind the heavy velvet curtain; her mother did not know she was there. Beyond the cold glass the sodden branches of the trees dipped and sighed in the wind, and now and then a fierce gust sent the first fallen leaves scurrying across the lawn. At the other side of the curtain she could hear the voices of her mother and Adam Hewitt as they sat facing each other across her father's desk,

223

discussing the mound of papers that lay between them.

Every now and then she would peep out and watch them. She knew that Adam Hewitt was something called a solicitor and they were discussing business, and from the grave tone of their voices she knew that it was very serious.

At one stage Mrs Simmons, the cook, interrupted them. She was dressed in a warm cloak and bonnet as if she was about to go out, but she was also carrying a tray of tea things. Agnes Bannerman looked up.

'Are you leaving us now, Mrs Simmons?'

The older woman appeared sad. 'Yes, Mrs Bannerman, and I'm sorry to go. If there was any way I could stay and help you – I've a bit saved, you wouldn't have to pay me until things are sorted out.'

Agnes sighed. 'That's kind of you. But I don't think things are going to be sorted out. Constance and I will be leaving Lodore House very shortly.'

'I'm sorry to hear it.' Mrs Simmons edged the tray she was carrying on to the end of the desk and Mr Hewitt quickly leaned over to pull assorted documents out of the way. When the cook straightened up again her face was red. 'I'll be off then. I've got me things packed and me sister's expecting me – I've got a cab waiting.'

Constance could see that Mrs Simmons was close to tears. Adam Hewitt cleared his throat and reached in his pocket for a coin. 'Here you are, Mrs Simmons. Thank you for the tea and cake; very thoughtful of you on such a miserable day. Now allow me to give you your cab fare – and let me help you out with your luggage.'

The young solicitor walked to the door with Mrs Simmons. When she heard their footsteps echoing across the marble floor of the entrance hall Constance peeped out at her mother. Agnes was sitting staring at the documents spread out on the

224

table in front of her as if, try as she might, she couldn't make sense of them.

Mr Hewitt returned and Constance withdrew slightly but he didn't glance in her direction. He gestured towards the tray and when her mother nodded he began to pour the tea. Agnes stood up suddenly and moved away from the table. The young man looked at her in surprise.

'I'm sorry,' Agnes said. 'Did I startle you? But I'm so cold.' She hurried away from him across the expanse of oriental carpet towards the marble fireplace where she stopped and stared down at the meagre, smoking fire. She picked up the coal scuttle and sighed with exasperation. 'There's nothing left but coal dust.'

'Shall I go and fetch more? Just tell me—'

'There's no more.' Her mother looked sad. 'No more coal, very little food, and the servants have deserted us. Mrs Simmons, good soul that she is, was the last to go.'

'Mrs Bannerman,' Adam Hewitt looked embarrassed, 'I didn't realize that the servants had all gone. I could arrange for a small payment – some kind of allowance – just to have someone here to help until . . . until you leave . . .'

He stopped when he saw the way Agnes was staring at him. Constance saw that the colour had drained from her mother's face; her black mourning clothes made her look slighter and frailer than ever.

'There's no need,' she said. She turned away from him and tipped the contents of the coal scuttle on to the hearth. A cloud of soot billowed out and she hurried back to her seat at the desk. 'No need, I assure you. Constance and I will be leaving as soon as I can arrange it. Now' – she made a sweeping gesture across the mound of papers – 'explain what I must do.'

'I will but, please, drink your tea while it's hot.'

225

Constance heard the concern in his voice and, even though she was only eight years old, she understood that Adam Hewitt was unhappy to be the cause of so much distress. After a moment he continued, 'It's very simple, Mrs Bannerman. Today I only need your signature on some of those documents and the business will be complete. As for the explanation, I thought that my father had already gone over everything in great detail.'

'He may have done but, if you remember, that was the day of my husband's funeral. My mind may not have been up to the task on such a day.'

Her tone was subdued; Constance saw the young man's look of dismay.

'Forgive me.'

'Forgive you? Whatever has happened, I know it isn't your fault. Now please . . .'

'Of course. As you know, Bannerman's has failed. Although your husband made his initial fortune in the chemical industry he had invested heavily in his new venture – the manufacture of electric lights—'

'It seemed to be doing so well.'

'At first, that's true. But he simply could not compete with Edison and Swan. It was their own invention, after all. And not only that, entirely against my father's advice, your husband had been making a series of extremely unwise investments abroad.

'I cannot help assuming that his heart attack was caused by the fact that he had already guessed at the size of his losses. His will may leave everything to you and the children but I assure you, Mrs Bannerman, there is nothing left for you to inherit.'

'Except debts.'

'No, Mrs Bannerman. At least we have been able to spare

you the burden of the debts, with the sale of the factory sites and all remaining stock, plus we have found a buyer for this house.'

'My home.'

'Yes. I – I – haven't met the party concerned; he prefers to deal only through his solicitor, but the offer was generous. You need have no fear of being pursued by creditors.'

'Only of having nowhere to live.'

'Ah well, as for your stepson, Robert, his mother's family are quite happy to provide a loving home for him.'

'Of course, but not for Robert's sister or me.'

'Half-sister. And, to be fair, why—'

'Why should they? Quite. Let us forget compassion and remember only that they have never forgiven me for marrying Richard so soon after Caroline's death. They thought we had offended their daughter's memory. They could never accept that it was because he had loved her so much that he was so in need of solace. I made him happy once more. Was that such a sin?'

'Mrs Bannerman, what will you do?'

Her mother didn't answer at once and Constance leaned out further from her hiding place behind the curtain. Agnes was staring at the solicitor as if she wasn't really seeing him. He repeated his question, 'You and Constance, what will you do? Where will you go? Have you no relatives of your own who would take you in? No money of your own to provide a place to live?'

'Don't worry, we shall be gone soon. I assume you will want to inform the new owner when he can take possession.'

'Yes, but please don't think that I don't care what happens to you and your daughter. I wish you could assure me . . .'

Her mother didn't seem to notice the young man's distress. She continued as if she hadn't been listening, 'I have no family.

227

My parents died young and any money they left me I gave, willingly, to Richard to invest in his business.'

It was said without rancour or regret and when, a moment later, Agnes Bannerman picked up the pen and began to sign the documents on the table in front of her, her hand was quite steady. Adam Hewitt stared at her throughout. Constance thought that she had never seen a grown man look so unhappy.

Eventually her mother laid the pen down and said, 'I have a little jewellery of my own.'

'Your own?'

'I mean the jewellery that I brought with me into the marriage, not that which my husband bought for me. I presume that that is still mine and that I will be able to sell it in order to provide some kind of home for Constance and myself?'

'Yes, yes, I think – I'm sure that will be quite in order.'

'Ought you to check with your father?'

'No, no, I won't even tell him. I mean, go ahead, sell it, raise whatever you can.' The solicitor sounded flustered. Constance formed the impression that he wanted to bring the conversation to an end. Hurriedly he gathered up all the documents and placed them in a large folder.

'Very well, Mr Hewitt,' her mother said as the solicitor tied the ribbons of the folder. 'Thank you for coming.'

'It was my duty. Mrs Bannerman, if there's anything I can do – anything.'

'I'll remember. Now can I offer you an umbrella? It's quite a walk to the High Street and the rain seems to be worse than ever.'

Her mother turned towards the window as she spoke and looked up into the grey skies. Constance tried to shrink back into the corner but she wasn't quick enough. Her mother gave her a startled look before turning back to speak to Mr Hewitt.

'Come, we have plenty in the cloakroom. I don't think

228

any of them are valuable enough to interest my husband's creditors.'

'How kind . . . I'll return it, of course.'

'There's no need. Come, I'll see you to the door.'

Constance waited until she heard the front door close behind Mr Hewitt before she emerged from her hiding place. Her mother was coming back into the room; she hurried over and kneeled down, taking Constance in her arms.

'Sweetheart, I'm sorry you had to hear all that.'

'It's all right, Mama. I knew we might be leaving here.'

'Who told you?'

'I overheard Robert's Grandmother Meakin when they were waiting to take Robert away after Papa's funeral. She told Robert's grandfather that as long as they could have Caroline's boy to live with them, you and I could go to the workhouse for all she cared.'

'Oh, Constance!'

'Are we going to the workhouse, Mama?'

'No, no, of course not. We're not going to the workhouse. You heard me telling Mr Hewitt that I had some jewellery to sell?' Constance nodded. 'Well, that will bring enough for you and me to find a cosy little lodging house somewhere, perhaps at the seaside. Would you like to live at the seaside?'

'Yes.'

'Well, then. Now let's go to the kitchen. I have an idea that Mrs Simmons has left us some raisin cake!'

Constance took her mother's hand and they hurried through the cold house to the kitchen. The fire in the range was still burning and, her mother had been right, there was a large slab of raisin cake left, as well as a pan of broth, a loaf, some cheese and the remains of a roast leg of lamb.

Those provisions as well as two large tins of biscuits kept them going until Agnes had sold her jewellery and they did find some lodgings by the seaside, although they weren't exactly cosy. Agnes' plans to support the two of them by taking pupils for deportment and elocution had kept them going for a while, but it hadn't been very long before the money had run out and they had ended up in the workhouse after all.

Constance looked up into the sky. Clouds the colour of slate were gathering and she wondered if it was going to rain. Above the noise of the wind in the branches she became aware of a faint creaking sound. A steady rhythmic creaking. When she realized what it was she felt her heart bang painfully against her ribs. There was someone on the swing.

She made her way cautiously along the path that led to the less formal part of the garden where her father had made a swing for her and Robert, slung from the branches of a sturdy old apple tree. The swing had always made a sound like that – it must be the same one – and Constance was consumed with curiosity to see who was sitting there.

'Be careful, sweetheart. Don't swing too high.'

She heard the voice before she had rounded the beech hedge and she stopped, tears burning in her throat and at the back of her eyes. It was a man's voice, and so like her father's.

Someone laughed and said, 'Don't fuss.' A girl's voice – a child?

Was she dreaming? Was she imagining things? Perhaps the emotions stirred by coming back here for the first time in ten years had summoned up the ghosts of her father and her former self . . .

Constance stumbled forward until she could see the apple tree and the swing gently to-ing and fro-ing beneath its gnarled branches.

It was no child; it was a young woman sitting on the swing.

Perhaps she was a little older than Constance, and she might have been pretty except that her fair complexion seemed unnaturally pale and, even from this distance, Constance could see the shadows beneath her eyes. Her light brown hair was caught back from her face with a ribbon, like a child's, and as she swung, Constance could see the reason for the man's concern: she was heavily pregnant.

'Iris, we should go indoors now,' the man said and, again, puzzlingly, he sounded just like her father.

The man stepped forward and caught at the ropes of the swing, stopping its motion. Almost unwillingly Constance looked at his face and, even although she had not seen him since she was eight years old, she recognized Robert, her half-brother.

She did not realize that she had cried out until she heard her name. 'Constance! Is that you? It can't be . . .'

The man was coming towards her. She stepped back, caught her skirts in the lower branches of a laurel bush, stumbled and would have fallen if he had not reached out and caught her. Her heart was pounding as she looked up into his face.

'Constance,' he repeated, 'I don't understand . . .'

They looked at each other and, although she was concentrating on the details of his grown-up face, she was aware that, behind him, the young woman, Iris, was moving towards them. Perhaps he heard the rustle of his wife's skirts on the grass but he smiled self-consciously, dropped his hands from her arms, and stepped back.

Suddenly he smiled. 'But this is marvellous!'

'Marvellous, Robert?'

'Of course. Do you know I never thought I'd see you again, and now – although I don't understand it – here you are!'

'Did you care?'

Robert, who had grown up to look so like their father,

231

frowned. 'Care? What do you mean?'

'Did you care that you might never see me again?'

'Of course I did!'

'And yet you made no attempt to find us – my mother and me.'

Robert pushed a lock of his dark hair back from his brow and Constance remembered with a stab of pain that their father used to make the very same gesture when he was vexed with them. 'Constance, that's not fair. I was only a child, eleven years old, when my grandparents came to take me to live with them. They promised me that you would be coming to visit.'

'They what?'

'They said that your mother had agreed to let you come and stay with me – for holidays – but you never came. They said your mother would not allow it.'

'I see.'

But Constance didn't see. Her mother had never told her about such an arrangement and, if it were true, she would surely have allowed her to go. Agnes Bannerman had loved her stepson; surely she would have made every effort to allow Constance and her half-brother to stay in touch.

'It's true, you know.' Robert was looking at her, reading the doubt in her expression. 'My grandmother wrote many times to your mother, but she never answered the letters. Eventually she told me that your mother probably didn't want anything more to do with me.'

And with those words Constance knew that none of it was true. Even though it would cause him pain, Robert's grandmother had told him a pack of lies. The truth was that the Meakins had wanted nothing more to do with the young woman who had married their son-in-law so soon after their daughter's death. They must still have hated Agnes Bannerman for taking their daughter's place even though she had proved a kind and loving mother to their only grandson.

'We never quarrelled when we were children, Constance.' Robert looked troubled.

'Are we quarrelling?'

'I hope not.' He reached for her hand. 'But we have so much to talk about. Will you come in to the house?'

'I suppose so. But perhaps . . .'

Robert sensed her hesitation and clasped her hand more firmly. 'No, you mustn't leave, not now. And you must meet my wife, Iris.' He turned and smiled at the young woman who was now standing at his shoulder, 'What do you think? This is my little sister, Constance. Isn't that wonderful?'

Briefly Iris's lips thinned into an uncertain smile, then she looked up into her husband's face. Her manner excluded Constance as she spoke. 'Robert,' she said, 'I'm cold . . . and tired.'

Immediately he let go of Constance's hand. His look became one of concern and she knew that, for a moment, she was forgotten. 'Are you, sweetheart? Then we must go in at once. A cup of tea will revive you.'

Their look was so intimate that Constance dropped her gaze. He is as protective of her as John is of me, she thought, and for the same reason. And yet there is something between them, something more personal than John and I have. It's not just the child that Robert is anxious for.

Constance was surprised at the insight she had just been granted and, unwilling to think about its significance, she forced a smile to her lips and looked at her brother's wife. The girl had turned to face her. She wasn't smiling.

'Come.' Robert had slipped an arm round his wife's shoulder and he gestured with the other one for Constance to join them as they walked towards the house. 'I want you two to become friends.'

233

'If you say so,' Iris replied, and Constance suspected that her listless tone had nothing to do with her condition.

My brother's wife doesn't want me here, she thought. If I had more pride I should make some excuse and slip away now, but I can't, not yet. Constance knew that having come so far at last, she had to set foot once more inside her childhood home.

Chapter Sixteen

They've ruined this room. Constance looked round in dismay.

Robert had led the way to the small sitting room where her mother had answered her correspondence and seen to the household business. But in Agnes Bannerman's day the room had been light and airy with oriental rugs scattered on the polished floorboards and the furnishing kept to a minimum. In fact, Constance could remember only her mother's elegant writing desk, a bookcase, an occasional table and an armchair at either side of the small hearth, nothing else.

Now, heavy carpet covered most of the floor. Dark green waxy-leafed plants and a profusion of pottery knick-knacks stood on occasional tables, and gloomy oil paintings featuring Scottish glens and romantically ruined castles obscured the walls. Her mother's elegant silk-upholstered furniture had been replaced by overstuffed leather and velvet chairs and embroidered cushions.

Constance took advantage of one of these cushions by stuffing it into place in the small of her back. Although she knew she didn't show it yet, she was nearly six months pregnant. The dresses that John had designed and made for her hid her condition very skilfully. John's inspiration had been fuelled by the desire to maintain reserve and respectability without harming the child she was carrying, and he had succeeded. She knew that if he worked hard enough he had the talent to become a fashionable couturier.

Today she was wearing a cleverly flared three-quarter-length woollen biscuit-coloured coat over a tailored walking dress of the same colour. Both dress and coat were trimmed with brown velvet the same colour and material as her toque. She had secured the hat on her piled-up hair with a creamy faux-pearl hatpin that John had chosen.

However, Constance knew that, no matter how proud John was of her appearance, he would not have been pleased if he knew she was still walking about so freely and so far from home. He didn't mind if she strolled as far as the park and he had even asked Mrs Green to accompany her on such jaunts and told them to treat themselves to cakes and tea at the Willow Tea Rooms. But he also wanted her to rest as much as possible. Today's excursion would not please him. However, she thought, he came home so late these days that there was no danger of him finding out.

It was obvious that Robert and his wife had not guessed that she was expecting a child. But then Iris was completely taken up with her own condition. Constance watched surreptitiously as her half-brother settled the sulky-looking girl in the most comfortable chair and brought her an embroidered footstool. Then he crossed to the bell pull near the hearth.

After he had tugged it once he kneeled to make up the fire. 'It's chilly, isn't it?' he asked over his shoulder. 'The May flowers may be in bloom but I think we're going to have to wait a little longer for any real warm weather.'

'At least it's warmer here than it is in Berwick,' Iris said, and she gave an exaggerated shudder. 'And, Robert, you shouldn't do that, you should wait for the girl.'

'I know.' He smiled. 'But the poor little thing is still getting used to being in service. And, while I'm thinking about it, perhaps I'd better go down to the kitchen myself and see that the tray is set up properly.'

'Really, Robert, there's no need . . .' his wife began.

'I think there is. You know you get upset when things aren't done quite how you like them.' He turned and smiled ruefully at Constance. 'Iris has very high standards and I don't want her to have to start training any more new maids, not now.'

Constance watched him go. How loyal he is, she thought. The truth of it is probably that his wife is a demanding and difficult mistress. I wonder how she would have coped with Polly? For a moment she felt guilty when she remembered her wedding day. She remembered how eager to please Polly had seemed and yet she had still been quick to find fault with the poor girl. Had she been too eager to establish herself in her new position as a mistress rather than a servant? Perhaps.

And yet Polly *had* needed the rough edges smoothing over. Well, anyway, they were rubbing along together well enough now, especially as Constance was willing to turn a blind eye to the number of times Albert Green found an excuse to call at the back door. Constance smiled.

'Do you find it amusing?

She turned her head to find Iris glaring at her crossly.

'Amusing?'

'The fact that my servants are impossible?'

'No, of course not. I know how difficult it can be training a new maid. In fact I've had some problems myself.'

'Have you?' Her brother's wife found this interesting and she studied Constance anew as if still trying to assess her position in the social scale. She allowed herself a brief conspiratorial smile. 'You know, I find the working people here are not as respectful as those in the Borders,' she confided. 'The girls from the families serving the big estates have been brought up to know their place. These town folk are a rebellious lot with too many ideas about their rights. *Rights*, for heaven's sake!'

Constance tried to imagine what would have happened if she had stood up for her rights when she had been working at the Sowerbys' house in Rye Hill – and failed. Either Iris had been very unfortunate in her choice of servants so far, or she was an even worse mistress than Mrs Sowerby. At the thought of the Sowerbys her mind gave the customary shudder and, quickly, she blanked out the unwelcome memories.

'Constance?' Her brother's wife was staring at her.

'Sorry. Did you say something?'

'Yes. I asked you why you came here today.' The warmth had dissipated and both her look and the tone of her voice were suspicious.

'Oh.' She ought to have been prepared for this question. 'I . . . I wanted to see the house. I was curious to see if was still as I remembered it.'

'If you mean you want a guided tour your curiosity will have to remain unsatisfied.' Her mouth clamped shut in a mean little line.

'Guided tour?'

'I won't allow you to go tramping through my home.' She gave the slightest emphasis to the word 'my'.

'I wasn't going to suggest such a thing.' Constance was shocked at the animosity.

'And do you live near by?'

'Not . . . not too far away.' Instinctively Constance knew that Iris would think it very strange that she had walked across the Town Moor unaccompanied. She would consider it not quite the done thing.

Luckily Iris hadn't noticed Constance's hesitation, and she continued, 'You really didn't know that your brother was living here?'

238

'No. How could I? You know that we lost touch with each other when . . . when our father died.'

'And do you want to renew your acquaintance now?'

'Acquaintance! We are brother and sister—' Constance broke off when the door opened and Robert hurried in.

He had caught her last words and he glanced swiftly at his wife who beamed a smile at him. 'Aah,' she sighed, 'the tea. How welcome.'

A very young girl followed him into the room carrying a tray. She stood uncertainly in the centre of the room while Robert lifted forward an occasional table. Before doing so he had had to remove a bowl of wax fruit, and both the young maid and Constance saw Iris's irritation as she watched him put the bowl in the hearth.

As soon as she had placed the tray on the table the girl escaped. As the door had closed behind her, Iris snapped, 'The fruit, Robert. It will melt!'

Constance felt sorry for her brother and she was amazed at his patience as, with a self-deprecating smile, he placed the bowl on another table a safe distance from the crackling flames.

'I don't know what I'd do without you, my love,' he said. 'I should probably live like a barbarian.'

He took over the duties of pouring the tea and, for a while, they were silent. By the time he was settled in his chair he seemed to have received some unspoken message from his wife, for when he spoke to Constance again, he sounded subdued. 'I can see that Iris is tired,' he said. 'I was going to suggest that you should stay for lunch but perhaps—'

'Of course,' Constance was quick to reply. 'I shall call another day.'

Her brother and his wife spoke together. 'Shall you?' Iris

asked challengingly while Robert smiled and said, 'Oh yes, Constance. I do hope so.'

He didn't see his wife's frown and continued, 'There is so much we have to talk about . . . so much I don't know about you. For instance, I can see that you are married. And from the quality of your clothes, forgive me if this is presumptuous, but we did grow up together, your husband must be . . . well . . . prosperous.'

Constance saw Iris's expression change to one of mild curiosity. Perhaps she was even wondering whether she should have been a little more welcoming. It pleased Constance to reply, 'Oh yes, John does very well. But now I must go.'

Iris remained where she was and Robert walked through into the hall with her. 'I mean it, Constance. You must come again.'

'Mm?' Suddenly she was distracted. Rather than her brother's voice she could hear voices from the past. Hers and Robert's as they ran shrieking up and down the wide sweep of stairs, the two kittens darting up and down ahead of them and in no danger of being caught. Her mother's voice gently chiding them but overcome with laughter at their antics. Their father's voice as he walked through the door . . .

'*What is the meaning of this uproar? Can a man not look forward to peace and harmony when he returns to his own home?*'

But he had been laughing. Indeed, he joined in the chase and soon there was an indignant kitten in each of his pockets.

'*Poor little things,*' her mother had scolded. '*Give them to me. They must go back to the kitchen at once for a saucer of milk . . .*'

Constance stopped in the middle of the hall and took hold of her brother's arm. 'Robert, what happened to the kittens?'

'The kittens?' He frowned.

'You know, when Papa ... when he died and we had to leave this house, Maggie Muff had two little kittens. I feel ashamed but I just can't remember what happened to them.'

Robert smiled. 'They came to Berwick. Maggie Muff and her two little kittens in one basket. There's no need to worry, Constance. My grandparents knew how attached I was to them and said that of course they should come with me. Grandmother grew quite fond of them and was very upset when Maggie died.'

'Died?'

'Old age, I should imagine. But her babies – grown cats they are now – are still there. Constance, what is it? Are you crying?'

She shook her head. 'No.' But her voice was small. 'Robert, may I go out through the garden room?'

'Of course. But why?

'Oh, the old superstition ... go out the way you came in ... you know?'

'I suppose so.' He led the way to the door at the back of the hall. 'But when shall I see you again? You and your husband, of course. John, did you say?'

'Yes. John Edington. But I'm not sure if he would be welcome here.'

'Whyever not?'

'I suspect we are not the kind of people that your wife would want to receive.'

Robert stopped by the French window of the garden room and frowned. 'What do you mean?'

'Trade, Robert. To put it bluntly, John is a shopkeeper.'

'Oh, I see.' Robert laughed. 'But then we're not exactly landed gentry – well, to be perfectly correct, Iris might be. However, that didn't stop her from marrying me.'

'You'll have to explain.'

241

'How do you think I can afford to live here?'

'Your grandparents . . . Captain Meakin . . .'

'And where do you think he makes his money?'

'I have no idea.'

'He owns a fleet of colliers.'

'Coal ships – then he must be wealthy.'

'I suppose he is. But it's trade none the less, and I was taken into the firm the moment I left school. No university for me. I had to pay my way by working in the family business and that's why I'm living here in Newcastle – to run the shipping office. Although Iris tries to keep me here at home with her as much as she can! So you see I am not going to allow you to cut yourself off from me through any ridiculous notions of snobbery.'

'Oh, Robert . . .'

'What is it? Why are you looking at me like that?'

'I was thinking how very like Father you are.'

'Am I?' And for a moment his eyes too filled with moisture.

Constance waited until he had taken a large white handkerchief from his pocket in order to brush at his eyes, then she murmured, 'Robert, I'm glad it's you that's living here.' Then she reached forward, opened the door and walked out into the garden.

'Wait, Constance,' he called when he realized what she had done. 'I don't know where you live. I don't know when I'm going to see you again.'

She stopped in her flight and waved. 'I'll come back, I promise,' she called, before turning and hurrying along the path towards the gate that led on to the moor. But she didn't honestly know whether she would be able to keep that promise. If she did then her heart might break all over again.

* * *

242

'That woman's here. She refused to go away. Said she would wait for you.' Constance had hardly closed the door behind her when Polly blurted out the information.

'Polly, what woman are you talking about?'

'That little – that little person that came to see you just after Christmas. Said she was a friend of yours.' Polly's eyebrows rose sceptically. 'Miss—'

'Nicholson! Nella! Where is she?'

'In the front parlour, of course.' Polly said this not so much because the front parlour was the right place to put a guest, but rather that there was no way she would have wanted her mistress's visitor to sit in the kitchen with her.

'Thank you, Polly.' Constance turned to open the door of the front room. Perhaps she ought to have told Polly that she should have called her visitor a 'lady', not a 'woman', but the atmosphere in the house was comfortable at the moment and she didn't want to upset it.

She had already opened the door when Polly said loudly, 'I told her that you would want your lunch when you came back but she still insisted on staying.'

Constance paused. She was vexed. Nella was bound to have heard the housemaid's words and the tone in which they were uttered, but she still didn't want a confrontation. She turned round to face Polly and smiled.

'Lunch. Thank you for reminding me. Would you set up two places in the dining room? My friend will be joining me.'

'But—'

'Thank you, Polly.' She walked into the room and shut the door behind her without giving the girl the chance to react further.

'Nella, I'm sorry . . .' she began, but her friend was smiling broadly.

'To think I actually felt sorry for that saucebox last time I

243

came here,' she said. 'Constance, are you sure you aren't being too lenient with the young baggage?'

'Nella, oh, Nella, what a wonderful surprise!'

'Surprise? Do you mean because I've come to see you at last – or is it because you just can't believe the sight you see before yer eyes? Constance, stop staring at me like that. Speak to me!'

'Nella, of course I'm surprised to see you. I thought that you'd forgotten all about me.'

'As if I would!'

'But you look wonderful!'

Constance stared unbelievingly at her friend. In fact she was wearing a very simple outfit. A long grey velvet cloak hung from her shoulders to the ground. Were her shoulders level? Was her back straight? Only the tips of shining patent leather boots were showing. But the velvet was pearl grey, somehow luminous and fluid as Nella moved slightly, and very good quality. Constance had learned something about fabrics from John and she knew that this material must have cost far more than Nella could afford.

The cloak was old-fashioned, of course, and a bit theatrical, but now that she'd had a chance to assess her, Constance knew why Nella had chosen it. Looking at her standing smiling in front of the fireplace like that you wouldn't think she was at all crippled or deformed.

And her face! She was still pale but she no longer looked washed out. Her sharp features had softened and her eyes were filled with – what was it? Happiness? Incredibly, Nella looked truly happy.

Her cloak fell open to reveal a day dress also made of grey velvet as her friend raised an arm to point to her hat. 'What do you think of the titfer?'

Constance stared at the confection of greeny-black feathers.

It was shaped like her own toque and was secured on Nella's shining curls with a glittering paste hatpin. 'It's . . . it's different,' Constance said. 'But it suits you.'

'Don't it just! Actually I borrowed it from Lucy. I divven't usually wear anything so fancy but Harry says I ought to get used to dressing more like a star now that I'm topping the bill.'

Lucy . . . Harry . . . star . . . topping the bill . . . What was Nella talking about?

Her friend's smile turned into a wide grin. 'Come and sit down before you fall down,' she said, 'and I'll explain everything!'

Constance moved towards one of the chairs by the hearth. She felt cold. The skies had clouded over completely as she'd walked back across the Town Moor from Lodore House and she had been worried that she might be caught in a sudden downpour. Luckily the rain had held off but perhaps she ought not to have hurried quite so much, not in her condition. She was aware that her head was aching and, before sinking into the chair, she reached up to remove her hat.

'Here, let me help you.' Nella had moved to her side. 'Are you all right, Constance? You've gone pale.'

'No . . . I'm fine.' Constance smiled up at her friend. 'It's just . . . it's just that I'm—'

'You're expecting!' Nella was staring down at her. 'That's wonderful! Ee, Constance, I couldn't be more pleased if it was me – not as if that'll ever happen! Now sit still while I fiddle with this hatpin. I divven't want to pull yer hair.'

Constance was happy to close her eyes and allow her friend to help her. Nella's misshapen fingers were surprisingly deft and she felt the pin pull out and then the hat lift from her head. There was a silence and, after a while, Constance opened her eyes. Her friend held the velvet toque in one hand and in the other she held the hatpin. She was staring at the hatpin ruefully.

'What is it?' Constance asked.

Nella quickly changed her expression to a genuine smile. 'Oh, nothing. Just admiring yer hatpin. Where shall I put this?' She gestured with the hat. 'Mustn't put it on a table. Bad luck.'

'I can't remember if you were always so superstitious.' She had warmed up a little and she began to undo the buttons of her coat. Languidly she leaned sideways and gave the bell pull a tug.

'What are you doing?'

'Ringing for Polly.'

'That's right. I keep forgetting you're a lady now!' Nella shot her a look that would have been sarcastic if it hadn't been so affectionate.

Constance looked at her friend askance but continued, 'The girl will take my hat and coat and your things too.'

'I'll keep me hat on, if you don't mind. Lucy arranged it for me and I'll nivver get it on again by meself. And, as for superstition, we theatre folk live and breathe it, you know.'

'Theatre folk? Nella, you're being infuriating. It's time you explained!'

'I will. I'll tell you everything. But wait . . .'

The door had opened and Polly swept into the room. Nella began to remove her cloak. It was only when the girl had gone again that Nella resumed speaking. 'Not in front of the servants!'

She sat down in the armchair at the other side of the hearth and, for a while, they couldn't talk for laughing. When Nella recovered herself she said, 'Remember that day I came to see you? The day after Boxing Day? Well, would you believe I nivver went back to the Sowerbys' house that night? In fact

I've nivver been back there from that day to this!'

'But, Nella, how . . .? I mean what have you been doing? Where have you been living?'

'I've been sharing diggings with Lucy Lovekins. She wasn't too keen at first but she wouldn't refuse Harry anything. But after a while I think she took to me. We've become bosom pals.' Nella grinned but then her expression grew more serious and she leaned forward and spoke earnestly. 'Of course, she would nivver mean as much to me as you do, Constance.'

'Nella, you still aren't making sense.'

'No, I suppose I'm not.' She leaned back contentedly in her chair. 'Well, it all started that day I last saw you, when I went to the pantomime. Lissen and I'll tell you.'

A little later there was a perfunctory knock on the door before it opened. Polly stood in the doorway looking tense and rebellious. 'The food's on the table.'

Constance sighed. 'I think you're supposed to say something like, "Lunch is served," Polly, but thank you all the same.'

She gave her the sweetest of smiles and, in spite of herself, Polly responded and relaxed a little. They had been getting along so well of late that Constance could only assume that it was Nella's presence that was upsetting her maid. Constance knew that most people found it difficult to deal with Nella's deformity, and she knew that she owed it to her own mother that it had never been a problem for her.

Agnes Bannerman had been one of those people who seemed to be totally free from prejudice. A person's character was more important to her than their outward appearance.

Constance led the way through to the dining room. Her head was still spinning with everything that Nella had told her. Truly it sounded like one of the stories in the penny

247

novelettes that their old adversary, Mrs Mortimer, loved to read. Her friend had saved all her money to go to the theatre and there she had been discovered by Harry Bodie, one of the most successful impresarios in the north of England, according to Nella. And now, only a few months later, she was a star. 'Top of the bill' as she put it.

If it had been hard work, if it had been painful, if it had stretched her physical endurance to its limits, then Nella seemed to be thriving on the challenge. And, of course, there was the money she was making. That was the most unbelievable part of all. Constance found that she was really glad for her old friend. After all, she would probably never marry, never have what she, Constance, had with John, never have children, so the fact that she would have money of her own was only fitting.

The fire in the dining room was burning cheerily and, in spite of the funny mood she was in, Polly had set the table with a clean damask cloth and the best silver cutlery. There was a jug of water and two crystal glasses. This room at the back of the house was always dark and, instead of lighting the gas mantle, Polly had set an oil-lamp, the best porcelain pillar lamp, in the middle of the table.

'It seems a pity not to use nice things when you've got them,' Polly said when she saw Constance's surprised smile. 'Albert's mother was just saying that it's a shame that you and Mr Edington don't entertain more. But then I suppose it wouldn't be right yet, you still being in mourning for Mrs Edington.'

'Albert Green is her sweetheart,' Constance explained to Nella when Polly had left the room. 'He's a fine handsome young man who lives next door—'

'Convenient!' Nella grinned.

'—And I just can't understand what he sees in Polly!'

248

Nella frowned. 'What are you talking about? There's nothing wrong with the girl. She's clean and respectable-looking.'

'She owes that to me. I told her that she must wash regularly. She can have as much hot water as she likes and I've treated her to some scented soap – she doesn't have to use the household stuff – and that she must also wash her hair and keep it tidy. Believe me, she looks a deal better than when I first came here but, be honest, Nella, she's not exactly pretty. And yet the young man seems to dote on her.'

'Nothing strange about that. You don't have to be a raving beauty to attract admirers, handsome ones at that.' Nella was smiling. Constance could have sworn the smile was smug . . . secretive . . . but Polly came back into the room and they held off talking.

'I hope Miss Nicholson likes calf's foot broth,' Polly said as she placed the soup tureen on the table.

'Oh, Polly, not again,' Constance sighed.

'I do like it. At least I think I do.' Nella sniffed appreciatively as the maid began to ladle the broth into the soup plates.

'It's good for you, Mrs Edington,' Polly said uncompromisingly. 'Master John wants you to have the best.'

'I know it's good for me but this is invalid food,' Constance protested. 'And I'm not an invalid, I'm just expecting a baby.'

Polly looked shocked. 'No need to shout it out like that.' Constance held her tongue; she knew it was no use arguing. 'And cheer up, there's lamb chops to follow and then raspberry blancmange and jelly with a dollop of cream.'

'Does she always speak to you like that?' Nella asked when the girl had gone.

'No, but John has asked her to look after me and she's taking it very seriously. Do you know, I shall be delighted when Albert Green finally plucks up the courage to propose to her.'

'Oh yes, the young man who lives next door. And talking about admirers . . .'

'Mm?' Constance sipped her broth, which was delicious, and looked across the table to find Nella looking like the cat that had swallowed the cream.

Nella kept her waiting. She broke her bread into her broth and ate three spoonfuls before saying, 'I'm sure Polly's young man is as good-looking as you say but he couldn't possibly be as handsome as my admirer.'

'Your admirer?' Constance tried to keep her surprise from showing and failed.

'Think that's a likely story, do you?'

'No . . . of course not . . . but your life has changed so much already that this . . . this . . .'

'Oh, don't worry, I can hardly believe it meself. But it's true, right enough. There he sits, in the best seat – usually the royal box – just staring at me as if I was the girl of his dreams and, ee, Constance, he's so handsome. Tall and dark and handsome just like in them stories. Harry Bodie says that the fella's a regular stage-door Johnnie except that he's not interested in any old chorus girl in search of a good time. He's just interested in me!'

Nella's eyes were shining and, looking at her, Constance could see how lovely her face was and, combined with her sweet singing voice, how easily she could attract a man. If only he could not see her malformed body.

'I know what you're thinking,' Nella said sharply. 'And he's nivver seen me close up. Also I divven't walk about much once I'm on the stage. In fact Harry's arranged it so that the curtain comes up on a blacked-out set and then the spotlight comes on, white as moonlight, and picks me up just as the music starts. Very poignant, he says, whatever that means.'

'Nella, I . . .'

'And then there's me cloak,' Nella hurried on. 'You noticed it, didn't you, when you first saw me today? I've designed it so that it hangs just so and disguises the way me poor little back is all crooked. And, do you know, I hev you to thank for that idea.'

'Me? How?'

'Tell you later. But anyways, Valentino's got no idea what I really look like. And there's the problem.' Her features pinched up with worry.

'You know his name?'

Nella sighed. 'Yes. Lucy recognized him, and so did some of the dancers. He's called Valentino Alvini and he owns the restaurant next door to the Palace. Lucy was taken there for dinner once or twice by one of her Johnnies, and quite a few of the troupe go to the coffee shop on the ground floor – and once seen never forgotten so they say. Ee, Constance, what am I gannin' to do?'

'Do? I don't understand?'

Nella fell silent while Polly came in and cleared away the soup plates. She served the chops and vegetables and left the pudding on the sideboard. Constance told her that they would go back to the front parlour for their coffee and then they were alone again.

Nella pushed one of her chops around her plate for a moment before she said, 'He wants to meet me. There's a young lad always with him, seems to be some kind of servant. He brought a bouquet of flowers to the stage door and left a message that his master would be pleased if Miss Nicholson would meet him in the coffee shop. He said I could leave word with the manageress as to what morning would best suit me. But I can't gan, can I?'

251

'I . . . I don't see why not.'

'Don't you, Constance? Don't you really?' Nella gave her a bitter look.

'Nella, you've been so brave . . .'

'Brave?'

'Yes, leaving the Sowerbys and starting this new life of yours. Every night you go on stage and stand before hundreds of people and sing. And, from what you've told me, they seem to love you.'

'But they don't know the real me!'

'But I do, and I don't find it strange at all that you've acquired a handsome admirer.'

'And he's rich an' all,' Nella couldn't help saying. 'Not that that matters; I'm making money of me own.'

Constance smiled. 'You can't run away from it, Nella. You've got to be just a little more brave and go and meet him. If he loses interest in you once he's seen you face to face then he doesn't deserve you.'

Her friend stared at her for a moment and then seemed to make a decision. 'You're right. I'll gan to the coffee shop. Lucy's promised to be me chaperone. Chaperone, that's what Harry calls it. It's really because he wants to keep an eye on the situation – doesn't want anyone running off with his bread and butter!'

'Bread and butter?'

'As me manager he's doing well out of me success.'

'Oh, I see.'

'You know, I'd prefer it if you came with me. Would you? I could write and tell you when it's to be.'

'We-ell . . .'

'Oh, do say you will!' Nella leaned towards her across the table. Her eyes were shining.

Constance smiled. 'I'll see.'

Nella seemed to accept this as an agreement.

When they had finished, Constance rang for Polly, and Nella told the girl that she had never in her life had such a tasty luncheon. It was blatant flattery but, as Constance observed the little scene, she realized what a good actress her friend was becoming. So good that Polly actually smiled at her and went on smiling as she served them coffee in the front room.

'Thank you for building up the fire,' Nella said. 'You wouldn't think it was nearly summer, would you?'

'No,' Polly replied, not quite sure how to react to all this charm from someone who had seen the sharp side of her tongue.

'And by the way,' Nella said, just before the girl left them, 'if I send you a couple of complimentary tickets to the next show at the Palace, would you hev anyone in particular you would like to accompany you? I'm sure Mrs Edington would give you the night off, wouldn't you, Constance?'

'Certainly.' Constance could barely refrain from laughing.

'I . . . oh! Yes, please Miss . . . Madam . . . yes, please!'

'Nella, I can hardly believe the change in you,' Constance said when they were alone. 'You have become such a consummate actress.'

'If consummate means I'm good, then yes I am. And perhaps I always was.'

'What do you mean?'

'How else did I manage to get through all those years at the workhouse and then the Sowerbys' house? Only by hiding what I really felt and putting on a show. Do you know what I mean?'

'Yes I do.'

'You did it too.'

'Yes.'

'But, anyways, I can't sit here all day, I'm a working woman. But I promised I'd tell you how I owed the cloak idea to you, didn't I?'

Constance nodded as she sipped her coffee.

'Well,' Nella said, 'it was that black cape you gave me. I went to the Grainger Market to do a bit of shopping and this young scallywag bumped into me and his ma apologized as if I was a proper lady. She didn't look horrified or disgusted—'

'Nella—'

'No, Constance. You know it's true. Just think what Polly was like. Well, anyways, she looked at me straight, as if there was nothing different about me and I realized that in the crush – the way I was standing – with the cape over me horrible little hump, I looked like a proper person. And that's how I came to design me stage outfit! Isn't that grand?'

'Well, yes, it is.'

'And now the reason that I went to the market in the first place.' Nella delved into her handbag, a more commodious item than the one she had had the last time she visited, Constance noticed, and brought out a red velvet jewellery box. 'Here, it's for you.'

Constance took the box, opened it and stared at the gold chain and locket that she had totally forgotten about. As she did, painful memories of the night that Nella gave it to her flooded into her mind. The chain biting into her neck when Gerald . . . when Gerald . . .

'Ee, don't cry, Constance. I didn't tell you at the time but I could see how upset you were about losing me present and I decided to get it mended. There you are – good as new – your initial and mine entwined to prove our friendship. You will wear it, won't you?'

'Of course.' There was no going back. She had lied when she told Nella that she had managed to fight Gerald off. So how could she tell her now that the chain brought back too many painful memories?

'Here, let me put it on for you. No, don't get up.'

Nella was bending over Constance, holding the ends of the chain in her hands when the door opened. Both of them turned to see John standing there, his face convulsed with horror.

'Constance!' he said. 'Who on earth is this?'

Chapter Seventeen

Nella stepped back and turned her head to look at John. Constance, distractedly, couldn't help noticing how the gesture emphasized the shape of her friend's humped back. She rose from her chair and stared at her husband. He had not moved from the open doorway and she couldn't understand why he looked so perturbed.

'John . . . this is my friend Nella Nicholson.'

'Your *friend*?'

'Yes, I . . . we worked together at the Sowerbys' . . .'

'Miss Nicholson is a servant?'

Constance hated the expression in her husband's eyes. 'She was a servant – just as I was.'

'Of course.' He made the effort to smile and walked into the room. But he left the door open.

'Nella is not working there now. She is – she has become a singer. She is successful . . .' Constance said.

John wasn't listening and he avoided her eyes. Neither did he look at Nella. He reached past Constance and pulled at the bell rope.

'What are you doing?' Constance asked.

'My dear, now that I have come home I'm sure that your friend— Ah, Polly,' he said as the girl came into the room, 'Miss Nicholson is leaving. Will you fetch her things?'

John went over to stand by the window.

Constance could hardly bring herself to face Nella. 'I'm sorry,' she murmured, 'I don't know what ... why ...'

'Hush,' Nella whispered. 'He's just disappointed because he wanted to come home and spend some time with you. Any young husband would be the same.'

Constance knew that Nella didn't really believe that. She was putting on an act for her sake, and she felt ashamed. And puzzled. She had always believed John to be kind and compassionate. One of the reasons that she had fallen in love with him was because it hadn't seemed to matter in the slightest that she was a servant. So that couldn't be the reason for John's shocking behaviour. No ... she knew what the matter was – and she could hardly believe it.

'Here,' Nella murmured as she pressed the chain and locket into Constance's hand. 'I said I had to gan, so it's not as if he's chasing me away.'

But he is, Constance wanted to protest.

Her distress must have showed because Nella gave her a lopsided grin. 'Don't upset yerself, Constance. I'll call and see you again, I promise.'

Nella allowed Polly to help her on with her cloak and then she reached up and kissed Constance on the cheek. 'Did that surprise you?' she asked when she saw Constance's eyes widen. 'I'm catching theatrical ways, you know. It's all kisses and "darlings!" backstage even when they can't stand the sight of each other!'

Constance managed a smile but in truth she hadn't been reacting to Nella's gesture. Over her friend's head she had seen John's look of horror and his visible shudder. He remained standing by the window when Polly ushered Nella from the room.

When the door had closed after them he hurried forward. 'Sit down, my love. You look tired.'

She obeyed him but she said, 'I'm not tired, John. Just upset.'

'Upset?' He took the chair opposite to her and smiled kindly. 'Has your . . . Miss Nicholson's visit been too much for you? Perhaps you ought to write to her and ask her not to come again.'

'Not to come again? My friend never to come and see me?'

'Never is a long time.' John looked uncomfortable and because of this Constance warmed to him a little. 'I don't know if I mean never. But perhaps just while you are . . . just until after our child is born. Or rather until you are done with nursing.'

'Oh, John, done with nursing? That is still a very long time. You might as well say never.' She was mortified to discover that a lump of misery had risen in her throat and her eyes were stinging.

'Sweetheart, don't cry!' John came to kneel at her feet. He took a clean white handkerchief from his pocket and dabbed at her eyes gently. 'You see, you are overtired.'

Constance caught at his hand and kept it in her own. 'I'm not tired. It's just that I think I know why you don't want Nella to call and I'm . . . I'm disappointed.'

'Does she mean so much to you?' He resumed his place on the chair.

Constance sighed. 'Yes, she does and I'm disappointed because I think I know why you dislike her so—'

'I didn't say I disliked her.' He looked uncomfortable and Constance smiled ruefully.

'You didn't have to. You could hardly bring yourself to look at her—'

'That's true,' he interjected. 'Oh, sweetheart, when I walked into the room and saw her standing over you all humpbacked

259

and crooked like Rumpelstiltskin, I was shocked to the core!'

'Why, John, why?'

'Because you are so beautiful and the child you carry, our child, is so precious, that when I saw that . . . that . . .'

'Don't, John. Don't say it!'

'When I saw her standing over you like an ogre in a fairy tale, I couldn't help myself giving way to superstitious dread. Will you forgive me?'

Constance stared at him. He looked truly sorry. 'I . . . I suppose so . . . but Nella . . . can she . . . is it all right if she comes to visit now and then?'

John could not disguise his shudder. 'If she must.' Then he surprised her. 'I'm glad I came home early today.'

'Why is that?'

'Because I've just realized that I have been neglecting you. Come, we'll go up to the sewing room and I'll show you my latest designs.'

He reached for her hands and pulled her gently to her feet. Once she was standing he leaned forward and kissed her softly on the forehead. Constance realized that he had no idea how much she yearned for gestures like this and how she wanted to be held even more closely. She put her arms around his waist and rested her head on his chest for a moment but, all too soon, he backed away.

'Come along, up to the sewing room.'

As she followed him upstairs she wondered if he realized that *her* sewing room had long ago become *the* sewing room and that it had been weeks since she had been allowed in there. But she was pleased to be going there now, to be part of John's dreams and plans for the future.

Then, as he pushed open the door, she heard him say, 'Sorry to have kept you waiting, Matthew. But I thought I'd bring Constance in today.'

'John ...' Constance caught at his sleeve. 'Matthew is here?'

He turned and smiled. 'Didn't I tell you? I brought him home with me and he came straight up.'

'I see.'

Constance tried to hide her disappointment and, as she followed her husband into the room and saw his friend standing there, a startling thought came from nowhere.

Is Matthew trying to hide his disappointment, too?

Nella climbed the stairs of the theatrical lodging house in Spital Tongues. It was a respectable establishment but the liberal use of lavender polish never quite overcame the odours of boiled mutton and cabbage rising from the basement kitchen.

Spital was just up the road from the Haymarket, and the terrace of houses looked on to the south side of the Town Moor. Mrs Small, the landlady, had been in the theatre herself and, as a former dramatic actress who had married a minor playwright, she thought of herself as being a step above the likes of Lucy Lovekins. But the house was clean and the food, although unimaginative, was supplied in generous portions.

Nella was still sharing a set of rooms with Lucy, because Harry thought it best, although she could well afford a place of her own now. Soon she would be able to buy a nice little house, somewhere she could retreat to and get away from the others in between engagements. And she needed somewhere private to keep the nice things she had started buying.

The wardrobe mistress who had made her first theatrical costume was an experienced needlewoman who didn't seem to mind the extra work it took to get a dress to hang just right from Nella's crooked shoulders. Apart from the outfits she wore on stage, Nella had started building up a wardrobe of her own to replace the sad collection of rags she had left behind at the Sowerbys' house.

She sometimes wondered what had become of them. She'd sent a letter to Alice, asking her to sort through and give the lot to the rag-and-bone man. She'd told her to keep any pennies he might give her. Alice had never written back: perhaps she'd never got the letter; perhaps she couldn't read. Nella didn't really care.

When the theatre she was appearing in was too far to travel back to each day, Harry had started getting her a room in a nice hotel as near to the theatre as possible. Nella questioned the amount she had to pay for the privilege but Harry said that she had to start living like a star. She couldn't afford to make herself look cheap.

Nella paused on the landing. Lucy was singing, practising her scales, and Nella grinned. She could understand why the other lodgers complained. Lucy had never had much of a voice and her dancing would never had got her out of the chorus line if she hadn't been so beautiful. Not beautiful in the way Constance was beautiful. Constance was refined and delicate, whereas Lucy Lovekins was bold and curvy and eye-catching. Well, she had been once upon a time, when she was a young soubrette; the effect now was a little overblown.

Poor Lucy, she'd never bothered to save up for her old age and she had no man to keep her when she retired. I won't let that happen to me, Nella thought. I doubt if I'll ever get a husband but at least I can start saving me money. Yes, and buy a nice little property somewhere. Not something like this – I divven't want to hev to take lodgers like Mrs Small – I'm aiming for something grander. Perhaps across the moor at Gosforth or Brunton, with a servant or two to keep the place in order for me . . .

Lucy stopped singing when Nella opened the door. 'Hello,

pet,' she said. 'Did you see your old friend, then?'

'Yes. Any chance of a cuppa?'

'Of course, love,' Lucy busied herself in the tiny kitchen. Mrs Small provided most of their meals on request, but they could always boil an egg or brew up tea or coffee for themselves. 'I bet she was surprised to see you!' Lucy called.

'She was.'

'And delighted, no doubt. I mean, she must have thought you'd forgotten all about her now that you're making your way.' Lucy appeared in the doorway bearing a tray.

Nella didn't bother to explain that Constance had known nothing about her new career until this very day. She simply grinned as she loosened her cloak and eased herself down on to a chair near the dark green chenille-covered table. 'Yes, I think she was delighted.'

Lucy put the tray down and began to pour the tea. 'And did you give her the present?'

'Present?' Nella frowned. She hadn't told her roommate about the broken chain and how she'd had it mended.

'You know,' Lucy put a small square of oilcloth on the table in front of Nella and placed her teacup on it, 'the bonny hatpin you bought for her, with a pearl as big as a pigeon's egg!'

'Oh, that. No, I forgot.'

'What a pity.' Lucy sat down at the table and stirred two spoonsful of sugar into her own cup. 'Never mind. Next time, eh?'

'Yes. Perhaps.'

But Nella hadn't forgotten to give Constance the hatpin. She had decided not to the moment she saw the one that her friend was already wearing. From a distance it looked the same but close up, when she had helped her remove it, Nella had seen there was no comparison. She didn't imagine that it was a real pearl, any more than the one she had bought in the market was. But the way it was set into the filigree, rather than clasped crudely between two claws, the way the 'pearl' glowed rather than shone like a painted bead, that told her how much more expensive it had been than her little gift. She simply hadn't removed it from her bag. Constance would never know.

She'd been disappointed, of course, but that disappointment was nothing compared to the pangs she'd suffered when Constance's husband had come home. Oh, she'd smiled and tried to tell Constance that John was simply peeved not to find his wife alone. But she'd known the truth of it straight away. She'd seen that expression too often. He'd taken one look at her and recoiled in disgust.

She drained her tea and gestured to Lucy that she'd like a fill-up. Constance loves the man, she thought, so I mustn't make a judgement too quickly. But I wish I didn't feel so uneasy . . .

Constance sat in the small armchair near the fireplace in the sewing room and John kneeled on the floor beside her, watching her face as she looked at the sketchbook. A small fire burned in the hearth, and husband and wife were enveloped in a circle of soft, warm light. Matthew, sitting at a distance by the sewing-table, felt excluded and it hurt.

How beautiful they are, he thought, like two fairy children. He smiled at his own fancy. For of course they weren't children and neither were they fairy folk, they were only too human and adult enough to be going to have a baby of their own. He was surprised that the idea of John as a father was so disturbing. They had both known that it was necessary in order for John to come into his inheritance and, indeed, they had planned it – in a way. They hadn't exactly set out to find a wife for John, but the moment they had met Constance in the park that day, their half-formed ideas had become reality.

The fact that Constance was beautiful had been more than John had hoped for. He had a keen sense of aesthetics. The fact that she was well-spoken and obviously used to a better way of life than that of a servant had not made him as curious as he should have been. He had been happy to accept Constance as an orphan – indeed her being an orphan with no family to take care of her was exactly what was required – but he hadn't seemed to care enough to want to know more about her.

I suppose that should make me happy, Matthew thought, the fact that he doesn't care. And yet what about ordinary human curiosity? No, I have to accept that John is too self-centred to wonder about other people's lives. Even mine . . . When we are together he is all that I want him to be but what if I had to leave him for any length of time? Would he wonder what I was doing? Whether I was happy? Or would he simply worry about the effect it was having on his own life? And how soon would he find someone else to take my place?

'John, these designs are wonderful,' he heard Constance say. 'I had no idea that you had done so much – worked so hard.'

'What do you think I do when I lock myself away in here?' John replied and then he laughed. 'Even when Matthew comes to visit I do not allow myself to be distracted. No – in fact I work even harder. Matthew is a hard taskmaster, isn't that right?' He smiled up at his friend.

John's eyes were shining as he sent an unspoken message of shared knowledge. Matthew felt a stab of excitement in his loins.

'Taskmaster?' Constance asked. 'Why should that be so?' She was frowning.

Take care, John, take care, Matthew thought.

'Because Matthew is investing money in my enterprise. Without his help I do not think I would ever be able to break free from the tyranny of Uncle Walter and the family business.'

'But I understand that the business will be yours one day. Esther has no brothers and your grandfather's will—'

'Yes, yes,' John said impatiently. 'But I cannot wait until that day in the future when Uncle Walter dies. He would never agree to anything so revolutionary as ladies' fashions. I must start now or my best years will be wasted. Don't you understand?'

'Of course.'

But Matthew guessed that Constance was puzzled. Not by her husband's desire to forge his own way – indeed, she obviously admired him for that. No, she was beginning to wonder why a man from his own background should be interested in helping John set up as a glorified dressmaker. Perhaps she was intelligent enough to have begun to wonder about their very unlikely friendship.

Constance leaned back in the chair and rested her head in her hand. Matthew could no longer see her expression. 'Are you tired, Constance?' he asked. 'John is so enthusiastic about his plans that it may not have occurred to him that you might like to rest a while before dinner.'

'Dinner?' Constance dropped her hand and looked at her husband. 'Will you be staying at home tonight?'

'I . . . I hadn't planned to. Matthew and I were . . . we . . .' John had the grace to look uncomfortable. He glanced at Matthew and, in that moment, Matthew felt a surge of dislike for his friend. He knew this reaction to be unfair. He was equally to blame for Constance's loneliness.

'John, I'm tired of dining alone!'

Matthew had never seen Constance look so mutinous and

he guessed that John hadn't either. Something had upset his friend's wife today, that was obvious, otherwise John would never have brought her into the sewing room like this. A friend of hers had been here when they arrived; had the friend been unsettling Constance? Hinting that her husband ought to spend more time with her?

'John, that little maid of yours,' Matthew asked suddenly, 'what kind of a cook is she?'

'Not bad. Why?' John frowned.

'Well, why don't we both stay here with Constance tonight? I'll go out and buy some decent wine and even if Polly can only come up with cold meats and salad, we'll make a feast of it.'

'Stay here? But—'

Matthew ignored him and turned to Constance. 'What do you say, Constance? Will Polly give notice if we ask her to provide a meal for the three of us?' He smiled his most engaging smile and he saw Constance begin to respond.

'No, she won't give notice. And she's not a bad cook; I've been teaching her . . . well, telling her about the things I like and she's always willing to try. And, tonight, I'm sure Mrs Green would come in and help her.'

'Mrs Green?'

'Next door,' Constance said.

'Oh, yes. Young Albert's mother.' He glanced at John, who smiled slightly and shrugged.

'Well, then. That's settled. Here,' he took a couple of sovereigns from his pocket, 'tell your maid that she must hurry out and buy anything she needs.'

'No, that's not necessary—' Constance began.

'I insist. It's my idea, my treat. Is that all right with you, John?'

John was looking sulky. 'I suppose so. But I thought we were . . . I mean . . .'

'If you mean that we need to be alone to discuss business then that's all right, too. Constance will go and instruct Polly and then she will go and lie down until dinnertime. No, Constance, I insist. We want to spoil you today.'

John's wife stared at him for a moment and then her shoulders seemed to relax. She arose from the chair and took the money from his hand although he could see that that made her uncomfortable. He would have to be careful. She may have come from the workhouse but she had more integrity than her husband.

John saw her to the door. 'Come down with me,' she said. 'Polly is less likely to make a fuss if the request comes from you.'

John smiled. 'Very well, sweetheart. And then I shall tuck you up in bed myself.' Matthew could see that his good humour had been restored.

While John was gone from the room Matthew wondered whether he should tell him what he had discovered. John may not have been curious about his wife's former life but Matthew had been. And, really, it hadn't been very difficult to discover her story. Bannerman was not a common name and people in the business community remembered how Richard Bannerman had gone bankrupt and then died.

Matthew had also learned that his widow and small child had ended up in the workhouse because the Meakins, the parents of his first wife, had refused to help. But they had taken their grandson to live with them. Constance had a family after all, a half-brother who was now living in Newcastle and managing the family shipping business; and not too well, if the rumours were accurate.

Matthew wondered if Constance knew the whereabouts of her half-brother, Robert Bannerman, and whether she would want to get in touch with him. If she did the brother might want to assume responsibility for her. John would have to take care how he treated her . . .

When John returned he was pleased with himself. 'Mrs Green is already installed in the kitchen, Polly has gone to the shops and I've sent Albert for the wine and a bottle of brandy. Hargreaves will put it on my account.'

Which, no doubt, I shall settle, Matthew thought; but all he said was, 'Albert?'

'Don't worry. I told him exactly what to buy.' He locked the door behind him and turned to face his friend. 'I've told them to take their time, to make sure everything is perfect.' He laughed. 'Mrs Green is actually pleased that we are entertaining. She thinks Constance needs cheering up.'

'And does she?'

John frowned and then he sighed. 'Yes, I think she does. I should have realized that my wife lacked company.' He moved over to the fireplace and rested one arm on the mantelpiece. 'You know, Matthew, when I returned home earlier and found her chatting with that . . . that little witch, I was shocked to the core.'

Matthew sat in the armchair that Constance had recently vacated and looked up at him. 'Yes, what was all that about? As far as I can make out you chased her friend away and dragged the poor girl up here.'

'She was pleased to come here. She's interested in my work.'

'But was she pleased to have her friend dismissed?'

'No. But, Matthew, if you had seen her!'

'What on earth is the matter with the girl?'

'She's deformed. Humpbacked and twisted. Rickets, I suppose, and that's sad, but when I saw her standing over Constance with her pointy face silhouetted against the firelight, it was as if she were casting a spell on my wife and my unborn child.'

269

'What nonsense! I had no idea that you were so ig— superstitious!'

John's face became suffused with temper. '*Ignorant*. That's what you were going to say, wasn't it? Well, perhaps I am. I haven't had the advantages of your upbringing and education. Your wealthy background!'

Matthew stared at him. He knew that it would be no use telling him that wealth had nothing to do with it. Nor even education. There had been other boys at Eton who would have been just as cruel about Constance's poor little friend, perhaps more so. No, prejudice was a character flaw that occurred in all levels of society and John should know that. After all, beautiful as he was to look at, there were aspects of his personality that would not bear scrutiny.

'John, don't let us quarrel.' He smiled. He knew that he had to charm John out of this mood otherwise their time together might be wasted and, although John did not know it yet, they might not have much longer.

'No,' John sighed. 'But, perhaps you would do me a favour?'

'If I can.'

'Persuade your sister to come and visit again. She will cheer Constance up enormously.'

'What? And expose your wife to my sister's dangerous views about women's emancipation?' He laughed.

'Oh, I care nothing for that. Women can do what they like.'

'Very well, then.' Matthew watched the petulance drain away. He guessed that John had given as much consideration as he was able to his wife's wellbeing. 'But now let us make the most of our time together. How long will we remain uninterrupted?'

John kneeled before him and looked into his eyes. 'Oh, a couple of hours at least.'

'Time enough,' Matthew said, leaning forward in the chair

to take John's hands in his. 'Time enough for me to play the taskmaster.'

Chapter Eighteen

Harry Bodie was waiting in the foyer of the hotel. 'There you are, Lucy my love. Did Nella get home safely?'

She felt like telling him that Nella was more than capable of looking after herself these days, but she knew how important the girl was to him. 'I went back to Mrs Small's with her and then told her I was slipping along here for a while to talk about the show. She didn't mind. She was dead beat.'

'We'll have to be sure we don't ask too much of her. Don't want her to burn herself out before—'

'Before you've made as much money as possible.'

Harry put on a hurt look. 'Before she's reached her full career potential, was what I was going to say. Now, what about you know who?'

'Valentino? No trouble. He watched us get into the cab and then went off with the lad as usual. He seems happy with the situation . . . for the moment.'

'Mm. That's what I want to talk to you about. But come through and sit with me in the lounge.'

Harry made a grand gesture like the actor he was and ushered her through as if she were a real lady. The dark panelling and the marble floor, along with the wide sweep of the oriental carpeted stairs, tried to give the impression of a gentleman's country house. However, the effect was unmistakably commercial. Still, it was one of the best hotels in Newcastle. Once upon a time he would have been sneaking me up to his suite, Lucy mused. Those were the days . . .

Harry turned and smiled. 'Would you like something to drink? The usual?'

'I don't mind if I do.' She sank gratefully into a red plush chair while Harry summoned a sleepy waiter and ordered their drinks, a port and lemon for her and whisky for himself. The usual.

They had opened at the Grand in Byker that night and it was late, but after the first night of a new show Lucy was never able to settle. She'd been pleased when Harry had asked her to come along for a chat, even though she'd been expecting it. She knew what it would be about.

The waiter appeared with the drinks on a silver tray. Lucy noticed how old he was, how his skin was like yellow wax, and his out-of-date black suit was threadbare and cheesy. Poor old thing, she thought, having to work at his age, and at this time of night. Still, Harry's a generous tipper; he'll not go unrewarded.

'There you are, my love,' Harry said as the old man retreated into the shadows. 'Chin-chin!'

'Cheers, Harry.'

They savoured their drinks for a moment in the dim, overfurnished room. It was late and the other hotel guests would be in bed; only theatricals kept eccentric hours like this. Lucy glanced around at the oil paintings in heavy ornate frames and the old-fashioned gaslight fittings. She was surprised that a hotel of this size hadn't gone over to electricity but apparently the clientele were a conservative lot. At least that's what Harry said.

'Why do you stay here?' she asked suddenly.

Harry looked surprised. 'I always stay here. In fact I keep a suite here permanently, you know that. Home from home.'

'But why a hotel, Harry? I mean, you could afford a nice little villa, keep it staffed.'

'I've got a nice little villa.'

'But that's in Kent!'

Lucy knew all about Harry's home in St Margaret's Bay, not five miles from Dover. That was where Harry went at least once a year and the base from where he set off for holidays on the continent. It was also where he kept Mrs Harry Bodie and the little Bodies. Or so he claimed.

Oh, Lucy believed in the existence of the villa all right. He'd even shown her photographs of it; some of them pictured him dressed in a linen suit and a Panama hat, sitting in a deck chair in the garden. But none of the photographs included his wife or family. Did they exist or were they a convenient fiction to prevent various lady friends getting ideas above their station? Lucy had once entertained such ideas. But that had been a long time ago.

'Another one?' Harry gestured towards her empty glass.

'We-ell . . .'

'Don't worry. I'll see you home safe.'

'Will you, Harry?' She raised her eyebrows and glanced sideways flirtatiously, but she knew he wouldn't respond, not now. 'Go on then. Just one more.'

The waiter appeared on cue and Harry ordered not just the drinks but also two rounds of cold roast beef sandwiches. 'Don't forget the horseradish,' he said. Then to Lucy, 'I'm feeling peckish, aren't you?'

'So-o,' he said a while later when they had done justice to the late night snack. 'How did it go?'

Lucy knew he didn't mean the show. Apart from Nella's act, there wasn't anything much new about the routines the troupe had performed tonight. No, he meant the meeting in

Alvini's Coffee House that very morning. The meeting between Nella and her faithful stage-door Johnnie. Harry had agreed to it, encouraged it even, but he'd asked Lucy to go along with Nella as a chaperone. At least that's what he'd called it. She suspected that what he really wanted was a spy, and this was the first chance she'd had to report back.

'It went all right.' Lucy paused as she remembered what had happened. 'But I suppose you know that Nella didn't really want me to go with her?'

'Did you tell her that it was right and proper? Her reputation and all that tarradiddle?'

'I did but she'd already asked an old friend of hers to meet her there.'

'Friend of Nella's? What – a servant girl? A skivvy from the house where she used to work?'

'No, I was surprised, I must admit. Constance her name was. Mrs Edington. And very well-dressed and respectable she was too.' Lucy didn't add that she had thought Nella's friend to be a real beauty, sensational, even. No need to tell Harry that.

'Well, well. There are things about little Nella Nicholson that we don't know, eh? Perhaps Mrs Edington was the lady of the house? No . . . I thought she worked for the Sowerbys. A married daughter perhaps?'

Lucy fidgeted uncomfortably. She didn't really care who Nella's friend was but she could see that Harry's curiosity had been aroused. He liked to know everything about everyone. That was the way he was.

'Never mind, Lucy my love,' he said at last. 'What I really want to know is how the meeting between our little sparrow and her devoted follower went.'

'Very well. Except—'

'What is it?'

'Harry, he's strange.'

'Strange? What on earth do you mean? He's tall and dark and outstandingly handsome and, as the master of Alvini's, he's worth more than a bob or two. He's ideal. Otherwise I wouldn't have agreed to it – wouldn't have taken advantage of it.'

'Advantage?'

'Look, Nella's got the voice and the face of an angel. That can't be denied. But the rest of her. Her . . .'

'Her body.'

'Yes, her body . . . well, all we can do is disguise it. And we can't keep it secret, much as I'd like to. The wardrobe girls, the stagehands, the other performers, we can't stop them talking. Nella's public is bound to know – or rather to guess that there's something wrong. So-oo,' he leaned back in his chair and took a drink of his whisky, 'an admirer, a possible beau who is every maiden's dream, can only help. That's why I planted the stories in the newspapers.'

Lucy smiled. 'I guessed it was you. The way it was written up in the *North Mail* it even sounded like your very words!'

'They were my words. The reporters on the regional papers are so short of imagination that they're grateful for handouts. They'll print it word for word.'

'*Mystery admirer!*' Lucy exclaimed. '*Who is the handsome gentleman who follows Nella Nicholson from theatre to theatre? Wherever the Little Sparrow appears you will find him sitting in the royal box! And so on!*'

'Good, aren't I?' Harry laughed. 'But go on, tell me. How did the lovers' meeting go?'

'Don't say that!' Lucy shuddered.

'What?'

'Don't call them lovers, Harry. Let's hope it never comes to that. That would be . . . would be . . . disgusting!'

277

Harry stared at her. His expression was unreadable and his voice subdued. 'Tell me why.'

Lucy didn't know how to express what she meant. 'I've told you. He's strange.'

'In what way?'

'He's . . . he's . . . Well, although he's a fine big man with a grown man's body, his mind is . . . is like that of a child.' Harry was nodding solemnly. 'You knew?' Lucy asked.

'I guessed the very first time I saw him joining in the sing-along at the pantomime. There was such a look in his eyes – innocent . . . childlike. And the woman with him, I guessed it was his mother, she was looking at him as if her heart would break.'

'Well, if you knew about him why are you encouraging this . . . this . . . What exactly are you encouraging, Harry?'

'I've told you. It will help Nella's career if she has a rich handsome admirer, especially when he's no real threat.'

'What are you talking about, no real threat? You should have seen the way he looked at her! I've never seen such . . . such adoration . . . devotion . . . worship. I'm not sure what it was. He listened to her every word as if she were the Queen of England – or the Queen of Heaven for that matter. And Nella—' She broke off.

'What about Nella?'

'We-ell, she's not daft. I'm sure she caught on straight away that he's not quite right, but, even so, she loved every minute of it.'

'Of course she did. Would you deny her that?'

'What do you mean?'

'Look, Lucy, Nella's never going to get married, never going to have a normal life, why shouldn't she have a devoted admirer to bring joy to her poor little heart?'

'I'm not so sure about that.'

'What?'

Lucy looked at Harry and wondered whether he realized that he might have miscalculated for once. 'That Nella is never going to get married. It wasn't just Valentino there today.'

'No, you said her friend Constance was there and I guess the young lad was there to keep an eye on him as usual. Yes, I guessed a long time ago that he was a sort of a minder.'

'His mother was there too.' Lucy was pleased to see that she had managed to surprise Harry at last. 'Not just his mother but his brother, Frank – the whole family in fact. Now, come on Harry, they're Italian. Valentino wouldn't have his ma along unless his intentions were serious, would he?'

'Well, I suppose . . .'

'There's no suppose about it. And that's what I find disgusting.'

'Matrimony – holy matrimony,' Harry rolled the words around his mouth and declaimed them like a preacher, 'the honourable state of matrimony! Disgusting?'

Lucy leaned forward on the edge of her seat. In spite of their old friendship – well, it was more than friendship to be honest – she found it difficult to say what had to be said. 'Don't make a joke of it. Wedding bells lead to the marriage bed and . . . and . . . oh, just think of it!'

Harry looked down into his glass. 'What's the problem, Lucy?'

'Don't pretend you don't know what I mean! Underneath that costume you've concocted for her, Nella is just a little scrap of twisted bones. She looks like a strong wind could snap her in two. If that great hulk of a man gets into bed with her, acts like a husband has the right to act, it would probably kill her!'

'Is that what you think?'

'Of course that's what I think. And so would any woman. Harry, you can't let this happen!'

'I may not be able to stop it. Supposing you're right, supposing Valentino wants to marry her?'

'I'm right, I'm sure of it!'

'Well, then, what if that's what Nella wants too?'

'Oh, she may like the notion of it, poor little morsel, but she can't have any idea what it would mean. Harry, you can't allow it!'

Lucy betrayed her agitation by the way she gripped her empty glass. Harry leaned forward and took it from her hands. He placed it on the table between them. 'Listen, Lucy, I trust your instinct about this and I think you're right. I think the great galoot may want to marry our little sparrow— Hush!' He raised a hand to stop her protest. 'Listen to Harry and trust me. As I say, even if he does want to marry her – and she him – I think it would be all right.'

'All right? How could it be?'

'Because I knew a man like that once before.' Harry settled back in his chair again and his eyes narrowed. 'When I was a lad, barely left school, I worked in the circus. Did you know that, Lucy?'

Lucy nodded tersely. She had heard the story many times and she didn't want to hear it again now.

'Well, anyway, one of the acts, the strong man, was even bigger than Valentino and probably just as slow in the head, if not more so. He had a tiny little wife, one of the circus midgets, and all the girls used to widen their eyes and shudder and pretend to be horrified when their marital arrangements were discussed. But they had no need to be. It was common knowledge that the little woman had nothing to fear.'

'Why not?'

'I don't want to be indelicate, Lucy, so you'll have to trust me when I say that I don't think Nella would have anything to fear either. But to set your mind at rest, if the courtship does develop that far, I'll have a word with the lad's mother, Madame Alvini – or perhaps it had better be his brother. Will that do?'

'I suppose so. But—'

'No buts, Lucy. Another drink?'

'Well, perhaps I'd better be getting along.'

'We could take the drinks up to my suite.' Harry paused. 'For old times' sake?'

Lucy smiled. 'Go on then.'

Frank Alvini stood at the bedside and stared down at the sleeping form of his older brother. The expression on Valentino's face was blissful; that was the only word that Frank could think of to describe it. He had never seen him look so happy. An oil-lamp burned on the bedside table and the soft glow highlighted the classic bone structure.

Such a beautiful human being, Frank thought. To look at his features you could have no idea of the sad and scrambled state of his poor mind. Frank covered the muscular shoulders with the bedclothes and stepped back. He turned the oil-lamp low but left it burning. Valentino Alvini still could not sleep soundly without a nightlight.

Jimmy Nelson moved quietly in the shadows as he tidied and folded Valentino's clothes. When he had finished he stood still and waited for Frank's nod before they both slipped quietly from the room. Noise from the dining room drifted up from two floors below, along with the odours of rich food, wine and tobacco. Frank realized that he had lived all his life surrounded by the ambience of the restaurant. He exchanged it daily for that of the medical school with its mixture of floor polish and antiseptic. How good it would be to go home at night to a normal sweet-smelling house.

Jimmy Nelson had paused at the top of the stairs and was looking at him hesitantly. Frank pulled his thoughts together and smiled at the lad. 'Here's your tram fare.' He dropped some coins into the lad's hands. 'Straight home, I think.'

'Won't Mr McCormack want me to wait on? They're still busy down there and every one of the private dining rooms is taken. Sounds like it's going to be a late night.'

'You're excused. I'll help out if needs be. I'll tell Mr McCormack. But, Jimmy?'

'Yes, Mr Alvini?'

'Do you miss it? Being a waiter, I mean. You don't mind having to . . . having to go about with my brother?'

'Bless you, I don't mind. Getting out and about, going to the theatre, having more money to spend. It's a great life. Except that . . .'

'Yes?'

'Well, I'm missing me training, aren't I? Some other young lad might come along and get promotion ahead of me.'

'Would you be sorry?'

'Well, me ma was pleased when I got taken on here. She thinks it's a good trade.'

'Better than being a manservant? A kind of valet?'

'Come again?'

'My mother and I have been talking about it. You handle . . . look after Valentino so well. He likes you.'

'And I like him!'

'Well, then. He's probably always going to have to have someone to help him . . . to keep an eye on him, because—'

'Don't worry, Mr Alvini, you don't have to spell it out. And, if you're offering me the job, I'll take it. But there's one thing.'

'What's that?'

'Does a manservant, a valet, get paid more than a waiter? I mean a waiter gets tips, doesn't he?'

Frank smiled. 'Don't worry, Jimmy. You'll be well rewarded. Just go on looking after my brother as well as you do now.'

'That's all right then.' Then the lad's ready grin suddenly faded. 'But what happens if . . .?'

'If?'

'If Mr Valentino was to get married. I mean, that's the way it's heading, isn't it? This morning's meeting with the family and all?'

Frank sighed and rubbed his eyes. He was dog-tired and he was being forced to face unforeseen problems. Problems that he just wasn't ready for. 'You may be right,' he said. 'We may not be able to prevent it.' He saw Jimmy raise his eyebrows and wished he hadn't said that. 'But, if he does get married he will still need a manservant. He will still need you.'

'All right then. Good night, Mr Alvini.'

'Good night, Jimmy.'

Frank walked down as far as the restaurant floor with him and, after Jimmy had gone, he had a word with Patrick McCormack as he had promised. They stood in an alcove out of the way of the hurrying waiters.

'I'll miss him. He's bright,' the head waiter said. 'But I can see why you want him to look after Valentino. Your mother's getting on in years and you have your medical career to think of.' He paused and looked serious suddenly. 'You don't mind my talking to you like this?'

'Of course not, Patrick. We couldn't manage without you. Even my mother has to admit that. And you're right about Jimmy. He's very bright. I want to take him on and train him now before it all becomes too much for my mother.'

'And before Valentino decides to leave home.'

'Leave home?'

'If he marries the little singer she'll want a home of their own.' Patrick frowned. 'And then, if you don't mind me saying so, they'll both need looking after.'

Frank stared at Patrick. 'Do you really think that's the way it's going? Do you really think my brother has marriage in mind? I mean, all this following the girl around from theatre to theatre – isn't that just being starstruck? You were an actor once, Patrick. You know what young men are like when they take a fancy to some actress.'

'Well, firstly some of them do marry the actress in question. And it works the other way round – sometimes a travelling actor marries a young lady admirer and settles down and changes his profession!' At the head waiter's smile Frank remembered that was exactly what had happened to Patrick. And why Alvini's had such a good employee. 'But secondly,' Patrick continued, 'your brother isn't like any other young man, is he? The little singer seems to mean the whole world to him. You may find this difficult to accept, Frank, but your brother is in love.'

Frank sighed. 'I know.'

'And then there's your mother.'

'My mother? What do you mean?'

'She knows very well that Valentino is always going to need looking after – a woman to care for him.'

'Yes, but—'

'And I believe she has accepted already that a mother's love is no longer what your brother wants. Forgive me, Frank, but Madame Alvini has never been able to deny Valentino what he wanted.'

'That's true.' Frank sometimes wondered if his mother's actions were spurred by guilt. If somehow she blamed herself for the difficult birth that had resulted in Valentino's less-than-perfect condition.

'Luckily, until now, his needs have been reasonable,' Patrick said. 'But if he thinks he needs a wife, your mother will not put difficulties in his way. His happiness means everything to her.'

'But the girl . . . the little singer . . . she's . . . she . . .' Frank hated himself for what he was thinking. He looked up to see a gentle smile on Patrick's face.

'She's the girl that your brother loves.'

'But my mother – do you think she realizes? I mean, the cloak the girl was wearing, it could have deceived her.'

'Frank, listen. Your mother would not be deceived. She knows that no . . . no normal girl could be expected to take on Valentino. I'm sorry, but that's true.'

'And the girl herself?'

'Bright as a button, I would say. No, you needn't worry that she would be under any illusions. She's a survivor. She'll take what she wants and if that's Valentino, she'll take very good care of him. Believe me.'

Frank stared at Patrick. He was more than just head waiter: he had become a friend and confidant. Without ever having been asked to, he had helped Frank and Madame Alvini cope with Valentino. 'So what do I do?'

'You get back upstairs to your studies and you allow me to send you up a tray. And look . . .'

Patrick stepped out of the alcove and drew Frank forward until he could see into the restaurant. The atmosphere in the room was livelier than usual and at one table a group of young men were being particularly boisterous. Frank recognized them as regular customers: Warren Carmichael, Leonard Russell nd Gerald Sowerby. Often their behaviour caused Patrick trouble but they were big spenders and he was reluctant to ban them. Frank bowed to Patrick's judgement but, in truth, he despised them. Gerald was a fellow student at the Medical School but

285

he was no friend. Indeed, he never missed an opportunity to mock Frank about his background.

There was a sudden burst of laughter from their table and an expletive that made heads turn. 'Don't worry,' Patrick said, 'I'll deal with them. But the reason I pointed them out was to remind you that your brother is no longer interested in their company. That's good, isn't it?'

'Yes, Patrick. That's good.' But Frank still sighed before he turned and made his way upstairs.

His mother had already gone to bed and he would be able to devote an hour or two to his books before he went down to oversee the clearing up in the early hours of the morning. Patrick was as good as his word and he sent up a substantial meal of oxtail soup, cold meats and salad, bread rolls, cheese and fruit; also a large pot of coffee. Frank resisted the temptation to pour himself a glass of brandy; he needed to keep his head clear for his studies. He had to catch up with the work he should have done this morning.

For a while he was able to concentrate, but a page of diagrams showing the effects of malnutrition on the human skeleton sent his thoughts tumbling back to that morning . . .

It had been sunny and Patrick's wife, Belle, who managed the coffee house on the ground floor, had ordered the waiters to put tables and chairs on the pavement under the striped green and white awning. Valentino was delighted and he told Belle to move two of the tables together and reserve them for his party.

Frank should have been working in the library at the Medical School but his mother asked him to stay and escort her down to meet Valentino's guest. Patrick came up to tell them when it was time to go. He seemed not to mind that Valentino had requested that he, and only he, should wait on his table. As head waiter of the restaurant he normally had nothing to do with the running of the coffee house but he made an exception that morning.

'I've served the coffee and the cakes and what a selection!' he said. 'But you know, my Belle can't refuse Valentino anything when he flashes those dark eyes of his.'

Frank watched as his mother reacted with pleasure to Patrick's words. She likes to pretend, whenever possible, that Valentino is normal, he thought sadly. But he blessed Patrick for his imagination and compassion.

Jimmy Nelson was holding sway and keeping them entertained. As Frank escorted his mother through the coffee house, past the tables full of morning customers with their newspapers and their shopping, past the gleaming counter and the hissing coffee machine, towards the bright sunshine streaming in through the windows and the open door, he could hear Jimmy dominating the conversation with reminiscences of the shows they had seen. Valentino was laughing with delight.

He's a godsend, that boy, Frank thought, intelligent and adaptable. He's just what we need.

Then they stepped out on to the pavement and Valentino and Jimmy rose to greet them and busied themselves settling Madame Alvini at a table. Frank stared at the girl sitting opposite. She was as lovely as his brother had told him she was. Her face was heart-shaped, her complexion fair with just a hint of golden tan as though she spent time, unfashionably, walking out of doors. Her eyes were a deep, dark blue; perhaps they were violet. She was wearing a hat – a ridiculous confection of feathers perched in amongst her piled-up golden curls.

Golden curls . . . He smiled to himself: what am I thinking of? And then he realized with a pang that not only was she lovely but that he was jealous.

He had never been jealous of his brother's looks before. He

287

would never match Valentino's height, his enormous strength, his perfect classical features; Frank was small, sinewy rather than muscular, and plain verging on downright ugly, or so he thought of himself. But thankfully nothing had gone wrong when he was born and he had the brain that God had intended.

As the brothers had grown up Frank had watched how women reacted to Valentino and yet he had known it would be more difficult for him to find a woman of his own. A normal woman, that is. So when he had learned of Valentino's passion he had made discreet enquiries and it hadn't been too hard to discover that Nella Nicholson was probably a cripple. But a cripple with the voice and the face of an angel. That's what they said.

And as he looked at her now, God forgive him, he couldn't believe that she would want anything further to do with his brother once she truly understood the truth about him.

'Mamma,' he heard Valentino saying, 'this is Miss Nicholson.'

Frank waited for the girl opposite him to react, to smile at his mother, but instead she turned her head to watch the person sitting next to her. Another girl, just as fair, almost as lovely, but her complexion was pale as though she never saw the sun and, when she half rose awkwardly from her seat, Frank saw that the line of her body was hunched and twisted.

'I'm pleased to meet you,' the other girl said, and his mother nodded and smiled.

'And who . . .?' Frank began, and Miss Nicholson's friend looked at him for the first time. Her eyes met his. He saw them widen. Then she smiled. He felt, his senses stir as they never had before.

'I'm Constance,' she said. 'Constance Edington.'

Chapter Nineteen

The room was warm, stiflingly so. Frank tried to concentrate on the notes he was making but his thoughts kept returning to the girl he had met that morning. Constance . . .

After introducing herself she hadn't said much. He had caught her looking at Valentino keenly but, when she'd become aware of Frank's gaze, she'd flushed slightly and turned her head away, though not with disapproval. She'd been content to listen to her friend, attentively at first, but as it had become obvious that Nella only seemed to want Constance there as an audience, Frank had seen the other girl relax and almost detach herself from the scene.

Then he had had time to notice the wedding ring and, with a pang, the swell of her body that revealed her pregnancy. But he had also noticed the faint air of . . . what was it? Sadness? No, it was not as definite as that. She did not look unhappy but neither did she look happy. Perhaps wistful was the way to describe that look in her eyes. He wished he knew what it was that caused her to look so wistful.

He took a sip of his coffee. It had grown cold. He could go down to the restaurant for another pot, but what was the point? It would soon be time for him to go and help Patrick close up. He picked up his books and took them to his room, then he went to the top of the stairs and looked down.

From above he saw the dark-suited gentlemen and colour-fully attired ladies making their way down to street level. He could hear the clatter of pans being washed and tables being scrubbed in the kitchen, and the voices of the waiters and catering staff rising cheerfully as they ended their night's work.

He saw Patrick coming up and stopping one floor below. The head waiter knocked respectfully on the door of one of the private dining-rooms. 'Your cab is here, sir,' he said.

A moment later the door opened and Patrick stood back respectfully as one of the North East's leading industrialists came out of the room followed by a much younger, richly dressed woman who was not his wife. 'The stairs are clear, sir,' Patrick said, and he preceded the couple all the way down to the exit.

Frank sighed and made his way downstairs. He knew what went on in the private rooms and, as Alvini's did very well out of it, he knew that he had no right to make judgements. His father had set the tone of the business many years before and his mother would never have questioned his wisdom. Frank knew that such a way of making a living was not for him. But, at the moment, he saw no way of escaping from it.

Just as he reached the next landing one of the other doors opened and he stood back as the guests began to emerge. There were two of them, both young men, with flushed faces and eyes slightly unfocused. He recognized them instantly for they had been here many times before. It was Matthew Elliot and his friend John Edington.

Edington! Of course ... Frank remembered that they'd even dined here alone together on John Edington's wedding day. Matthew had mentioned the bride's name. Constance. Poor Constance. Now Frank thought he knew the reason for that look in her eyes.

* * *

The weather was warm and, although Constance had shed her corsets long ago and wore only loose-fitting day dresses, she could no longer sit comfortably for any length of time. Even in bed at night, it was getting more difficult to find an easeful position. And as for walking for any distance, that was impossible. The last time she had been any further than the row of shops in the next street had been almost a month ago when she had gone with Nella to Alvini's Coffee House.

She'd gone to please Nella who had been so happy to have an admirer of her own. A rich handsome admirer who seemingly didn't care that the object of his devotion was not quite as other women. But, of course, Valentino was not like other men, Constance had realized that at once.

But she had also seen how much his family loved him and wanted him to be happy. His mother had hardly spoken but she had watched over him so tenderly. And his brother, Frank, had watched over both his mother and his brother and seemed to have no thought for himself. Until the moment that they had looked at each other.

Constance remembered that when their eyes had met, hers and Frank Alvini's, she had seen something there that made her own eyes widen with dismay. But she was not dismayed to see that he thought her beautiful. It was her own response to him that alarmed her. The sharp tug at her senses . . . the stirring of a desire that she had no right to feel . . .

'Are you all right, Mrs Edington?'

'Mm?' Polly was standing over her and she hadn't even heard her enter the room.

'I did knock.'

'No, that's all right, Polly. And I'm fine, really, just a little tired.'

'And sick of yourself and your own company no doubt.

Well, cheer up. You've got visitors. It's Miss Elliot and Miss Beattie. Shall I show them in?'

'Of course.'

'I hardly know what to say. I have neglected our friendship, haven't I?' Rosemary Elliot seemed taller than the last time she had been here, and slimmer and more boyish-looking, Constance thought.

'Sit down, Rosemary,' Hannah Beattie told her. 'You are tiring poor Mrs Edington with all this pacing around.'

Constance smiled her thanks at Rosemary's companion. 'Miss Beattie, would you pour the tea?' she asked. 'When I lean forward this bump seems to get in the way.'

'Just sit back and relax, my dear.'

'Really, Constance!' Rosemary seemed shocked that Constance should refer so openly to her pregnancy, and she flopped down in a chair by the window and started fiddling with the sash of her white muslin dress. She must be sixteen now, Constance thought, but she was still happy to dress like a schoolgirl.

Hannah Beattie, wearing a sensible lightweight grey walking costume, had poured the tea, and Constance took her cup and carefully eased herself back in the chair. Now, in her seventh month, there was no disguising her condition.

'I really am sorry, you know,' Rosemary said after she had sipped her tea and nibbled at a coconut macaroon. 'I should have called to see you without having to be reminded by my brother.'

'Reminded?'

Hannah Beattie pursed her lips and Rosemary had the grace to look embarrassed. 'Well, yes, I mean your husband had mentioned to him that you might be feeling lonely and would appreciate a visit from a friend.'

'I see.' And Constance did see, and more than the girl

could realize. She remembered her wedding breakfast when John's cousin Esther had hinted that Rosemary Elliot's friendship might not be sincere. Or rather that her friendship, even if it were sincere, would be short-lived. What was it Esther had said? '... *She will forget you as soon as she takes up with another of her lost causes* ...'

Lost causes ... Had she, Constance, been simply a lost cause to the rich young woman? She had arrived at the Elliots' house in the middle of the night, distressed and dishevelled and with nowhere to go, and Rosemary had been kindness itself. But even at the time Constance had suspected that the girl had been moved by the romance of the situation, a friend of her brother's marrying a servant girl, rather than any genuine desire to make a new friend.

Constance suppressed her irritation. She wasn't annoyed with Rosemary; she supposed she had known all along how immature she was in spite of her obvious intelligence. No, she was annoyed with John, who must have urged Matthew to persuade Rosemary to call and see her. John's motive may have been admirable but she didn't want friends who had to be reminded of her existence.

However, that part of it wasn't Rosemary's fault so she summoned up a smile. 'Well, I'm pleased you are here now,' she said, 'but you mustn't feel that you have to come and see me, you know.' She hadn't realized that she was going to say that and she bit her lip as she watched the girl's discomfort.

Hannah Beattie rescued the situation. 'In fact, we will not be able to call for some time. We are going up to the house in Coquetdale for the rest of the summer so that Rosemary can have time to think about her future.'

'I have decided that I don't want to be presented, you see,' Rosemary added.

'Presented?' Constance looked questioningly at Rosemary, who was scowling.

'Young women of Rosemary's class are expected to be presented at court and to take part in all the traditional rituals of a London season—'

'The purpose being to marry you off to some suitable young man and – oh, Constance, I don't know if I do want to get married. At least not for ages and ages!'

Hannah Beattie smiled. 'She's getting herself in a pet again,' she said to Constance, 'but there's no need. She has the kindest parents in the world. They don't mind being considered eccentric by the rest of society and they won't force her to do anything against her will. They have simply asked her to think very hard about what she wants to do. And they think it best if she does this thinking in the seclusion of the house in the Borders.'

'And what do you think you want to do?' Constance asked the girl.

'I don't *think*, I *know*! I want to go to university, I want to travel, I want to be independent. Above all, I don't want to have to answer to some man!'

'And, of course, Rosemary is lucky enough to have the means to live however she wants to.'

Constance looked at Beattie in surprise. She had actually sounded waspish and out of sympathy with her young charge for once.

Rosemary got to her feet clumsily. 'But perhaps we should go now. We mustn't tire Constance with my worries. She has enough cares of her own, what with the . . . the expected event and with moving house.'

'Moving house? What do you mean?'

'You didn't know?' The girl looked mortified. 'Oh no, it must have been a secret. Beattie, what have I done?'

'I'm not sure what you've done,' Beattie said drily, 'but sit down, girl, and tell Constance what you know. It will only vex her more to know half a secret.'

'Very well.' Rosemary flopped down again but then she suddenly reddened and shot an anguished glance at her companion. 'Beattie, I can't . . . I mean, you know what I said!'

Beattie sighed. 'Very well, I'll do my best to explain.' She turned to Constance. 'When Matthew asked Rosemary to come and visit you she said—'

'No, Beattie, don't!'

'Rosemary made some remark about the inconvenience . . .'

Constance saw Rosemary's astonished expression and guessed that the truth was being doctored.

'The inconvenience of visitors in this little house.' Beattie stopped and looked embarrassed.

'I see,' Constance said, and although she could guess the true nature of the spoiled girl's response she added, 'That was thoughtful of her.'

Beattie's smile was genuinely grateful and Constance had the feeling that they were conspirators as the older woman continued, 'And Matthew happened to remark that it wouldn't be long before her friend Constance would be able to receive her in a much larger and more gracious house. That's all, really.'

'Oh, Constance, you mustn't let John know that I've said anything. I can only imagine that he wants it to be a lovely surprise,' Rosemary said.

'Don't worry, I won't say anything. But I really would be very grateful if you would tell me where this new house of mine is going to be.'

'I don't know, really I don't.' And Constance could see that she was telling the truth.

295

Not long after that Rosemary and Miss Beattie took their leave and, in spite of her assurances to the contrary, Constance wondered if she would ever see the girl again. She realized, sadly, that she didn't much care. What was much more worrying was that her husband's friendship with Matthew Elliot seemed to be so close that it was possible for John to trust Matthew with intimate details of his marriage, such as his wife's loneliness, and even to discuss and plan moving house.

After Rosemary's visit, which she owed to John and Matthew apparently, she felt more isolated than ever.

'Sit down, everyone. Make yourselves comfortable. I have engaged this private dining room so that we will not be disturbed,' Harry said.

Harry looked good, Lucy thought. The occasion, afternoon tea at his hotel, was only semi-formal so he had chosen to wear a light grey flannel lounge coat with matching waistcoat and trousers. He could not altogether disguise his theatrically florid good looks, but this afternoon he was playing the part of a respectable and prosperous businessman. But then, Lucy mused, there was no real deception involved, for Harry Bodie had made a success of his theatrical career as both actor and manager and he was indeed prosperous.

At Harry's request Lucy had attired herself in her most tasteful outfit. She loved colourful fabrics with lots of frills and beaded embroidery. However, today she had allowed herself only a scattering of pink satin rosebuds sewn on to the high-standing collar of her cream satin blouse. Her tailored costume was of moss-green lightweight woollen cloth. She thought the shade went perfectly with the delicate red tint she had applied to her hair.

Nella, on the other hand, seemed to have made no attempt

at all to pretty herself up. Lucy turned her head and stared critically at the girl sitting next to her. Even though they were indoors Nella was wearing her cloak. Well, she would have to, Lucy supposed, but she could have chosen a bonnier one.

The cloak was one of the smoky-grey velvet ones that Nella wore on stage, and Lucy could glimpse that, underneath it, she wore a matching dress. Perhaps she feels most comfortable in those clothes, Lucy thought. But I wish she had let me do something to her face. She stared at that face now. Nella's delicate features were attractive enough – in fact very fetching, Lucy acknowledged grudgingly – but they were so pale. The girl had refused all Lucy's attempts to get her to wear some make-up.

'*I don't want to look like a painted doll!*' she'd said.

But she had, at least, made an effort with her hair. Piling it up on top of her head like that was the latest fashion and it suited her heart-shaped face. The soft tendrils of curls that she had teased out around the hairline looked more natural than artful. And, yes, perhaps the girl was right, make-up would have spoiled that delicate effect. Then Lucy sighed as she remembered that the illusion of grace and beauty would be shattered as soon as Nella took off her cloak.

Valentino looked as if he was going to burst with excitement. He was sitting, good as gold, between his mother and his younger brother, and the three of them looked like something out of a melodrama, dressed all in black as they were. Madame Alvini has probably worn black ever since she was widowed, Lucy thought, but why do the boys have to wear dark clothes? Probably because they know how attractive it makes them look. Even the younger one looked masterful.

Frank Alvini might not be big and handsome like his brother but there was something about him, something in those intelligent dark eyes that suggested hidden depths. Lucy wondered if he was spoken for and then laughed at herself for being taken with a boy young enough to be her . . . She didn't let herself finish that thought.

'No, don't leave us, lad. Here's your place, next to Miss Nicholson.'

Lucy looked round to see Harry gesturing to that young scarecrow Jimmy Nelson to come and join them at the table. The lad looked respectable enough in a suit that was certainly new but he must have been unsure whether he was welcome to join the family at the table. He had been about to leave the dining room.

Bless Harry, Lucy thought. It's good of him to include the boy; he probably knows how important he is to Valentino.

'And I'll take the chair at the head of the table.' Harry took his place with an expansive smile. 'The paterfamilias, yes?'

Harry couldn't resist showing off. Lucy didn't know what paterfamilias meant and she doubted if any of the rest of the guests did either, although she saw Frank widen his eyes and then conceal a smile, so perhaps he did. But then he was educated. A medical student, wasn't he?

So there they all were: Harry at the head of the table with Madame Alvini on one side of him, Valentino next to her and his brother Frank next to him. Lucy sat at Harry's other side, with Nella next to her and Jimmy Nelson at Nella's other side. The result of this seating arrangement was that Valentino, towering above the savouries and the sandwiches and the cream cakes, could stare straight across at Nella to his heart's content. And stare he did. He looked as if he intended to eat her up. Lucy controlled a shudder of unease.

She glanced across at Madame Alvini and got a shock. The old lady was looking at Nella, too, and she was smiling as if there was absolutely nothing wrong with the girl. But surely she knew . . . Well, if she did she had obviously decided to ignore it.

'Let us enjoy this repast before we discuss those matters that are dear to our hearts,' Harry said, and Lucy wondered if he had been carried away by the occasion and had slipped into one of his old acting roles in some high-falutin family drama. She supposed he couldn't help himself. And then he turned to the old lady with an expression of sincere humility. 'I do hope these refreshments will meet with your approval, Madame Alvini.'

The poor old thing looked puzzled. 'My approval?'

'After all,' Harry continued, 'I am perfectly aware that your renowned establishment has set the standard for all other restaurants in Newcastle.'

On her right Nella suppressed a giggle and Valentino, no doubt seeing her smile, laughed out loud. Although he hasn't a clue what he's laughing about, Lucy thought, he's simply happy because he thinks Nella's happy.

After that Harry had the sense to keep quiet while they all tucked in and, when the waiters had cleared the table, he asked them to bring fresh pots of tea and coffee.

'And, now,' he said, 'the reason that we're here.' He paused and the silence went on for so long that Lucy wondered if he was flummoxed for once; Harry Bodie actually lost for words. 'We're here because . . . because Nella and Valentino . . . these two fine young people . . .'

His words trailed away and Madame Alvini stared at him anxiously. 'My son—' she began, but Frank Alvini interrupted her.

'My brother has expressed a wish to marry Miss Nicholson.'

There, he's said it, Lucy thought and everybody turned to look at Frank. There was something about the younger Alvini that was altogether impressive, she thought. Sitting there so composed and confident and so completely in control of the situation.

'Er, yes,' Harry said. 'And Nella . . . er, Nella thought it best that certain things should be made clear—'

'It's all right, Harry.' This time it was Nella who interrupted. She pushed her chair back from the table as she spoke.

What's she going to do? Lucy wondered.

She stood there quite still just as if she were on the stage at the beginning of her act, but instead of a spotlight, the afternoon sun streamed in through the ceiling-high windows to bathe her in a shaft of golden light. Her fine blonde hair shone like a halo. Very dramatic, Lucy thought. She's a born actress. And then she held her breath as Nella raised her hands to pull at the ribbon ties of her cloak. When she had loosened them she pushed the cloak back ever so gently and let it fall gracefully on to the chair behind her.

'Valentino,' she said.

'Nella?' The big man looked at her expectantly. He frowned slightly with puzzlement.

She didn't say any more. Instead she began to turn round so slowly that, no matter where they were sitting, everybody at the table would get a good look at her from all angles. Three-quarters of the way round she stopped so that she was almost sideways on to Valentino. He couldn't possibly fail to see the way her twisted shoulders threw up the hump in her back. Lucy could hardly believe what she was seeing. Was the girl totally without common sense? Was she trying to put Valentino off?

Eventually she completed her turn and looked straight at her would-be suitor. So did everybody else, Lucy noticed. He was still staring at her with a half-puzzled smile. There was no sudden shock or expression of disgust, only the same adoring expression as before.

'Valentino,' Nella said, 'do you still want to marry me?'

He looked amazed. 'Of course.' He glanced round at everyone present and smiled at them as if Nella might have just made a joke but he was prepared to indulge her. 'That's why we are here, isn't it? So that our wedding can be arranged?'

'Yes, my son, that is why we are here.' His mother was looking at him lovingly and, if she had been shocked at what she had just seen, then she was concealing it very well.

Frank said nothing but Lucy could see no objection in his gaze, only a kind of sadness. She heard Harry clear his throat.

'Well said, young man,' he mumbled, and something about his voice made her glance at him swiftly. She was just in time to see him take a clean white handkerchief from his pocket and dab at his eyes.

Nella sat down again and Lucy turned to look at her. She was smiling a funny little smile and Lucy saw with dismay that her eyes were moist too. Lucy leaned towards her. 'For goodness' sake,' she whispered, 'don't start blubbing or you'll set me off as well.'

She was relieved when Harry stood up and smiled down the length of the table at Jimmy Nelson. 'Jimmy,' he said, 'may I prevail upon you to go and attract the attention of the wine waiter? Tell him it's time to bring in the champagne.'

Chapter Twenty

'Nice place you've got here.' Nella stood in the middle of the airy drawing room and raised her eyebrows appreciatively. 'And from the looks of you, you've moved house just in time!'

Constance, lying with her feet up on a new chaise longue, smiled at her friend wearily. Nella looked more theatrical than ever. Today a confection of silk flowers and lace seemed to be woven into her hair and a few soft wisps had been teased out to frame her face. The fabric of her dress, sheer delaine, Constance knew to be a mix of wool and cotton; John had experimented with it for a series of graceful day gowns. He had rented tiny shop premises in Northumberland Street and installed a manageress and two seamstresses. There was no need for his uncle, Walter Barton, to approve this venture as Matthew Elliot was still funding the enterprise.

But it was easy to see that Nella's outfit had been made by someone with an eye for drama rather than high fashion. The cerulean fabric seemed to be moulded to Nella's body at the front, accentuating her tiny waist, but at the back the fabric hung from a high yoke in the graceful folds of a false cloak and almost obscured her deformity. It's like an optical illusion, Constance thought.

'What're you grinning at?' Nella demanded suddenly but she grinned herself before taking her place on a small sofa.

None of the furniture had been arranged properly yet and there were still a few packing cases ranged together near the door.

'I'm smiling because I'm pleased to see you,' Constance said. 'Polly and Mrs Green won't let me do anything to help—'

'I should think not!' Nella interjected.

'—and, to tell you the truth, I'm going out of my mind with boredom.'

'So that's why you sent me the letter and just happened to mention that John was away at some mill looking at new fabrics.'

Constance was embarrassed. 'I sent you the letter to let you know my new address.'

'Of course you did. And it's all right, I know that John doesn't like me to visit you.'

'Nella, that's not—'

'Constance, you divven't hev to lie for him, and I divven't think any the worse of you. I'm just pleased that you still want to see me, what with all yer high-class friends.'

'I haven't any high-class friends,' Constance said quietly. And she knew that to be true. She was glad that Nella didn't pursue the subject.

Instead her friend asked, 'Do you get along with John's relatives at all? I mean, he has an aunt and a young female cousin, hasn't he?'

'John's Aunt Muriel thinks that he has married beneath him.'

'What a cheek!'

'And I think his cousin, Esther, wanted to marry him herself; consequently she dislikes me thoroughly.'

'Is she in love with him?'

'Maybe. But more importantly, the family business will go to John when her father dies.'

'But that's dreadful,' Nella said, and she sounded genuinely shocked. 'Surely she didn't want to marry him just for the money?'

'It happens.'

Constance tried to find a more comfortable position on the chaise longue. Although the day would seem merely pleasantly warm to most people, Constance found herself perspiring constantly. The loose folds of her muslin day dress clung to her body damply and no matter how she sat, the baby seemed to press on something inside that hurt her.

Nella had noticed her discomfort and she frowned with sympathy. 'Poor Constance,' she said. 'I don't suppose you can get about much now.'

'No.' Constance sighed.

She managed to stuff a plump cushion into the small of her back and then, unconsciously, she began to fiddle with the locket that she wore around her neck. When she saw Nella looking at her attentively, she dropped her hand. She hoped that Nella couldn't read her mind – couldn't guess that she had sat at her dressing table a full five minutes before putting it on. The memories of the night she had lost it were still too vivid . . .

'It can't be much fun being in that condition in the summer heat,' Nella said. 'And, I hope you don't mind my saying so, Constance, but I got a shock when I saw you.'

'Why?'

'Well, it's probably not very ladylike to say this but what a size you are! And it seems to hev happened so suddenly.'

Constance frowned. 'I know, but Dr Mason has assured me that everything is all right.'

'A doctor?'

'John insists I visit Dr Mason, just as he has insisted that I take great care of myself. And apparently, you can carry the child high at first and hardly look pregnant until the baby starts moving into the right position to be born.'

'Have you long to go?'

'Not too long.' Constance hesitated. 'You know I'm not sure about these things – I had no mother to teach me – but according to Dr Mason it should be sometime in August.'

'Next month? But we're almost there! So why on earth did John choose now to move house?'

'He was adamant that we should move before the baby is born. The old house wasn't big enough.'

'Not big enough? There were four rooms upstairs, weren't there?'

'We need a nursery.'

'Yes, but—'

'And a room for the nursemaid.'

'But—'

'John was reluctant to use his mother's room for any other purpose. You know she died of consumption and he was afraid of lingering infection.'

Nella nodded.

'But there are other reasons,' Constance said. 'Now that John can afford to live a little better, he thought Polly should have a room of her own instead of having to sleep in the kitchen.'

'Quite right too. Although I'm not sure if the little tartar deserves it!'

'And John needs a larger sewing room.' Constance realized that she had referred to the sewing room as John's domain but she didn't think that Nella had noticed that she seemed to have given up all claim to it.

'Well, whatever the reasons, this is a grand place to live,' Nella said, 'tucked away at the end of this blind terrace, and

306

you can look out on a nice bit of green from this tower or turret or whatever it is.'

Nella got up and walked over to the hexagonal bay that formed the corner of the room. The turret that jutted out from the corner of the house rose up over all the three storeys and even here, on the ground floor, there was a fine view of the adjacent park.

She stood for a moment watching the children playing and the nursemaids strolling with their perambulators. 'Can you get into the park from the end of yer street or do you hev to gan right round?'

'There's no official way in, but John has discovered a gate in the back yard, although he says it doesn't look as though it's been used for years. The padlock is old and rusted.'

'Hevn't you seen it yerself?'

'To tell you the truth, Nella, I haven't even been up to the top floor yet. I just seem to drag myself around, getting through the day as best I can.'

'Who would be a woman, eh? Now, shall I gan and hurry that young maid of yours up? I'm dying for a cup of tea!'

Nella didn't have to go, thank goodness, for Constance knew that Polly was harassed enough with overseeing the final touches of the removal. She had her younger sister Jane to help her, and in fact Jane would be coming in every day from now on to take over most of the rough work.

But Mrs Green had also been helping out and it was she who appeared almost as soon as Nella had spoken, bearing a tray laden with tea and home-made scones.

'Here you are,' Constance's former neighbour said. 'I'll put everything on this little table and perhaps Miss Nicholson could see to things.'

'Of course.'

Mrs Green smiled warmly at Nella. 'I want to thank you

for sending those tickets to Polly. She took my Albert with her, you know. They did enjoy themselves. Polly says she feels quite proud that she actually knows you in person.'

Constance saw Nella's eyebrows shoot up and she shot her a warning glance. 'Well, well,' Nella said, and she covered her mouth with her hand, apparently suffering from a short burst of coughing.

'Mrs Green,' Constance said, 'I can't thank you enough for helping out like this.'

'You don't have to thank me, Mrs Edington. I was very fond of your ma-in-law and I'm pleased to be able to do anything I can. Besides, I feel like one of the family, what with Albert walking out with Polly and your John being so good to him, an' all.'

'John is good to Albert?' Constance was surprised.

'Oh yes, I told you when we first met that Mr Edington gives my son samples from the shop. Well, at first it was just nice shirts and socks and handkerchiefs and the like, but lately he's given him a couple of decent suits and no charge wanted.'

'Well . . . that's nice.' Constance was perplexed. She had often been unhappy at the way John treated Mrs Green almost like a servant rather than a friendly neighbour, so if he was being kind to Albert that was good. It meant that in his heart he acknowledged how much he owed to this kind family. And yet he had never mentioned his generosity to her. Constance supposed that made it all the more admirable but yet she wasn't sure . . .

'And now, if you don't mind, I'll leave you two to have a good gossip. I've promised to help Polly get the larder sorted out before I go home.'

'Does young Albert still live in yer kitchen, then?' Nella asked when the door had closed behind Mrs Green.

'If you mean does he still visit almost every day, then the answer is yes.'

'Here's yer tea. Can you reach if I put it on this daft little table? Now I'm gannin' to cover a couple of those scones with that delicious-looking raspberry jam. And do you allow yer staff to entertain admirers like that?' Nella suddenly asked, changing tack.

'*Allow my staff to entertain admirers?* Are you joking, Nella?'

Nella placed the plate with Constance's scone next to her cup of tea and took her own back to the sofa where there was another occasional table. She smiled but, when she spoke, the tone of her voice was serious. 'Yes, I'm joking. But you do seem to be familiar with the servants, as they say.'

'Mrs Green isn't a servant. She's been a good friend.' Constance felt uncomfortable when she remembered that she had often puzzled over the exact place in society of Mrs Green, but she hurried on, 'And as for Polly, well, I'm . . . I'm training her. She's improved a lot.'

'Ee, Constance, don't take on. I wasn't being serious and what I really wanted to say was that you seem to hev learned a lot from Mrs Sowerby.'

'Mrs Sowerby! I have learned from Mrs *Sowerby*! Whatever can you mean?'

'Calm down, for goodness' sake, or you'll start something off! What I meant was that never in a thousand years would you ever be like her. I know very well that you and your mother were used to better things – that you were gentry – but your years in the workhouse and then working at Rye Hill have made sure that no matter how rich you become, you'll never treat poorer folk like scum. There. That's what I meant.'

Nella bit into her scone and Constance watched her obvious enjoyment. She was aware that she had probably overreacted but she would never have jumped to conclusions the way she just had if it wasn't for the fact that any mention of the Sowerbys was still agonizing for her. After all these months her violation at Gerald's hands still conjured up feelings and images that were almost too painful to bear.

Nella finished her scone, took a sip of tea and dabbed at her lips with a napkin. Then she looked at Constance. 'That's right, drink yer tea – and try to finish that scone; you're supposed to be building yer strength up, aren't you?'

Constance laughed. 'Oh, Nella, you're as bad as the rest of them. John, Mrs Green and Polly – they have been pampering me as if I were an invalid instead of someone who is simply fulfilling one of life's natural functions.'

She had imagined that Nella would laugh but, instead, she looked concerned. 'Natural it may be but I'm sure that you remember as well as I do that women in the workhouse died performing that function.'

'Yes, but many of those poor women were weak from years of hard work and ill-feeding.'

'Well, doesn't that prove that John is right to look after you?'

Constance stared at her friend and burst out laughing. 'I'm outnumbered. I give in. They can pamper me as much as they want to.'

'That's settled, then. Now, let me fill up yer cup and how about another one of these scones? I'll hev one even although I might hev to take out a few tucks in me wedding dress.'

Constance accepted the scone without protest but her laughter died.

'Go on, say it, then,' Nella said when she had settled herself back on the sofa.

'Say what?'

'Whatever it is that's worrying you. Don't deny it,

310

Constance, I saw it in yer eyes the minute I said "wedding dress".'

'We-ell . . .' Constance began, but realized she didn't have the words to express her fears for her friend.

'Oh, all right then, I'll say it for you. You don't think I should marry Valentino, do you?'

'Nella, I'm not sure—'

'Yes, you are and I think I know what's bothering you.'

'Do you?'

'It's obvious, isn't it? If John treats you like an invalid because you're expecting, you probably think that having a baby would kill me; that I'd die in childbirth just like the poor women in the workhouse. That's it, isn't it?'

'Yes.'

Constance wanted to say that it was much more than that. That she hadn't even got as far as thinking of Nella being pregnant, the truth was she had balked at the very idea of Valentino and Nella in bed together. He was such a giant of a man and she such a twisted little scrap – the marriage act itself would be sufficient to damage or even kill her friend.

'Well, you needn't worry about that.'

'About what?' Constance knew that she was blushing. Had Nella read her thoughts? She hoped not.

'You needn't worry about me getting pregnant. There won't be any children.'

Constance dropped her eyes and sipped her tea. She sensed that it would be less embarrassing simply to let Nella talk without interruption.

'Valentino's a big handsome man.' Nella was smiling but Constance saw that the smile was tinged with sadness. 'A giant of a man, in fact, and probably as strong as Samson in the Bible. He looks like the perfect specimen of manhood, doesn't he?'

311

'Yes.'

'But you've guessed that he isn't perfect, hevn't you? Gan on, admit it, you knew what was wrong only a minute or two after meeting him.' Nella sighed. 'He's what unkind folks would call simple. Valentino has the mind of a child – an innocent child.' She shot Constance a keen look and then said quickly, 'And there's another bit of him that's like a child too. The important bit. Get me meaning?'

'I . . . I think I do.'

'Me manager, Harry Bodie, had guessed as much and he had a long talk with Valentino's brother, remember him? He had coffee and cakes with us that day, although he didn't say much.'

Constance looked away. Of course she remembered Frank Alvini. In fact he'd crept into her idle thoughts quite often now she had so little to do. She had been disturbed by the way he had stared at her across the table although she had tried to act as if she hadn't noticed. She hadn't even spoken to him other than to tell him her name. But when, at last, their eyes had met something had passed between them . . . something that didn't need words . . .

'Constance!' Nella's voice rebuked her.

'What?'

'You're woolgathering!'

'I'm sorry, it's the— I'm so warm . . .'

Nella's eyes narrowed. 'Are you sure that's all it is?'

'What else could it be?' Constance stared down into her empty teacup.

'I'm not sure . . .' Nella looked hard at Constance for a moment, then she shrugged and smiled. 'Well, anyway, I was telling you, Harry had a chat to Frank and then he got Lucy to explain things to me. But to tell you the truth, I think I already knew.'

312

'How could you?'

'The way Valentino looks at me . . . it's not like . . . I don't know how to say this . . . it's not like the way the other stage-door Johnnies look at the chorus girls as if they're imagining what they'd look like with no clothes on. Oh dear, I've shocked you. I keep forgetting that we theatre folk are more free and easy than respectable people!'

Constance managed to smile.

'That's better,' Nella said. 'And don't worry about me, I know what I'm getting myself into. I won't be heving any children – but I'll hev my career on the stage and I'll hev a big handsome husband who thinks the sun shines out of me and who wants to be with me every blessed minute of every blessed day. That's more than I ever hoped for!'

'Well, then, I'm very pleased for you,' Constance said. And she was. In many ways Nella's life would be more satisfactory than her own. Valentino was handsome, that couldn't be denied, and many women who didn't know the truth would be envious of Nella. But even more important was the way he loved her, the way he wanted to be with her all the time. Nella would never be left at home wondering where her husband was and whether it was her fault that he spent less and less time with her . . .

Nella finished her second scone and drained her cup. 'I must gan. Do you remember Alice? No, of course you wouldn't. Alice was the little lass who came to the Sowerbys after you left. Well, Alice has written to me saying that she's coming to see me this afternoon. I'll hev to hurry home and see what she wants before I get off to the theatre.'

When she stood up Nella walked over to the fireplace and rose on tiptoes to fiddle with her hat and her hair. She turned and smiled her new, confident and infectious smile. 'I know I'm vain, you don't hev to say anything! Now, if I give this bell pull a tug, do you think you could get yer hoity-toity little maid to run along and get me a cab?'

'Of course.'

After Nella had gone Polly came into the room to collect the tea tray. 'Mrs Edington, you look tired,' she said accusingly.

Constance admitted that she was and allowed Polly to help her upstairs. Her bedroom was clean and fresh-smelling, and the lace curtains were moving gently in the breeze from the open window.

'Why don't you take your clothes off and get into bed and have a proper rest?' Polly said. 'Here, I'll help you.'

Constance submitted herself to the maid's kindly ministrations and settled back into the mound of freshly laundered pillows.

Polly paused at the door. 'Mrs Edington, why don't you just stay there? Mr Edington isn't coming home until late tonight so I can bring your meal up on a tray.'

'All right, Polly.' Constance sighed and after the door had closed she mused, *I might as well be alone in this room as in any other*.

'What are you thinking of, sitting on the doorstep like that?'

Nella had just paid the cab driver and she turned to stare down at the unhappy girl. As the cab clattered away across the cobbles, Alice shaded her eyes with one hand and squinted up against the dusty city sunlight.

'Miss Nicholson,' she said.

'That's right, but answer me. Why didn't you ring the bell?'

'I did and the woman said you weren't back yet and I didn't know what to say so she shut the door.'

Nella could just imagine Mrs Small's impatience at being confronted with poor Alice. Mrs Small, who was politeness itself to her lodgers, was known to be a tartar with her staff or anyone she deemed further down the social scale than herself and Mr Small. On top of that she had just lost a little maid of all work: the girl had had the temerity to get a better job in a big hotel.

Alice scrambled to her feet and, although she could only have been thirteen by now, she towered above Nella.

Nella put her head on one side and squinted up at her. 'You should hev told her that Miss Nicholson was expecting you and you could hev waited in me sitting room.'

'Could I?'

Nella frowned. She had known from the start that Alice was slow, but she wasn't stupid, and Nella suspected that there was something worrying her that was more serious than the fact that she had got the worse of an encounter with Mrs Small.

'Oh, hawway, lass,' Nella said suddenly. 'I'm as bad as you, just standing here instead of getting inside. Now ring that bell for me, will you?'

Mrs Small was full of apologies. 'I'm so sorry, Miss Nicholson,' she said, 'but the girl didn't make herself clear. I imagined that she was a member of your devoted public come to pester you for some token.'

'Did you?' Nella was surprised. She knew she had admirers – large numbers of them followed her from theatre to theatre – but no one had ever come to her lodgings before.

'Oh yes,' Mrs Small shook her head sympathetically, 'I know what it's like to be loved by the theatre-going public. Before I retired from the stage I used to have to disguise myself in order to get even from the stage door to the waiting hansom cab.'

'Fancy that.' For a moment Nella wondered whether it was permissible to ask this famous actress to bring her up a plate of sandwiches but then she remembered that she was paying good money to live here.

'Of course, Miss Nicholson,' Mrs Small said. 'I've got some nice boiled ham. And I'll bring them up myself. You know that I'm managing with only the cook and one skivvy, don't you?'

Nella took that as a reproach, but nevertheless she hurried upstairs to her rooms with Alice following on and breathing heavily. When they reached Nella's landing she turned and looked at the girl critically. Alice's usually pasty cheeks were flushed and her breast was heaving.

'You need to lose some weight, girl,' Nella said. 'Although how you've managed to get like that on the rations old Mortimer doles out, I'll never know.'

Alice looked as though she was going to cry. 'I'm not greedy, really I'm not. Mrs Mortimer says that I must be sneaking down into the kitchen at night and pinching anything I can find – but there's never anything missing when she checks – but she shouts at me all the same and says I'm growing into a fat, ugly lump. But, honestly, Miss Nicholson, I think I'm just made this way.'

'Of course you are. Come on in, pet, and divven't fret yerself.' She raised a finger to her lips. 'We'll hev to talk quietly because Lucy, that I share with, will be heving a little nap in her room.'

Nella led the way into the sitting room. She hoped that she hadn't upset the poor lass too much. She, of all people, should have remembered what it was like to be mocked for her appearance.

'Now, do you think you could get yerself into that little kitchen through there and make us a nice pot of tea to gan with the sandwiches that Mrs Small will be bringing up?'

Nella wasn't really hungry. She had indulged herself with Mrs Green's home-made scones and she never liked to eat too much before a performance. It wouldn't be too long before Harry called in a cab to take her and Lucy to the station where they would meet up with the others and catch the train to Shields. When she got back here after the show, she and Lucy would have whatever Mrs Small had left out for them. She doubted if she was doing her constitution much good with these midnight feasts but after the show she was usually ravenous.

Alice polished off most of the sandwiches and drank two cups of tea, then she sat and stared at the floor.

'So what is it, then? Why did you come to see me?' Nella asked.

'Oh!' Alice raised a hand to her open mouth in a startled gesture. 'Ee, Miss Nicholson, you must think I'm daft!'

'No, pet, I don't, but whatever it is you've come to see me about, you'll hev to look sharp. I'll hev to get ready to gan quite soon.'

Alice thrust a hand into the pocket of her skirt and brought something out. She held her hand out across the table and Nella could see a small coin resting in her palm. 'I've brought this. It's yours.'

'Sixpence?'

'Yes, for your things. You know, you told me to give them to the rag-and-bone man and he said that's what they were worth.'

'You sold all me worldly goods for a tanner!' Nella said theatrically, and the girl looked frightened. 'Ee, Alice, divvent look like that, pet. I'm not angry with you! In fact I'm surprised he gave you so much for me bit rags. But I wrote that letter months ago.'

'I know, but . . . but . . .'

'And I said you could keep whatever you got for them. So what's brought you here now? Alice, whatever is the matter?'

317

Nella watched in consternation as the tears welled up in the younger girl's eyes and then spilled out and ran down her cheeks. At first she cried quite silently and then she began to sob, louder and louder as she tried to gulp back her grief.

'There, there, bonny lass.' Nella got up and went to put an arm round the girl's shoulder. She noticed how soft and cushiony it was. 'Now, are you gannin' to tell me what this is about?'

'I shouldn't be surprised if it's a man that's the cause of all this commotion – that's usually the case.' It was Lucy who had spoken. Alice stopped halfway through a sniff and she and Nella looked towards the open doorway of Lucy's bedroom.

Nella's roommate was wearing a silk robe loosely tied around her ample figure and her hair was in curling rags. She never looked her best without her make-up and, at the moment, she looked both sleepy and cross.

'I'm sorry, Lucy,' Nella said, 'but me little friend seems to be in some kind of trouble.'

'I can see that.' Lucy's expression softened when she took in the young girl's distress. 'Look, my dear, you've come to the right place. You can confide in me and Nella and we'll help you if we can, but first I'm going to make a fresh pot of tea, and you can tell us all about it while I start doing my hair.'

Alice remained completely silent while Lucy made the tea and then she watched in awe as the older woman began to untie the rags in her hair and drop them on the table.

'Come along then,' Lucy said. 'What's the matter? Are you in the family way?'

Alice shrieked and half rose from her chair. Nella thought the lass was going to run from the room, and she grabbed at one of her hands and tugged until she sat down again. 'It's all right, Alice,' she said, and the girl shot her a wide-eyed look

318

of panic which made her add, 'I think you'd better answer the question.'

'No, I'm not,' Alice said defiantly. 'I'm a good girl.'

'Well, thank goodness for that,' Lucy said drily. 'So what is it? Has some little errand boy broken your good little heart?'

Alice pursed her lips and looked sulky.

'Give over, Lucy,' Nella said. 'The girl's upset. You shouldn't tease her. Now, come on, Alice, we hevn't got much longer before I'll hev to go.' Alice glanced at Lucy, who was still taking out her rags and Nella continued, 'Don't be fooled by her manner. Lucy Lovekins has a heart of gold. Who else would look after me the way she has? Now, come on, you can trust her.'

'So, it isn't a man?' Lucy prompted.

'Yes, it is, it's him . . . it's Master Gerald . . .'

'Gerald Sowerby . . .' Nella breathed, and her anger rose in her throat like bile to choke her.

Chapter Twenty-one

'Who is Gerald Sowerby?' Lucy asked.

'Dr Sowerby and Mrs Sowerby's pride and joy!' Nella said and when she saw Lucy raise her eyebrows she added, 'The son of the house where Alice works – where I used to work.'

'And I take it you have cause to dislike him?'

'I hate him!'

'But why? He didn't . . . I mean . . . surely he wouldn't . . .'

'Fancy me?' Nella laughed, but it was a dry, cracked sound. 'No, he didn't try anything on with me. But he did with a friend of mine.'

She realized that Alice was looking at her curiously and she brought her thoughts back to the present problem. 'But it's this poor bairn we're concerned with now.' She looked straight at the girl. 'What did he do to you?'

Alice flushed crimson. 'Well . . . he'd been following me about for days.'

'Following you?'

'Well, you know, catching me at the top of the stairs when I was carrying a pile of clean linen – or standing watching me when I filled up the coal scuttles, or saw to a fire.'

'But he did more than just watch or you wouldn't be sitting here telling us all this,' Nella said.

Alice's lower lip began to tremble and the tears spill from

her eyes again. But this time she went on with her story. 'Just last week I was cleaning the bathroom . . . I didn't even hear him come in . . . I was bending over the bath when I thought I heard something. I looked up and saw his reflection in the mirror and I nearly died of fright.' The girl's eyes widened and she bit on her lips so hard that Nella thought they might bleed.

'He was standing behind me,' Alice went on, 'so close that I couldn't have moved back without bumping into him. I tried to straighten up but he pushed me down over the bath and kept me there with one hand and then . . . then he started to lift my skirt—'

'Why didn't you yell blue murder?' Lucy asked.

'I was going to. I took a deep breath and he grabbed at my hair and pulled it and said that if I made a noise he'd kill me.'

'Oh, Alice . . . Alice . . .' Nella said.

'I believed him! You should have heard the way he said it! I thought if he didn't get me there and then he'd get me later.'

'All right, pet,' Nella said soothingly. 'What happened next?'

Alice blushed scarlet, then she dropped her head and looked fixedly at the carpet. 'He pushed my skirt up . . . and he was pulling at my . . . at my drawers . . . you know . . . and at the same time he was moving sort of funny . . . sort of pushing himself against me.'

'Dirty bastard!' Lucy exclaimed.

Alice looked startled and Nella said, 'Lucy! Language! She's only a bairn!'

'That's why he's a dirty bastard and so's any man that'll try to have his way with children!'

'It's all right,' Alice blurted out. 'He didn't – I mean it didn't come to that.'

'What happened?' Nella asked.

322

'Miss Annabel . . . she came into the room and she shrieked—'

'I bet she did!' Nella found herself laughing with relief.

'Master Gerald cursed something awful and he went chasing after her and . . . I heard him shouting her name but I don't know what he said.'

'So who's Annabel?' Lucy asked.

'Gerald's little sister,' Nella told her. 'And I bet he'll hev persuaded her not to tell on him. Has he bothered you again?'

'I've been dodging him,' Alice said. 'But I just don't know how long I can keep out of his way.'

'Don't worry, you're not gannin' back there tonight – nor ever again,' Nella said.

The girl's eyes filled with hope. 'Do you mean I can stay with you? That's why I wrote to you. You were so kind to me when I started working at the Sowerbys' that I was sure you would help me.'

Nella remembered how she had been so upset at losing Constance that she had had to force herself to be even civil to the poor lass; and yet the girl had remembered her as a friend. Well, she would be her friend, and she would help her.

'You did right. You can stay here—'

'Wait a minute—' Lucy began.

'Mrs Small, our landlady, needs a housemaid,' Nella said. 'Would you like me to arrange for you to get the job, Alice?'

The girl stared at her. Relief at not having to go back to Rye Hill fought with fear of the formidable Mrs Small and Nella laughed.

'Ee, don't worry, pet. She's a bit of a tartar but she's good at heart, and if you work hard she'll treat you right. And the grub's better than you'd ever get at Rye Hill,' she added.

And that seemed to do it. Alice's smile was like the sun

coming out. 'Oh, thank you, Miss Nicholson, I'll stay – that is, if she'll have me.'

'Don't worry, she will. But you'll be starting work tomorrow. Tonight Lucy and I are taking you to the theatre.'

'He looks so happy.' Madame Alvini smiled as Valentino and Jimmy Nelson made their way downstairs from the family apartment at the top of the old building in the Haymarket. A cab was waiting at the door of the restaurant to take them to the station and here they would catch the train for Shields.

'Of course he's happy,' Frank said. 'He's going to the theatre to see his sweetheart. He goes to the theatre to see her every night and never mind that it's costing us a fortune.'

Frank regretted his words the moment he had said them and he regretted them even more when he saw the smile drain from his mother's face. She turned her beautiful eyes on him with a look of anguish. 'But, Frank, we can afford it, can't we? I mean, we have sufficient money to be able to make your brother happy?'

He reached for his mother's hands and held them as he spoke. 'I'm sorry, Mamma. Of course we can afford it. Valentino asks for so little in life whereas I—'

'You are talking about the cost of your studies. That is something I would pay for even if I had to go out scrubbing floors. I will be so proud of my son the doctor!'

Frank laughed. 'You go out scrubbing, Mamma? My father would rise from his grave and haunt me if ever I allowed you to spoil these beautiful hands in such a way.' He raised them to his lips and kissed them. 'Now, come in and sit down. You have nothing to worry about. Jimmy will take good care of Valentino, and I have some studying to do.'

Frank sat at the table and spread out his books, and a little later his mother brought him a pot of coffee and a slice of almond cake. 'When they are married Valentino will not have to pay for his tickets,' she said.

With an effort Frank tore his eyes away from the page in front of him and frowned up at his mother. 'Not pay for his tickets? What are you talking about?'

'Mr Bodie explained to me that once Valentino and Miss Nicholson are married there will be complimentary tickets – and probably for Jimmy, too.'

'That's good. But, Mamma, I was wrong to complain about the cost of the theatre tickets. It really doesn't matter.'

'So what is it that does matter?'

'Mamma?'

'Something is worrying you, Frank. Making you angry.'

His mother pulled out the chair opposite to him and sat down. He knew that his studies would have to wait. He sighed. 'Very well.' What should he say? He didn't know how to begin to express his worries for his brother's future without causing his mother distress. 'I'm not angry. I want Valentino to be happy just as you do,' he began cautiously, 'so I would like to be sure that it is correct for him to marry.'

'Are you worried that Miss Nicholson isn't a Catholic? She has agreed to take instruction. The children will be brought up in our Church.'

Frank struck the edge of the table with both hands and his mother's eyes widened. 'Mamma, you know there won't be any children!' he said. 'You know that this will not be a proper marriage.'

His mother flushed but her reply was spirited. 'And what is a proper marriage? I thought a marriage was when two people promised to love each other and look after each other and make each other happy for the rest of their time on earth!'

Frank stared at her. Her cheeks were flushed and she was

325

breathing quickly. 'I'm sorry, but you know what I mean,' he said.

There was a silence as his mother's breathing returned to normal. 'I know what you mean, Gianfranco.'

Suddenly she looked so sad that he wished he could change the world for her. He wished that he could turn the clock back to the time of his brother's birth and somehow perform some miracle of modern medicine that would either make Valentino normal, or prevent him from being born at all.

Frank groaned when he realized what he had been thinking and his mother got up and came round the table. She rested a hand on his shoulder. 'I know that there will be no children and I know why. It is just that I am a foolish old woman and I like to pretend sometimes that . . . that . . .'

He heard the sob in her voice and he turned towards her and looked up into her face. 'I know, Mamma, I know.'

His mother took his face in her hands and bent down to kiss his forehead. 'You are a gift from heaven, Gianfranco. A good son. I don't know how I could ever carry my burden without you.'

After that she left him to get on with his studies but Frank found it difficult to concentrate when he knew that his mother would be sitting alone at the kitchen table determined not to do anything further to distract him.

A little later he realized that he had turned page after page and couldn't remember one single word that he had read. He rested his head in his hands. It was true that he had reservations about his brother's marriage – but that was natural in the circumstances, wasn't it? But he shouldn't have worried his mother . . .

He sighed and closed his books. He would go into the kitchen and ask her to warm him some soup, then sit with her for a while. She was always so pleased to do anything for him.

Thank goodness she could have no idea of the other cause of his distress: his hopeless longing for a woman he had met only once and who could never be his.

Constance didn't know what it was that had awakened her.

It was late and the room was shadowy. It had been warm and she'd asked Polly to leave the window open and not to draw the velvet drapes. So now the moonlight filtered in through the lace curtains that moved like pale ghosts in the breeze.

She heaved her bulk into a comfortable position on the feather mattress and then lay still, listening for the sound to repeat itself. But what sound? Not the rustling of the leaves of the trees in the nearby park; that sound was too gentle to have disturbed her.

Had it been footsteps? Yes, perhaps it had been Polly going to bed, but Polly didn't have to pass this way in order to get to her room. Constance turned over and picked up the clock from the bedside table. She brought it forward into the moonlight and stared at it. Three o'clock. No, in any case it couldn't have been Polly; she should have been in bed hours ago.

John, then. John had said that he might not return until the morning but, instead, he must have caught a late train back from Manchester and he'd gone straight to his room instead of coming in to say good night. It was so late that he wouldn't want to disturb her.

Didn't he realize that she wouldn't have minded? That she longed for him to come to her room? That she hated the fact that he had not shared a bed with her for months and that she would dearly like him to. Just to be able to lie within the circle of his arms.

Then she heard it again. It was the sound of voices – low,

but unmistakably the sound of two voices. She held her breath and lay very still and listened. The voices seemed far away and she couldn't hear what was being said, but there was that pattern of sound – of one voice and then another in some kind of conversation. But where was it coming from?

Constance pushed the eiderdown aside and positioned herself at the edge of the bed before lowering her feet to the floor. She gasped with pain when the child inside her protested and pressed, briefly, on a nerve. She walked to the door, opened it, and stood listening. Silence.

She started to walk along the passage towards the stairs that led down to the half-landing. Polly's small room was there, next to the bathroom. Did she have someone in her room with her? Could she have allowed her young sister Jane to stay for the night?

Constance stopped and gripped the stair-rail. If that was so she would leave them be, although she might say something in the morning about talking the night away and disturbing her sleep.

But while she hesitated, the conversation started again. It drifted down the stairwell from a room on the third floor and, although it was indistinct, it didn't sound like Polly and Jane. One of the voices was definitely that of a man. Could Polly have taken Albert Green up there?

What should she do?

Constance turned back and began to walk towards the stairs that led to the third floor. She knew that she ought to see if John were home yet, she ought to ask him to deal with whatever it was that was going on up there, but she didn't want Polly to get into trouble. If their maid had her sweetheart in the house in the middle of the night John would have no option but to dismiss her instantly. Constance didn't want that. She would have to deal with this herself – speak to Polly and warn her that this must never happen again.

As she went up the stairs, she found that the gloom was relieved by moonlight streaming through the open doors of the upper rooms. When she reached the top and turned to look along the landing she saw the collection of buckets, brooms, mops and dusters. Mrs Green, Polly and Jane had obviously not finished up here.

Only one door was closed and that was the door at the very end of the landing that opened into the room with the bay in the turret, the room that John had chosen as the sewing room. That's where the voices were coming from.

Constance paused with her hand on the door knob. Should she knock? This was her own house and the idea seemed ridiculous. And yet if she didn't knock, what would she find when she opened the door?

And then one of the people in the room spoke quite loudly. It was a man and judging by the cultured tones, it certainly wasn't Albert Green. Constance tried to control the sudden pounding of her heart.

'. . . but this is a marvellous place,' the voice said. 'It will do very nicely for us. It's like a tower in a fairy tale. Are you being kept prisoner here by the wicked sorceress?' He laughed. 'Rapunzel, Rapunzel, let down your hair!'

Whoever he was speaking to laughed too, lightly, flirtatiously, and Constance puzzled over the sound which was both familiar and yet strange.

'Come here,' the first voice said. 'Let me look at you.'

She knew that it would be easier to turn and walk away. To go downstairs and back to bed and lie there pretending to be asleep until morning, when she could persuade herself that this had been a dream . . . or a nightmare.

But she found herself gripping the door knob, turning it, and pushing the door open as softly and as silently as she could.

329

They hadn't heard her and they were so absorbed with each other that they didn't see her standing there. One figure, tall and dark and handsome in the warm light of the flickering candles that had been placed around the room, was Matthew Elliot, as Constance had already guessed.

But who was the woman that was standing before him? She was wearing an evening gown of dark blue velvet; smooth white shoulders rose from the low-cut neckline and her fair hair was covered with a gauzy veil.

Matthew took hold of the woman's hands and drew her towards him. 'Come here, your ladyship,' he murmured.

There was something about the way he said it that reminded Constance of that day long ago, before she had been married, when she and Matthew and John had been walking through the arcade and they had stopped to look at a display of new fabrics in a shop window.

'*Do look at that blue velvet. What do you think, John?*'

'*It's charming!*'

'*Not charming – magnificent! I can't wait to see her ladyship draped in that!*'

Constance had smiled as she had listened to their banter. She had imagined that John was going to make her an evening gown from the blue velvet. But in the months since they had been married he seemed to have forgotten about it. Once, when she reminded him, he'd said, sensibly, that they should wait until after their child was born.

But now she saw that Matthew hadn't been referring to her at all. The blue velvet had never been intended for her . . .

As her husband's friend took the smaller figure in his arms, the veil dropped back, revealing the angel-blond hair that was much too short to be that of a woman. Their faces moved together and Matthew's lips claimed the other's in a long, deep kiss.

330

The figure in the blue velvet evening dress was her husband. Constance felt something move within her, a falling sensation. She grasped the door and hung on to it with both hands. Her mouth felt dry.

'John!' she called, but no sound came from her lips.

She tried again and, at the same time, she let go of the door and took two faltering steps into the room. Still they hadn't heard her and she was sickened to see how closely they embraced and to hear their soft moans of pleasure.

She stooped to pick up one of the candlesticks from a small table and her hand shook so that the shadows leaped and danced about the room as she held it high. She felt as though her tongue had swollen up to fill her mouth but she forced herself to speak.

'John!' she cried again, and this time they heard her.

The figures sprang apart, their eyes widening with shock. Constance saw her husband snatch at the veil and try to draw it over his face but Matthew stopped his hand.

'Too late, my dear,' he said, but as he spoke he looked straight at Constance, his expression watchful. And then he took hold of John's shoulders with both his hands and turned him round to face her. 'Too late,' he said again. 'It is time to tell Constance the truth.'

Matthew stepped forward, took the candle from her, and held it steady.

She had time to register that John's initial shame was draining from his face to be replaced with defiance and excitement before the pain ripped through her. The falling sensation accelerated and something inside her gave way; a hot gush of water surged out from between her legs, soaking her robe. She clutched at her belly with both hands and she saw the expression on both of the men's faces turn to horror as she sank, moaning, to the floor.

Chapter Twenty-two

January 1908

The applause went on and on, filling the theatre, echoing round the auditorium, rising from the pit to the gods and back again to surge across the stage and engulf the exultant cast of the pantomime. They bowed and curtsied repeatedly, smiling as they took their share of the approval until, one by one, they crept away to leave her standing centre stage and alone. And then the audience went wild.

'*Nella! Nella! Nella! One more song! "The Song of the Sparrow"!*'

They stamped and shouted until she took one step forward and gestured towards the conductor of the orchestra, who raised his baton and half-turned towards the cheering crowd. He posed theatrically with his head thrown back and his arm raised until they settled in their seats again, waiting for complete silence before he turned and gave the signal for the musicians to start playing.

Nella began to sing and, at that moment, she felt as though she were Queen of England and every one of the people sitting out there was her loyal subject. She never got tired of singing this song, the song that had started it all in this very theatre just over a year ago.

When the last note had died away there was a moment of complete silence before the applause began again. But there was no encore. This was the end of the matinée and there would be another full performance later that night. Nella, even more than the others, needed to rest.

The house lights came up as the curtain swept down and, for a moment, Nella was alone on the stage before Valentino strode out from the wings and picked her up in his arms. He carried her to her dressing room and laid her gently on the day bed.

With her arms still round his neck, Nella looked up into his face. His expression was solemn and tender and infinitely proud. Proud not just of his talented wife, but proud because he had something important to do: he had to take care of her; that was his purpose in life. Nella kissed his face before he relinquished her and began to loosen the ties of her cloak. Freda, Nella's dresser, was waiting to help but Valentino gently removed the cloak himself.

'Shall I go now?' he asked.

'Yes, I have to rest before the next performance.'

Nella smiled up at her husband and for a moment he looked uncertain, then he handed the cloak to Freda and quietly left the room. Both women waited until the door closed and then they relaxed as though they had been holding their breath.

Freda hung the cloak with the other costumes behind the screen and then brought a jar of cream and a clean rag and began to remove Nella's stage make-up for her.

'I'll do that,' Nella said. 'Just pull that mirror forward a bit, will you? That's better.'

Freda watched her for a moment. 'I know some that don't bother to clean off in between shows,' she said.

'And they end up with skin like old boots. I divven't want to ruin me best feature!'

Freda left her to get on with it and lit the small gas ring. 'I've often wondered,' she said, 'where he goes.'

Nella knew whom she meant. 'Usually he just sits somewhere in the theatre and Jimmy Nelson keeps him company, but when we're here at the Palace, he gans home to tell his mother all about the show – even though she's heard it all over and over again.' Nella grinned. 'Now how about a cup of tea?'

'Coming up. And I got the cream cakes for your guests as you requested.'

'Thank you, Freda. That's very good of you.'

'It was easy. I just popped next door to the coffee shop and asked Belle McCormack to put up a nice selection. They'd do anything for you, you know. They're so grateful that you've made Valentino happy.'

Nella looked thoughtful. 'Yes, I know. And you would have thought that I should be the grateful one. I mean, getting a husband at all, being the way I am.'

'Get away with you,' Freda said, but Nella was grateful that the older woman didn't try to contradict her. Freda had worked in the theatre since she was twelve years old and, although she respected talent and hard work, she was completely realistic about her charges once they were off stage. She would never have resorted to false flattery, no matter how big the star.

Freda busied herself setting up a small table with the tea things. 'But why do you send him away? Valentino would sit in the corner and never say peep if you told him to.'

'I know. And he would watch me all the time. Never take his eyes off me. I wouldn't be able to relax.'

'I suppose not.' There was a knock at the door. 'That'll be your guests. Are you ready?'

'Yes.' Nella reached over and put the jar of cream and

335

the rags on the dressing table. 'Now, would you pass that rug?'

Freda arranged the rug over Nella's legs. Although the dressing room was cosy enough, the Palace was a draughty old theatre and it was the dead of winter. Nella cooled down so much once she came off stage that she was frightened of catching a chill.

'Come in,' Freda called, and Jimmy Nelson popped his head around the door. 'Tell Mrs Alvini I've found them.'

Freda tut-tutted. 'Miss Nicholson, you mean. Your master's wife is Miss Nicholson when she's in the theatre.'

'Sorry, keep forgetting, don't I?'

'No you don't. You're too smart to forget anything. You just do it to annoy me.' Freda wasn't angry and they both laughed. 'Now don't keep those poor folks waiting in that draughty passage, show them in.'

The door opened further and Constance's housemaid, Polly, walked in, followed by Albert Green. Nella smiled a greeting.

'I'll go now,' Jimmy said. 'But save me a cream cake, Freda.'

'I might.' She shut the door after him and began to pour the tea.

'Sit down, won't you?' Nella said to her guests. 'Albert, would you bring those two chairs forward? You got me letter, then?'

'I did, thank you, Miss Nicholson. And the tickets. It's very kind of you,' Polly said.

Polly sat on the edge of her chair. She looked very smart and Nella wondered if Constance had had some influence on her taste. She wore a black and white check three-quarter-length coat over a grey skirt. Her black hat was tied in place with a wispy bit of veil. Nella saw that Polly was the kind of girl who, realizing that her face was never going to be her

336

fortune, had decided to make the best of her trim figure.

And a very nice figure it was. Now my face and voice with a figure like that, Nella thought, and there'd be no end to the kind of roles I could play.

Albert was even better dressed than his sweetheart, Nella noticed with surprise. Polly's clothes were stylish but cheap; Albert's suit looked like it was made from a very nice piece of cloth. Like something Valentino or Frank would favour. She wondered how Albert could afford such a suit on a railway clerk's pay.

Freda had given the young couple a cup of tea each and had placed the cream cakes on a small table near by. Albert was eyeing them with delight. 'Go on, help yerself,' Nella said. 'You mustn't mind if I don't join you but all I take is a cup of tea between shows.'

'It was wonderful!' Polly said suddenly. 'I couldn't believe it when everything went round and the kitchen just seemed to turn into fairyland and you came up out of that silver cauldron looking like a fairy princess!'

'No, Polly,' Albert contradicted. 'Miss Nicholson was the fairy godmother, she wasn't a princess.'

'I know that. But she looked so beautiful, just floating there above the mist.'

Nella smiled. She hadn't been floating anywhere: Harry wouldn't risk her in the wires, so the effect had all been stage mist and optical illusion. But she certainly had popped up out of nowhere. She had balanced herself on a piece of stage machinery: a lift that came up from below the stage, far too rapidly for Nella's liking.

'And this is a treat too,' Polly said. 'Coming to meet you backstage like this. We waited in our seats like you said, and it was so exciting when that young lad came and told us you were ready to see us.' Then the girl's smile faded a little. 'But

337

I think I know why. I mean it wasn't just to talk about the show, was it?'

Nella was grateful that she didn't have to explain herself. 'No, Polly. I can see that you've guessed why I want to talk to you.'

'Of course. You want to know about Mrs Edington. I'll tell you what I can.' She glanced at Freda, who had taken a seat half behind the screen and had started on mending and repairing some stage costumes.

Nella smiled and said, 'It's all right, Polly. Freda nivver repeats anything she hears in the dressing room. She would hev lost her job in the theatre long ago if she hadn't learned to be discreet. So,' her smile faded, 'tell me, is Constance well?'

Polly thought for a moment and then said, 'She isn't ill. But the birth was difficult.'

'She had a bad time?'

'Yes. You know it was early. But the doctor said that twins often come a little sooner than one baby.'

'Twins . . . two girls . . .' Nella breathed.

'Yes, and they're so beautiful. They're like two little angels – big blue eyes and fair, curly hair. Oh, Miss Nicholson, if only you could see them!'

'If only. But, you know, I've tried.'

'I know. And I felt dreadful turning you away but she wasn't well – really she wasn't – and Mr Edington was quite right to say she must have no visitors. He didn't even allow his Aunt Muriel and his cousin Esther to visit until just before Christmas, and then he sat with them and watched over her the whole time.'

'Why did he do that?'

Polly frowned. 'In case they tired her out, I suppose.'

'But Mrs Edington's a lot better now, isn't she?' Albert said suddenly. 'I mean, she's started going out again.'

'Out?' Nella asked. 'Does she gan visiting? Does Mr Edington take her out?'

'No,' Polly said. She looked troubled. 'In fact I'm not sure if he knows about it.'

Nella saw that the girl was torn between her loyalty to John Edington and her obvious fondness for Constance. 'Tell me, Polly, tell me what's the matter,' she said.

'Oh, I don't think that there's anything the matter. It's just that before Christmas, about the same time that Mrs Barton and her daughter came to see the babies, Mrs Edington started to go for long walks again.'

'Constance always liked walking. Perhaps that's a sure sign that she's getting better.'

'Yes . . . well . . . perhaps. But the weather's been dreadful and she stays out so long. It's almost as if she doesn't want to come back to the nursery.'

'She doesn't want to be with her babies?' Nella was puzzled. She had imagined that Constance would be a loving mother.

'No – I mean, yes. It's hard to explain,' Polly said. 'Sometimes Mrs Edington will spend hours just . . . just looking at them. And then other times she stays away for hours and leaves everything to Flo.'

'Flo?'

'The nurserymaid.'

'I can't understand it.'

Albert cleared his throat and Polly glanced at him and said, 'Mrs Green, Albert's mother, says we're not to worry, that Mrs Edington'll come round in time – that a lot of women are a bit strange after childbirth.'

'Let's hope she's right,' Nella said. 'But, meanwhile, I want you to do me a favour.'

'If I can. What is it?'

'The next time I come calling I want you to let me in.'

339

Polly looked as though she was about to protest and Nella hurried on, 'Now wait a minute, pet – just listen. If Mr Edington is at home just tip me the wink and I'll go straight away. But if he isn't, then divven't tell yer mistress I'm there, divven't given her a chance to think about it, just take me to see her and I'll try to find out what's bothering her. You do want to help her, don't you?'

Polly took so long to answer that Nella thought her loyalty to John Edington was such that she couldn't allow herself to deceive him. But eventually she nodded. 'All right,' she said.

After Polly and Albert had gone Nella tried to sleep but she couldn't stop thinking about Constance. She could just about understand her friend not receiving visitors, especially if her husband was making difficulties, but she could not understand why Constance had not replied to her letters.

Well, she *had* replied to the wedding invitation. Constance had sent a brief note saying that she regretted that she would not be able to attend the ceremony in St Mary's Roman Catholic Cathedral nor the wedding breakfast at Alvini's. She was still not quite strong enough after the birth of the twins to face such a big social occasion, she explainèd, and, of course, John would not feel that it was proper to come without her. She hoped that Nella would understand and she wished her and Valentino every happiness. She had sent them a beautiful Crown Derby tea service.

Had Constance ever received the letters, she wondered now. It occurred to her that John could have been intercepting them. She ought to have asked Polly. But would Polly say anything that might imply criticism of John Edington? Suddenly Nella had the strangest feeling that whatever was the matter with Constance might not be so much a result of childbirth as something that had happened between husband and wife.

Even though her rest had been so disturbed, Nella's performance that evening was as good, if not better, than ever. Once she stepped on to the stage, once the curtains rose and the show began, she was able to leave her everyday life behind her and lose herself in the wonderful world of make-believe. The lights, the music, the give and take of the other performers and, above all, the wonderful warm feeling that reached towards her from the auditorium, never failed to uplift her.

Afterwards, after the last encore, after the audience had streamed out reluctantly into the Haymarket, Valentino picked her up and carried her out of the theatre and into the entrance of Alvini's next door, then on up the stairs.

The restaurant was still busy and Nella glimpsed the head waiter dealing with a group of rowdy, well-dressed young men. In that brief glimpse she had before Valentino swept on up the stairs, she thought that one of them looked familiar. They seemed to be arguing over the amount of their bill but, as usual, Patrick McCormack was being both firm and courteous. Nella had no doubt that the incident would end without trouble.

On the next floor she noticed that the doors of the private dining rooms were all closed, which meant that they were occupied, and she wondered, as she often did, about the lives of the women who were taken there. In spite of her own deformity and what it had meant to her chances in life, she pitied the poor souls who had to rely on beauty alone.

The last flight of stairs took them to the family's apartment at the very top of the building. For the moment they were living there. Their married home was Valentino's old bedroom, which was large enough to house a sofa, a small table and an armchair. But they took their meals with Madame Alvini and Gianfranco. Meals which Madame Alvini liked to prepare herself, unless they were more than usually late – in which

341

case Frank would insist that she go to bed and he would have a tray sent up from the restaurant.

Tonight Valentino's mother was waiting. The table was set with a large tureen of oxtail soup, bread, apple pie and a jug of cream. Nella was ravenous as she always was after the show, but she wondered how long she could go on eating meals like this before the little lost sparrow became a plump little partridge. If she didn't do justice to the meal Madame Alvini would be hurt. Valentino ate like a horse – and that was another problem. The more he ate at night the longer he stayed awake and wanted to talk to her about the show he had just seen and, particularly, her part in it. She would have to think of something if she were to get sufficient rest.

But those worries were nothing compared to the uneasy feeling she had about Constance . . .

Gerald Sowerby staggered out of the dining room and down the stairs. His companions, Warren Carmichael and Leonard Russell, went ahead of him. They were sniggering because they thought they had got the better of McCormack over the matter of the drinks bill, but Gerald was not so sure.

True, the headwaiter had seemed to allow them to convince him that they had had only four bottles of wine. But he had given in too easily. Perhaps he had seen Warren forcing the cork back into one of the bottles and hiding it under the table earlier, or later slipping it into the inside pocket of his opera cloak.

Then, instead of taking issue with them and causing an unpleasant scene, Gerald guessed that the cost of the wine had simply been spread over the rest of the items on the bill. Carmichael hadn't really checked it, he had been so obsessed with the idea of cheating Alvini's out of a bottle of wine.

'Hurry up, Sowerby!' Leonard Russell called. The other

342

two were waiting on the pavement outside.

'What's keeping him?' Carmichael asked.

'Perhaps he's gone upstairs to the private rooms – perhaps he's got an assignation up there,' Russell replied.

They both turned to look at him as he joined them. Their smiles were foolish but Gerald was always aware that he was the outsider. They both came from much wealthier families than his own and if they needed a butt for their jokes it was usually he.

'What exactly do you mean by that?' He tried to sound aggressive but was aware that he was enunciating his words a little too carefully.

'Oo-ooh! He's cross with me!' Russell said. 'I simply meant that I saw you watching that big booby Valentino carrying the woman up the stairs, and I wondered if you fancied going up and showing him how.'

Gerald relaxed and laughed with them. 'Even if I wanted to show him I don't think I'd succeed,' he said.

Russell frowned. 'What do you mean by that? Something the matter with you?'

'Not me; nothing wrong with my performance.' Gerald leered suggestively. 'But I'm not even sure if Alvini's got what it takes to please a lady – and even if he has got one, I shouldn't think he knows what to do with it.'

There was a moment's silence as his words penetrated the drunken fog and then both his companions hooted with laughter. Then Carmichael turned and called loudly for a cab.

'Good night, Sowerby,' he said, and he and Russell made their way across the frosty cobbles to the cab stand.

On their way, Leonard Russell caught the heel of his shoe in a metal tramline. Gerald watched with amusement as he struggled to free himself while one of the new electric trams, known locally as a coffin, rumbled towards him. Carmichael reached out to help, the bottle of wine fell from his cloak and smashed on the road and he collapsed with laughter. In the end, the waiting cabby had to run and pull Russell free. Gerald heard his friend's howl of pain turn to rage as he realized that he had left his shoe behind for the tram to run over.

Just before he followed Carmichael into the cab Russell turned and yelled indignantly, 'Thanks a lot, Sowerby, thanks for your help, I'm sure!' Then he turned and vomited on to the cobbles.

Gerald lit a cigar before strolling over to get a cab for himself. On the way home he thought about what Russell had said earlier. It was true, he had watched as Valentino Alvini had carried the woman upstairs. But what had intrigued him was that he thought he knew who the woman was. And yet he could hardly believe it. She had been bundled up in a voluminous velvet cloak but her hood had fallen back to reveal the pale blonde ringlets tumbling down over Valentino's arm.

It was the luxuriant hair that had attracted him. And then he had seen her face – or rather her profile. His admiration had turned to incredulity and then disgust. Impossible as it seemed, the well-dressed, attractive woman being carried upstairs in her Valentino's arms was none other than Nella, the little humpback skivvy who had left the Sowerbys' house on Rye Hill one night about a year ago and never returned. Her features may have filled out – the cheek he had glimpsed had been more rounded than before – but the profile was the same. She still had the sharp nose and the pointed chin of a witch.

Now, on the way home, he thought about her again and he couldn't even begin to imagine the circumstances that had brought her to Alvini's. Suddenly he recalled the way she had looked at him that day in Annabel's bedroom . . . when had it been? He couldn't remember for sure but he had known in that instant that she despised him. But why? He had never harmed her. She'd had no cause to look at him like that ... unless ... unless ...

Gerald remembered the other little maid who had left their employment a short while before Nella had gone. Constance, her name had been. Had the girls been friends? Had Constance told the other one what he had done? Had the little witch sworn to put a curse on him? In spite of himself he shivered.

In that case it was just as well that the creature had left his mother's employment. Valentino was welcome to her.

Chapter Twenty-three

Constance pushed the gate and found that it was blocked by a drift of snow. The path across the moor was almost clear, with heaps of grey-looking sludge lying amongst the brownish straggles of grass but, here in the sheltered grounds of Lodore House, the thaw had been slower. She pushed harder and the gate gave way, skidding across the snow so quickly that she almost fell into the garden. She stopped to take her breath.

The air she gulped in was cold, catching at her throat painfully. The garden looked desolate. Although the bare branches of the trees lent a certain stark beauty, the shrubs had grown unchecked and the rose bushes remained unpruned with a few late roses, their petals brown-veined and shrivelled, clinging to the thorny stems. Constance was sad that her brother seemed to care so little for the garden that their father had loved.

She almost turned to go back at that point, but curiosity got the better of her. She had no intention of making her presence known. She would look and then leave again, just as she had the last time she had been here a few weeks ago, just before Christmas . . .

That time she hadn't planned to come at all. She had been driven out of her own house by her ever-growing sense of restlessness – and by anger and the need to try to forget the remarks of John's Aunt Muriel and her daughter, Esther. The two women had peered into the babies' cribs, their faces pinched with curiosity.

Aunt Muriel had been holding her breath. She'd let it out slowly and remarked, 'Fair hair.'

'And blue eyes,' Esther added unnecessarily.

Aunt Muriel straightened up. 'They're fine babies, Constance,' she said grudgingly. She paused and added, 'But they did come a little early, didn't they?'

John stepped forward. 'Dr Mason told me that that's not unusual for twins,' he said.

Constance could barely control her anger. She knew that John was anxious to assure them that everything was normal because he never wanted anybody to know what had happened that terrible night in the turret room – what had caused the shock which sent her into labour. But she also knew that Muriel Barton had been implying that the twins had come when they did because she, Constance, had been pregnant before she got married. She realized then that the poisonous woman had even been hinting at that at the wedding breakfast . . . and perhaps at something more.

After they had gone and John had made some excuse to leave the house, Constance had left Florence in charge of the nursery and set out to walk off her rage. The walk had become longer and longer until she'd found herself halfway across the Town Moor.

And then, of course, it had seemed inevitable that she should go on and enter the gardens of Lodore House. The day had been bright, and a fresh fall of snow had sparkled in the sunshine. Constance had felt a sense of exhilaration and excitement as she'd peered surreptitiously through the windows of her childhood home.

The sitting room at the side of the house had a large bay

window and she pressed herself close to one of the stone stanchions and peered round into the room. A fire blazed in the hearth and, in one corner, a giant Christmas tree shimmered with tinsel and shining glass ornaments. The people in the room were too interested in the baby sitting on Iris's knee to thank about glancing towards the window. Constance was safe to observe them.

Iris still looks pasty, Constance thought, but she is obviously devoted to the sturdy, rosy-cheeked child on her knee. Constance couldn't tell whether the dark-haired baby was a boy or a girl but her brother's child looked to be some months older than her own daughters.

Robert stood behind his wife and child and Constance couldn't see his expression. He was bending towards the baby and dangling something that twisted to and fro on the end of a ribbon. It was a silver rattle and the baby followed its progress with its eyes. The child was laughing with delight. The scene of domestic bliss was being played out before Robert's grandparents, Captain and Mrs Meakin, and a middle-aged couple whom Constance took to be Iris's parents. They all stared at the little family group with self-satisfied absorption.

The pain that gripped her heart was almost physical. For the first time since the birth of her own babies it struck her that there was no one to hold her and her daughters in such a cherished gaze. Their father rarely visited the nursery and her children had no grandparents to dote on them. Her eyes had filled with the tears that never seemed to be far away these days.

The scene before her had blurred and, sobbing convulsively, she had turned and run from the garden.

Today the scene was different. The tree and the Christmas decorations had gone and only a small fire burned in the hearth. At first Constance thought the room was empty until she saw a movement in one of the armchairs near the fire. A man sat there reading by the light of a lamp on a table nearby; the movement that had attracted her attention had been the turning of a page. Was it Robert?

She stared at him. The figure in the chair was so still that she thought he might have fallen asleep. She pressed her face right up to the glass. She saw that it was her brother and that one hand held the book steady on his knee while the other rested along the arm of his chair and supported his head. His attitude suggested weariness or dejection.

Then, without warning, he looked up and saw her. He rose to his feet and the book fell to the floor. She stayed long enough to see him begin to walk towards the door of the room, before she turned and began to retrace her steps through the garden. She had almost reached the gate on to the moor when she heard him call out to her.

'Constance! Don't go!' When she turned to face him he stopped and reached a hand out towards her. 'For goodness' sake, don't run off like you did last time. I'm all alone here. At least come in and take a cup of tea with me!'

She stood watching him for a moment. He looked sad, she decided. Why should her half-brother look so sad? Slowly she began to walk towards him.

It was a different little maid who brought them tea and a plate of rich fruit cake. Constance wondered how many unfortunate girls Iris had seen off since the last – and first – time she had visited them in late spring. This one seemed cheerful enough, but perhaps that was because Iris and the baby – a son, Robert had told her – were away staying with her parents in Berwick.

When the girl had gone, Robert built up the fire and then sat down and smiled at Constance. 'It's so good to see you,' he said.

Constance sipped her tea before replying. 'Robert, what did you mean just now when you asked me not to run off like the last time?'

He looked at her solemnly. 'I saw you that day, looking in at us. But before I realized fully who it was, you had taken off. None of the others had seen you so I didn't say anything.'

'I don't suppose Iris would have made me welcome.' She realized how crabby she must have sounded and added, 'I'm sorry.'

But she noticed Robert didn't contradict her. 'I thought it was because my grandparents were here. I thought that perhaps you might . . . you might . . .'

'Bear them a grudge?'

'Perhaps.'

This time it was Constance who made no contradiction. 'But, Robert, how could you have seen me?' she asked. 'You had your back to me. You were engrossed with your son.'

'It was Douglas who saw you.' He smiled when he saw Constance's frown of puzzlement. 'He was following the movement of the rattle with his eyes. He's so alert, you know! Well, anyway, he suddenly looked beyond the rattle towards the window, as if he had seen something. I looked round and saw you, you had a hand to your eyes. I barely had time to register the fact that it was you before you turned and hurried away.'

'I see.' Constance smiled. 'Clever baby.'

Robert's response was immediate. 'Oh, Constance, he is! He's so bright. I think I spend more time in the nursery than Iris does . . . and I hate having to leave him and go to the office!'

'And what does Iris think of that?'

'She encourages me.' He sounded embarrassed but, at the same time, pleased. 'She resents the time I am away at

351

business, anyway. She would rather we spent the whole day together.'

'And you? Do you want to spend the whole day with Iris?'

Robert looked at her keenly. 'Constance, I know that she didn't make you welcome. I was very sorry about that, and it's going to be a problem—'

'Why a problem?'

'Well, now that I've found you again, I want to keep in touch. And this time I'm not going to allow you to leave without your telling me where you live. But Iris . . . Iris . . .'

'She doesn't like me.'

'No, it's not that. I mean, well, it's not just you. She is jealous of anybody that I spend my time with. She seems to need to keep me all to herself. In fact that's why I am abandoned here alone now. My grandfather thinks that I am neglecting the business. He persuaded Iris's parents to ask her to visit them – on the pretext of allowing them to spend time with their grandson. But it's really so that she will not distract me.'

'And did Iris agree to this plan?'

'She's a dutiful daughter and a fond mother. She found it hard to resist her parents' desire to make a fuss of Douglas.' He smiled self-mockingly. 'But she was very reluctant to leave me behind!'

'And do you mind such possessiveness?'

'I wish she could be different . . . but I love her. I don't know exactly why. Who can define or explain love?' He laughed self-consciously.

Constance remembered how patient Robert had been with his wife when she was being difficult with the housemaid. She said without thinking, 'So you're prepared to put up with her high-handed ways?'

He looked taken aback and Constance thought that she

might have gone too far. 'Robert, I'm sorry. I shouldn't criticize your wife. I promise that I won't do it again. There, that's the second time I've had to apologize.'

Her brother looked away for a moment and then he said, 'My little family is so important to me. When we were all together – my father, your mother . . . you and me – life was perfect then, wasn't it?'

'Yes.'

'I think I've been trying to make such a home again . . . will go on doing so . . . if we have other children. Do you know what I mean?'

'Of course I do.'

He looked concerned. 'But I want you to know that my grandparents were very kind to me.'

'I'm sure they were. But—'

'So I could never tell them how much I missed Mama.'

'You mean—'

'Your mother. I hardly remember my own. I think about her – my own mother – more now that I have a child of my own. I'm so sad that she and Father are not here to see their grandson.'

'Oh, Robert, I know how you feel.'

'Do you?' At that moment she would have told him about her own children and her own feelings of loss but he hurried on, 'And Mama Agnes, too. She always behaved towards me as if I were her own child.'

'I know that she loved you.'

'And I loved her.' Suddenly he grinned. 'How fortunate that my father chose to go to Le Touquet!'

Constance smiled. She remembered how, when they were children, their father would begin their favourite story with those words. He would regale them with the tale of how he and Robert had been walking up a steep path from the beach when an old lady in a bath chair had come hurtling towards them. Robert had tugged at his father's sleeve and pointed in wonderment as the chair drew nearer and the old lady's terror became evident. A young woman was running down the path behind the chair but it was obvious that she wasn't going to catch up with it.

Richard Bannerman pushed his son aside on to the grassy bank and grabbed at the chair, hanging on to it for dear life as the young woman caught up with it and collided with him. She only had time to breathe her thanks into his waistcoat before the old woman turned round and, instead of being grateful, began to hurl abuse.

At this point Constance and Robert would always ask, 'What did the old woman say?' and their father would reply, 'Words that I'm glad my little boy couldn't understand!'

The old woman, Mrs Stanton, was a wealthy widow who had come to Le Touquet hoping to relieve her arthritis by partaking of the mineral salts of its waters. The young woman had been Agnes Lowe, her companion, who had been instantly dismissed over the runaway bath chair.

No matter that it had been her employer's own fault; when Agnes had advised against taking the steep path, Mrs Stanton had grabbed at the wheels wilfully, and set off anyway. Agnes was to take her back to the hotel and pack her own bags and be gone. It would be easy enough to find another improverished, orphaned English girl amongst the English expatriate community who would be grateful for the pittance paid by Mrs Stanton.

Richard Bannerman used to laugh when he told them he had been tempted to carry Agnes off immediately and leave the difficult old person stranded on the beach to be carried away by the incoming tide. But Agnes's sweet nature had prevailed and they had taken Mrs Stanton back to her hotel together. She had even stayed with the old ogre until the next unfortunate companion was established in her duties.

After that their father had always ended the story by telling them that he had offered Agnes a new position on the spot. That of looking after Robert – and himself. Agnes had accepted the job of nursemaid and, before very long, his heart as well, he said. By the time they returned from Le Touquet, Agnes had become the second Mrs Bannerman.

Constance and Robert remained silent for a while, each lost in memories of their shared, happy childhood. The fire crackled in the hearth and, outside, the sky darkened. It was only when the windowpane began to rattle in a rising wind that Constance's reverie was broken.

She looked at the clock on the mantelpiece with alarm. It was half-past four and it would take her more than an hour to get home, longer if the weather worsened. She would not be in time to feed Beatrice and Amy . . . Florence would have to manage with the feeding bottles again . . .

'Constance, what is it?' Her brother had risen from his chair and he looked concerned.

'Mm?'

'You look worried.' Again she could have told him about her own children but she simply said, 'I've stayed too long. I should go now.'

'I'll take you home.'

'Take me?'

'I have an automobile – such fun! Have you ever ridden in one?'

'Yes.' She saw his questioning look and added, 'A . . . a friend of my husband owns one. He took me to the church on my wedding day.'

* * *

John knocked peremptorily on the door of the nursery and opened it without waiting for an answer. He didn't want to give Constance the chance to send him away. She was sitting on the padded seat that formed the corner of the fender, holding some baby clothes towards the fire. Florence and Polly held a twin each; the babies were wrapped in large white towels. They had just come out of the bath. The room was filled with the scent of soap and baby powder.

He caught his breath. The scene looked so peaceful, so normal, such as was enacted in hundreds of other households every evening. How could he fail to be happy? How could he fail to love the beautiful children that Constance had given him? He felt a deep regret that he didn't spend more time here . . . he knew that it was his conscience that was keeping him away. For at the heart of this picture there was a lie.

Constance didn't speak; she just looked towards him politely. She was always so icily polite.

'Will you be long?' he asked.

'Long?'

'Will our daughters be in bed soon?'

'Yes, soon.'

'I should like to speak to you.'

'Well, speak.'

'Alone.' He controlled a spasm of anger. 'I mean alone.'

'Flo and I can finish in here,' Polly said. 'You run along if you want to, Mrs Edington.'

'No, that's all right, Polly. I should like to see Amy and Beatrice into bed.'

John saw the two young women exchange looks. Constance's visits to the nursery were erratic. She came when it suited her and could not be counted on to stay. Tonight it suited her to stay here and thwart him.

'We'll just be another ten minutes or so, Mr Edington.' It

was the nurserymaid, Florence, who spoke, no doubt worried that he would blame her for any delay. She flushed when she saw Constance's look of displeasure.

Amy, who was on Florence's knee, began to grizzle as if she had sensed the new tensions in the erstwhile cosy room. Beatrice turned her head to look at her sister and gave out a bellow of rage. John watched helplessly as both his daughters began to sob, egging each other on, unwilling to be the first to be comforted.

He saw a smile pass across Constance's face before she said, 'It may take a little longer to settle them now, John.'

Florence and Polly looked down at the floor and Constance watched him expectantly. He bowed his head in acknowledgement of her victory and left the room.

Once her daughters were settled in their cribs Constance told Florence that she could go down to the kitchen and have her tea with Polly; she herself would be happy to sit here until dinner was ready.

As soon as their regular breathing signalled that Amy and Beatrice were sleeping soundly, Constance left her chair and went to look at them. As usual the tears came to her eyes. They were so beautiful, and she wished she could love them wholeheartedly as they deserved. Mrs Green had assured her that many new mothers took time to adjust and it was quite normal to feel weepy now and then. Especially after such an unexpectedly protracted labour.

But Constance could honestly say that the physical pain she had suffered was easily forgotten. She was young and healthy and she had certainly been pampered throughout her pregnancy.

It was the other events of that dreadful night that she was still trying to come to terms with. The nightmare of finding

357

her husband dressed like a woman and in the arms of another man. Even now she only half understood what kind of man John might be. And there was no one she could ask, no one she could confide in.

After that first shocked moment Matthew had been the first to realize what was happening. John had looked utterly horrified – and helpless. He'd stood there with one frilled strap of the ridiculous blue velvet gown falling down his shoulder, and the white flower in his hair – yes, there'd been a flower in his hair – was swooping down towards one eye.

Even in her pain, Constance had felt the urge to laugh. In fact she thought that she probably had laughed but the hysterical sounds she made had been mistaken for cries of pain and terror.

'John!' Matthew had commanded. 'I think your child will be born tonight. Go and get changed as quickly as you can and then rouse Polly. I shall go for your doctor.'

Neither of them had thought to lift her on to the sofa or even give her a cushion or two. She had heard a whispered conversation at the door before she had been left alone. She didn't know how long she'd lain there, she only knew that her birth pains had started.

When John returned, Polly was with him. 'When I came home I brought some samples of cloth upstairs,' Constance heard him saying as they entered the room. 'Your mistress must have heard me and she came up to see what I was doing. She shouldn't have climbed these stairs, should she?'

Polly seemed to accept this attempt at an explanation. 'Didn't you think to take her back to bed?' she said. And that was as near as she'd ever been to criticizing him. And, of course, Constance could never tell Polly, or anyone, what she had just witnessed and what had really brought on the labour.

And how could she ever explain to Mrs Green that her state

of mind was not just that of a new mother? That it was more than just feeling weepy after childbirth? For since her daughters had been born – two babies instead of one – there was something else that was troubling her. Something so crazy to contemplate that she feared she was losing her mind.

She looked at her daughters now. They were turned towards each other even though they were in separate cribs. 'Faces like little cherubs,' Polly would say, 'and golden hair like halos.' Albert was fond of remarking that they were like peas in a pod. But they weren't. And surely it couldn't only be Constance who had noticed the differences . . .

Yes, their hair was blonde. But Amy's hair was as pale as an angel's whereas Beatrice's hair sometimes glinted red-gold. Both were healthy but already it was plain that Amy was going to be dainty, whereas Beatrice was more robust. Amy was easy to please, easy to placate, whereas her sister, older by ten minutes, was more demanding and less biddable even at this age. And there was something else about Beatrice . . .

When Polly informed her that the evening meal was ready, Constance said that she felt tired after the long walk she had taken earlier and that she would be grateful if Polly would bring her a tray to the nursery.

'Oh, and tell Florence she can keep you company until it's time for the twins' last feeding bottle,' she added.

Polly hesitated. 'What shall I tell Mr Edington?'

'Tell him what I have just told you. And say that I hope he enjoys his dinner.'

When she had finished her meal, she sat by the nursery fire until Florence returned with the bottles and they managed the feed together. And, even then, when the girls were washed and changed and put down for the night, and Florence was yawning and glancing meaningfully towards her bed, even then Constance lingered until she heard two sets of footsteps mounting the third-floor stairs.

On the floor above her the door to the room that she would never set foot in again opened and closed. She knew that John would be there for hours – probably all night.

Only then did Constance leave the nursery.

Sleep didn't come easily. Constance tried to push from her mind all her anxieties about John and her daughters, and what their life together had become.

She tried to imagine life as she thought it should be. John hurrying home to her each night and taking her in his arms . . . Going up to the nursery with her to play with their much-loved children . . . The girls looking just like their father . . .

She realized that she had sobbed out loud and she turned her face into the pillow. She remained like that, shoulders tense, crying silently until she managed to banish all disturbing thoughts from her mind.

But then, as so often, another image came to disturb her and she was frightened by her own response to it. She tried to resist, she knew that she ought to, but the image was insistent. And finally, with a sigh, she relaxed and allowed herself the luxury of thinking about Frank Alvini.

It was always the same. She saw his kind, intelligent face, his dark eyes, the way they seemed to search and find answers without his having to say a word.

As she drifted off to sleep Constance prayed that she would not dream.

Chapter Twenty-four

'Why don't you stop pacing about and tell me why you are so agitated?'

Matthew was sitting by the fire in the sewing room. He looked up at John curiously. He had never seen him so fretful. Was there any way he could have heard the news? No, there had been no announcement . . . so it was something else.

'John, did you hear me?'

'I'm sorry.' He came and sat on the ottoman at the other side of the hearth but he looked as if he might take off and start pacing again any minute.

Matthew sighed. He had planned that tonight would be so different. He had wanted it to be something special because he had something to tell John. But it was obvious that his news would have to wait. 'So, tell me what's upsetting you,' he said.

John sat hunched and miserable; he stared into the fire rather than look at him. He looks like a cross child, Matthew thought. Or a child who has been crossed. He smiled at his own whimsy.

John turned his head and looked at him. 'I'm glad that you are amused,' he said.

'For goodness' sake, don't snap at me; just tell me what the matter is.' Matthew knew he had sounded sharp but he was pleased to see that it had had the required effect.

'It's Constance,' John said without further preamble.

Matthew was puzzled. Not surprisingly there had been a coldness between husband and wife ever since that dreadful night when she had found John and Matthew together. But now that he was a father, John had not seemed to mind too much that he and Constance were living like strangers under the same roof. 'Is she still refusing to talk to you about anything but the essentials?' Matthew asked.

'Yes.'

'Surely you had realized that you might have to explain one day? Hadn't you prepared her at all?'

John looked at him. 'What are you talking about?'

Matthew stared back, equally at a loss. At last he said, 'I thought you were upset because you had been trying to make things better with Constance . . . trying to explain what kind of man you are.'

'How could I ever do that?'

'It's not impossible. And if you promised her that you would always look after her – that, in fact, she might be lucky—'

'Lucky!'

'Well, there would never be another woman, would there? There would be no mistresses.'

John's smile was rueful. 'You don't know Constance, do you? I have come to realize that my wife wants much more from marriage than to be looked after. But that's not the point. I wanted to talk to her about something in particular and, as she often does, she managed to evade me.'

Matthew saw his plans for the next few hours evaporating. He leaned forward and took up a bottle of red wine from the hamper at his feet. 'I'll open this and pour us both a glass. And you must tell me what it is that is ruining our evening together.'

John had the grace to look contrite. He waited until Matthew had handed him his glass of wine and then he began, 'When I came home today Polly told me that Constance had gone for a walk.'

'In this January weather?'

'She's always liked walking. That's how we met her, remember? Anyway, it was getting dark and cold, and I suppose I was worried—'

'You only suppose?'

'Don't tease. Yes, she is my wife and the mother of my children; I'm not heartless. I was worried. So, not knowing what to do, I walked along to the end of the terrace only to find her waving goodbye to a man in an automobile.'

'She had been out with a man? Constance?' Matthew supposed that he should not have been surprised. After all, Constance was young, beautiful and healthy, and John had not proved to be the husband she had hoped for.

'She said it was her brother.'

'Aah.'

Matthew watched John's eyes widen. 'You believe that?' John asked.

'Yes.'

'Why?'

'Because I knew. I knew Constance had a brother – half-brother, actually – and I thought it might not be too long before they found each other.'

'Why have you never told me?'

'Because I didn't think you were interested. Oh, I didn't know from the start; I only found out later. But does this worry you?'

'Why should it worry me?'

'Because Constance is not the friendless orphan that you – we – thought she was. There is someone to care what – what

363

sort of man she has married; someone she may confide in.'

'You'd better tell me what you know.'

'I will. But first let's dive into this hamper that I've brought. There're all kinds of treats in there. Do you remember when we used to have feasts in my father's old stables?'

Matthew watched John's expression lighten and then his pleasure grow as he began to explore the contents in the hamper. What a child he was sometimes, and how easy to please. Matthew realized how very much he was going to miss him.

As they shared the game pie, the cheese savouries, the Turkish delight and the chocolate, Matthew told John as much as he had been able to find out, first, about Constance's father, Richard Bannerman, and how disaster had overtaken his family when he had gone bankrupt; and, secondly, about Constance's older half-brother, Robert, who had gone to live with his grandparents, the Meakins.

'Meakin? Do you mean Captain Meakin? But he owns a fleet of colliers,' John said. 'They must be wealthy. How did Constance and her mother end up in the workhouse?'

'The worthy couple wanted nothing to do with their son-in-law's second family. They hardened their hearts, I suppose.'

'And Robert? Did he harden his heart?'

'He was only a child himself. He can't have known what had happened to Constance. But now . . .'

John put down his wine glass. 'Do you think she will confide in him?'

'That is something you will have to find out. But I don't think so. I would judge that she has too much delicacy, too much pride. And there's something else. I think Robert Bannerman may have troubles of his own.'

John shrugged as if the other man's troubles could not possibly interest him but Matthew continued, 'The rumour is

364

that Meakin leaves everything to Robert Bannerman and that he has been neglecting matters of business: not maintaining the boats properly, painting over the rust just in time for the Lloyd's inspectors – and they aren't always as thorough as they might be. I've heard it said that Meakins are underinsured. If they're not careful they could end up in Carey Street.'

'Bankrupt?'

'That's right.'

John stared into the fire moodily. Matthew was relieved that he hadn't thought to ask how he had come by all this information. That part of the story could come later, although Matthew didn't know how much longer he could delay the telling of it.

He reached for John's glass and filled it. 'Drink up,' he said. 'And don't sit so far away from me. In fact, why don't we spread this rug on the floor like we used to in the tack room? That's right, toss those cushions down.'

He sat on the floor next to John and they made themselves comfortable amongst the blankets and the cushions.

'This is our magic place, remember,' Matthew said softly, 'our room in the tower . . . where just for the moment we can be alone together . . . and I need so much to be alone with you tonight . . .'

Nella was bone-weary and it would have been so easy just to sink into the comfortable feather mattress and go to sleep, but there was something she had to do. She lay on her side, propped up on a mound of pillows, supporting her head with one hand while she watched her husband. His eyes were closed and his breathing was even. Soon it would be safe to go. As she waited, she thought about the first night they had slept together.

She remembered that, even though Valentino's mother,

helped by his brother, Frank, had explained to her that she had nothing to fear, she hadn't been able to help worrying just a little when at last they were alone. It had been a strangely wonderful day, she remembered now, like a dream.

The wedding had been arranged to take place during the brief break before the pantomime opened. Harry had cancelled rehearsals and the whole cast came to sit on Nella's side of the cathedral. They were her family, along with Lucy, Alice, and Mr and Mrs Small and their lodgers. But Constance, the nearest person to family that Nella had ever had, had been unable to come.

On the bridegroom's side were Italian relatives from all over the north of England, along with prosperous business folk and almost the entire staff of the restaurant. Jimmy Nelson, in the best suit he had ever owned, was instructed to look after Madame Alvini and keep her supplied with clean handkerchiefs.

Outside, in the streets, crowds of people waited to catch a glimpse of the golden couple: Nella Nicholson, the famous stage star, Tyneside's own Little Sparrow, and Valentino, the handsome master of Alvini's.

When Harry escorted Nella down the aisle there was a gasp of wonder from the congregation. Her ivory satin dress was covered with hundreds of seed pearls and the train, carried by two small Italian cousins, was arranged so skilfully that it completely obscured the shape of her shoulders.

The candles, the incense, the scent of the massed white flowers made Nella think she was living a romantic dream. Valentino was waiting with Frank by the altar and, when he turned to face her, and she lifted back her veil, his expression of wonder was enough to fill her heart with love for the rest of her days.

When they left the church the crowd cheered and threw

rice and flower petals. The cheering continued as the carriage took them up Grainger Street, then along Neville Street, where the cast from the Empire came out to wave them by. Another crowd was waiting in the Haymarket and they roared with delight when Valentino descended from the carriage and then lifted Nella up into his arms to carry her into Alvini's.

During the wedding breakfast he had not stopped smiling until the last guest had gone. He had been almost like an actor, Nella thought, playing the part of the happy bridegroom. He knew what was expected of him. But once they were alone the smile had been replaced by a slight frown.

In fact there had been a moment when he had seemed puzzled that his new wife intended to share his bedroom. When Nella had emerged from behind the screen where she had undressed and put on her nightgown, she'd found him standing frowning uncertainly in the middle of the room.

Before she could say anything there'd been a knock on the door and his mother came in carrying a tray with two cups of warm milk and honey. 'Here you are, Valentino,' she had said. 'One for you and one for your wife.'

'Ah yes, my wife.' His smile had returned and he'd climbed into the bed, which was big enough for the two of them to lie there all night without bothering each other.

He was so childlike that Nella sometimes wondered why he didn't at least want a cuddle, but she supposed that it was better that he didn't. There might just be enough manhood there to cause her trouble if he got roused.

So tonight, like every other night, he had been content to get into bed and close his eyes almost as if she wasn't there. When at last she was sure that he was fast asleep, she eased herself away from him to the edge of the bed and then lowered her feet to the floor. Her limbs jolted painfully. Even though she didn't walk about much on stage, she had to stand a lot and it was beginning to tell.

Harry had mentioned that he might devise an act for her where she could sit on a swing and move gently to and fro while she sang. She had quite liked the idea until Lucy reminded them of Rose Kelly, billed as 'The Little Flower Girl', who used to swing out over the audience tossing scented paper rose petals as she sang. Her career ended one night when she fell off the swing into the orchestra pit and broke her back. So Harry was having to think again.

By the light of the oil-lamp that was always left burning low on the bedside table, Nella reached for a large paisley shawl and draped it round herself. She pushed her feet into her slippers and left the room as quietly as she could. Late as it was, she could hear sounds from the restaurant echoing up from below, so Frank would not be in bed yet. Good.

He was alone and the room was quiet. He sat at the table with his books, illumined in a pool of light, and he looked up in surprise as Nella came in and shut the door behind her.

'Is something wrong?' The muscles of his face, slack with fatigue, suddenly tautened with alarm; he stood up, pushing his books aside. 'Valentino? Is he—'

'Valentino is sleeping like a baby,' Nella laughed softly. 'Why do they say that? Sleeping like a baby? The babies I remember from the workhouse seemed to cry all night and keep everybody else awake.'

'Come and sit down.' Frank pulled one of the chairs away from the table. 'I think the saying means that babies are so innocent that they have no wicked thoughts to keep them from sleeping. But the poor scraps of humanity in the workhouse were probably too hungry to sleep.'

Nella settled herself in the chair and waited until Frank resumed his place at the other side of the table. She looked at the books and papers spread out over the chenille cloth. 'You work so hard,' she said.

'It's what I want to do.' He smiled and she saw that you didn't have to be handsome to be attractive. 'But why are you out of bed when you should be sleeping?' he asked. 'Are you ill?'

'No, although it's a wonder I divven't hev indigestion every night, the amount of food yer ma expects me to eat.'

'She enjoys looking after you.'

'I know, and I'm grateful . . .'

'But?'

'Frank, I've thought about how I was gannin' to say this but there's no other way except to come right out with it. I want to leave here.'

'You want to leave Valentino? It would break his heart.'

'Divven't look at me like that. Of course I divven't want to leave Valentino. I want him to come with me. I can afford to buy me own place – and before you object, I can afford to pay people to look after us, Jimmy Nelson included. In fact I want a house big enough to allow the lad to live with us so that he can get more sleep than he does now.'

Frank stared at her. He had picked up one of his pencils and he was twisting it round. Nella noticed how well-shaped and supple his fingers were. 'That would make sense, of course,' he said, 'having Jimmy and perhaps your own personal maid to live with you and be there all the time.'

'I've already got a lass in mind for the position: Alice, a girl I used to work with. She's young but she's strong and I think I could teach her my ways.'

'Whereas my mother is old and getting weary – and she would never learn new ways!'

'God bless her, why should she? But she still wants to treat Valentino like a child . . . and me too. It might seem odd to

369

you, being the way we are, but yer brother and I are like many another married couple – we'd be better off in our own place. And you know that you would nivver hev to worry about Valentino; not while he has me.'

'Yes, I do know that and I think my mother sensed it right from the start too. She saw what kind of person you are.'

Nella grinned. 'And what kind of person is that?'

'Someone who can be trusted. Someone who would not break promises. Someone who would be loyal and true.'

'Give over!'

Frank laughed when he saw her expression. 'I'm not joking. And I think you are right about leaving here. And right to come to me; I'll explain things to my mother. She will understand that a woman wants to be mistress of her own kitchen.'

'Kitchen!' Nella assumed an expression of mock horror. 'After the years I spent in the kitchen at Rye Hill, I nivver want to set foot in a kitchen again. And if you mean cooking, then I intend to hire the best cook I can afford!'

'Then be careful that my mother does not apply for the job.'

They smiled at each other and Nella thought how much she liked this man. When he fulfilled his ambition and became a doctor, his patients would be very lucky.

'That's that, then. I'd better get back to bed,' she said.

'Wait, Nella. There's something I want to ask you.'

He looked embarrassed and Nella thought that he might be going to question her about his brother . . . about whether everything was working out all right as far as the marriage bed was concerned.

So she was surprised when he said. 'Your friend . . . the girl who came to the coffee shop that day . . .?'

'Constance?'

'Yes, Constance Edington. How did you meet her?'

She wanted to ask him why he wanted to know, but she saw that he couldn't meet her eyes. Suddenly Nella remembered Constance staring down into an empty teacup when she had mentioned Frank and she felt the same twinge of unease as she had done that day. She hoped she was wrong. There was no hope down that path.

She saw that Frank was gripping his pencil so tightly that she feared it might snap. 'Constance and I worked together at the Sowerbys' house,' she told him. 'But we first met when we were children.'

'How?' At last his curiosity made him look up and Nella saw that he was trying to imagine how two such different children could possibly have crossed paths.

'In the workhouse when she arrived there with her ma.'

'I see. Poor Constance.'

'Poor me!'

'Of course . . . I'm sorry.'

'Oh, divvent worry, I know what you mean.' Nella sighed. 'Constance is a lady, there's no question. And me? Well, I don't even know who me feyther is.' She grinned ruefully. 'See? I can't even speak proper!'

'Don't, Nella. You have done very well and I'm sure Constance values you for what you are.'

'Do you, Frank? Well, I always hoped so. But since she got married I just divvent know.'

'She married John Edington.'

'You know him?'

'He comes here, to the restaurant . . . or rather to one of the private dining rooms.'

'With a woman?' She couldn't disguise her dismay.

'No, not with a woman. With a – a friend of his, Matthew Elliot. They – they like to be alone together.'

371

He looked at her as if he wanted to say more and, after a short silence, she answered his unspoken question. 'I understand.'

'Do you?'

'I've learned a lot in the theatre besides how to work an audience, Frank, and I've nothing against those fellows. Live and let live is what Harry says. But I still can't help thinking poor, poor Constance.'

'Yes, poor Constance,' Frank echoed, and the pencil he was holding snapped in two.

It was still pitch-black when Polly opened the back door. She was expecting to see her sister, and Jane was standing there sure enough, but so was Albert Green.

'What are you doing here at this time of the morning?'

'That's a nice way to greet your sweetheart!'

Jane burst into giggles and slipped by into the kitchen. Polly smiled. 'Come on in out of the cold, you big daft lump. I've just put the kettle on. Jane, have you had any breakfast?'

Her younger sister shook her head and Polly brought a loaf of bread and a bowl of dripping from the pantry. 'Here you are.' She gave Albert the bread knife. 'Make yourself useful and cut us a slice each. Jane, when you've hung your coat up, fetch the cups and saucers. Lucky I got the fire going, isn't it?'

'Oh, you'll make some lucky fellow a grand wife,' Albert said, and he winked at Jane, who giggled even more than before.

'Hush!' Polly admonished. 'We don't want to wake anybody up before we've had this little time to ourselves.'

For, of course, she hadn't really been surprised to see Albert. He had taken to calling by first thing whenever he was on early shift, just to spend some time with her, even though it meant getting out of bed at least an hour earlier than he needed to.

Polly relished the early mornings. She didn't mind getting up to get the range going, though, strictly speaking, that was one of Jane's duties now. In the morning, when the house was quiet, she could spend time with her sister and spoil her a little, for God knew how hard the girl's life was in the overcrowded slum where the rest of the family lived.

And when Albert planted his big feet under the scrubbed clean table she could even pretend for a while that this was her kitchen; her own happy home. And it was only now, before anyone else was up and stirring, that there was any happiness in this house, it seemed.

She smiled with contentment as she watched Albert standing by the table and slicing the bread. 'Albert Green, take your muffler off or you won't feel the benefit,' she ordered.

He snapped to attention and pretended to salute. 'Yes, ma'am.'

If Jane hadn't been there she would have kissed him. In fact she would probably have ended up sitting on his knee instead of across the table from him, watching him spoon out the dark brown jelly from the bottom of the bowl and mixing it with the dripping on the doorstep that he'd cut for himself.

'Pass the salt, pet,' he said to Jane, and for a while none of them said anything as they washed down their breakfast with hot, strong, sweet tea.

When they had finished, Polly washed the dishes herself and sent Jane up to start the fires. 'Flo will be down any minute for boiling water for the babies' bottles,' she said. 'As soon as you hear her up and stirring, go and see to the nursery fire – you can mind the girls till Flo gets back.'

'Right oh.' But Jane hesitated by the door.

'What's the matter?'

'What about the sewing room?'

'What do you mean?'

'Am I to do the fire in there?'

'Of course. The room must be kept warm all day. When Mr Edington comes home from work he goes straight up there.' And I wish he didn't do that, Polly thought. I wish he would make the effort to spend more time with his wife.

Jane made no move to go. She looked worried.

'What's the matter with you?'

'Well . . . I think Mr Edington and . . . I think he's still in there.'

'That's right, Polly,' Albert volunteered. 'I met up with Jane at the end of the terrace and when we got to the gate we saw that the lights were on in the room in the tower.'

'I suppose Mr Edington could have left the lamps burning – forgotten to turn them off. I mean he works so late in there on his designs for his shop, perhaps he was too tired to notice.'

'No, he's in there. We saw him,' Jane said.

'They're both there,' Albert added. 'Him and his friend.'

'Mr Elliot put the money up for his shop,' Polly said, glancing towards her sister. 'He has every right to be there, checking the designs and such like.'

'I know, I know,' Albert said. 'Well, they must have been working all night.'

'You definitely saw them?'

'Yes, Polly.' It was Jane who answered. 'And I don't know about working, but they were standing by the window, close together . . . and the curtains were open and . . . they looked like they were arguing.'

'Arguing?' Polly didn't know why she was relieved that her sister had said arguing. She had worried for a long time now about the amount of time that Mr Edington spent with his

374

friend and she remembered how his mother hadn't exactly welcomed Mr Elliot to the house when she was alive.

She had heard the rumours about Mr John's father and why he had left home but she had only half understood them. Once she had tried asking Albert but he had only blushed and told her not to believe everything she heard. The trouble was that Polly had never completely understood what she had heard or what it was that people had been hinting at.

But now it seemed that the master had stayed in his sewing room all night and whether he was with Mr Elliot or not didn't matter. What did matter was that his poor little wife had been left alone once again. Polly knew about babies – her mother had had enough of them, hadn't she? And she knew that Mr Edington could have gone back to his wife's bed months ago – if he had wanted to.

Poor Mrs Edington. Oh, she had had some funny ways at first but her heart was in the right place and she knew how to treat her servants; she had learned quickly. Polly couldn't have asked for a better mistress.

'Just leave the sewing-room fire, Jane,' she said. 'It's his own fault if the room gets cold.'

Constance awoke to the sound of sobbing. At first she thought the sounds were coming from the nursery and she half rose from her bed but, when the sleep cleared a little, she realized it could not be either of the children, neither could it be Florence. The sobs were ragged and of too low timbre to be those of a woman. It was a man who was crying. It must be John.

But why should John cry? Surely not because of the pain he had caused her? He had never explained his behaviour – he had left her alone to try to make sense of this strange marriage of theirs. Sometimes she believed the only escape from her tormented thoughts was in sleep.

The room was dark. There was only a faint glow from the hearth. The fire had been banked up the night before and the embers were glowing. In the morning, before it was light, Jane would come and rake it and blow some life into it with the bellows before building it up again, and then Polly would bring her a cup of tea . . .

Constance lay back and pulled the bedclothes up around her shoulders. She went back to sleep.

'Please calm yourself! You will rouse the whole household.'

Matthew gripped John's shoulders and tried to hold him still. It was early morning and still dark outside. He caught sight of their reflections in the window behind them and it crossed his mind that, if anybody saw them, it would look like a scene from a melodrama – as though he was about to murder his friend.

Gradually the sobs subsided. Matthew couldn't make up his mind as to whether John's tears had been prompted by rage or sorrow. Surely not sorrow? Surely John's emotions didn't run deep enough for him actually to love someone and to feel grief because they must part?

He had loved John, there was no question of that, but he had always accepted the little shopkeeper for what he was: an enchanting, beautiful boy who demanded his attentions and his gifts as of right. If the truth were known, he was the one who was heartbroken, not John.

Rage then. Or rather outrage because something he had enjoyed was over and he had not been consulted about its ending. The sobbing had stopped and John was glaring at him.

'Let go of me.'

Matthew felt his heart contract. John's hair was dishevelled, his complexion pale and his blue eyes huge. Matthew saw more clearly than ever what he was losing. But he had no choice.

'Only if you promise to sit down and listen to reason.'

John nodded sullenly and Matthew dropped his hands. His friend turned abruptly and went to sit by the dying fire. 'Explain,' he said. 'Explain, if you can, why you should treat me like this.'

'I've told you.' Matthew followed him warily, not wanting to do anything that might start another fit of hysteria. 'I am to be married.'

John remained staring sullenly ahead. He didn't say anything, so Matthew sat down in the chair opposite.

'I am married,' John said at last. 'What difference does it make?'

'The difference lies in the girls we've chosen. Eleanor Heslop is from a different world to your sweet Constance.'

'Don't patronize me. What you mean is that you are frightened of her father the coal baron!'

John's statement was close enough to the truth for Matthew to simply shrug and say, 'Perhaps it's Eleanor herself that I am frightened of. She's a veritable amazon.'

In spite of himself, this roused John's curiosity. 'Is she not beautiful? I couldn't bear to think of you with some ugly old hag!'

The note of hysteria was creeping back and Matthew reached for John's hand. He didn't shake him off.

'Eleanor is neither ugly nor old,' Matthew said. 'She is tall and lithe and beautiful, and her mind is razor-sharp. And she is the same age as I am, twenty-five.'

'On the shelf, then?'

'She has remained unmarried only because her father is wary of fortune-hunters.'

'And they couldn't accuse you of that.' John snatched his

hand away. 'For goodness' sake, Matthew, your family is fabulously wealthy; it can't be the money you're after!'

'Not exactly. It is expected of me that I make a good marriage. You've always known that, admit it.'

John's frown deepened. 'Of course I've known, but I didn't expect that it would make any difference to us – to you and me!'

'I've told you, Eleanor is—'

'Eleanor Heslop is different. But she wouldn't have to know.'

'I think she already does.'

'What?' Matthew could see that that had startled him. 'But how? How could she?'

'Well, she doesn't know the details – about you and me, I mean. But the circles she moves in are very worldly and I suppose there have been rumours about my . . . predilections.'

'And she doesn't mind?'

'Eleanor will close her eyes to it as long as I am a dutiful husband and I am discreet about any unhusbandly activities.'

'Well, that's easy!' John's smile returned, his eyes shone. 'We can be discreet! We need never meet anywhere except here – who would know?'

'It's no use. We've been seen going to Alvini's. People already know. And, in any case, Eleanor does not want to live in Newcastle, she wants our main residence to be in London.'

John looked sulky again. Suddenly he said, 'You said, "Not exactly." '

'I beg your pardon?'

'When I said that surely you didn't need the money, you replied, "Not exactly." '

'You noticed.' Matthew smiled at him. 'You have always surprised me by how quick you are. Don't scowl – I'm not patronizing you; I'm paying you a compliment. Yes, we are rich – all that land, all those sheep. But we are nowhere near as rich as the Heslops. No, don't interrupt. Eleanor is an only child: eventually, the coalfields, the steel mills, the munitions factories, the shipping – everything, will pass to her children – who will also be my children. Can you imagine what a dynasty that will be?'

'And that's important?'

'Of course it is. Surely your shopkeeper's soul can comprehend that!'

When he saw John's expression he knew that his momentary burst of irritation had been unwise. He rose from his chair in unison with his friend and they stared at each other angrily.

'That's all I've been to you, isn't it?' John said. 'Someone from the trading classes, someone so far below you who you can take up with for a while, to amuse yourself, and then discard when you are tired of me.'

'I'm not tired of you. I don't think I could ever tire of you, believe me. But this has to be.'

It hurt Matthew to see the look of disbelief and scorn in John's eyes. 'Go, then,' he said. 'There's no point in staying longer.'

'John . . .'

'Oh, and you'd better take your property.' John gestured towards the hamper Matthew had brought. It was on the floor near the hearth and so were the blankets and the cushions where they had lain all night.

'Keep it.'

'I don't want it. Or any of that Lady Bountiful stuff. Take it back.'

'Very well.' Matthew kneeled down to gather up the remains of the feast and put them in the wicker basket. When he looked up again John had moved away and was standing by his work table.

'Was this all a game to you?' he asked. 'Encouraging me to open my own shop, design my own clothes?'

'Not a game. I think that you are talented. And whatever your uncle says, there will be enough money in the account to keep the business going until it is established.'

'It *is* established and my uncle is willing to take it into the business. I don't need your money. In fact I will soon be able to pay back every penny of your investment.'

Matthew saw the satisfaction it gave John to be able to tell him that so he did not press the point. 'Very well, if that's what you want.'

He picked up the hamper and moved uncertainly towards the door. 'I suppose I'd better take my leave before your household awakes.'

'Yes.'

'Well, would you be a good chap and run along and get me a cab?'

'Get your own cab.'

Matthew glimpsed a viciousness in John's expression that he had never seen before but then his friend turned away from him to stare out of the window at the sky above the houses at the other side of the terrace. It was streaked with red.

Matthew looked around the room in the tower for the last time and then left it to move as quietly as he could down the stairs to the front door. On the ground floor he noticed a little maid entering one of the rooms carrying a bucket of coal, but he wasn't sure if she saw him.

Chapter Twenty-five

March

Nella pulled her cloak around her for warmth and sat down on a mossy rock in the forest glade near the stream. But there were no sounds of rushing water; neither did the branches of the trees move in any passing breeze. That was because both the trees and the stream were painted on a backdrop, and the rock was merely a stage prop made of canvas stretched over a wooden frame and painted brown and green. And the paint was old, and it didn't smell too good.

Only the working lights were on above the stage and the auditorium was dim. Nella stared out into the red and gold cavern, at the rows of empty seats, remembering and savouring the thrill of pleasing the audience and the cries of 'Encore! Encore!'

She had told Valentino that she wanted to be alone on the stage for a moment, that she needed to think about her songs and he understood that. Nevertheless, he had not gone far away. He was in the royal box, where he had sat with his mother the very first time he had seen her. He watched her patiently.

She couldn't see him but Nella knew that Jimmy Nelson

would be sitting at the back of the box, keeping an eye on her husband, as usual. The only time the lad wasn't there to help her was at night when she and Valentino were in their room above Alvini's. And that would change the minute she found a house of their own. It would be easier for her if she knew that Jimmy was near by even though she wouldn't bother him unless she had to.

'This is a funny place to sit, Nella.' Harry strolled on from the wings. He looked pleased with himself but tired, as they all were at the end of the pantomime season.

'I like it here. This is where I can live that other life – do you know what I mean, Harry?'

'We all need that other life, not just you, Nella, otherwise we wouldn't be in this crazy business.'

'It's not crazy. It's magic.'

'Go on feeling that way.' Harry bent down to close the lid of a trunk that was full of props – stage goblets, swords and a couple of fairy wands – and then sat on it.

Nella had edged round so that she was facing the backdrop. 'I mean, even from here it looks as though that path is winding through the woods towards that castle on the hill, doesn't it?'

Harry smiled. 'And that hint of blue under the trees . . . it could be bluebells . . . an enchanted forest.'

'And look at the clouds,' Nella said, 'look at that wonderful sky! It's like some faraway country that just might exist somewhere.'

'But that's the whole point of it all,' Harry said. 'When you look at it from out there,' he gestured towards the auditorium, 'when you're sitting in the dark in a warm theatre, and trying to escape from your mundane and sometimes difficult life, and you're willing yourself to believe that everything that happens up here in front of your eyes is real . . .'

'Or at least possible . . .' Nella grinned.

'That's right, Nella. If we can just persuade the poor souls, for a little while, that anything's possible, and send them away happy, then we've done our job.' They were silent for a moment and then Harry said, 'But back to business. Thank you for coming in this morning. I wanted to talk to you when the others had gone.'

'What about? Hev you found a new star? Do you want to get rid of me?'

'That'll be the day! Nella, I wish you'd take up my offer for you and Valentino to come to my house in Kent for a month. There'd be room for Jimmy. You need a break and the sea air would do you good. You could even pop over to France if you wanted to – and Mrs Bodie would love the company.'

'There is a Mrs Bodie, then?' Nella glanced at him slyly and Harry laughed.

'You've been listening to Lucy.' Harry smiled at her. 'As a matter of fact there *is* a Mrs Bodie and she holds a diploma in elocution. She could teach you to talk like the rich lady you have become.'

'Give over, Harry. I know that you want me to talk proper now that I'm a star, but it wouldn't be me. I'd frighten meself silly every time I opened me mouth.'

Harry sighed. Ah, well, I suppose it's all part of your persona.'

'Me *what*?'

'You know ... your magnetism ... your allure ... your fascination ...'

Nella grinned. 'Oh, haddaway with you! I'm sorry, Harry. Mrs Bodie isn't going to make a lady out of me!'

It suddenly occurred to Nella that the Mrs Bodie to whom he was referring could be his mother, but she didn't intend to go all the way to St Margaret's Bay to find out. 'I'm going to use the time to look for a house of my own,' she said.

'You may be travelling further afield in future; you'll soon be outgrowing the Northern Circuit.'

'I know. But it will be somewhere to keep my nice things and somewhere to come back to – just like you hev yer house in Kent.'

He nodded. 'And I'll be using up the time thinking of a new routine for you, Nella. Some kind of act where you don't have to stand all the time. I know how hard it's been for you and I'm going to try and make it easier. Will you trust me to come up with something?'

'I'll hev to – but remember I'm enough of a cripple already; I can't risk any accidents.'

'I wish you wouldn't talk of yourself that way.'

'Why not? It's the truth. I'm a cripple.'

'Not when you sing.' She could have sworn that his eyes were moist. He stood up.

'Are you off now, Harry?'

'Yes. So you won't be coming down to join me?'

'No.'

'Ah well. The cab's waiting to take me to the station.'

'Goodbye, then.'

'Not goodbye – just *au revoir*.'

Nella laughed. 'Whatever that means.'

Frank was sitting in the restaurant examining the accounts with Patrick McCormack. They didn't open at lunch time but the head waiter always came in about now to start organizing the evening's menu. As well as the ledgers there was a plate of cold roast beef sandwiches and a pot of coffee on the table. The cleaners were still at work all round them. The velvet curtains had been drawn back and the long windows opened to help disperse the odours of wine, tobacco and last night's food.

Frank and Patrick were so engrossed in the facts and figures that they did not see Nella, Valentino and Jimmy Nelson standing in the arched entrance. Or rather Valentino and Jimmy were standing. Nella was held in her husband's arms, for he had, as usual, carried her up the stairs.

The first indication Frank had that they were there was when he heard Nella say, 'Put me down, sweetheart.' He looked up. 'Go up with Jimmy,' Nella continued. 'I want to speak to yer brother.'

Frank saw Valentino's brow crease. His diminutive wife smiled up at him. 'It's to do with the books. Look, they're adding all the figures up. I want to tell Frank that he must be sure to report to you when he's finished.'

'Ah, yes, the books.' His brother smiled and followed Jimmy Nelson up the stairs obediently.

Nella came over to the table and Patrick stood up and pulled out a chair for her.

'Thank you.' She sat down and loosened her cloak. 'Now how about a cup of hot coffee? It's perishing cold in that theatre when there's nobody there.'

'Do you want a sandwich?' Patrick asked. 'I can get some more made up.'

'No, thanks. I'm not working tonight so I'll hev no excuse not to eat whatever huge meal Mamma has waiting for me!'

'Do you really want to see the books?' Frank watched her curiously. Could it be that his little sister-in-law had some idea of wanting to get involved in the family business? He hoped not . . . not after what Patrick and he had just been discussing.

'God love you, of course I divven't!' But she must have caught his look of relief because she added, 'Is there a problem?'

385

She was quick, Frank thought, and she might prove a useful ally. 'Not exactly a problem . . .'

'But?'

'You have no interest in running Alvini's?'

'None whatsoever.' She frowned. 'Is this what the meeting is about? Are you worried that because I'm married to yer older brother I might want to take over?'

'It hadn't occurred to me until now,' Frank said.

'But I've told you! I've got me career—'

'I know but, nevertheless, it's something I should have considered before I had this talk with Patrick.'

'Ay, now the plot thickens!' she said.

Frank looked puzzled and Patrick explained, 'That's a line from an old play,'

Nella smiled at him. 'Of course, you used to be an actor, didn't you? A real one like Harry sometimes pretends he was. He's fond of quoting that line when he senses a mystery.'

'No mystery,' Frank said. 'I'll tell you all there is to know. Valentino will never be able to be the master here.' Nella nodded. 'My mother is getting old and I—'

'You want to be a doctor. Else what's the point of all yer studying?'

'That's right.'

'So why not let Mr McCormack run the place for you? He's just about doing that already.'

'You mean as manager?'

'Yes. He could train up another head waiter to take his place.'

'That's one option,' Frank said. 'Patrick is willing to try that, but I don't think it would be fair to him.'

'Why not?'

'Because I happen to know that, for a long time, Patrick has wanted a restaurant of his own, where he would have a completely free hand to run it the way he pleases. One day I would lose him – no, Patrick, you might swear to stay as long as we need you, but I can't let you do that.'

'So let him buy this one. That's why you're poring over the books, isn't it?'

Frank caught Patrick's eye and saw the agreement there. 'All right, Nella,' he said, 'this is the problem. You and Valentino will be leaving soon and when I'm qualified I want to buy another property somewhere in the suburbs, perhaps at the coast, and start my own practice. Of course my mother will come with me.'

'So?'

'Patrick isn't in a position to buy us out yet. This is a big building on a valuable site in the city centre. We've been trying to work out how long it will take . . .'

'And from those glum faces I can see that it's gannin' to take too long. So why divven't you sell him the restaurant, the business only, and hang on to the property – rent it out to him? You can decide later on whether you want to part with the bricks and mortar as well.'

Both men looked at her for a long time and then Frank said, 'I think we were just about to reach that solution to the problem before you interrupted us.'

'Like hell you were! Whoops, I forgot I was a lady, didn't I? Put it down to yer bloomin' cheek!'

Frank reached across the table and took her hand. It was so small, like a child's hand. The fingers were slightly crooked but her skin was soft. Frank guessed that that hadn't always been so. 'I'm glad my brother married you.'

'And so am I,' Patrick said, and they both looked at him in surprise. The head waiter smiled. 'Valentino never comes to the restaurant in the evenings now. Sometimes it was taking all my acting skills to refrain from telling those so-called friends of his what I really think of them. You know who I mean . . . Carmichael, Russell and Sowerby.'

'Sowerby?' Nella's eyes widened.

'Yes.' It was Frank who answered her. 'Gerald Sowerby. He's a student at the Medical School; I think he may be the son of the family you used to work for.'

'And does he— Do they still come here?'

Frank wondered what was bothering her. 'They do, and they still try Patrick's patience now and then. But you have no need to worry. Valentino isn't interested in their friendship now.'

'Good,' she said, but Frank had the feeling that there was something he didn't understand and he could see that Nella wasn't going to tell him.

'But why did you come in just now,' he asked, 'if it wasn't about restaurant business?'

'I mean to ask you a favour. I want to visit a friend tomorrow and I would be grateful if you could find something for yer brother to do. He worries when I'm away from him; he thinks it's his duty to go with me everywhere. It's getting worse, Frank.'

She broke off, and Frank wondered why he hadn't noticed before that his brother's attachment to his wife could easily become a dangerous obsession.

'Look – don't worry,' she said quickly. 'I've been thinking about it and, in a way, Valentino is like an actor. He needs to be told what part he's playing. In this instance, do you think you could tell him man to man that husbands are not expected to accompany their wives when they visit nurseries?'

'I'll talk to him,' Frank said, 'and my mother will too.'

'Perhaps I'm the one to do this,' Patrick said. 'After all, I'm a married man. Send him down in a moment, tell him we need him to look at the books, and I'll ask him how it's going and put him wise about the ways of women, man to man, like you say!'

'Thank you,' Nella said, and she stood up to go.

'I'll help you up the stairs,' Frank said and, not trusting himself to look at her, he asked, 'is it Constance Edington that you're visiting tomorrow?'

'Yes. You know she had twin girls? They must be eight months old now and I hevn't seen them yet.'

Constance woke during the night to hear her daughters crying. She pulled on her robe and went into the nursery. Florence was already out of bed and kneeling by the hearth, building up the fire. She saw Constance when she rose. She smiled and then went over to pour water into a bowl on the washstand. She washed her hands.

'Don't worry, Mrs Edington,' she said quietly. 'It's just teething. I'll rub the balm on their gums and then perhaps they'll need a bit of a cuddle to get them back to sleep.'

She went to the cribs and picked Beatrice up. Constance had noticed that Florence, and Polly as well, usually reached for the older and more demanding baby first. Once Beatrice was settled, Amy would often settle herself. She was the more placid twin and usually took the lead from her more difficult sister.

Difficult? Was Beatrice difficult, Constance wondered. Even if she was, she was certainly the more interesting of the two . . .

'Let me see to Beatrice,' she said.

The balm didn't settle them entirely so Constance joined Florence by the fire, one each side of the hearth, as they sat and rocked the babies in their arms. The only sounds were the soft hushing sounds they made to the girls and the crackling of the coals.

Here in the warm shadowy room that smelled of soap and talcum powder and freshly washed baby clothes, with the softly whimpering child held close to her breast, it was easy for Constance to close her eyes and pretend that Florence and Amy were not there. To pretend that there was only one baby. She wished with all her heart that that was so. But here was the agony of it: if what she suspected was true, the baby she should be holding to her heart was Amy.

Once she was back in bed, she slept deeply and barely stirred when Jane came in to see to the fire. Now she realized that there had been no early morning sound from the nursery. Her daughters must be sleeping later than usual because of the disturbed night.

There was a knock on the door and Polly came in, not just with a pot of tea but with a breakfast of boiled eggs and toast on a tray.

'Flo came down to have breakfast in the kitchen. She said the girls were still fast asleep and not to worry.' Polly put the tray on the bedside table and stacked the pillows up. 'There, sit back.'

'Thank you,' Constance said as the maid first placed a linen cloth over the bedclothes and then carefully put the tray on top. 'But why are you spoiling me like this?'

'I don't know, I'm sure.' The girl smiled briefly and left the room.

When she had finished her breakfast Constance put her tray aside and poured a second cup of tea, leaving it on the tray. She picked up her library book. She had got into the habit of reading in bed, both night and morning. She suspected that Polly and Mrs Green thought that reading was an idle habit, but for Constance it had become a very necessary escape.

The book she was reading now was set in America about a

390

hundred and fifty years ago. Constance knew the story to be melodramatic; the misery and suffering the wretched heroine had to endure was almost unbearable. But now she was beginning to suspect that, unlike other such stories, there was not going to be a happy ending.

She resisted the temptation to turn to the end and allay her fears. She, along with Audrey, ought to see it through step by step. However an aspect of the girl's background which Constance had found intriguing, the fact that she had a trace of 'savage' Indian ancestry, looked as if it was going to bring about her doom. Other characters referred to her as having 'tainted blood'. Therefore, it seemed the poor creature was not entitled to her place in society – and might even have to die to satisfy proprieties.

Constance laid the book aside. Could blood be tainted? Could any child be condemned because of its ancestry? She remembered the Bible tracts that Mrs Sowerby had handed out to the staff at Rye Hill. Is this what was meant by 'the sins of the fathers'?

By the time Constance was dressed John had already left the house. She was glad of that. The situation between them was no better. She was aware, of course, that Matthew Elliot no longer called here, but when he first stopped coming, she thought that they might be meeting elsewhere, although she didn't know why they would do this. Surely they hadn't suddenly decided to respect her feelings?

But then she had a letter from Rosemary, telling her with great excitement that she was going to be a bridesmaid at her brother's wedding. Matthew was engaged to Eleanor Heslop, the daughter of the great industrial magnate, and the wedding would be in London.

After receiving the letter Constance wondered briefly if the absence of Matthew would make any difference to their own marriage but John spent even more evenings away from home than he had before. Although now and then, very late at night and in the early hours of the morning, Constance was sure she could hear movements and voices from the room on the third floor. Perhaps John had found a new friend to bring home. Someone else he would rather spend his time with. She did not let herself imagine what they might be doing there.

When she was dressed she went into the nursery where the twins were still fast asleep in their cribs. She was ashamed to see that Florence looked surprised. She knew that her appearances here were erratic and she suspected that Florence and Polly gossiped about her seeming lack of interest in her own daughters. She guessed also that Albert's mother had made excuses for her, and told them that she would come round eventually.

She could have told them that many mothers who could afford to have other people look after their children took even less interest in nursery doings than she did. But she did not respect those mothers herself – and, anyway, she could hardly pretend to have a busy social life.

She knew that she would never be able to confide in anyone the real reasons why she stayed away from the nursery . . . the suspicions and the fears that were in danger of poisoning her natural feelings of love for her children.

But this morning she found herself drawn to the comfort of the nursery fireside. Florence had set up the baby bath at a safe distance from the hearth and was filling it with warm water from a jug. The water was steaming and Constance frowned. Florence looked up and saw her expression.

'Don't worry,' she said, 'I always test it and add cold water if necessary. But the girls are still asleep so I thought I'd have that cup of tea first. Do you want one?' Constance shook her head. 'Well, I'm going to sit down and enjoy this, if you don't mind, Mrs Edington.'

'Of course I don't mind. I don't want any tea but I'll stay here with you until they wake up. If *you* don't mind.'

Florence smiled and sipped her tea. Constance had said that because she wanted the girl to know that she respected her authority over the day-to-day running of the nursery.

Nevertheless, when the twins began to whimper and stir, Constance was the first to rise. She took Beatrice from her crib and watched in wonder as the blue eyes opened and stared at her. She caught her breath and then smiled. Why did Beatrice's stare always seem so challenging? Or did her daughter save that look just for her mother? Amy, as usual, looked angelic on wakening and she smiled and made soft chattering sounds on Florence's knee.

'Would you like to bath Beatrice this morning, Mrs Edington?' Florence asked.

'Yes, I think I would.'

'Well, take this pinny to save your pretty frock.'

'Thank you.'

Florence helped her tie the pinafore and then Constance sat down and began to take off her daughter's nightclothes, marvelling at the small, firm, exquisitely shaped limbs.

'Well then, Constance, I've managed to catch you in at last.'

Constance turned to see Nella standing just inside the door. Polly was hovering behind her, looking uncomfortable.

'Divven't blame the girl,' Nella said. 'This time I wouldn't take no for an answer. I threatened to make a scene in the street. I would, you know.'

Constance held Beatrice closer but she didn't say anything. However, her eyes must have betrayed her alarm for Nella said, 'Divven't fret, I asked Polly if John had left for business.

393

I don't want to cause trouble between husband and wife.'

'It's not that – I mean, I will see my friends when and where I want to.' Constance was aware that both Polly and Nella were frowning.

'What is it, then?' Nella asked.

Constance didn't answer her. She smiled somewhat frostily at the maid. 'Polly, would you take a tray of tea and biscuits to the morning room? Miss Nicholson and I will leave Florence to bath the twins and we'll come downstairs.'

'Hold on,' Nella said quickly. 'I'd like to hev a look at these gorgeous babies first. If we come downstairs Mrs Edington can ring for you.'

Constance was furious and in the moment of shocked silence Polly made her escape.

'Since when do you give orders in my house?' she asked when the door had closed.

Nella grinned and cast her eyes towards Florence, who was clutching Amy to her in her embarrassment. '*Pas devant*,' she said in a stage whisper. 'Do you know what that means? It means, not in front—'

'Yes, I know.'

They glared at each other and it was Constance who crumpled first. 'You'd better sit down,' she said.

'I will, but not until I've had a proper look at them. After all, it wasn't you, my forgetful friend, I came to see, it was yer innocent daughters. Ee, Constance, she's a little angel!'

Nella was standing over Amy, and Florence was only too happy to show the baby off. The nursery maid had already stripped off the baby's nightclothes and she was sitting wrapped in a towel waiting to go into the bath. 'If you don't mind I'll go ahead and bath her. The water will be just right now,' Florence said.

'I don't mind,' Nella assured her and she watched, fascinated as Florence lowered the trusting child into the baby bath.

'She's like a baby doll,' Nella said. 'One of those beautiful German porcelain cherubs, the ones that look like real babies.'

'I know the dolls you mean,' the nursery maid said. 'They have real hair, don't they? But it's usually thick straight hair whereas Miss Amy's is soft and fine and curly.'

'It is indeed,' Nella agreed, 'and so fair that it's almost white. As I said, she's like an angel.'

'Would you like to hold her while I bath Miss Beatrice?'

'Oh, may I? I mean, we must ask Mrs Edington.'

Florence coloured. 'I'm sorry, of course. Mrs Edington, is that all right?'

'Yes.' Perhaps that was the best thing, Constance thought. Nella would be so occupied with Amy that she might not notice . . . might not notice . . .

Nella had taken off her cloak; she took one of the clean towels from the clothes horse and sat down. Florence, who had dried Amy a little, placed the baby on Nella's knee. It was one of Amy's good points that she would go to almost anyone. It was as if she sensed that all who saw her adored her, and she was more than willing to be adored. She had even sat happily on Muriel Barton's knee one day when John's aunt had grudgingly admitted that the babies were 'as pretty as pictures', especially this one.

Constance remembered being surprised that she had been hurt by Muriel's preference for Amy. Beatrice was pretty, too, although admittedly not as delicate or as fine-boned.

She glanced at Nella, who was gazing at the baby on her knee with wide-eyed wonder. Perhaps she would be so enchanted with Amy that she would not really look at Beatrice.

'Shall I take Beatrice now?' Florence was standing over her.

'Yes, I suppose so.'

Constance handed her daughter over reluctantly, securing the all-enveloping towel more tightly as she did so. She watched as Florence kneeled by the baby bath and eased the towel away before lowering Beatrice gently into the water. She heard Nella's soft gasp of surprise.

She turned her head and saw that Nella was staring at Beatrice with horror. Nella sensed her gaze, turned to look at her, and then dropped her eyes for a moment. After a moment's silence she said, 'Well, then, Constance, if you'll help me dress this baby of yours, we'll leave Florence in charge and gan down to the morning room for that cup of tea you promised me.'

Chapter Twenty-six

Frank gripped his brandy glass as he stared across the table at his brother's wife. He had been just about to put his books away when she had crept into the room wrapped in her outsize paisley shawl, as pale and distracted as a ghost in a melodrama. Her expression had brought him to his feet, his stacked books and papers spilling across the table.

Seeing his alarm, Nella had clutched her shawl about her with one hand and raised the other, at the same time shaking her head. 'No, it's all right,' she said. 'Valentino is sleeping peacefully. It's not him I want to talk about.'

He'd gestured towards the table and then, he wasn't sure why, he'd walked over to the heavy old sideboard, opened it and brought out a bottle of brandy. He'd poured them each a shot, sat down and listened to what Nella had had to say.

'So you're absolutely sure?' he asked her now. 'About the birthmark, I mean?'

'As sure as I can be. Everyone in that house knew that that was why Mrs Sowerby wore them old-fashioned high-boned collars. Even when she was giving a dinner party she nivver wore a low-necked gown. Isabelle had seen it many a time when she helped her dress and so did I once when Miss Annabel had been sick all over her and I had to gan and help her change. And that was the first time I saw that Miss Annabel is marked too. It's like a red stain from her neck all the way down across one breast. A family curse!'

'Not a curse, a birthmark,' Frank murmured.

'Well, a mark like that is as bad as a curse to a woman. And I'm telling you, Constance's baby has the same mark except it's not quite so angry red. And I may not be studying medicine like you are, but I know what that means. That bastard Gerald got at her that night no matter what she told me later! And that's why she's been avoiding me!'

Frank was shocked at his own surge of hatred. He could taste the bile in his throat. It had been bad enough imagining Constance Edington in the arms of her husband but at least he had been able to take some selfish comfort from the thought that, knowing John's predilections, it could not be much of a marriage. But now to learn that Gerald Sowerby had undoubtedly raped her was almost more than he could bear. It was all the more agonizing because he knew he had no right to feel this way. Constance was not and never could be his.

'Just the one baby?' he asked. 'You said that only—'

'Beatrice. Only Beatrice has the mark.' Nella sipped her brandy and stared into the shadows for a moment. 'And that's really why I want to talk to you. If it had just been that Gerald had attacked her, I would have kept her secret. But Constance is making herself ill with worry over something else. I think it's stopping her loving her daughters the way she should.'

'Loving them?'

Nella's lips twisted into a smile. 'Yes, it's strange, isn't it? No matter how a baby was got, a woman usually ends up loving it. After all, it's not the poor bairn's fault, is it, if its father's an animal?'

'So you're sure the other baby doesn't have the birthmark?'

Nella nodded and pushed her glass across the table. Frank poured more brandy for both of them. 'Yes. I helped bath her.

Amy's skin is completely unblemished.' She stopped and stared into the shadows again, shaking her head as if she didn't believe what she was about to say.

'So?' Frank prompted. 'It's not unusual for one or more children not to carry a family trait.'

'Especially if it isn't one of the family.'

'What are you saying?'

'Constance believes that only Beatrice is Gerald Sowerby's daughter. She's persuaded herself that Amy is her husband's child.'

'Why does she think that?'

'The girls look different and Constance says that as they grow the differences have become more marked.'

'But that's possible in twins. They may not be identical – that is, they may not have grown from the same seed.' He looked to see if Nella was embarrassed by his plain-speaking and saw that she wasn't. She was listening intently. 'They may be what we call fraternal twins. That is, two separate babies right from the start.'

'So they would be like normal sisters?' Nella asked.

'Yes.'

'But could they hev different fathers?'

'Constance really believes this?'

Nella frowned. 'Amy has hair like white gold. She has blue eyes and fair skin just like John. Beatrice's hair has a reddish shine and her eyes arc a deeper blue—'

'Like her mother's,' Frank said, and Nella gave him a strange look. He would have to be careful.

'Yes, like her mother's. But it's more than the way they look. Amy is an easy baby, gentle and placid, no trouble to her nursemaid, whereas Beatrice, who came into the world first, by the way, is already showing signs of being strong-willed and difficult.'

'Those physical differences still don't prove anything. Look how different in appearance my brother and I are. And he was blessed with all the good looks.' Frank smiled self-deprecatingly.

'I know, I know. I've tried to tell her she's imagining things but she won't hev it. I think it's driving her crazy. That's why I've come to you. I thought with your medical knowledge you might know if it can be true. If it is medically possible for two babies who shared a womb to hev different fathers.'

'I'm not sure, but I may be able to find out.' Nella looked relieved. 'And you think this will help her?'

'Yes, I do.'

'What is the answer she wants, do you think?'

Nella frowned. 'What do you mean?'

'Surely Constance wants to hear that her intuition is wrong. Surely she would wish both children to have been fathered by her husband?' Frank tried not to show how much he hated those words, 'her husband'.

'Rather that than both fathered by Gerald Sowerby!' Nella's eyes glittered dangerously. 'But the birthmark – there's no getting over the birthmark, is there?'

'No, I suppose not.'

'And she loves the child, you know . . .' Nella shook her head wonderingly. 'I've told you, there's no accounting for mother love. But that makes her feel guilty – as if she's cheated her husband – broken her vows.'

Frank gave way to a surge of anger. 'What happened wasn't her fault!'

He thought of Constance as having been doubly betrayed. First she had been grievously wronged by the dissolute Gerald Sowerby and then, in all likelihood, trapped into a marriage with a man who needed the respectability this would give him.

400

Nella looked straight into his eyes. He could tell that she knew. Her words confirmed it. 'Of course it wasn't. We know that because we love her . . . don't we?

'Yes.'

Nella's smile was sad. 'I'm sorry. I guessed the way it was with you and yet I still asked you to help. It must be torture for you. But believe me, I know that it would ease her mind if she could believe that Amy, at least, was John's daughter.'

Frank waited until he could speak without betraying any emotion. 'Then I will do what I can.'

'Aunt Muriel, I wish you would wait for John to come home.'

Muriel Barton and her daughter, Esther, had called to take afternoon tea with Constance, and now John's aunt had suddenly announced that she wanted to inspect John's work-room.

'And when will John be home?' she asked.

'After business hours . . . I mean . . . he doesn't always come straight . . .'

'Exactly. And I want to have a look at the place now. So shall we go up? It's at the top of the house, isn't it?'

Muriel Barton led the way up to the top floor with Esther following and Constance trailing miserably behind. She had never set foot in the sewing room since the night her daughters were born and she had never intended to go there again, but she could hardly begin to explain this to John's aunt and cousin. She was pleased to note that the older woman was flushed and out of breath by the time they reached the top landing.

'Well, lead the way,' Mrs Barton said, and Esther smirked and stood back to let Constance pass.

Constance paused with her hand on the door handle. For a moment she considered that John might keep the room locked; after all, it had become so much his private domain. But the handle turned, the door opened, and her hope died. She stood back and let the other two women enter before her.

Muriel Barton took a few steps into the room and looked round suspiciously. Constance wondered what she was expecting to see. Esther had hurried straight over to the dressmaker's dummy and was gazing raptly at a half-finished evening gown of blue velvet. Constance felt sick as she remembered the last blue velvet gown she had looked at in this room.

'What is it, Constance? You're not expecting again, are you?' Muriel Barton was staring at her.

'No, of course not!'

'There's no need to bite my head off and there's no of course about it. I only asked because you looked so pasty-faced for a minute.'

'I'm sorry, but I can assure you that I'm not expecting another child.'

'Noo-oo,' John's aunt drew the word out thoughtfully. 'More's the pity. I imagine that John feels that he's done all that's required of him.' She glanced uneasily at Esther as if wishing that she hadn't said that, but her daughter had moved across to the work table and was leafing through some of John's sketches.

Constance imagined that John would be irritated by the intrusion but she felt powerless to stop it – also she didn't know if she cared sufficiently to do so.

'But these are wonderful,' Esther said. 'Oh, Mother, you must persuade John to let me work with him!'

Constance stared at the girl in astonishment. In the romantic novels that she brought home from the library and devoured with a kind of guilty pleasure, John's cousin would have been described as a striking dark-haired beauty, vivacious but self-seeking, and ready to make the heroine's life a misery in one way or another. But neither in the pages of a novel nor in real life would such a young woman want to work!

Muriel Barton was smiling wryly. 'I can guess what you're thinking, Constance, but my daughter is actually quite talented. She's what I call artistic. You might not think so to look at her but she makes a lot of her own clothes – including the outfit she's wearing now.'

Constance glanced at Esther and her eyes widened.

Muriel Barton's smile was smug. 'Good, isn't she?' It was a statement rather than a question.

Esther's dress was of dove-grey wool crepe with a belt and buttons covered with scarlet satin. Her black strap shoes could be glimpsed because the skirt was a little shorter than usual, and that was the latest fashion. But what was really noticeable was that it was what was known as a hobble skirt, not so tight that it restricted her movement, but tight enough to require small slits at each side to make walking easier.

'She's very good,' Constance said, and she meant it.

'And there's no need for her to do all that – we can afford to buy her anything she wants. But she says she likes to keep ahead of fashion, not follow it.'

John's cousin had gone over to the shelves to look at the bales of fabric. She was stroking and fingering the cloth almost lovingly.

'Is that why you've come here?' Constance asked. 'To ask me if I'll persuade John to let Esther work with him? Because if you have, I must tell you that I have no influence with him.'

Muriel Barton's dismissive tone was almost insulting. 'No, Walter will tell John that he must take Esther into his enterprise—'

'*Tell? Must?* But John's shop is managed separately from the rest of the business; he is responsible for his own accounts and he's doing very well,' Constance said.

'Yes, yes,' the older woman sounded impatient, 'but now

that his friend Matthew Elliot is no longer financing him – don't look surprised; everybody knows that Elliot no longer has time for John now that he's taken up with the Heslop girl – John will need more funds if he wants to expand – open more shops, perhaps in other cities. And I'm sure that he does.'

'So why have you come here today?'

'Two reasons. I wanted to see for myself, or in this case, let Esther see. You see, on this matter I trust her judgement. If Esther still wants to go ahead with her plan after having a look around here in the workroom, then I will tell Walter to talk to John.'

'I see.'

Constance imagined that no matter how talented Esther Barton might be, she might also prove difficult to work with. She remembered John telling her in the early days of their marriage how much he wanted to be free of the constraints of working entirely for the family firm. She wondered whether she now cared much that he might be trapped after all . . .

'And the other reason?' she asked. Aunt Muriel frowned. 'When I asked why you came here today you said there were two reasons.'

'Ah. Yes.' She turned to look at her daughter. 'Esther, I want you to go and wait for me downstairs.'

'But, Mother—'

'You can come here again, but now I want to talk to Constance alone. Go to the nursery, if you like. Go and look at the twins.'

As if my daughters were an exhibit, Constance thought. She was irritated that John's aunt should give orders like this in her house but she had neither the energy nor the will to oppose her. She observed Esther's sulky expression as she left the room; John's young cousin was not the least bit interested

404

in looking at the twins but she probably did not want to argue with her mother at this stage. Not when she needed her to further her plans. Constance sighed. The girl would probably be a disruptive presence in the nursery and she would have to apologize to Florence when the Bartons had gone.

'Now, Constance, shall we sit down?' Muriel Barton led the way to the other end of the room near the fireplace. 'My, he has got this cosy, hasn't he?' She was staring at the small sofa, the occasional tables and the easy chairs grouped around the hearth. The floor at this end of the room was covered with a small but luxurious Persian carpet.

Constance didn't look at her as she took her place unwillingly in one of the velvet upholstered chairs. 'That's because he spends a lot of time up here. He – he works late. Sometimes all night.' She didn't know why she had added that last sentence and she looked up quickly to find the older woman regarding her with narrowed eyes.

'And does he work here all alone?'

'Why shouldn't he?' Constance was aware that she was flushing and she was uneasy as to where this conversation was leading.

There was a small silence and then Muriel Barton said, 'Constance, I owe you an apology.'

'What! I mean, I beg your pardon?' Constance was completely taken aback. John's aunt actually laughed. 'That startled you, didn't it?' And then her smile faded. 'Am I such an ogre?'

'No. I mean—'

'Don't bother to contradict me but I hope you will understand why I acted like I did if I explain something.'

She stared into the hearth as if gathering her thoughts. The fire had been laid but not lit and, although the fire surround was decorated with colourful Dutch tiles, it somehow looked cheerless. Outside the window a bank of clouds moved across the sky and obscured the sun. The room darkened. When John's aunt turned to regard her again, Constance could not quite make out her expression.

'I wasn't very pleasant to you on your wedding day; I didn't make you welcome, did I?'

'No.'

'My husband, who is a much nicer person than I am, took to you straight away. He said that you were just what John needed.'

'Needed?'

Muriel Barton ignored the interruption and went on, 'But I was convinced that you had latched on to John because it was you who needed something . . . A husband.'

'I don't understand.'

'I think you do. You're not stupid, Constance, far from it. I think you knew straight away what I was hinting at.'

'I . . . you thought I had married John for his money. You thought it was a way to escape the drudgery of life as a servant. You did not believe that I loved him.'

'And did you?'

'Of course I did.' Had the other woman noticed the past tense? And was it really in the past, her love for John?

'I believe that now. Poor Constance.' She dropped her eyes. 'But it's worse than that, I'm afraid. God forgive me, when young Elliot turned up at the wedding I even imagined that he had got you in the family way and John was marrying you as a favour to his rich friend.'

'That's disgraceful!'

'I know. And I acknowledge freely that I was wrong. You only have to look at the little ones, Amy in particular, to see that John is the father.'

Now it was Constance who could not meet the other

woman's eyes. She gripped the arms of the chair and stared into the intricate patterns of the oriental rug at her feet.

'I can see how angry you are and I don't blame you. But there's something else you have to understand. I believed that John would be only too pleased to accept such a bride – a bride who was already pregnant because . . . because . . . Oh, for goodness' sake, Constance, I don't have to spell it out, do I? You must know by now what kind of man he is!'

She didn't answer. She went on staring at the rug.

'But what I didn't know at the time was that Matthew Elliot is that kind of man, too. And I can't help feeling sorry for Eleanor Heslop in spite of all her money!'

At last Constance looked up at her. 'Why have you decided to tell me all this now? No matter what you say, I can't entirely believe that it is because you feel that you have misjudged me.'

'No.' She sighed. 'You're right. I did misjudge you and I'm sorry. All the more sorry because I upset Frances when I knew she was desperate for John to make a happy marriage . . . after what Duncan did to her.'

Constance stared at her. 'Did to her? You know, at first I thought John's father was dead, and then, when his mother was dying she said . . . she said that he had loved her but that there was someone that he loved more.'

'There was. It was another man.'

'I see.' Something, some thoughts, fell into place in her mind like the pieces of a puzzle fitting together. 'No wonder John's mother told me that the family would rather he had died than leave her in such a way.'

'Can you blame us, Constance? We are not so rich that we can ignore the constraints of society. Any hint of scandal could have destroyed the family business – and it still could – which is one of the reasons I wanted to talk to you today.'

'I see.' She rose from the chair. 'Forgive me, but I think you should go now.'

'No, Constance, listen to me. Since Elliot left town John has been seen with more doubtful friends ... People are talking ...'

'What do you expect me to do?'

'Talk to him ... Ask him to spend more time with his wife and family. If you cannot change his ways at least beg him to be discreet. Tell him that you would like another baby ... After all, surely he would like a son to inherit the business ...'

Constance found that she was shaking with rage. Muriel Barton's eyes widened and she rose from her chair slowly and began to edge away. Constance moved round behind the chair she had been sitting in and gripped the back of it. She was unaware that she was sobbing until she heard the other speak.

'Constance ... don't ... I haven't been tactful ...'

'Just go.'

John's aunt began to back away.

'Go!'

She heard the woman gasp as she turned and fled. Constance went on gripping the velvet upholstery of the chair and staring down into its cushioned depths until she heard Muriel Barton hurry out of the room, along the landing and down the stairs.

She looked at the marks her fingers had made on the velvet ... the blue velvet ... and she felt sick. Suddenly she whirled round and hurried across to the work table. She snatched up a pair of scissors and returned to the chair. She barely knew what she was doing when she raised her arm and brought it down with all her force. The points of the sharp blades met a moment's resistance before tearing into the velvet fabric.

Her rage was all the more intense because she couldn't give it voice. She didn't have the words to express the hurt that John had caused her, the disappointment of unfulfilled hopes and dreams, the humiliation of knowing that the man she had loved so much preferred the kisses of another – a man.

She slashed into the blue velvet again and again until her arm grew tired and she could no longer see what she was doing for the scalding tears that filled her eyes and streamed down her face.

Then, mercifully, the rage subsided. Her arm dropped limply to her side. She sank down on to the floor behind the chair and drew her limbs in to her body so that she was curled up as tight as possible.

Hours later, when Polly came looking for her, she was still there.

Chapter Twenty-seven

Frank sat on the edge of his seat. He had not wanted to come but Nella had insisted that her friend needed a doctor.

'I am not a doctor yet,' he'd told her.

'As good as,' was her terse reply and she'd hurried him down the stairs and into a cab with her, ordering Valentino, Jimmy Nelson and Albert Green, who had brought a message from Polly, to follow them in another.

Polly must have been watching from the window of this very room for she snatched the door open even as they hurried up the path.

'Any change?' Nella asked.

'Well, I've got her into bed but she still won't say anything. She won't tell me why she was crouching behind the chair in the sewing room. She must have been there ever since Mrs Barton and Esther left. And another thing – she was clutching a pair of dressmaking scissors.'

'Had she tried to harm herself?' Frank asked.

'I don't think so. But you should see the state of the chair,' the maid added grimly.

It was only then that he had begun to understand that the situation might be serious. 'I'd better go up and see her,' he said.

'No,' Nella told him. 'I want a moment with her first. You wait downstairs with the others.'

So here he was, sitting with his brother and Jimmy Nelson in a room which the lamplight revealed to be both tasteful and comfortable; but none of them had been able to relax. No one had drawn the curtains, and from the sofa where he was sitting, Frank could see out of the window to the houses at the other side of the terrace. It was dark enough for lamps to be lit and some curtains to be drawn, but light enough for him to see John Edington if he should arrive home.

He couldn't stop himself from watching out for Constance's husband and he hated how furtive that made him feel. He forced himself to turn away from the window and look into the room once more.

Valentino had somehow ended up on a chair which seemed too small for his giant frame, but he remained there obediently, with only a slight frown betraying his confusion. Jimmy Nelson, as watchful as ever, had spread his long limbs across a large ottoman and, if he was wondering what was going on, he was too tactful to say so. Now and then he turned to glance at the door and, eventually, Frank asked, 'Is something bothering you, Jimmy?'

'No, I was just wondering what happened to that cup of tea Albert promised.'

Albert Green, whom Frank understood to be Polly's young man, had vanished in the direction of the kitchen as soon as they had arrived. It seemed that he'd been sitting there when Polly had first discovered her mistress in the sewing room, and just as well.

The young maid had been worried sick and, as the master of the house was not at home, and apparently not likely to be coming home soon, Polly had sent her sweetheart to tell Mrs Edington's friend, Nella, what had happened, and beg her to come as soon as possible. And that was why they were here.

'Ah,' Jimmy said, 'that's better.'

The door was opened by a waif who looked as though she might be related to Polly, and Albert Green came into the room carrying a large tray. But Frank didn't stay to sample the tea or the roughly sliced cake for, a moment later, Polly popped her head around the door and said, 'Will you come up now, Dr Alvini?'

'I'm not a doctor y—' he started to say but she hurried away ahead of him across the hall and on, up the stairs.

Nella was waiting outside one of the bedroom doors. Her body was a hunched-up bundle of tension and her expression a mixture of worry and vexed frustration. 'I haven't been able to get a word out of her,' she told Frank. 'She's just lying there with her eyes closed but I know very well that she isn't asleep.' She turned to question Polly. 'What do you think brought this on?'

'I've no idea. Perhaps it was something that Mr Edington's aunt said. Her daughter was making a nuisance of herself in the nursery when Mrs Barton came hurrying down and sent Jane along for a cab. Then the pair of them took themselves off.'

Nella shook her head. 'Well, unless Constance decides to tell us, it will remain a mystery.' She turned and took hold of the door knob. 'Gan on in, Frank. See what you think.'

'Wait, Nella.' He reached out and placed a hand on her arm. 'I'm not sure what you expect me to do. You know I'm not qual—'

Nella raised her other hand to stop him speaking. 'Polly,' she said, 'you must show me that chair in the sewing room. I'll follow you up in a moment, but if it's as bad as you say, you'd better go ahead and hunt around for a piece of cloth we can make a temporary cover with.'

Nella waited until Polly had hurried up the remaining flight

413

of stairs to the top floor and then she said quietly, 'I know you're not qualified, Frank, and I divven't expect you to do anything – to give her anything. I just want you to use yer judgement and tell me whether this is serious – whether Constance has lost her wits . . . gone mad.'

Suddenly she gripped his arms and looked up at him with real fear in her eyes. 'You see, I love her so – I just divven't know what I'd do if . . . oh, Frank . . .'

He took hold of her shoulders and held her for a moment; he could feel the tremors that shook her slight body. He said gently, 'All right, Nella. I'll go in to her. But you mustn't expect too much of me, you know.'

'Bless you, Frank. I know that I do.'

She opened the door and ushered him into the room. Then, as she left him, she would have closed the door, but he seized the handle firmly and made sure that the door was left ajar. Here, in John Edington's house, feeling the way he did about John Edington's wife, he knew he must be careful to observe the proprieties.

Her eyes were closed and her bright, beautiful hair was spread out across the pillow. She was very pale and her high-necked, white nightdress made her look virginal, somehow untouched – in spite of everything that he knew had happened to her. Her arms were stretched down on top of the bedclothes at either side of her body and Frank suddenly noticed that her hands were clutching at the padded eiderdown – completely destroying the effect of repose.

He sat down on the bed and reached for her hands. He took them firmly in his own and lifted them up, breaking the grip of her fingers on the cloth. He had acted without thinking and, for a moment, he was able to do no more than savour the feel of her soft cool flesh against his. He fought to control his own racing pulse as, first, he felt for hers and then he began to make soothing circular motions across her palms with his thumbs.

'Constance,' he said.

She wished they would all go away.

She had not protested when Polly had made her come down from the sewing room and helped her undress and get into bed. Why should she? Bed was as good a place as any, for at least here she could close her eyes and pretend to be asleep. That way they might leave her alone.

But Polly had sent for Nella and Nella had fussed and begged her to talk to her – to tell her what the matter was – when all she wanted to do was sleep and forget it all. She couldn't understand, when she was so weary, why she couldn't go to sleep.

Then Nella left the room and Constance thought that she was going to be left in peace at last, but the murmur of voices outside the door told her that they were still there. Didn't they realize how irritating it was when they tried to talk quietly like that?

When the door opened again she thought that Nella had come back and she wondered why her friend was standing so quietly looking down at her. In sheer exasperation she gripped the eiderdown even more tightly and it was then that she felt her hands grasped and held and heard someone – a man – she didn't know call her name.

Shock made her sit up and open her eyes.

The man smiled at her, a sad, gentle smile and she realized that she did know who he was. But what was Frank Alvini doing here? She frowned. Was it possible that he knew how often she had thought of him? Had he answered some deep unspoken need? No . . . that couldn't be.

Nella. That was it. Nella had brought Frank here to see her

because he was studying to be a doctor.

But he shouldn't be holding her hands like this. His touch, the feel of his skin on hers, the warmth that flowed from his fingers was disturbing.

She pulled her hands from his grasp and hid them under the bedclothes. She drew her knees up protectively and began to shake her head.

'What is it, Constance?' he asked, and his voice was almost as sad as his smile.

She looked straight at him. 'Nella shouldn't have brought you.'

'Perhaps not, but she was worried about you.'

'Why?'

'Do you need me to tell you?'

She was rebuked by his cool scrutiny. 'I'm sorry,' she said.

'Why are you sorry?'

She felt a spasm of irritation. What did he want of her? 'I'm sorry to have caused so much bother.'

She wasn't sure if she quite understood the way he was looking at her. His dark brown eyes were warm, but there was something more than sympathy there. It was as if he could see her pain but, more than that, he was sharing it.

'Nella thinks that you might be going mad,' he said at last.

'I'm not. I'm just unhappy. Unhappy. Do you believe me?'

'Yes, I do.'

Instinctively, she withdrew her hands from under the bedclothes and reached for his. She wanted to feel his touch. She needed to. This time his grasp was comforting. She began to cry and instead of the painful sobs that had racked her body before, the tears flowed gently. And the wonder of it was that he was crying too.

* * *

416

The journey back to the Haymarket would be all too short so Nella began to question Frank as soon as the cab set off.

'So she's not losing her wits?'

'Far from it,' he said. 'Constance is quite sane. She's unhappy and has been too proud to tell anyone. What happened today was simply the release of tension.'

Nella moved as far away from him as she could within the close confines of the cab and tried to study his expression in the light of the streetlamps they passed. At the moment his face was in shadow, but she could see his eyes glittering with some unexpressed emotion. She suppressed a wave of pity. She knew what he must be feeling and she wished there was something she could do about it. But Constance was married, and there was no help for him.

'She'll be all right then?' she asked.

'Constance is a survivor,' Frank told her. 'And she has you for a friend. She's lucky in that.'

'You know, I used to think Constance was the lucky one,' Nella said.

'Lucky?'

'Oh, I know she and her ma ended up in the workhouse, but she's so beautiful and clever and spirited – she nivver let anything that happened get her down – and when John proposed to her I thought that all her troubles were over. I thought she was gannin' to be happy ever after! And instead . . .'

'Instead, if what you tell me is true, poor Constance was raped the night before her wedding.'

'By Gerald Sowerby. This state she's in now – it's all his fault!'

'Not quite, Nella. Think of everything else that has happened. You say she grew fond of her mother-in-law.'

'She did. They got on well, even though the poor lady was dying.'

'Exactly. Constance lost a friend in that house when Mrs Edington died. And then there was a difficult childbirth and her worries about the twins—'

'She wouldn't have that worry if it wasn't for Gerald Sowerby!'

Frank turned away to look out of the window at his side of the cab before he murmured, 'And her marriage has not been all that it should be.' But Nella had not heard him.

'Hev you found anything out yet, Frank?'

He turned towards her again and she saw him frown.

'About the twins,' she prompted. 'You know . . . whether it's possible for them to hev different fathers?'

'Nella, there's barely been time—'

'Of course. I'm sorry.'

'But, yes, I think it *is* possible.'

'It is? But how?'

'I found a paper in the library at the Medical School, it's about multiple births on the slave plantations in America in the last century.'

'Multiple births?'

'More than one baby.'

'Of course.'

'Anyway, it was noticed that in some cases twin babies born to black women could have different racial characteristics.'

'Frank!'

'One baby would be black like its mother and her slave partner, and the other would have fairer skin, sometimes almost white.'

'But what can that mean?'

'That the woman had been . . . taken . . . by the slave owner, or the overseer or some other white man.'

'The evil bastards!'

'It was not always rape, Nella.'

'Mebbe not. But what choice did the poor women hev? Anyway, can any of this be proved?'

'Not proved exactly, but I can make out a pretty convincing case. There's a doctor at a university in America who I'm going to write to. He's made a study of these births. When he replies, I promise I'll put it as simply as I can. But you'll have to tell her. Not me.'

'Of course.' Nella reached across in the semi-darkness and took his hand. She did not realize how tightly she gripped it. 'When the child grows,' she said, 'that mark will grow. It will nivver go away, and Constance will nivver be able to forget what happened. She will know in her heart, whether you can find anything to prove it or not, that Gerald Sowerby is Beatrice's father.'

Suddenly Nella remembered a promise she had made to herself the day she had found the little gold-coloured heart she had given Constance in the turn-up of Gerald's trousers. She had vowed that if ever she discovered that Gerald Sowerby had hurt her friend then she would find a way to kill him.

'Stay in the shadows, sweetheart!'

Nella reached for her husband's hand and pulled him closer to her as they hurried up Westgate Road. He didn't protest. In fact he hadn't said a word, bless him, since she had placed a finger to her lips and mimed the need to be silent just before she opened the door to their room and led him quietly along the top landing, past his mother's bedroom, to the door that led to the back stairs.

He hadn't even questioned her when she had dressed him in the oldest clothes she could find in his wardrobe and wrapped a muffler round his throat and lower face so that he looked like a working man. He had watched, with smiling

419

eyes, while she put on an old dress and pulled a woollen shawl up over her head like a beggar woman.

It was the outfit she wore in one of her acts when she took the part of an old street singer; and perhaps Valentino thought that that was what they were going to do now – go on the stage.

When they'd left, the restaurant had still been busy. Nella knew that Gerald Sowerby and his friends were there because, when Jimmy Nelson went home, she'd made some excuse to walk part of the way down the stairs with him until she could see through the arched entrance and look at the crowded tables.

In the family room Frank was working at his books as usual and had probably been quite pleased when Nella said that she and Valentino needed an early night. Please God he thinks we're sleeping soundly now, she thought, instead of sneaking out the back yard of the restaurant and then hurrying through the streets towards Rye Hill.

She'd decided that they had to walk. They couldn't risk taking the tram or a cab because a couple so distinctive – Valentino so big and powerful and herself so small and oddly shaped – would probably be remembered.

Her knees began to hurt as the way grew steeper and she had to rest for a moment on the corner of one of the streets that cut down at a right angle towards the river. She grasped the iron railings of the house behind her and breathed hard, motioning for her husband to wait by her side.

Before she had caught her breath she heard the clip-clop of hoofs on cobbles and the jangle of a harness. She looked down the way they had come and saw coach lamps cutting through the damp night air. Could this be Gerald coming home? It was probably about the right time. She looked round in panic and then realized with relief that they were there. This was the street where the Sowerbys lived.

She took hold of Valentino's hand and pulled him round the corner. She knew that the cab would stop at the top of the street because the cab drivers were unwilling to negotiate the steep gradient of the streets that led down to Scotswood Road. So they should have time to reach the house before he did. But, almost immediately, they had to slow down again. The damp air had made the paving stones slippery; they would have to take care.

Nella heard the cab driver shout, 'Whoa!' and the cab come to a stop just as she and Valentino reached the Sowerbys' house. She looked around . . . she wanted to surprise him. She didn't want him to be on his guard. The area yard . . . that was it . . .

Swiftly she pulled Valentino down the stone steps until their heads would be hidden from street level. She could hear footsteps coming down the street towards them. They were slightly unsteady. There was a streetlamp not far away so they had to crouch low but, as the footsteps came nearer and nearer Nella raised her head and craned her neck round until she could peer up the street. It was Gerald – she was sure of it. They had got here just in time.

And then, as the bulky figure drew nearer and began to slow down a little, Nella wondered what she was doing there. Did she really intend to kill a man tonight? She glanced round at her husband, waiting obediently and unquestioningly a few steps below her. Valentino adored her; he would do anything she asked him to.

At the moment he was gentle as a lamb – with her he always had been. But Frank had told her that before she had come into his life and given it a purpose, Valentino had shown signs of a developing a dangerous rage.

Those big hands, which could span her waist with room to spare, and which were so gentle when he picked her up and held her in his arms, could just as easily snap somebody's neck – if she wanted them to.

Suddenly Valentino tilted his head a little so that the lamplight fell across his face. He was smiling at her. He thinks this is all a game, she thought. He's an innocent. She felt uneasy; did she have the right to turn him into a murderer?

But then she remembered that just below them, on the rough concrete of the yard, Gerald had raped Constance and destroyed her happiness.

Gerald knew he'd had too much to drink. Russell and Carmichael had had to get him into the cab and he could barely remember the journey home. Then the driver had got down to haul him out and had hung on to him until he was steady enough on his feet to dig into his pocket for the fare.

Had he given the correct fair? He remembered digging into his pocket for his loose change and holding his hand out so that the driver could choose the coins himself. He hoped he hadn't been cheated. If I find out he's cheated me I'll see he loses his licence, Gerald thought.

And then, even though the man had said, 'Now get along carefully, sir,' he'd shown no respect. The fug in his brain had cleared enough for Gerald to sense that he was laughing at him.

Whoops! The pavement was damp and greasy, and he found himself sliding down hill like a boy on a frost slide. He managed to grab on to the railings and right himself. He giggled. But, a moment later he sobered up as he anticipated the undoubted confrontation that awaited him with his father.

The old man had taken to waiting up for him. He'd have to face another interminable lecture about the evils of drink and letting it get the better of you. Sometimes his mother would be hovering on the landing bleating on about him neglecting his studies and how all she wanted was for him to qualify and be a respectable doctor.

Well, there was one thing she didn't know yet. As soon as he was qualified he would be off to find a home of his own. He wouldn't stay here and be treated like a child one minute longer than he had to.

'My God, who are you?'

Gerald pulled up short just a few yards way from the steps that led up to his front door. A diminutive figure – a woman – seemed to have jumped up out of the ground and now she was standing before him, stopping him from going any further.

'Get out of my way! Did you hear me? Be off with you!'

The woman had a shawl pulled up over her head. Gerald stared at her blearily. It looked like the old beggar-woman who sometimes came up the street from Scotswood.

'Here,' he said, and brought out a couple of coins and held them out to her. 'Take this and go away.'

She raised her hand and knocked his viciously, sending the money flying. He stumbled backwards in shock. 'Steady on,' he said. 'What'd you do that for?'

He had fallen back against the railings and he stayed there staring at her owlishly.

'I know what you did,' she said, and even in his fuddled state he detected the hatred.

He pushed himself upright. 'What are you talking about?'

'You know very well what I'm talking about. I know what you did that night and it's time you paid for it.'

Gerald frowned; he thought he recognized the voice and yet it couldn't be . . .

'Who are you?' he asked, and he began to feel uneasy.

The woman pulled the shawl away from her face and let it fall down on to her shoulders . . . her crooked shoulders . . . and the look in her eyes turned his unease into fear. 'You 'know who I am and you know why I'm here,' she said.

Suddenly Gerald saw the absurdity of the situation. Here he was, confronted outside his own front door by this ridiculous creature who, for some reason, had got herself up in a strange collection of old clothes. If he was honest he did have some idea why she was haunting him like this: it would be something to do with the other maid she used to work with – the tasty baggage with ideas above her station. But this one was such an insignificant little bag of bones that all he had to do was push her out of the way.

He began to laugh. 'Joke's over,' he said, and he raised a hand to give her a shove.

And then he felt his arm seized from behind and yanked with such force that he felt his shoulder dislocate. Spinning round in pain and fury, he found himself facing Valentino Alvini.

'What . . .? Where . . .?'

Gerald was shaking with rage and fright. He realized that Alvini must have been waiting down the steps in the area yard – and so must the woman. That was why she had seemed to spring up out of nowhere. And, of course, the little witch was married to the big dimwit, wasn't she? What a pair – a crookback and an addlehead. God help the world if they ever had children.

But he didn't like the way Alvini was looking at him. 'Look,' he said, 'I wasn't going to hurt your wife. I just want her to get out of the way so that I can go home.'

Gerald saw the big man glance sideways and he turned to see Nella walking round to stand next to her husband.

'Should I let him go home, Nella?'

To see the giant of a man waiting obediently for orders from the diminutive woman was so bizarre that, in spite of the pain in his shoulder, Gerald began to laugh. He held his right arm close to his body, supporting his elbow with his left hand and began to back away from them, all the time making strange choking noises that were halfway between a laugh and a sob.

'No, Valentino, he can't go home. This man hurt me.'

'Hurt you?' Valentino's brows drew together in a puzzled frown.

By God he's trying to think, Gerald thought, but his scorn turned to apprehension as he saw confusion begin to give way to anger . . . and then rage.

'Yes, sweetheart. This man hurt me badly.'

'I didn't!' Gerald screamed as Valentino took a step towards him, one powerful arm raised threateningly. 'I never hurt you – I never even touched you! Why are you lying like this?'

'You know why,' Nella muttered, and she took a step backwards.

Her husband had caught the movement from the corner of his eye and turned his head. 'Nella, what do you want me to do?'

Gerald watched as the woman stared up into her husband's face. What was she thinking? Why was she just looking at him like that instead of provoking him to violence as she had so obviously intended? Slowly she reached up and placed a hand on the big man's arm. She pulled it down.

'Nothing, sweetheart,' she said. 'I don't want you to do anything except take me home.'

Gerald had been holding his breath. Now, as the strange pair looked at each other and he saw that they were actually smiling, he let his breath out slowly and turned to go. He was safe. Facing his father's tirade would be nothing compared to what might have happened if the strange creature hadn't suddenly called her bruiser off.

The small hands landed in the middle of his back with such force that he lost his footing and began to fall. He flung his

425

arms out and tried to grasp the iron railings but he missed and, slipping on the top step, he began his headlong progress down into the area yard.

The pain when he hit his head was excruciating. He lay amongst the coal dust feeling sick and disorientated. He looked up and saw the globe of the streetlamp hanging above him. And something else. The little crookback was standing on the top step looking down at him. He moaned and felt hot vomit rise in his throat.

'That's right,' he heard her say. 'You can lie there and die for all I care.'

And then a mist obscured his vision and her face dissolved and became part of the light . . . the light that was fading . . . slowly . . . until the world went black.

Chapter Twenty-eight

The tram came to a shuddering halt in the Haymarket and Constance made her way to the rear platform. She paused in dismay. The rain, which had not seemed so bad viewed through the steamed-up fug of the windows, was heavier than she'd anticipated. The sky had not even been cloudy when she left the house and she had not thought to bring an umbrella. She should have done; April was living up to its reputation.

'Hurry up, pet, there's folks has got shoppin' to do!'

Constance turned to see a stout, cheery woman standing behind her. 'I'm sorry,' she began, but the woman smiled and nudged her to one side.

'Here you are,' she said as she leaned out of the tram and opened a large black umbrella. 'You can share this.'

As she stepped down from the tram, she held the umbrella high above her head with one hand and pulled Constance towards her with the other. 'Hawway, pet, grab me arm and run, or you'll get that bonny blue coat splashed. Them automobile drivers never slow down when it's wet. They divven't seem to care!'

The two of them set off together across the cobbles and the tram tracks until they reached the pavement, laughing and breathless. Constance turned to face her new friend and smiled. 'Thank you,' she said.

'Where are you going now?' the woman asked. 'You can walk along with me until we get to the shops. Are you going down Percy Street?'

'No, that's kind of you, but I'm going right here – the coffee shop.'

'All right then, pet. I'll walk you to the door. There. Tarra, then.'

Her saviour hurried away and Constance dived into the warm, steamy atmosphere of Alvini's. She almost hadn't come here today. She wanted to see Nella, that was true, but she had also hoped that she might see Frank. And that hope had unsettled her. But the absurd little episode with the umbrella had left her feeling exhilarated. She was smiling as she went up to the counter.

'Sit down, madam, and I'll send a waiter.' The tall, handsome woman smiled at her. 'Oh, but wait a minute, it's Mrs Edington, isn't it?'

'Yes, but—'

'Belle McCormack. I remember you from that day when you came with Miss Nicholson – Mrs Alvini, now – to meet the family.'

'Well, it's Nella I want to see, actually. That's why I came.'

Mrs McCormack frowned. 'Oh dear, I think you've missed her.'

'Is she . . . is she at rehearsal?' Constance had a very hazy idea of how Nella's days were spent when she wasn't actually appearing on the stage but she had thought that she might catch her this early in the morning.

'No, not today. But, look, if you go and sit at that table over there, I'll send word up to the family and see if they know when she's coming back.'

Constance made her way to the table by the window. Her dash through the rain and the resulting feeling of wellbeing seemed to have sharpened her senses. The smell of the customers' damp clothes, the pervasive odour of coffee, the sounds of the coffee machine and the hum of conversation were all heightened.

She had barely taken her place at the table when a young waiter brought over a pot of coffee and a slice of almond cake. 'Mrs McCormack's compliments,' he said.

Constance smiled her thanks and removed her gloves. The hot coffee was just what she needed and the cake looked delicious.

After a while she turned to stare at her own reflection in the window. The fur trimming on her hat sparkled with a spattering of stray raindrops and the spray of feathers attached to the hat pin was drooping limply. She raised a hand and brushed a loose tendril of hair back from her face and laughed softly.

Beyond the café window people hurried by as quickly as they could. Two or three market stalls on the opposite corner were braving it out, their owners huddled under dripping tarpaulins. The cab drivers sat stoically in their cabs, dressed in long waterproof capes; she felt sorry for the patient, steaming horses.

'Mrs Edington?' Constance looked up to find Frank Alvini looking down at her. 'May I join you?'

She had hoped for this and yet dreaded it. All she could do was nod in agreement as he took the seat opposite to her. His black hair was brushed back severely from his high brow and his dark suit made him look quite forbidding. Until he smiled. His smile transformed him. His dark eyes and irregular, mobile features radiated wit and warmth. Constance wished she could share that warmth more often.

He turned and raised an arm and, immediately, the same young waiter hurried across with a fresh pot of coffee.

'You came to see Nella?'

'Yes.'

'My brother and his wife are out looking at houses. They want to buy a place of their own.'

'I see.'

'Are you so very disappointed that she isn't here?'

'Disappointed, yes. But why do you ask?'

'Because a moment ago, before I joined you, I saw that you were smiling – you looked happy. But now your smile is gone and you are barely speaking above a whisper. But maybe that is my fault.'

'Why should it be?'

'Perhaps you are remembering the last time we met . . . the circumstances. Perhaps you don't wish to be reminded.'

Constance remembered how he had taken her hands in his. The feel of his skin against hers. The sensations his fingers had aroused as he brushed them across her palms . . . She lowered her gaze. 'Well, yes, I don't like to think about it, but the fact is, that was why I wanted to see Nella – to tell her how grateful I am that she came that day. And that she brought . . . brought you with her.'

'And why is that?'

'Because you believed me – believed that I wasn't mad. Do you know, I'd begun to convince myself that I might be. But I behaved like that because I was unhappy, I was driven to it by . . . by . . .' She faltered and stared at him helplessly.

'It's all right. You don't have to tell me.'

Frank reached across the table and took her hand. She was shocked by her own reaction. She felt the same excitement as last time only now, if possible, it was more intense. She stared at her hand in his. Suddenly she found it difficult to breathe.

She heard him sigh and looked up to find that he was

430

staring down at her hand – at her wedding ring. She pulled her hand away.

They sat staring at each other, then, 'And are you happy now, Constance?' he asked. 'Did you come to tell Nella that everything is all right now?'

'No.' She knew it would be pointless to lie to him. 'But to assure her that she need not worry. Her friend is quite sane and . . . and has much to be thankful for.'

Frank looked away. 'I'll tell her that.' He stood up and looked out of the window. 'I think the rain is easing off; please wait here as long as necessary. But I mustn't be late for lectures. Goodbye, then, Constance.'

'Goodbye.'

She watched him go. He didn't look back. Constance was dismayed to discover how much that hurt her.

'Nella, it will be at least a year before the girls can wear these!'

'That's the idea. I want to be able to take them out walking in them.'

'They're beautiful.' Constance held up one of the white satin dresses and examined the delicate, self-coloured embroidery. 'Far too good for these little rogues. They must have cost you a fortune!'

They were in the nursery and the twins were sitting on a large rug spread out on the floor. They were surrounded by soft toys but they were more interested in sucking on the biscuits that Nella had just given them – which she would never have dared to do if Florence had been there.

Nella looked at them and smiled. 'There's nothing too good for them bairns! And, as I'm nivver gannin' to hev any of me own, you must allow me to spend me money on your children. That's the next best thing.'

431

Constance laid the dresses back in the box and folded them into the tissue paper. 'Very well.'

She stared out of the window. The branches of the trees were bending and swaying in the wind, but at least it hadn't rained today. She wondered whether it grieved Nella that she would never have children, that she would never have a normal marriage. But then, what was normal? Certainly not her own marriage and even her two daughters had not been . . . were not . . .

'Ee, Constance, look at this mess!'

She turned to find Nella on the floor with the girls, trying to wipe the dribbled, sticky crumbs from their faces. Amy submitted to her ministrations patiently but Beatrice howled with rage and squirmed out of the way.

'She's a bad 'un!' Nella said, but she smiled in spite of herself.

They both looked at Beatrice and neither of them spoke for a while. Then Nella crawled over to an easy chair, just as one of the children would have done, and pulled herself up. She settled back amongst the cushions with a sigh. Constance sat down at the other side of the hearth. She guessed that her friend was going to tell her something. And what it would be.

'It is possible, Constance,' Nella said finally, 'because of what happened to you only one night before yer wedding night, and the evidence of the birthmark, it is perfectly possible – and likely – that the girls hev different fathers.'

Constance stared at her. 'You asked Frank Alvini, didn't you?'

'How do you know that?'

'Because you're talking like a textbook – and who else do you know who is studying medicine?'

'Yes, I asked Frank. Do you mind?'

'It's too late if I do.'

432

'Divven't look at me like that. You can trust Frank. And he doesn't think any the worse of you, if that's what's bothering you. He's not the kind of man that would think it the woman's fault for being raped.'

'Hush, the children!'

The twins had lain down where she'd left them and were looking drowsy. Nella glanced guiltily at them and then she smiled ruefully. 'I don't think they understand what we're saying, but I'll keep me voice down, anyway.'

'So tell me, what did Frank say?'

Nella told her of the papers that he'd found in the library of the Medical School, and then of the correspondence he'd had with an American professor about the births in the slave plantations.

'But I can't prove it?' Constance asked finally.

'There is no proof that would stand up in a court of law, although Frank thinks that one day there may be,' Nella said. 'But right now at least you know that there's a very strong chance that you're not imagining things.'

Constance remained silent.

'And does that make you any happier?'

'A little. At least I can believe that Amy is my husband's child. That she is rightfully part of John's family. And, Nella,' she glanced at her daughters, whose eyes were now closed, 'we must never speak of this again. As Beatrice and Amy grow older I never want them to hear anything that might . . . that might . . .'

She broke off when she realized that there were tears in her eyes. Nella pushed herself up and came to put her arms around her.

'I know, Constance, I know.'

Later that night, when she was alone in bed, Constance thought about Nella and herself and the way their lives had changed so dramatically since they had worked together at the house on Rye Hill.

Who would ever have believed that Nella would become rich and famous and marry such a handsome man? And who would envy her if they knew the truth about her marriage or the pain her work caused her frail, twisted body? And yet, she seemed to be happy.

And me. What of me? Constance thought. I am also married to a fine-looking man. I have my own home, two beautiful daughters, all the clothes that I could ever wish for and servants to look after us. A lot to be thankful for . . . She remembered her words to Frank Alvini in the coffee house that day. And it was true, she supposed, if a good life meant wanting for nothing material.

Was it so wrong to want more?

Dearest Constance,

We are to be parted again. Iris and I are leaving Lodore House, and this time I do not see how I can ever return. Believe me, I did not know for many years that it was my grandfather who had bought the house from our father's creditors. I suppose that he wanted to save my childhood home for me. But not for you. And, for that, I am sorry. It was gracious of you to tell me that day that you were glad it was me that was living there.

I hope that you will believe me when I tell you that I was overjoyed to find you again and I fully intended that we should remain close. I am sure that Iris would have come round in time. Especially when she learned that you and she had so much in common as the mothers of young children. Why did you not tell me about your children, Constance? I had to learn from gossip in the business community that John Edington and his beautiful wife had twin daughters.

Whatever the reason, I know that you will make a wonderful mother because you are so much like your own mother. I will never forget how she took me to her heart and made me believe that I was as important to her as if I were her own son. I bless her memory.

But now I must beg you to answer my letter and I hope that we will become regular correspondents. For, you see, I am leaving the shipping office; I am a failure as a business-man. My grandfather has decided to salvage what he can by selling the fleet to George Heslop; who will now have his own colliers to carry his coals from Newcastle.

Iris and I are to live in Berwick and, although I do not need to find employment, I believe that my father-in-law hopes to train me up to manage his estate, but with the 'help' of his trusted land agent. Iris is delighted.

And what of Lodore House? My grandfather has decided there is no further use for it and a buyer has already been found. In fact I have met her. It is a lady who is buying it, apparently, although her husband came with her – a big handsome man who followed her round obediently while she did all the talking.

Oh, Constance, if you could have seen her: such a strange little woman and yet strangely beautiful. She had a sweet face and such expressive eyes. And I wish you could have seen how tenderly she addresses her husband – and he her. It pleases me to think that they will be happy in this house, even although it distresses me that you and I will never be able to meet here again.

But I hope fervently that we will be able to meet again sometime, somewhere.

With love from your affectionate brother,
Robert

Constance put the letter aside. How odd that Nella should be buying Lodore House, for, of course, it must have been Nella and she couldn't have known that that was Constance's childhood home. She sat for a moment waiting for the tears. None came, although she felt sad for Robert.

She realized how much she liked him. He may have failed in business but he was a nice man – just as their father had been. Surely he had noticed Nella's crooked back and the fact that Valentino was slow-witted? And yet he had simply said that she was a strange little woman and that the man had let his wife do all the talking. And then he had mentioned their good qualities.

And he had said that she herself would be a good mother because she was so like her own mother. Well, she loved her daughters, there was no question of that. Whatever had happened had not been the fault of two innocent babies. And she was learning to deal with her feelings and keep them separate from her children's needs. Ever since the day she had given way to her emotions so dramatically, it was getting better. She had learned to accept those things that she couldn't change.

She hoped that Robert would be happy with his domineering young wife – but she feared for him.

Still dry-eyed, Constance glanced out of the window. This year's April showers had gone on well into May and, in addition, there had been some high winds. The trees in the garden looked drenched through and some of the spring flowers had been flattened by a combination of non-stop rain and worrying winds. But the clouds were clearing; she could even see a patch of blue above the roofs of the tall houses at the other side of the terrace.

She rang for Polly. When the maid came, Constance

436

asked her to bring her hat and coat. She would go out for a walk.

As soon as the rain stopped Belle McCormack hurried out of the coffee shop and looked up into the sky. She had to judge whether it would stay dry enough, for long enough, to allow her to set up some tables on the pavement. The coffee shop was so busy nowadays that, at certain times, the customers had to queue up for tables. They didn't like that and sometimes the impatient ones decided to take their custom to the inferior establishment at the other side of the Haymarket.

Belle stood in the doorway and pushed a wisp of hair back behind an ear. She was a calm, thoughtful woman who never panicked, and who never had to raise her voice to command obedience. But latterly she had been burning with an inner excitement. She could hardly wait for the day when Patrick took over the restaurant. It wouldn't be long now.

She must have been smiling because she noticed a few heads turning to look at her. And the glances the men gave her were appreciative. The people hurrying by were beginning to furl their umbrellas and the sun that had broken through the clouds was actually warm. The flowerseller was setting out her baskets on the opposite corner. Belle made her decision: she would bring out the tables.

A short time later Nella and Valentino sat at one of the tables to have coffee and cakes before leaving to catch the train to Middlesbrough. Belle was overseeing the packing of a hamper for them to take. Patrick came out to join them.

'Well, then, Patrick,' Nella said. 'It won't be long now.'

He knew what she meant. 'No, and my Belle can hardly wait.'

'Won't she mind living here, above the shop, in the centre of town?'

'Alvini's is hardly a shop! And, no, she'll love it. But you, will you miss it?'

'I suppose I will. But it will be marvellous to hev me own house – me and Valentino, I mean.' She smiled fondly at her husband, who was enjoying his favourite chocolate cake. 'And it's such a grand place, Patrick. I'm so lucky to hev found it – and I can't wait to show the house to me friend Constance. I hevn't told her about it yet; I want to take her there and surprise her!'

'And Madame Alvini? How is she taking the move?'

'She's sad, of course. She lived here with her husband and she brought up her boys here. But Frank has convinced her that she will enjoy living at the coast and being a doctor's mother!'

An automobile went by and sent up a spray of puddle water. Nella lifted her feet and twisted aside in her chair. 'Careless beggar,' she said, but she was laughing, and Valentino, seeing her smile, joined in.

'Do you know, I'm thinking of buying one of those things,' she said, 'but Jimmy Nelson will hev to learn to drive it because I divven't think Valentino or I could master it.'

'Why would you want an automobile? Surely the trains can take you anywhere you want to go – and they're quicker.'

'Well, not quite everywhere – for instance, we might want to bowl along on a trip to the country. And, anyway, I believe that's the future, Patrick. That's the way the world's gannin'.'

'And talking of gannin', that's what we'll be doing as soon as Jimmy arrives. You know we've decided to stay in Middlesbrough for the length of this engagement? It's too trashing coming back every night.'

'Very wise. I'll see if Belle's got your hamper ready. I told her it's only just over an hour's journey, but she likes to spoil Valentino – and you, of course.' Patrick got up to go.

'Wait, Patrick.' Nella paused. She'd rehearsed many times how she was going to say this but she still found herself hesitating. 'I . . . I wondered . . . them young hooligans, the ones that used to pester Valentino . . . do they still come to the restaurant?'

'Yes, they do.'

'Oh.'

It was no use; she just couldn't think of a way to ask the question that needed to be asked. But, after a slight pause, Patrick sat down again.

'At least two of them do,' he said. 'I doubt that Gerald Sowerby will be bothering us again.'

'Why's that?' Nella had to use all her acting skills to keep her voice from trembling.

'Well, we all knew that he was drinking too much. They all were, but Sowerby didn't seem to have any control over his appetites.'

Nella hoped Patrick hadn't noticed her shudder.

'One night – I remember it – his pals had to carry him down the stairs and put him in a cab. One of them should have gone home with him but, in my opinion, the other two never really cared for him.' Patrick frowned.

'So . . . what happened?' Nella prompted.

'Oh well, he didn't make it. He almost got home – right to the front door, in fact, but then he must have slipped or taken a drunken fall. He landed down in the area yard – where he was found amongst his own blood and vomit the next morning.'

Nella gasped and raised both hands to her face.

'I'm sorry,' Patrick said. 'I shouldn't have spoken so plainly.'

'Was he . . .?'

'Oh, he didn't die, but he'd taken a severe blow to his head. They say his brains are scrambled. He can't even remember what happened, and now he can neither walk nor talk properly. They don't think he'll ever recover sufficiently to complete his studies. His parents are heartbroken.'

He glanced at her keenly. 'Nella, I shouldn't have told you this story. You're too tender-hearted. I've upset you.'

'Upset . . .'

'Let me get you a shot of brandy.' Patrick McCormack rose and hurried into the coffee house.

'Nella?' Valentino had finished his coffee and cake and was staring at her worriedly. 'Are you upset?'

'No, my darling. Everything's fine.'

'Where shall I serve the coffee, Mrs Edington? In the front room or the conservatory?'

'The conservatory, please, Polly. It's such a pleasant evening, don't you think, John?'

He didn't reply but he smiled and went ahead to light the lamps, although, at almost midsummer, it wouldn't be truly dark for more than an hour yet. They didn't have a garden at the back of the house, only a yard, but the conservatory, built out from the dining room, was large and, thanks to Albert Green and his father, it was beginning to rival that of John's uncle and aunt at their grand villa in Jesmond.

John held her chair for her and when she was settled, he sat at the other side of the engraved brass-topped table and smiled ruefully. 'I wish Polly would say "drawing room" not "front room". Can't you train her any better?'

Constance controlled her own irritation. 'She's doing very well, John.'

She would have liked to add that, although she was doing her best to educate their maid, she herself was beginning to question some of the trivia of social niceties, but she held her peace. After all, it was only recently that John had started dining at home again and, as he was obviously trying to please her tonight, she did not want to upset him.

She was glad she'd kept quiet when he said contritely, 'I'm sorry. You've been marvellous. Our servants . . . this house . . . our daughters . . . You are a good wife and mother, Constance, and you are more than I deserve.'

He turned to look out of the window, or rather at the massed plants standing between him and the glass, but he had not been quick enough and Constance had seen the sheer misery in his eyes.

'And yet you are not happy.'

She said it so quietly that she was not sure that he had heard her. He remained staring into the waxy green foliage until Polly arrived with the tray, then he turned and smiled up at her.

'Thank you, Polly. And thank you for the lovely dinner.'

'It was only brisket,' Polly said, and turned to go.

'Wait a moment.' John called her back. 'Did Albert like the silk scarf?'

'Yes he did, thank you. But I'm not sure when he's going to wear it.'

When she had gone, John raised his eyebrows. 'My goodness,' he said. 'She's grumpy, tonight.'

'I think she's a little jealous.'

'Jealous?'

'Of the fuss you make of Albert.'

John was silent for so long that Constance wished she could recall her words. But then he said, 'I'm not sure what you mean.'

'Well, you know, you have been generous . . . you give him gifts—'

'They're usually samples.'

'That may be. But sometimes when they go out together

Albert looks much smarter than she does. Perhaps Polly feels belittled.'

She wished she'd had the courage to say what she really believed. That Polly had guessed that her master was in some way attracted to Albert. Constance saw that John was staring at her. Had he read her mind?

'That's nonsense!' he exclaimed. But he smiled. 'Well, if that's what it is, I can easily put things right. You know the new shop is specializing in a line of ready-mades? When I saw all the little shop girls gawping at the display in the window – and some of them were making sketches – I realized there was another market out there! Well, anyway, it would be easy enough to bring a sample home now and then for Polly. Do you think that would put things right?'

'It may do, John, and that would be kind of you.'

'Good. Do you mind if I have a cigar? I'll open the outer door and stand there. But don't go away, will you?'

'Please go ahead. I'm going to have another cup of coffee.'

Did all husbands and wives talk to each other like this, Constance wondered. Like polite strangers? She watched John go over to the doorway, open it and begin the business of lighting his cigar.

When they were first married, she mused, Polly would never have spoken to John like that. In the maid's eyes, John Edington could do no wrong, and she and Polly had got off to a bad start. But she had made every effort to put that right and now she could count on Polly as an ally.

Ally . . . what was she thinking of? Did she need an ally? Was John her enemy? Were they at war? No, of course not. But neither were they loving friends as she had imagined they would be . . . and she had imagined that they would be so much more.

Although John had been making an effort lately, the

442

atmosphere between them was entirely artificial and more than a little strained. For example, he had never questioned her about the destruction of the chair cover in the sewing room as surely a normal husband would have done.

And he had been so pleased just now to accept her explanation of why Polly was jealous – the gifts of clothes. But Constance suspected that it was more than that. Even if Albert refused to acknowledge it, his sweetheart knew what kind of man John was, and she was worried that one day he might expect a certain kind of gratitude.

'You were right, of course.'

She looked up to find him staring out into the yard; the smoke from his cigar curling out into the dusk. 'Right?' she said.

'About my not being happy.'

'Oh, John, I—'

'In fact I am most unhappy about my uncle's latest suggestion. Suggestion! That's what he calls it but it is more like an order. You know what I'm talking about, don't you? My cousin Esther has persuaded her parents that she should work with me.'

'Would that be a bad thing?'

He turned and glared at her. 'How can you ask? Of course it would. I want this venture of mine to be completely separate from Barton's. My aim is to be completely free of the family.'

'Then you must say no.'

'Would you support me?'

'Why do you look so surprised? Of course I would.'

'Well, that day they came here – Aunt Muriel and Esther – and persuaded you to show them my workroom . . .' He hesitated and Constance wondered if, at last, he was going to ask her what had happened in there that day. But then he continued, 'I thought they had persuaded you to influence me.'

'Goodness, no. Your aunt knows that I have no influence with you.'

She was surprised by the look he gave her. It was one of consternation. 'Oh, Constance, I'm sorry. Have I been such a bad husband?'

'John . . .'

'My uncle told me that I had, you know. He said that I had been neglecting you shamefully – that I should spend more time with my wife and family.'

'Is that why you've been coming home for dinner lately?' she asked sharply. 'To please your uncle?'

'No! Not to please my uncle. It's because I saw the truth of his words. I have been neglecting you and I felt ashamed.'

'But not ashamed enough to stop bringing—'

'Go on, what were you going to say?'

'Nothing, John. I'm glad that you have been coming home to dinner with me.'

'But you are still unhappy?'

She shrugged.

'Constance, my uncle said that you might want another baby. Is that true?'

'I think that idea came from your aunt.'

'But is it true?'

'I . . . I don't know, John.'

'Well, anyway,' he looked relieved, 'it's something to think about, isn't it?'

He smiled at her and her heart ached to see how handsome he still was – in spite of the dark shadows under his eyes. He always looked tired these days and Constance had no way of knowing how much sleep he got. Her husband may have returned to the family table but he still had not returned to her bed.

'Well,' he said, 'I think it's time to go out and check the

444

gate, see that we are locked up securely for the night.' He stepped out into the yard and then half turned and said, 'I won't be long.'

Constance put her coffee cup on the table and rose from her chair. In spite of John's good intentions he had probably just lied to her. He checked the gate that led into the park every night but she had known for some time that he wasn't always locking it. On the contrary, some nights her husband would be making sure that the gate remained unlocked.

That way the visitors that he imagined nobody knew about, the new friends who came when everybody else was in bed, did not have to walk down the terrace past the houses of all their respectable neighbours. They could come unseen across the park and John would no doubt meet them at the conservatory door before taking them surreptitiously up to his room at the top of the house.

Constance had sometimes heard the whispers and the stifled laughter as they mounted the stairs and she burned with shame to think that Polly and Florence might hear them too.

She had no idea who these men were, for of course, the visitors were men. Sometimes there was only one visitor; now and then she heard two. But none of them spoke in the cultured tones of Matthew Elliot.

She didn't wait for John because she knew that she wouldn't be able to face him and pretend that nothing was wrong. With a last regretful look into the musky night, she turned and hurried up to bed.

Chapter Twenty-nine

'Go on – eat some. It's good.'

'What is it?'

'Goose liver pâté.'

'Ugh!' Declan pulled a disgusted face.

John smiled. 'Just try it,' he said. 'It's made from goose, bacon, wine, brandy. Here, take this knife and put a little on this biscuit . . . let me . . . there you are, open your mouth.'

Declan took a bite gingerly and then looked up and grinned. 'I like it.'

'Have some more. Help yourself – and try the cheese . . . and the pigeon pie. I'll pour you some wine.'

'I'd rather have a glass of stout.'

'No doubt you would, but I haven't got any.'

'Gin?' Declan raised his dark brows hopefully.

John laughed. 'No. You're going to have wine, and a good one at that, although I doubt if your uneducated palate will appreciate it.'

Declan scowled. 'What's readin' and writin' got to do with wine?'

'What are you talking about?'

'You've just said I'm uneducated. It's never bothered you up to now.'

He put down the knife he'd been holding and hunched

forward on the chair, clenching his huge fists on his knees. John noticed how the firelight glinted on the signet ring he wore and how it highlighted his swarthy features, making him look sinister, menacing almost. But that was part of the attraction, he supposed, the hint of danger was exciting ... stimulating. Nevertheless he decided to tread carefully.

'I didn't say that you were uneducated. What I meant was that, as you are not used to drinking wine, it may take some time – and several bottles' – he grinned, hoping to coax a response – 'before you begin to appreciate the difference between one wine and another. That's what I meant. Really.'

'Really?'

'Yes.'

Declan relaxed and unclenched his hands. He reached for a large slice of cold pie and put it on his plate. 'You know, John,' he picked up the plate and sat back, 'sometimes you talk a load of horse manure. I wouldn't put up with it if I didn't love you, would I?'

John shook his head faintly and sat down on the other chair. He leaned back into the cushions until his face was in shadow and watched as Declan wolfed down the pie and then reached for another slice. At one point he paused and, with a scattering of flaky crumbs, he said, 'Aren't you going to have anything?'

'I might ... later. But go on. I like to watch you enjoy yourself.'

'Right. Suit yourself.'

John closed his eyes and tried to conjure up the little feasts that he and Matthew had shared together. Matthew had always provided them, bringing the delicious titbits from Moorside Towers. Sometimes there were things in his hamper that John had never seen, never tasted before. Had Matthew been trying to educate him just as he was trying to educate Declan now?

He supposed he must have been but it had been done so subtly that John had never felt as though he were being patronized.

Declan was smart enough to know that he was. But he had obviously decided not to be offended. Why should he be? He'd done well out of John ever since the night they'd met in Pink Lane. John had been drawn to him immediately. Declan was tall and dark, just like Matthew, but there the resemblance ended. Matthew had been slim and elegant; Declan was burly and flashily dressed.

John was trying to do something about that too, and, if the truth were known, that was probably the reason that Declan was so compliant. Why should he argue if acquiescence not only meant fine food and wines but a whole new wardrobe?

And of course he was well paid for his services.

John felt the emotion well up and burn at the back of his throat: a mixture of grief and shame. Why had Matthew deserted him like that? If they had still been together he would not have had to go searching for relief and comfort from the kind of men who hung around the more questionable establishments. Men who were waiting for men like John, with plenty of money in their pockets.

He had been seen. There had been talk and it had got back to his uncle. He still burned with anger when he remembered the day that Walter Barton had called him into his office.

'I always feared this day would come,' he'd said sorrowfully, as if John had brought a plague of biblical proportions down on the family. 'But I hoped that your marriage to Constance might have kept you on the straight and narrow. But now I see that it was all a sham. Poor Constance.' His uncle had looked genuinely sad. 'John, I do not hope for miracles but I can only urge you to be more discreet . . . to spend more time with your family. Would you not like a son to inherit your part of the business one day?'

449

How dare he talk to him like that? How dare he make him feel guilty because of what he had done to Constance? It hadn't been a sham, had it? He had been attracted to her beauty; he had been genuinely fond of her, hadn't he?

He had taken her from a life of poverty and hardship and given her a comfortable home, an allowance of her own, beautiful clothes, designed especially for her. And she had the girls, their daughters, to look after. Wasn't that what women wanted? Babies to love and care for? Some wives were grateful if their husbands left them alone – why did Constance have to be one of those women who wanted more?

John heard a slight sound and he opened his eyes and looked up to find Declan standing over him, his right hand reaching out towards the watch chain looped across his waistcoat. He shivered. 'What do you want?'

Declan straightened up and stuffed his hands in his pockets. 'Did I frighten you, darlin'?'

'Of course not.'

'You nearly jumped out of your skin. I thought you'd gone to sleep. Thought you was too tired for any fun. I was just going to check your watch. I was wondering whether I ought to scarper.'

John glanced quickly at the clock on the mantelpiece and away again. 'No, don't go.' He was aware that he was gripping the arms of the chair . . . the chair that had recently acquired a new loose cover.

Declan stepped back. 'Go on then. I'll sit down and have another glass of that wine while you get ready . . . put your bonny frock on. That's what you want to do, isn't it?'

'Yes.'

'Which one will it be tonight? The blue velvet or the green taffeta?'

'I don't know. Will you help me choose?'

'Sure thing.' Declan grinned salaciously and sipped his wine.

John stood up and took off his watch. He put the watch and the chain along with his pocket book on the mantelpiece next to the antique carriage clock that had been his father's only gift to his mother. He was aware that Declan was watching him, slanting his gaze up over his wine glass. But that was part of the game, wasn't it? The game he was playing with fate. He had not yet discovered how far he could go.

For a while Constance wasn't sure whether the sobbing was part of her dream. What had she been dreaming about? She tried to hang on to the sounds, the images, but they curled away like snaking ribbons back into the shadows and they were gone. When she opened her eyes and sat up she could only remember that she had been frightened.

Now, with the morning sun streaming across her bed, she ought to have felt reassured. But she didn't. Polly was standing over her with a face as white as paper – and she could still hear the sobbing although it had softened into a kind of stifled whimper.

'The twins are still asleep, thank God,' Polly told her before she could ask, 'and so is Florence, although I don't know how after the commotion Jane made.'

'Jane?'

'My sister. She works in this madhouse, remember?'

'Polly, what is it? What on earth is the matter?' Constance began to push the bedclothes aside.

Instead of answering, the maid went over to the door, which Constance noticed had been left ajar, and reached out to pull her younger sister, who was crying, into the room. She shut the door behind her and took hold of Jane's shoulders. 'Try to stop that,' she said. 'I know you've had a shock, but it isn't over yet.'

By the time Constance had got out of bed and pulled on her robe, the girl was quiet.

'Now be brave,' her sister told her, 'and tell Mrs Edington what you saw.'

'Why can't you tell her?' the girl whimpered.

'Because you were the first one to go into the sewing room and I want to be absolutely sure that we get it right.'

Jane turned to look at Constance but she still didn't say anything.

'Go on, pet,' Polly said. 'Look, I'll start you off. You went upstairs to clean the hearth in the sewing room and you noticed the door was open . . .'

'. . . the door was open,' Jane said in a thin childish voice as if she were repeating a lesson. 'So I went in . . . and I saw the lady on the floor . . . and she had a bruise across her face and there was blood on the carpet . . . and I think she's hurt real bad . . . and I screamed and I dropped the bucket – and there's coal all over the floor, I'm sorry – and I ran back downstairs to the kitchen . . . and I told Polly. Polly went up and had a look but I wouldn't go in there again. That's it.'

When she'd finished the litany she took a huge breath and immediately looked as though she were going to collapse like a rag doll with the stuffing knocked out of it.

Polly took hold of her shoulders again and looked her straight in the face. 'Good girl. Now go downstairs as quiet as a mouse and make a pot of tea. Do you think you can do that?'

Jane nodded. 'Yes.'

'And you don't have to say anything more to anyone, ever.'

'Don't I? Not never?'

'Not ever. Not even to our mam.'

Jane glanced at her sister gratefully and fled the room. Polly turned towards Constance. 'Now you and me had better go upstairs.'

Constance followed Polly up to the top floor. Even though it was very early, the house was warm and the scents of the garden drifted in through the open windows of the upper floors of the house to mingle with the smell of lavender polish. She could hear a blackbird singing his heart out in the park nearby. She concentrated on enjoying all the signs of a beautiful summer's day – anything rather than contemplate the horror of what she knew lay ahead.

The door was open but Polly stopped outside. She turned and faced Constance. 'Two things,' she said. 'You know it's not some lady, don't you?'

'Yes. And . . .?'

'And it's not just a matter of being hurt real bad. I think he's dead.'

He lay on his back on the fireside rug, his head turned to one side and his beautiful eyes wide and staring into the cold ashes in the hearth. Jane had been right. There was a terrible mark across his handsome face with trickles of dried blood running down from his brow on to his neck and his bare shoulders. A lace shawl had been pinned to his hair with a tortoiseshell comb, which now stood up at a cruel angle as if it were poised to pierce his skull.

This time her husband was dressed in emerald taffeta. What was it Matthew had said that day? That day which seemed so long ago now, when the three of them had been walking through the new arcade? John's eyes had sparkled when he pointed to the display of fabrics in the shop window and said, '*What about the emerald taffeta?*'

'*No. too bold . . .*'

Too bold, Matthew had said.

Even though Constance had thought her husband and his friend had been discussing a new wardrobe for her, she had been aware of a sense of exclusion that day. They had been discussing their own plans, planning their own pleasure, and she was simply the means to achieve it. She had been used.

She sank to her knees beside her husband and Polly gasped. 'Mind your robe,' she said, and she pointed to a dark stain on the rug.

'I think it's wine,' Constance said.

A wine bottle lay on its side not far from the body and another, nearly empty, stood on the low table beside two glasses and the remains of a pigeon pie.

'I wondered where that pie had gone,' Polly said inconsequentially. 'And the cheese . . . the cheek of it. Feedin' his guttersnipe pals like that – and look where it gets him!'

Constance wondered how much Polly knew about the men that John had been bringing home and whether the tears that were coursing down her cheeks now were for John or for all of them, caught up in this nightmare.

'It stinks in here!' the maid said suddenly. 'I'll have to open the windows.'

She hurried over to the windows, still crying, and opened them wide to release the odours of tobacco, wine, stale food and . . . what was the other smell? Was it blood, or fear? Had John been frightened before he died and did his terror linger?

Constance found herself looking around for the weapon. Some weapon must have been used to strike such a terrible blow. She saw that the poker had gone from the hearth.

'The clock's gone,' Polly said suddenly. 'The beautiful little carriage clock that Mrs Edington was so fond of.' She had come back over and was staring at the mantelpiece. 'What are we going to do? Call the police?'

Constance sat back on her heels and looked up at Polly. 'I suppose we'll have to,' she said. 'But I think Mr Barton should be here.'

Polly looked relieved. 'Of course, John's uncle. Do you

want me to go for him? I can run. It should only take me about twenty minutes.'

'Will Jane be all right?'

'I'll tell her that I'm going for the doctor. I think it's best if she doesn't know the truth of it – at least not until my brain can come up with some kind of explanation for what's happened here tonight.'

'I'm sorry, Polly. So sorry . . .' At last Constance began to cry.

The maid kneeled down beside her swiftly and took her in her arms. 'There then,' she said. 'You haven't got time for that, Mrs Edington, dear. Save those tears for later when we've got ourselves out of this awful muddle somehow.'

Constance moved back out of Polly's arms and wiped her cheeks with her fingers. She smiled. 'Go on, then. But don't tell Mr Barton too much. Just say that there's been an accident. I – I don't want Mrs Barton and Esther to know.'

'I understand,' Polly said.

But, of course, Polly couldn't understand fully because she didn't know what Constance was going to do.

'And shut the door behind you,' Constance continued, 'I need to be alone with my husband.'

They were standing in the darkened sitting room. 'I hate leaving you here alone, Constance,' Nella said.

'I'm not alone. I have my daughters, Polly, Mrs Green . . .'

'Maybe, but the girls aren't old enough to know what's gannin' on and I'm certain sure you're not gannin' to invite either Polly or Mrs Green to sit in here with you and hev a good chinwag. You're just gannin' to stay here all alone and brood.'

'Nella, I'm not going to brood, believe me.'

'I don't believe you!'

They stared at each other challengingly and then, suddenly, they both smiled. 'Ee, Constance,' Nella said, 'times hev changed but we hevn't, hev we? We can still argue like bairns in the school yard!' Constance laughed. 'And what do we look like now?' Nella continued. 'A couple of old crows, dressed all in black and flapping our wings and squawking at each other!'

They hugged each other for a moment and then Constance drew away. 'Sit down,' she said. 'Have you time for a cup of tea with me before you go?'

'Just about. It feels wrong heving to gan work on such a day but I hev to, you know that, don't you?'

'Of course I do. I'll ring for Polly and explain that she'll have to be quick.'

'And, while you're about it, could you ask her to open these curtains? It's nearly midday and the room's like a tomb— Oh, what have I said!'

Constance sighed. 'It's all right, Nella, but we can't open the curtains, not on the day of John's funeral. I'll get Polly to bring in some more lamps.'

As they drank their tea, Constance and Nella discussed quietly what had happened that morning. The children had been considered too young to attend a funeral and had stayed in the nursery with Florence, where they still were. And Nella had not brought Valentino. She'd explained to his mother that she wanted to be able to concentrate on Constance's wellbeing and, besides, she knew that the funeral would upset him.

John's uncle, Walter Barton, had arranged for the ceremony to take place very early, before the streets were busy. One or two of Barton's senior managers had attended the church as a sign of respect, but only the family had come back to the house for the funeral 'tea', except that it was early enough to be a late breakfast.

'So you'll be all right financially?' Nella asked now. 'John has left you well provided for?'

'Yes. Uncle Walter is to come back and explain everything to me after he's taken Muriel and Esther home. But he says I'm not to worry.'

'Then I'll be off now, Constance.' Nella rose but looked reluctant to leave. 'I wish I wasn't gannin' to Scotland next week. If there was only some way to cancel it . . .'

'What, and disappoint the whole of Edinburgh? No, you must go and win over a whole new audience! Come, I won't ring for Polly; I'll see you to the door myself.'

John's uncle looked haggard. Apart from the horror of the events he had had to deal with, Constance knew that he was genuinely grief-stricken. He had loved his only sister and, for her sake, he had cherished her son. It was not just Constance that John had hurt by behaving as he had.

After reading through various documents with her and making sure she understood them, he said, 'All that this means is that the house is yours. But the shares in Barton's will be held in trust for your daughters. I'm sure you will agree that that is fair.'

'Of course.'

Constance averted her eyes. What else could she do but agree? If the truth were known, it wasn't fair. Amy alone should be John's heir – but for her daughters' sakes, both of them, that was a secret she would have to keep.

'I'm sorry if this conversation is upsetting for you; that's why I wanted to explain things myself. When there are papers to be signed I'll make sure Silverman comes here, rather than have you go to his office, and I'll come with him.'

Constance remembered another occasion when papers had to be signed. Her mother had had to face the ordeal alone.

457

How much worse it must have been for her when her marriage had been so happy; when she had loved her husband so very much . . .

'Constance? Are you all right? I'll ring for Polly, shall I?'

'No, I'm fine. And thank you for coming; you've been very kind.'

'Right then. Anything you need, you just have to tell me, you know that, don't you? And I'll tell Muriel and Esther to call by. That will be a comfort for you, won't it?'

Constance nodded to hide her expression of dismay. 'Oh, yes,' she said faintly. 'A great comfort.'

'It's Dr Alvini, Mrs Edington. Shall I show him in?'

Constance looked up in surprise. She saw that Polly was surprised too. 'I suppose so . . .'

Polly hesitated. 'I think it will be all right. I mean, I know you're in mourning, but he is a doctor, isn't he?'

'Yes. Well, show him in.'

Frank stood just inside the room and regarded her gravely. Constance understood the questions in his eyes and fought to suppress an upsurge of emotion.

No . . . this is wrong . . . I cannot cope with this . . . not now.

'Will you sit down?' she asked.

She noticed how Polly smiled at Frank and asked him, without being instructed, whether he would like tea or coffee. She guessed that Frank, without trying, had this effect on most women.

'Coffee, please, Polly,' he said and then when she had gone: 'Have I made a mistake?'

'Mistake?'

'Asking for coffee.'

Constance thought of the delicious coffee served at Alvini's and she laughed. 'Probably. But Polly will do her best.'

'Good. But I'm not a doctor, you know. Not yet. That was just Nella's way of making it look official that day – that day when—'

'Yes. Quite. But why have you come today? Is that Nella's doing too?'

Frank smiled. 'Of course. Nella is fretting away up in Edinburgh and wishing she could be with you. She telephoned me—'

'Telephoned?'

'Yes, we have a telephone now and so has the hotel in which Nella and my brother are staying. Anyway, she telephoned me and asked me to call and see if you were coping.'

'Really.'

'She said that you might be cross.'

He paused while Polly brought in the coffee and by the time they were alone again, Constance remembered uneasily another favour that Nella had asked of Frank Alvini . . .

She watched him sip his coffee. 'Is that to your taste?' she asked.

'Not exactly. It's dreadful.'

'What!'

'Have I spoken out of turn? Was that not polite?'

'Of course it wasn't. Oh, Frank, you know it wasn't and you're doing it deliberately.' She began to laugh weakly.

Suddenly he put his coffee down and came and stood beside her. 'Constance,' he said, and took her hand.

'No, don't.' She snatched her hand away, and rose and backed away from him. 'You must go now,' she said. 'You have done what Nella requested, you can see that I am coping and that I can even laugh. Now please go.'

'Forgive me. But may I offer you my friendship?'

'I don't know. I don't know if you and I could be friends,

459

Frank. There's something . . . something . . .'

'Something else? Some barrier between us rather than your too recent loss?'

She didn't answer.

'It's the children, isn't it?' Once more she got the feeling that he could read her mind. 'It's because of what Nella asked me to find out for you . . . because I know—'

'Yes, you know,' Constance said quietly.

'Constance, listen to me. What do I know? I know that you were badly, shamefully, treated. That nothing that happened was your fault. And that if Gerald Sowerby had not had a drunken accident and become a shambling, useless wreck, I would probably have killed him at the first opportunity.'

She stared at him. His eyes were glittering with the kind of passion she had never seen before. She did not doubt that he meant every word. 'Accident? Gerald Sowerby?' she whispered.

'Yes, he will never be able to harm another woman as he has harmed you.'

After he had gone Constance wondered if Nella could have the faintest inkling of what she had done. Her friend couldn't have known that the manner of John's death would leave Constance with a burden that she would have to carry for ever . . . that she would never be entirely free from the past. Perhaps Nella had had the best of intentions when she had sent Frank Alvini to see her, but she had only succeeded in upsetting the fine balance of emotions Constance had fought to achieve since John's death.

Chapter Thirty

March 1909

'Can't you sleep?' Nella asked.

Constance turned away from the window of the garden room to find her friend coming towards her. Instead of a robe, Nella clutched a large paisley shawl around her shoulders; she looked tired.

'I'm sorry, did I disturb you?' Constance said.

'No, Valentino's the one who disturbed me! He's snoring like the proverbial pigs being driven to market and, as a result, he drove me out of bed! I was on the way down to make meself a drink of hot milk and honey in the kitchen, but I saw the light on in here.'

Constance smiled. 'Does he often snore like that?'

'Only when he's excited – as he is about the wedding tomorrow. But why aren't you safely tucked up and getting yer beauty sleep?'

'Too much to think about.'

'I know. But what on earth can you be looking at at this time of night?' Nella stood next to her and peered out. There was a moon but the light was intermittent as the clouds scudded across the sky, driven by the wind.

'Just the trees,' Constance said. 'Look at the branches swaying . . . I think I can hear the swing creaking.'

'The swing yer father made for you and Robert?'

'Mm. For Robert, really. He lived here before I was born.'

'And now I live here. I had no idea when I bought it, you know. Do you mind?'

'I would rather it were you and Valentino living in Lodore House than anyone else. I can see how much you've grown to love the place.'

'And you are welcome here always. You know that, don't you?'

'Yes, I do.'

'But for goodness' sake come away from all this cold glass, you just in yer nightgown and robe and all.' Nella shivered dramatically, as if she were on the stage. 'You'll catch yer death if you stand here much longer. Come away down to the kitchen with me. It's not a room I normally visit so you can show me round!'

Nella insisted that the house should be kept warm and, as they went through the door and down the stairs that led down to the domestic quarters, the comforting smells of Constance's childhood rose up to greet them: the smells of warmth and cleanliness and recent baking. When they reached the bottom and opened the door that led into the kitchen, Constance almost expected to see Maggie Muff and her kittens curled up in the basket near the range.

'Are you crying, sweetheart?' Nella had switched on the light and she paused to look up into Constance's face.

'Perhaps. But I'm not sad.'

'Gan on, then – gan and sit down by the table. I think I can just about find me way into the larder and discover where the cook keeps the milk.' Nella opened one of the doors that led off the kitchen and a draught of cool air wafted in. 'If I don't come back, come and rescue me!'

A short while later they were sitting facing each other across the table, cradling the warm drinks in their hands.

'Nella, you're tired; you should have let me make the drinks. I'm sorry.'

'No, I wanted to do it. Tomorrow's yer big day.' For a moment her smile faded and she looked sad. 'I said something like that once before, didn't I?' Then she shrugged and grinned. 'And you're wrong; I'm not tired, I'm exhausted. But now that the pantomime season's over I'm gannin' to take Harry up on his offer to stay at his villa in Kent. I'll hev a little holiday, time to recuperate. That's a big word for yer little friend to come out with, isn't it?'

'Oh, Nella, you're wonderful, you know.'

'Oh, aye, Aa'm a proper mazer, amman't Aa? Just amazing the lass is!' Nella slipped stagily into an exaggerated version of her accent, and they both laughed. 'That's from part of me act, you know. Harry dreamed up a new character – a rough little street urchin who's discovered sitting on a dustbin when the lights gan up. That way I get a break from standing – and the lid's got a specially made soft seat.'

They sipped their milk in silence for a while and then Nella said, 'I'm glad you agreed to this . . . to coming here with Beatrice and Amy the night before the wedding. But I should have realized that it might be painful for you.' She looked at Constance anxiously.

'Painful?'

'Yer childhood home . . . all those memories . . .'

'No, it's good . . . the memories are happy. And my mother and my father . . .' Constance stopped and shook her head.

'I know, pet. You don't hev to say anything. They would hev wanted this, wouldn't they – for you to be married from yer own home . . . from yer father's house?'

'I don't know what I would have done if you hadn't suggested this,' Constance said. 'I love Frank so much but I couldn't have got married from ... from John's house. It wouldn't have seemed right.'

'Why? Because it's so soon ... less than a year? Because people will talk?'

'They've never stopped talking!' Constance said bitterly. 'But it's not just that ... I mean, John ... the way he died ...'

'I know, poor man. But what was he thinking of coming home across the park like that?' Nella shook her head. 'Fancy losing yer life for a gold watch and a few banknotes.'

Constance looked down at the scrubbed table top. That's what Nella believed, that John had been waylaid by a thief as he came home in the early hours. The thief had never been caught. Only Constance, Polly, Walter Barton and one other person in the entire world knew any different.

As for Jane, she believed to this day that there had been two accidents that night. A lady had fallen and hit her head on the fender in the sewing room and, presumably, had gone home after the doctor had been called. And, worse, poor Mr Edington had been robbed and murdered in the park.

Even Walter Barton did not know as much as Polly. By the time he had arrived at the house that morning last summer, John was still lying on the floor in the sewing room, but he was dressed as a man. It had taken an almost inhuman effort for Constance to strip off the emerald taffeta gown and stuff it in the cupboard, and then, crying as though she didn't know how to stop, she had manipulated her husband's poor stiff limbs into his own clothes again.

She had known that she could not let him be discovered dressed the way he was. No matter that their marriage had not been what she hoped for, no matter that she had been unhappy, she knew that John was not really a bad man; only a weak one.

She had at least to endeavour to give him back his dignity.

Walter Barton had been crying too, as he'd lifted his only sister's son into his arms and gone silently down the stairs, with Polly leading the way and Constance following. They had left by the conservatory and then gone through the private gate into the park. John's uncle had gone as far as he dared along the paths sheltered by the overhanging branches of the old trees before gently lowering the body on to the ground.

It was better this way, he had told Constance, though there was no chance she could escape the unpleasantness altogether. She would probably have to live with ugly rumours about the way her husband had lived, the people he mixed with, for the rest of her days. But at least, by doing this, the death seemed a little less scandalous. He was doing this not just for the good name of Barton's, but also for her, John's uncle had assured her, and for John's daughters. Constance had not been able to meet his eyes when he'd spoken about John's daughters.

'I shall sell the house, you know,' she told Nella now.

'Quite right. You divven't need it now that you'll be living at Seaton. I suppose Florence will be coming with you, but what about Polly?'

'She's getting married.'

'Albert's popped the question!'

Constance smiled. 'They're going to rent a house just near his parents and Jane's going to live with them. I shall miss Polly.'

Nella sniffed and Constance remembered the old jealousies. She smiled and changed the subject. 'But I can't move far enough away from Aunt Muriel and Esther!'

'Now then, Constance. By all accounts they've been trying to be kind to you.'

'They've been insufferable! You know that some women, no matter how hard they try to be sympathetic, just end up

465

being patronizing. They think they've been doing me a favour by dropping in to see me all the time. They chatter on about how wonderful Esther has been to take on John's side of the business – the ladies' fashions – and they think they're being so brave, so noble.'

'Brave? Noble? What on earth do you mean?'

'Well, you know, standing by the poor little widow in the face of scandal and rumours.'

Nella gave her a cool look. 'And in their lights that's just what they've done. Stood by you.'

Constance sensed her disapproval and she felt ashamed. 'I know that, Nella. I'm too critical sometimes . . . I'm sorry.'

Nella reached across the table and took her hands. 'You divven't hev to apologize to me, pet. And, divven't fret, none of us is perfect!'

'Sometimes I think you are – the perfect friend, I mean. I think I could come to you whatever kind of trouble I was in, and you would try to put it right, wouldn't you?'

Nella gave her the strangest look before she removed her hands. 'Yes,' she said, 'I'd try.' And then it seemed to Constance that her friend had to bring herself back from some dark place before she asked, 'But you're happy now, aren't you? I mean, you and Frank . . . you divven't mind that I told him . . . that I involved him—'

'I don't mind,' Constance said quickly. 'I've told Frank everything. Everything. There are no secrets this time.'

Nella didn't say anything and Constance guessed that her friend knew that she was referring to the secret that she had kept from John – the fact that Gerald Sowerby had raped her the night before the wedding. But, of course, John had had his secret too: his love for Matthew. Constance wondered now if she and John had really had any chance of finding happiness together.

She had thought it so romantic, the way they had met in the park that day with the band playing. John had been so handsome . . . not handsome, beautiful, she had thought, like a painting in the art gallery, not like a flesh and blood man at all.

Frank wasn't handsome; he was kind and funny and intelligent and very, very real, and he made her feel as though she mattered more to him than anyone else in the whole world. At first she had accepted his offer of friendship. He had not pressed her for more and the friendship had grown and deepened until the time came that she could trust him with her burden . . . her final secret.

She told him what she had done to protect John's memory and then what she and Walter Barton had done to protect the family – especially her daughters. He had not condemned her. Frank had told her that she must forget that now, that she must leave the past behind. Then he had taken her in his arms. But he had not kissed her. Not then.

It had been here, in the garden of Lodore House, that she had finally admitted that she loved Frank. Nella had insisted on having a Christmas party for her family before she opened in the pantomime at the Palace on Boxing Day. She invited them all to stay. Constance and her daughters were part of Nella's family.

Nella and her mother-in-law doted on Beatrice and Amy and, at the end of a happy day, they had asked if they could help Florence bathe the little girls and see them into bed. Valentino and Frank had been ordered to clear up the toys. Constance, remembering past Christmases in this house, had put on her coat and had slipped out into the garden.

The night was cold and very still. There was a bright moon and the grass beneath her feet was crisp with frost. She made her way across the lawn to the old tree and the swing her father had made. She stood and looked at it.

In the stillness she imagined that she heard the excited, childish voices of herself and her brother calling out to their father to push them higher and higher, but there was no pain. Not now. It was ironic, she thought, that because of Nella's love for them, it would be her children who played here, not Robert's.

'Constance?' She turned to find Frank standing behind her. 'Are you all right?'

'Yes.'

He stood watching her, making no move towards her, and she understood that he was waiting. She also understood that he must wait no longer. It was time. She slipped off a glove and reached across the space between them to place her hand on his face. His skin was cold. But his lips, when he turned his head to kiss her palm, were warm.

He moved his lips across the soft flesh and the sensations he aroused were indescribable. Constance was trembling as she took the step that closed the gap between them and found herself in his arms. He held her close to him and she could feel his breath in her hair as he murmured, 'I love you.' Then he took her face in his hands and moved back a little so that he could see her expression. 'But you know that, don't you?'

She looked into his eyes and she saw the hint of a smile. 'Yes, I know. And I love you.'

His kiss was tender but she was overwhelmed by her own response. She clung to him frantically, welcoming his caresses, until it was Frank who had to break away.

'We'd better go in, now,' he sighed. 'But, Constance, we won't wait too long.'

And after that there had been no barrier between them, no pretence, and no denying the fact that they must marry as soon as possible . . .

468

'I divven't know what you're thinking, Constance, but judging by the look in yer eyes and the way you've gone all pink, I think that's just as well!' Nella said suddenly.

Constance laughed softly. 'Is it that obvious?'

'It's that obvious. And now, madam, I insist that you gan to bed so that you'll be all bright and beautiful for yer wedding tomorrow.'

'Thank you, Nella.'

'What are you thanking me for?'

'For sending Frank to me. For arranging my wedding. For persuading my brother and his wife to come. For buying the flowers . . . ordering the carriages . . . oh, everything!'

'You couldn't hev stopped me! I only wish it could hev been a grander affair, but you being a widow and all . . . Do you know that Patrick and Belle had a fine old job persuading me that they should provide the wedding breakfast in the restaurant?'

They smiled fondly at each other and got up to leave the kitchen. Constance put an arm round her friend and helped her up the stairs. On the landing outside Nella's bedroom they paused to say good night.

'Ssh!' Nella whispered. 'If we wake Valentino he'll talk the night away!'

Once back in her own bedroom Constance didn't go straight to bed. She went over to the dressing table and opened her jewellery box. She took off the wedding ring that John had given her and placed it inside and then she took out a little gold-coloured chain. A chain with a heart that didn't open like a proper locket.

The necklace lay in her hand. It was hardly any weight at all. She remembered the way the chain had cut into her neck that night outside the Sowerbys' house and she waited for the waves of pain and distress. They didn't come. She would never

469

be able to forget what had happened, not while Beatrice lived and breathed, but the hurt had faded. The links of the chain had been mended just as her life had been renewed with love and friendship.

She held her hand out under the pink silk-shaded lamp and looked at the heart and the two letters engraved there. *C* and *N*, the first letters of their names. She remembered their words to each other the night Nella had given the chain to her . . .

'*And wear it every day, mind, especially tomorrow, yer wedding day, promise?*'

'*I promise . . .*'

Constance fastened the chain around her neck. This time she would keep her promise.

The Gilded Cage

Josephine Cox

Powerful, hard-hearted Leonard Mears ruthlessly presides over his wife and children, exiling them from the outside world and brutally punishing any disobedience. But he is also a man with a dark secret; an illegitimate daughter whom he forced his sister to bring up. The girl is now a young woman who, unbeknown to him, is determined to find the father that abandoned her.

James Peterson, a gifted young man, runs Mears' factory with more success than Leonard's own sons. He lives for the day he can have his own business and make his fortune. Only then will he be able to declare his love for beautiful Isabel Mears who he means to release from the gilded cage her father has created. But then the lonely, lovely Sally comes into his life, turning his heart and dreams upside down.

'Impossible to resist' *Woman's Realm*

'A Cookson by any other name' *Birmingham Post*

'Driven and passionate' *The Sunday Times*

0 7472 5756 6

HEADLINE

The Ties That Bind

Lyn Andrews

Tessa O'Leary – the only daughter in a family of fatherless boys, when her mother dies she's her brothers' lifeline to survival. So for Tessa the privations of war are just another battle to be fought for a young woman who was born fighting . . .

Elizabeth Harrison – oppressed by her shopkeeper mother's snobbish expectations, it seems the coming war offers an escape from her family's emotional ties – but at what cost?

The Ties That Bind – the unputdownable story of two young girls in the slumlands of war-wracked Liverpool, bound together by a friendship that surmounts disaster, poverty and heartbreak . . .

'A great saga' *Woman's Realm*

'A compelling read' *Woman's Own*

'Gutsy . . . a vivid picture of a hard-up, hard-working community' *Express*

'Spellbinding . . . the Catherine Cookson of Liverpool' *Northern Echo*

0 7472 5808 2

HEADLINE

Now you can buy any of these other bestselling books from your bookshop or *direct from the publisher*.

FREE P&P AND UK DELIVERY
(Overseas and Ireland £3.50 per book)

My Sister's Child	Lyn Andrews	£5.99
Liverpool Lies	Anne Baker	£5.99
The Whispering Years	Harry Bowling	£5.99
Ragamuffin Angel	Rita Bradshaw	£5.99
The Stationmaster's Daughter	Maggie Craig	£5.99
Our Kid	Billy Hopkins	£6.99
Dream a Little Dream	Joan Jonker	£5.99
For Love and Glory	Janet MacLeod Trotter	£5.99
In for a Penny	Lynda Page	£5.99
Goodnight Amy	Victor Pemberton	£5.99
My Dark-Eyed Girl	Wendy Robertson	£5.99
For the Love of a Soldier	June Tate	£5.99
Sorrows and Smiles	Dee Williams	£5.99

TO ORDER SIMPLY CALL THIS NUMBER

01235 400 414

or e-mail orders@bookpoint.co.uk

Prices and availability subject to change without notice.